DUDLEY PUBLIC LIBRARIES

The loan of this book may be renewed if not required by other readers, by contacting the library from which it was borrowed.

About the Author

Lynda Renham writes romantic comedy novels. Lynda's novels are popular, refreshingly witty, fast paced and with a strong romantic theme. She lives in Oxford UK and when not writing Lynda can usually be found wasting her time on Facebook.

"Lynda Renham is right up there with chick-lit royalty! I'm not talking princess either, for me, the Queen of Chick-lit". – *Booketta Book Blog.*

Lynda is author of the best-selling romantic comedy novels including: *Coconuts and Wonderbras, Pink Wellies and Flat Caps, It Had to Be You and The Dogs Bollocks.*

Lynda Renham

The right of Lynda Renham to be identified as the author of the work has been asserted by her in accordance with the Copyright, Designs and Patents Act 1988.

ISBN 978-0-9571372-0-2

third edition

Illustrations by Tiffany Avery

Printed in Great Britain by SRP
Copyright © Raucous Publishing 2014

www.raucouspublishing.co.uk

Chapter One

Don't you just hate weddings? Well, maybe you don't. Generally I don't either but when it is your own wedding things just get so stressful. Jesus, I feel like I am having my nineteenth nervous breakdown. I mean, there is the dress nightmare for a start. I can't even look at a Hobnob, without everyone going into a massive panic and screaming, *'you will never squeeze into the dress if you eat that'*, while removing the offending Hobnob and plonking a Ryvita into my hand. I mean, seriously, like one Hobnob will make that much difference. This is, of course, bearing in mind I am a size ten and if I say so myself, with an enviable figure. So, it comes to something when I am denied the basic human right of a Hobnob. Anyway, back to weddings, or at least *my* wedding. There are just so many *what ifs* when it comes to weddings. You know, *what if* he isn't the right one? *What if* after the wedding you find that sharing a duvet is just too big a sacrifice? Worst of all, *what if* the second thoughts you are having are for real and you ignore them? I find myself spending the mornings worrying about the big day and the afternoons worrying if it is all a big mistake. I can't decide if the terrible churning in my stomach is simply wedding nerves or if I am really having serious doubts. So I decide to visit my mother a few hours before my flight. Not the best decision of my life. The front door is flung open and before I can say 'hello', Candice mounts me dramatically and I fall backward, pulling the seam on my new Yves Saint Laurent blouse on the coat rack and landing with a thud on the new shag pile carpet. Don't you just hate bloody dogs?

'Shit. Damn animal, get the hell off me, you monster.' I attempt to push her back with my hand but only encounter her cold wet nose. The house is stiflingly hot and I feel myself perspiring. I swear a sauna is cooler than my mother's house.

'Darling, I thought you were coming for lunch.' My mother's voice somewhere beyond the great hound that is licking me to death.

'Candy, down now,' commands my dad, who shuffles into the hall, wearing his gardening gloves and carrying a knee rest. His old gardening trousers are scuffed at the knees, and there is a contented look on his face.

'Hello darling.'

'Dad, can you get this bloody monster off me. God almighty, this dog is so over-the-top affectionate,' I puff as I battle to get up. The smell of freshly baked cake reaches my grateful nostrils. I feel so emotionally exhausted from all my wedding worries that even fighting off a dog arouses a chocolate craving.

'Language please, Bels,' scolds my mother, who emerges from the kitchen decked top to bottom in Boden Country Casuals and smelling of Estee Launder White Linen and Elnett hair spray. I scramble to my feet.

'What? I didn't swear and ooh that's nice,' I say stroking her cashmere cardigan.

'I heard you say S-H-I-T and B-L-O-O-D-Y,' she says, spelling out the words.

'Oh Mum, come on really.'

She sighs. I hug her, and she enfolds me within her bosom. Her perfume is decidedly comforting. My old-fashioned mum who has never sworn in her life, drinks only sherry on a Friday and wouldn't know Germaine Greer if she fell over her. But, ask my mum about fashion and she is a guru. Her wardrobe is an absolute delight.

'Come along, I have made a lemon drizzle cake for you. Take Candy out, Julian. Bels and I need to talk, and do change that hideous jumper.' We both give the offending jumper a sizable dirty look. I slyly turn down the central heating thermostat as I pass. I watch as Dad raises his eyebrows. I smile and give him a conspirator's wink. He gives me a quick bear hug.

'It is lovely to see you Annabel. Right, come on Candy, we have our orders,' obeys Dad, shaking a lead. Candice bounces towards him while I exit to the kitchen. The door slams and Mum pushes me into a chair at the table. I check my blouse and see the damage is not as bad as I had imagined, thank goodness.

'Why didn't you get a chihuahua? I thought that was what you wanted. That dog is huge, I hate it,' I say checking my skirt for hairs.

'Candice is a loving dog, and hate is a very strong word. Now, come on, tell me everything that is on your mind.'

I watch as she places a large slab of lemon drizzle cake onto a plate, followed by a smaller piece of fruit cake. I take a deep breath. Christ, where to start. What exactly is on my mind? I am living every woman's dream. My job is fantastic. Okay, so I am almost thirty, but I am features editor at *Versity*, the top fashion magazine. I have even managed to combine my wedding trip to Rome with a fashion show in the city. I mean, some of the world's top models are on my wedding guest list, just how cool is that. My future husband is handsome, spectacularly rich and exceptionally kind. What more could a girl ask for? Okay, a Hobnob right now would be nice, or even a simple digestive, but generally though, life is pretty good. And it would be even better if I didn't have these terrible second thoughts.

'God Mum, is it too quick?' I blurt out.

She hands me the cake which I put to one side.

'Mum, you know I can't eat cake, I have to get into my dress,' I protest somewhat feebly.

'Oh a small piece won't hurt darling,' she says confidently, clicking on the kettle.

She cuts an even larger piece for herself. I take a bite of the lemon drizzle and savour the tangy lemon sponge, quickly following it with a chunk of still warm fruit cake.

'Darling, you are thirty, how can it be too quick? I was actually starting to wonder if you were, well you know, batting for the other side,' she says sheepishly.

I choke on a raisin.

'Why would you think that?' I ask shocked.

'Well, you work with all those women models and... Well, you only have to watch films to know what happens. Anyway...'

She places a mug of tea beside the cake and I wrinkle my nose.

'Oh Mum, can I have proper tea?'

'Green tea is proper tea,' she says, looking insulted.

'Oh I thought it was that elderflower stuff,' I say, relieved. The elderflower stuff tastes like a combination of coconut and cat's piss.

'This cake is divine, Mother.'

'Do you think it would be healthier if it were made with wholegrain flour?'

I shrug. I've never baked a cake in my life but I feel sure that somehow it would not taste half as good made with wholegrain flour. My mother, the middle-aged health-food addict. Last year my parents went to Tibet and Mum returned with strange tinkling bells and even stranger ideas. Tetley tea bags were replaced with weird herbal ones and my mother started an enlightenment group called 'Touch the Spot', which I always thought sounded more like a mutual masturbation group, but I knew better than to say anything. She meets with fifteen other weirdoes once a month where they meditate, burn incense and share together and I wouldn't be at all surprised if marijuana were involved somewhere.

'I can't seem to get that elderflower tea anymore,' she says thoughtfully. 'Jane said, she thinks you can buy it in Harrods. Maybe you can get me some. Anyway, seven months is not too soon, and Simon is ideal for you. And who gets to have a fairy-tale wedding in Rome? Oh dear, I still think I should wear Stella McCartney for the ceremony, what do you think? I mean, the Dior is nice but I think I should be more with it as mother of the bride. Kat said, you know, our cleaner, that the bride's mother is the second most important person at the wedding. By the way, did I tell you her boyfriend is going blind?'

I yawn, my mother, the archetypal do-gooder.

'Yes, you did Mother,' I say feigning interest.

She nods and her face brightens.

'And the fund-raising thing we are doing with Waitrose?'

I nod emphatically.

'Surely, though, that would be Simon wouldn't it?' I say thoughtfully.

She looks confused.

'What would be Simon, darling?'

'The second most important person at the wedding, wouldn't that be the groom?'

'Ah, good point. I must tell Kat... her boyfriend...'

'Mum,' I snap.

Christ, does anyone care about me and my future? Jesus, I have known the guy for seven freaking months, he could be a closet alcoholic for all I know. Then there are his parents, oh shit.

'I have not even met his parents yet, I mean they could be like something out of the fuckers,' I say, feeling decidedly depressed.

'What?'

'God sorry, I meant the *Fockers*. God, I am so stressed.' Waves of exhaustion seem to engulf me.

'Well, I am sorry Annabel. Even stress is no excuse for the 'F' word. Now, listen to me. In a few hours you are flying to Rome to meet your in-laws, by the way I meant to tell you, I have been learning Italian.'

Clearly delighted, she reaches behind me to the large oak dresser and grabs a book. Oh for goodness sake, am I under some silly illusion that my mother wanted to discuss my future? I indulgently swallow another chunk of lemon drizzle and gulp down some tea.

'Look, I have been using this, with a CD. But, anyway, the good thing is I will be able to converse with your mother-in-law. I have been practising on your father.'

I sigh and wipe my hands on a piece of kitchen towel. What a waste of time this is. Any minute now I will hear how my heavily pregnant sister is making a big sacrifice by getting on an aeroplane.

'Mum, she may be Italian but she lived in England up until a year ago. I have already told you this. They live in Rome now because they retired. She speaks perfect English.'

'Yes, but she *is* Italian and we must make an effort, I mean your sister Alex...'

Here it comes.

'Heavily pregnant as she is, Alex is still making the effort to come to your wedding. I just hope, I really do, that she will be okay. What with you being thirty and not married, Alex almost forty and finally pregnant and I thank God every day for that, it makes me realise we just can't be picky Bels.'

I play with my cake.

'I'm not picky. I just don't want to make a mistake. I mean, even the *getting married in Rome* thing, I just feel you know, kind of bullied. Surely, I shouldn't feel like that,' I say dipping into the biscuit barrel.

She nods knowingly.

'Have you been meditating like I told you?'

Oh God.

'But, what if he is not *Mr Right*, Mum?' I ask, feeling that churning again.

She clutches her breast.

'Oh Annabel, tell me, tell me, how this cannot be Mr Right? Huh? A man running his own law firm...'

'His father's law firm,' I correct.

'His father's, his, whatever, it is all the same thing. It is family. Oh and how you met, so romantic,' she says dreamily.

It was?

'On a boat, it's romantic, it was fate.'

'I had far too much to drink Mother. I almost fell into the Thames, along with my phone, and it was more sordid than romantic. Okay, he rescued me, kind of, if you call yanking me back by my skirt rescuing me.'

I have found a Hobnob and feel decidedly better. I guess she has a point though, I mean, let's face it, just how much longer can I wait for Mr Right? After all, Simon feels like Mr Right, I think. How do you know when it is Mr Right anyway? If I leave it much longer I'll be so old and wrinkled and all the Mr Rights will have been spoken for. Yes Mum knows best, I must stop being picky, but hell this is the rest of my life. My Blackberry shrills and I yank it out of my bag, it is flashing *Kaz*, my assistant, best friend and courier for my wedding dress. Oh God, something must have happened to the dress.

'Oh no, what's happened, did you spill wine on it or something? I swear I will cut out your heart and sell it to Satanists. You haven't ripped it have you?'

Mum gasps and Kaz whistles.

'Geez Bels, thanks for that vote of confidence. You are evil do you know that? Actually, I was just phoning to let you know the dress is on its way to Rome. Are you still at your mum's? Christ Bels, get to the airport. Love you and see you in two days.'

I throw the phone into my bag and hug my mother.

'I've got to go Mum. Off to get married to Mr Right. Thanks for the chat, I feel loads better.'

The hell I did.

'See you in Rome,' I call back with a wave.

Rome here I come, and I just hope you're ready for me because I certainly am *not* ready for you.

Chapter Two

So here we are, or at least here I am, at the airport, trying to control the fluttering of my heart. Oh how I wish I had flown out two days ago with Simon. The thought of arriving in Rome, and going straight to dinner with my future in-laws is a bit daunting. I check the flight board and sigh with relief when I see my flight is on time. I pull my phone out and text Simon that all is on schedule. I take a deep breath, remind myself I had signed India Milano for our fashion shoot and let out a relieved sigh. I head for the loo to tidy up and after just one look at myself in the mirror I want to die. 'Shit, shit,' I mumble, as I spy a small red welt on my chin. Bugger, a pimple sprouting right now is not what I need. I comb my hair quickly and take a few seconds to admire my long flowing auburn locks before splashing my face with cold water and heading for duty-free to buy future in-law presents. My phone bleeps and I read Simon's text. *'Great your flight is on time. Mum and Dad have booked a table at Mangiamo, for eight, you will love it, the place is always booked months in advance. Your flight lands at six so we will have to go straight there from the airport. Make yourself beautiful darling, but I know that is not hard for you to do.'*

Oh God, why now the bloody pimple? God, what if Simon's parents have high expectations? He is a solicitor after all and will soon be in charge of his father's law firm once the contracts have been signed over, providing of course that Simon's horrid brother doesn't make a fuss. I don't fancy meeting him much. He sounds a real arse. Simon says he is far too irresponsible to run a law firm and he is nothing but a trouble maker. Oh God, what if they expect me to be highly intelligent and all political? I'll just tell them I didn't believe there were WMDs and that Tony Blair was a prick. They are bound to be Conservatives, so I'll just say good things about David Cameron. I wonder if I should buy *Politics for Dummies* but decide against it.

They should love me for who I am. I dive into duty-free and wander around the perfumes for what seems forever. I finally buy myself some Chanel, a Fendi handbag for my future mother-in-law and two bottles of whisky. My mouth is now so dry that my lips are cracking, and my hair so static it is almost standing up on its own. I am so hot I feel sure I will spontaneously self-combust. Why are airports always so bloody hot? Oh what I would do for a shower. I hand over my credit card relieved that the present buying is over.

'Boarding pass please.' The cashier flutters her false eyelashes at me.

For a second I just stare at her bemused.

'Sorry. What?'

'I'll need your boarding pass,' she repeats with a smile, and I spot pink lipstick on her teeth. Oh I so hate that. I mean, how can that happen? Do women just miss their lips or are they just plain blind? What did I do with the bloody boarding pass? I push my hand into my new Anya Hindmarch handbag and fumble around. A useless fumbling really, as all I pull out is one grubby ear plug. I exhale loudly, but there is no response from the assistant. Right, if she is really going to persist then there is nothing else for it. I clear the counter and begin emptying my handbag. The assistant sighs heavily.

'Right,' I declare, 'one mobile phone, one diary, one purse.' I fumble in the purse but alas, no boarding pass.

'What's that?' she shouts excitedly, pointing to a scrap of paper.

'Ah, my to-do list,' I cry triumphantly. 'Now, where is the other to-do list that had 'find to-do list' on it? I lost the original you see,' I explain, trying to ignore her bored expression. I am now a force to be reckoned with. I pull out a pack of contraceptive pills, a solitary tampon and, with a grimace, a bottle of black nail polish.

'Yuk. I thought I had thrown that away. Do you want it?' I offer. She shakes her head.

'I only bought it for Halloween,' I explain to the man waiting behind me who yawns in response and averts his eyes.

'Do you have the boarding pass?' the assistant asks irritably.

A stupid question really as obviously I don't. I give an apologetic look and shake my head as I slap more things on the counter. My hands touch on something hard and, with a sinking heart I pull out a Lovefilm DVD.

'Bother. I should have posted that. Is there a post-box near here?'

She yawns and shakes her head. A family size bar of Cadbury's Fruit and Nut follows the DVD.

'For a big night in,' I joke.

I pull out a pair of knickers and cringe.

'Not part of the big night in,' I snort. 'I assure you, they are clean.' I laugh, but she doesn't. I find a scribbled note which I struggle to decipher, then a tangerine, followed by a much bruised apple.

'Useful,' I mumble.

I look at the cashier's miserable face.

'You still need it do you?' I ask politely.

'I'm afraid so,' she replies through gritted teeth.

'Doesn't she have it Jade?' calls her colleague from the other till.

I drop a handful of coins, a pair of Christian Dior sunglasses, and a spoon onto the counter.

'For my yogurt,' I mumble. 'No boarding pass. Make-up bag, bag within a bag, tissues, ah... what is this, bag with bills inside, I bet I put it in there.'

'My God, I can't imagine what is in your main luggage,' utters the man behind me.

'I am prepared for everything,' I retort, placing my Rescue Remedy and my *Along the Road Less Travelled* book onto the ever-increasing pile.

'Yes, except to pay for duty-free.'

Really, some people are so rude. I continue emptying the bag until I finally pull out a mouldy packet of mints which are stuck to the elusive boarding pass.

'You can't take those on the flight,' Jade says firmly. I look at the packet of mints wondering why not, but as I follow the cashier's eyes I realise she is referring to a bottle of Clarins perfume and a jar of Jo Malone face cream.

'I've already been through security,' I reply, pushing my credit card at her again while trying to separate the mints from the boarding pass.

'No, you can make a bomb with those,' she replies indignantly, tossing back her thick mane of blonde hair and licking her pink lips.

I burst out laughing. If I were chemically minded I would be more inclined to make a Botox mix as opposed to a Semtex one. Besides, do I look like a terrorist? Do I have a beard for Christ's sake?

'Is this a joke?'

'Not to mention the spoon,' quips the man behind me.

The assistant eyes me up and down, and looks over to her colleague.

'Tracey, how many *mills* can you take on a flight? She has enough here to make a bomb.'

Christ, did she have to say it so loudly. Everyone turns to look at the potential terrorist. Tracey looks in horror at my perfume bottle.

'Oh no, you can't take those, you could make a bomb, Jade is right, you're right Jade,' she echoes.

'You don't say. Do I look like a terrorist to you?' I ask, trying to keep the sarcasm out of my voice.

They both give me a look which indicates they clearly think I do.

'They don't all carry holdalls and have beards you know,' chips in the man behind me who is now pointing earnestly at the solitary tampon. 'Your handbag is seriously worrying, and that is highly suspicious. You should get security to check that out.' He wags his finger at the inoffensive tampon.

'What are they saying?' calls a woman from the back of the queue.

'She is trying to blow the plane up,' another replies loudly.

'She tried to hide a bomb in a tampon.'

'I thought she looked suspicious wandering around the perfumes.'

Oh for God's sake. Why don't they body-search me and be done with it? Jade lifts the tampon and everyone gasps. I watch wide-eyed as she tosses it into a bin.

'For goodness sake, my fiancé is a top solicitor,' I say proudly.

'They all say that,' says the man nodding at me.

'Can you please just take my credit card,' I urge, throwing my things back into the bag.

11

'I still need your boarding pass,' she replies stubbornly, 'preferably without the mints.'

Perspiration is now trickling down my back. Great, I will arrive with a blackhead on my chin and smelling like a tramp. I remove the mints and hand the sticky boarding pass to her and take a deep breath. Okay, calm down. Plenty of time still.

'Oh you're flying to Rome, how lovely.' She smiles, handing me the bag with my goods. 'Didn't they just call a flight to Rome?'

She can't be serious. I race outside and check the board. Shit, it is my flight. I look anxiously for a Boots chemist and feel myself perspire even more. The chemist is just ahead and I start to run, but stop with a skid when I see the queue at the till. I close my eyes, think of the plane and picture myself relaxing with my book. With a new surge of energy I dive in and grab a small can of dry-shampoo, some pimple ointment, face-cleansing tissues, deodorant and a small tin of Vaseline, and squeeze into the queue. Thankfully it moves quickly and I fly out of the store and aim for gate fifty-seven, with my heart beating like a drum. I crash into a buggy and drop my purchases. Horror-stricken, I watch my can of dry-shampoo roll into a Sushi bar. Bother. I follow it with my eye. The Sushi bar is heaving with people. I freeze. Good Lord, is that Simon? What is Simon doing here, and in a Sushi bar? He hates Sushi. Then, of course, I realise it isn't him, it's just some guy wearing the same Marc Jacob cashmere jumper that Simon's mother had bought him for Christmas. I take a deep breath. I must be stressed because this guy doesn't look in the least like Simon, now I come to think about it and absolutely nowhere near as good looking in the jumper. I watch fascinated as he fills his plate until it is brimming over. My God, the way he is piling it on you would think they were giving it away. I reach the can and quickly throw it into my bag.

'Calling all passengers on flight 735 to Rome. You are advised that this flight is now boarding and the gate will close in fifteen minutes.'

Damn, damn. I turn and knock over a chair where the Simon lookalike is casually eating from his overflowing plate. Shaking my head in disbelief I stride towards gate fifty-seven, loaded down with duty-free, a laptop, and an oversized handbag in which I fumble for my passport. I remember the Clarins which is still sitting with Tracey at duty-free, oh bloody hell. I dither, and decide it is not worth the hassle and possible arrest as a terrorist. Finally, I am at gate fifty-seven and boarding the plane. Once inside I squeeze along the gangway towards the loo, where I lock myself in and stare at my face in the mirror with dismay. The pimple is redder. Hurriedly I wash and apply cream to the spot. I pull off my blouse and bra and give myself a quick scrub, and roll the deodorant everywhere. God, this is turning into the flight from hell. Oh I so wish I had a change of clothes. Just a simple Marks and Spencer black dress would do, and then my newly cut hair would look so much better. I apply a thin layer of foundation and smooth some blusher onto my cheeks. I appraise my appearance and nod contentedly at myself. My eyes are shining and my hair falls over my shoulders in gentle waves. I slowly make my way back and look for my seat. To my disappointment I find myself sandwiched between an academic with a tatty book twice the size of *War and Peace* on his lap, and a middle-aged, overweight, red-faced businessman, whose neck seems imprisoned in his tight shirt collar. The academic acknowledges me over the thick dark-rimmed glasses which hover on his beaky nose. I climb over his *Clapham Market Rules* carrier bag and try to ignore the tattered rustic jumper that covers his lanky frame. C&A is still alive and well in Clapham it seems. I fall into my seat and lean my thumping temples against the headrest. The businessman is tapping away furiously on a laptop. I give him a sideways glance. He seems to sigh heavily each time he hits the space bar.

'Miss Annabel Lewis?'

I jump at the sound of my name and look up to see a poker-faced stewardess looking at me. Don't tell me that Tracey and her friend have reported me.

'Oh God, what is it now? Here, search it search it, bloody war on terror.' I shove my handbag past the face of Mr Academic.

'Actually, it should be war on terrorism really, I mean, war on terror, that can't be grammatically correct can it?' I ask Mr Academic. 'That's right isn't it? You should know.'

'Why should I know, I'm a mathematician,' he says irritably, pushing back his seat so I can lean across him. Oh shut the hell up Bels. I try to ignore the shocked look on the stewardess's face when she is confronted with my handbag and with a cringe accept the bra she is handing me.

'I think you left this in the toilet,' she says softly.

'Right, yes, thank you. Sorry about the terrorist stuff, bit nervous of flying,' I mutter.

Mr Academic passes my handbag back to me.

'I know karate,' he says without looking at me. I find myself attempting to visualise his lanky body performing a karate move and fail miserably. I slide down in my seat.

'Cool, always good to know karate,' I respond, carefully removing my book. The plane is starting to fill up now and I begin to relax. In just over two hours I will be in Rome, and heading to the restaurant. The overweight businessman is fidgeting in his seat and sighing. I take another deep breath and close my eyes.

'For pity's sake,' he mumbles.

I turn to see him looking at his watch.

'Are you all right?' I ask politely.

'I would be if the plane took off. It is fifteen minutes late now. I have a business meeting in Rome. For God's sake, why can't they get these things off on time?'

I feel my heart lurch. I can't be late. As it is I have just an hour to freshen up before dinner. I cannot spare any more time. I was even hoping to quickly retrieve my Donna Karan dress from the suitcase.

'Ladies and gentlemen thank you for flying with Easyair. I am afraid we have a bit of a delay...'

The man beside me sighs heavily and I see perspiration running down his temples.

'We are still awaiting one remaining passenger who is joining us from a connecting flight.'

I tap my fingers on the armrest.

'Lady, are you trying to turn me into a nervous wreck? What is it with the tapping? I am trying to chill here,' quips Mr Academic.

Bloody hell, do I need Mr *socially inept and badly in need of a haircut* and Mr *stressed out get me to Rome yesterday*, sitting in the same row as me.

'And I am trying to get to Rome to get married, and I am supposed to be having dinner with my future in-laws, so I am a little nervous.'

'Do I need to know this?'

'Can someone please tell me who the fuck is holding up the plane?' shouts Mr Businessman who is now on his feet and, oh Jesus, his face is very red. I can see the perspiration on the back of his pale blue shirt. He rubs his hands together nervously.

'Please stay calm sir, we understand the passenger is on his way and will be boarding soon.'

Oh thank God.

'It's not right to delay a flight for one passenger,' he asserts.

I nod emphatically.

'Chill man,' advises Mr Academic. 'Statistically it is very improbable that we will arrive later than ten minutes after our scheduled landing time, in fact, statistics show that 90%...'

'Oh shut up geek. What do you know? I don't imagine you have ever had to be anywhere in a hurry. Whichever way it goes we are going to be late – so who gives a 90% shit,' snaps Mr Businessman.

Oh dear, this is not the best place to be. The stewardess seems to be greeting someone.

'I think he is here. We will be going soon,' I say, relief flooding through my body like a drug.

'Ladies and gentlemen, we will be departing in a few minutes,' announces the captain, sounding as relieved as I feel.

Some passengers applaud while others sigh. As the stewardess is showing the late passenger to his seat I spot the Marc Jacob jumper. It's the guy from the Sushi bar. What a sodding cheek, making us all wait while he has his bloody lunch. Well, I shall give him a piece of my mind. He casually walks past our row smiling, seemingly oblivious to the bad karma emanating from Mr Businessman, and then backtracks. My God, he is sitting in front of me. I watch as he squeezes into his seat. Connecting flight my arse, stuffing his bloody face with food more like. I attempt to push him from my mind and try again to relax.

'I won't make it, I know I won't. Christ, this is an important contract too.' I turn slowly to Mr Businessman and pretend I haven't seen his now even redder face. He is fumbling with his seatbelt and his hands are shaking with anger. Oh dear, this is so not good.

'We'll be up soon,' I say cheerfully, helping him

'Not before bloody time, bloody connecting flights.'

Together we clip the seatbelt on and I debate whether to mention the Sushi bar but decide on reflection it might be a bad idea. A terrible fight may ensue and someone might get knifed or shot or at the very least, punched and then I may never get to Rome, let alone to the sodding dinner. No, at times like this when violence is a probability, it is best to keep one's mouth shut. The plane starts taxiing and I decide to push the Sushi guy from my mind and relax with my book. I will still make it, maybe a bit harassed but I am sure Simon's parents will understand. I flex my feet and start reading. I feel a sinking in my stomach when the pilot announces we have missed our scheduled slot for departure thanks to the *stuff as much as I can into my mouth* late passenger. Obviously he doesn't call him that but we all know he is the cause of the delay. I almost hope a lynch mob may descend on him but of course being British we just mumble swear words instead. The lady opposite me even offers her Revels around. I am sorely tempted but point to my waistline and roll my eyes and she seems to understand. Ah, the language of women. Mr Businessman fidgets in his seat and repeats the 'F' word several times.

'Got any great numbers you want to offer, like whether he may kill someone before we even take off is like 95% probable?' I ask Mr Academic.

'Well, statistically speaking...' he begins.

'Yes, well, don't worry about it,' I interrupt as a load of paperwork spills into my lap. I hand the papers back to Mr Businessman, who I see from the headed paper is in fact a Mr Kevin Manning.

'I need to get on another plane. Someone get me on another flight. My whole bloody business depends on this meeting. I shall never fly with this airline again.'

Yes, well I think we all agree on that. I hand him the papers, along with a glass of water that the stewardess had given me. He snatches it, gulps it back in one hit, and fumbles with the papers.

I am beginning to feel very tense and reach into my handbag for my Rescue Remedy. I throw my head back and let three drops fall onto my tongue and immediately feel better. I hear a throaty chuckle, jerk myself up and feel the remedy catch in my throat, making me choke. My eyes stream and I sneeze uncontrollably. God, I feel sure I am going to die. Jesus, *Remedy Rescue*, is that a joke? Mr Academic bangs me on the back just a bit harder than is needed. I struggle to get my breath.

'That stuff will be the death of you.' I barely hear the crystal clear voice over my choking. Looking up through watery eyes I spy the head above the Marc Jacob jumper. He is mocking me while handing a large white handkerchief over the back of his seat. I respond with an enormous sneeze and notice his bright blue smiling eyes and ruffled brown hair. God, he is handsome, rather like a Greek God where everything is perfection. He laughs again revealing white even teeth.

'You surely don't believe in that crap? I suppose you swallow Evening Primrose capsules too, and burn incense,' he mocks me.
I feel the blood rush to my cheeks. How dare he? Posh bugger. I am just recovering when the seat belt sign *bings* and the stewardess asks him to take his seat. Damn it, not even time for a sharp retort. I close my eyes as the plane shoots down the runway and force myself to think of the fashion show that I will be attending in Rome. We are up and I am finally on my way. I feel my shoulders relax and lean down into my handbag to retrieve my iPod. I am just about to sit back when *he* reclines his seat, knocking the iPod out of my hand. What an inconsiderate git. I shove it forward, harder than necessary, in a vain attempt to break his neck.

'Do you mind?' I say angrily.
No response, typical. I fumble around Mr Academic's leg trying to find the music player.

'Hey. Easy tiger,' he coos and winks at me.

'Don't worry, I can resist you, trust me. It is just by your *I Love Clapham* bag, can you reach it?'

'*Clapham Market Rules,* actually. Here.'
He kicks the iPod towards me. I settle again in my seat, open my book, and prepare for the third time to chill. I turn to Kevin and gasp at his pale face. My God, he looks awful.

'Are you all right? Do you want some more water?' I offer.
Kevin shakes his head, the effort to speak seeming too much for him. I hold out my Rescue Remedy but he waves it away.

'Let me know if you need anything,' I offer as I push my earphones back in.

Closing my eyes I drift with the music. I picture Simon and feel a warm sensation. Mum is quite right of course, this is the one. It is perfectly normal to have pre-wedding nerves. After all, it is going to be a big affair, although that had been Simon's parents' choice. The chapel I had chosen in London was considered too small by his mother and suddenly we are being married in a small church on the outskirts of their village and having our reception in the grounds of their villa. I still find it a bit disconcerting that just a few days before my own wedding I still have not seen where the ceremony is to be held. I push silly negative thoughts from my mind and attempt to read my book. The movement of the plane lulls me to sleep. The next thing I feel is Mr Academic waking me up, pulling me from a nice cosy dream. The stewardess is offering coffee and packets of nuts. I prick my ears up as the stewardess offers drinks to the row in front. I hear that clear voice again and feel instantly angry with myself when I feel my heart beating a bit faster. For God's sake Bels, you are on your way to be married, what is wrong with you?

'Do you have anything else apart from nuts? It is just I have an allergy you see,' he asks politely.
The stewardess looks thoughtful.

'We have Toblerone, sir,' she offers.

'Yes, well that has nuts too doesn't it?'
She looks embarrassed.

'I think we have a few snicker bars,' she says helpfully.
I stifle my laughter.

'Yes, but that also has nuts doesn't it?' There is a hint of humour in his voice.

'Oh yes, silly me,' blushes the stewardess.
Oh really this is just too silly to be real. He surely can't be hungry after stuffing himself with so much Sushi.

'We have some cakes,' offers another stewardess, smiling sweetly at him. Oh for God's sake, throw yourselves at him why don't you? She hands him a small wrapped cake and I attempt to stifle my giggle but fail miserably.

'Ah, excellent, except Bakewell tart has nuts in it too doesn't it?' he says patiently, seemingly not hearing my laughter or deliberately ignoring it.

'Jesus,' exclaims Mr Academic and I follow his eyes to where Kevin is slumped in his seat.

Oh Christ, why did I have to be in this row? Kevin is clutching his chest and moaning quietly. For a second, only a second mind you, I wonder if I ignore the whole pain in the chest scenario, maybe it will all go away. Mr Academic leans over me and prods Kevin.

'Is he breathing?'

Oh God, I hope so. I touch Kevin's clammy skin and gulp.

'Kevin, what's wrong?' I ask softly.

He opens his mouth to speak but nothing comes out. Oh shit.

'Do you have any sandwiches?' I hear Marc Jacob jumper say and I see red.

'Oh please, give him something to shut him up, preferably a peanut butter sandwich, and then put out a plea for a doctor, I think this guy is having a heart attack,' I say angrily.

Suddenly he is leaning over his seat.

'Is there a doctor on board, can we have some oxygen here?' he calls out.

Mr Academic jumps from his seat as a man whom I presume is a doctor, sprints down the aisle towards us, while I gently wipe the perspiration from Kevin's face.

'This is your fault,' I say to the guy in front of me.

'My fault, why what did I do?'

'If you had not been stuffing your face in that Sushi bar, you would not have held the plane up and Kevin would not have got worked up and now be having...'

I am thrown from my seat by the doctor.

'Out, and can we please get this seat back,' he orders.

I am standing in the aisle now, face to face with the enemy, well you get my drift.

'Look, I am sorry about your boyfriend...' he begins.

'He is not my boyfriend. I have only just met him,' I interrupt, feeling furious. Good God, does he think I can't do better than Kevin? Not that there is anything wrong with Kevin, of course. He is probably very nice but it is obvious he is much older than me and not at all my type. He just shrugs however.

'Whatever. Your private life is none of my business, but his heart attack is nothing to do with me.'

The captain's announcement quietens everyone.

'*Ladies and Gentlemen this is your captain speaking. Unfortunately one of our passengers has been taken ill and it is necessary for us to make an unscheduled landing at Chatillon-Sur-Seine. We would ask that you disembark in accordance with health and safety regulations, and request you take any hand luggage with you should we need to change planes. Once the passenger has been collected by the emergency services we will recall you onto the flight. We apologise for any inconvenience. Please be assured, Easyair always maintains customer well-being as our top priority.*'

What the hell does he mean by *customer well-being*? I am getting so stressed trying to get to sodding Rome that I may also have a heart attack. Some customer well-being.

'Classic,' I mumble.

Chapter Three

So here we are, or at least here I am, at another bloody airport. The place is packed and there is not a solitary seat to be found. I fish my mobile from my bag to text Simon but find I have no signal. To top it all I am now somewhere in bloody France. I check the time on my phone. Bugger, if I am lucky I will make it with about fifteen minutes to spare. What a bloody first impression this is going to make. God, I am so thirsty but I cannot face the queues.

'Hey, *Rescue Remedy*,'

Oh no. Please God, not him. I pretend to ignore him and trundle towards the flight board.

'Buy you a coffee?' he persists.

I turn and see him. My God, the guy is the ultimate human dustbin. He has a large plate of croissants and jam.

'Join me. I can't eat all this myself.' He points to a chair.

'I am sure you will manage to force it down,' I retort scornfully, while staring enviously at his coffee.

'You surely aren't bearing a grudge are you? Come on, there is nowhere else to sit.' He is leaning back in his chair and carefully replacing a newspaper on a stand behind him. His jeans hug his thighs and I try not to look. His eyes beckon me. He is right of course. The place is packed, hot and noisy. Reluctantly I head towards him. The truth is I am so desperate for a coffee I would have sold my soul to the devil to get one. I squeeze past customers coming out of the café and sit down with a sigh and watch him spoon layers of jam onto a croissant.

'You like croissant with your jam then?' I say sarcastically, pouring myself coffee from his coffee pot.

He smiles and looks at me with that twinkle in his eye.

'I thought you would be with your boyfriend,' he says casually and then yawns.

21

Honestly, I cannot recall meeting a more unpleasant person. I grab a croissant.

'I already told you, he is *not* my boyfriend. I only met him on the plane,' I say crossly.

'Oh, so you did. I forgot.' He pops a sugar cube into his mouth. Probably, you were too busy thinking of food, I think. I spoon a small amount of jam onto my croissant and realise that I am quite hungry. He leans back in his chair and watches me. I feel myself blush. He yawns, leaning further back. I notice his hair is expertly cut and in a style that suits him perfectly.

'Sorry, late night last night and early flight from New York this morning. So, what's your reason for going to Rome then?' he asks yawning again.

What a bloody cheek, as if it is any of his business and am just about to tell him so when some idiot pushes past my chair, knocking the croissant out of my hand and on to my blouse. Jesus, I really cannot believe this.

'Oh God, now look, I can't arrive in Rome like this,' I fume.

Unperturbed he pours more coffee and I have an overwhelming urge to throw mine over him.

'The loo is just along there, can't you wash it off?' he says, casually pointing across the departure lounge.

Really, it is only possible to feel contempt for such a moron.

'This is an Yves Saint Laurent blouse, you know, you can't just scrub away at it with soap.' I do not even try to hide my contempt for him.

'Yves Saint Laurent? Wow that is some blouse then.'

I ignore his mocking tone and bite back the stinging comment I was about to make about his jumper when a muffled announcement drones from the public address.

'Passengers for flight 735 to Rome, this flight will be re-boarding in forty-five minutes from gate two'

Okay, there is time for me to wash the offending mark. I rush to the loo after making the human dustbin promise to bang on the door if there is any news. So here I am, back in an airport loo staring at myself in the mirror, and I swear to God I have aged in the short time it has taken me to fly here. Red raspberry jam sticks unmercifully to my blouse and my hair looks lifeless and, to my horror, I am wearing only one earring. I look around and scramble on the floor. Oh good God, what if I dropped it on the plane? It was the pair Simon had bought me to celebrate our engagement. I am getting to the stage where there is only my mind left to lose now. I pull the other earring out and throw it into my make-up bag. After soaking a whole roll of loo paper in hot water I dive into a cubicle. The sound of soft jazz and the occasional mumbled airport announcement make me anxious. I mean, seriously, how much worse can this get? All I want to do is get to my fiancé, preferably on time, and in one piece, and not looking like a cabbage patch doll. I pull off the blouse and rub frantically at the jam and succeed in making an even bigger pink stain that is covered in bits of loo roll. Sod it. Obviously, it is cheap loo roll and not that nice soft, perfumed one you buy in Waitrose. Slowly, I pick them off. Oh, this is terrible. Angrily I rub at the blouse until it is very wet. I throw it back on and come out of the cubicle and stand in front of the noisy hand-dryer in an attempt to dry the blouse. The wet patch sticks to my Victoria Secret bra and I feel myself wanting to cry. How could a journey be so stressful? After what seems an eternity, the blouse is drier, although a bit sticky, and dotted with specks of toilet roll. I pull a hairbrush from my bag and tidy my hair. Satisfied that I look reasonably presentable I walk out of the loos. You know that feeling you get when you know something is just not right, that things seem somehow different? Well, I have that feeling right now. I realise the airport lounge is practically empty. Marc Jacob jumper is nowhere to be seen, and the café bar is deserted. I spy the offending croissant sitting on the table and, as my eyes scan the airport lounge I see him. The bugger is fast asleep on a bench, and oh God, out of the window I see my plane racing along the runway. I run to the café and madly raid the cutlery tray selecting my weapon of choice.

'You stupid bloody wanker, I told you to bang on the door.' I seriously cannot believe I am holding a fork to his throat while grabbing his jumper with my other hand.

He yawns, looks at me, then at the fork.

'You plan to stab me to death with a plastic fork? Good luck,' he says calmly.

'We have missed the flight, you arrogant bastard,' I throw the fork at him in my frustration. 'Just be grateful it is plastic.'

He is staring at my blouse.

'What is wrong with you?' he asks casually as he sits up and stretches.

'Don't push me, don't you bloody push me, I am just about managing to stay calm.' I feel my heart thumping. All I can see are flashbacks from the *Psycho* movie, and I so want *him* to be in the shower scene right now.

'This is calm? Remind me to stay away from you when you are in a temper. I'm sorry, I fell asleep. Anyway, take some responsibility - you must have heard the call,' he says nonchalantly. Jesus, this guy really is the limit.

'Don't come anywhere near me, do you understand, *ever*,' I say, breathing fire at him.

He feigns a salute.

'Yes ma'am. Believe me, after the plastic fork attack it will be my pleasure to avoid you at all times. I wouldn't want to be around when you perform your party piece with a screwdriver.'

I take a deep breath and calmly pick up my bags. This really is becoming unbearable. I can scarcely get my legs to move towards the check-in desk. Oh God, what if I collapse here? What if the next big event in my life is my funeral? That man will have killed me. Well, I am not going to let him have that pleasure. Looking like something the cat has dragged in, I approach the desk.

'Excuse me. I don't suppose anyone has handed in a white gold diamond stud earring have they?' I ask hopefully trying to ignore her pained expression which clearly indicates she does not believe I was wearing white gold diamond earrings.

'I can check for you, madam.'

I shake my head.

'No, it's okay. I was on the flight to Rome, the one where the guy had a heart attack, and I got jam on my blouse and well, I need a flight.'

Her eyes lock onto my blouse and I feel sure she smirks.

'Ah, that flight has gone.'

Yes, well I bloody know that, don't I?

'What time is the next flight to Rome?' I ask patiently.

She shakes her head.

'We are a small airport. We have no scheduled flights to Rome, madam,' she says apologetically.

'What? But I have to get to Rome. You're an airport aren't you, well not you personally, of course,' I say loudly, 'you don't understand, I have to be in Rome for dinner at eight this evening. It is a matter of urgency.'

This is an airport, how can they not have flights? I hear a snigger behind me. Oh how I wish I had a real fork.

'Compared to world peace and the end of civilisation as we know it, I have to agree. Dinner at eight, in Rome, must certainly qualify for a private jet.'

I ignore his irritating voice and give the girl a pleading look.

'It really *is* important. I have to get to Rome by eight.' Oh God, am I begging? The tears I had struggled to hold back suddenly pour forth against my will. Oh, is it not enough that I have wedding nerves without all this too?

'One moment madam, I shall see what I can do.'

Oh thank God. I turn from the desk, expecting to walk into Marc Jacob jumper but he has gone. I fall into the nearest seat. I am beginning to think someone is trying to tell me something. Maybe I am not meant to marry Simon. I try my phone again but still have no signal. Then, I remember my laptop. Yes, I can email him. He will get the email on his Blackberry. For the first time in hours I start to feel a little more relaxed. I open my laptop and get into my emails, but, oh, shit, there is no bloody connection there either. What the hell is it with airports? Seeing the assistant has returned I slam the lid shut and rush over to the desk.

'Well?' I ask anxiously.

'We can get you on a flight to Marseille, and from there you can get a flight to Rome,' she announces, cheerfully, while looking at the computer screen, and I feel my spirits lift. I look at the time on my phone. Okay, I will be a bit late but at least I will get there.

'Oh that is great, thank you so much, what gate do I go to?'

'The flight isn't scheduled to take off until ten o'clock, but it will get you there in plenty of time for the connecting flight to Rome.'

This cannot be happening. It is a bad dream.

'Is that the best you can offer, ten o'clock tonight?' I say dabbing away at my tears again.

Okay, so, I will miss dinner, but at least I will be there tonight. And even if I miss dinner at least I will be in plenty of time for the rehearsal.

'No, madam, you misunderstand. The flight to Marseilles is tomorrow *morning* at ten. The onward flight to Rome is some hours later at about six in the evening, so you should arrive in Rome by about eight tomorrow evening.'

Shit, bugger and sod it. At the rate I am going I may not even make the rehearsal. I am slowly losing the will to live.

'Are you mad? I have to be there before tomorrow night,' I murmur. What is it with these people? I struggle to control my tears and lift my bag onto the desk where I begin emptying it until I find my bottle of Kalms. I shake out six and swallow them in one hit. Oh what the hell, I shake out two more and throw them back. Oh my God what the hell do I tell Simon? The thought of trying to explain all this over the telephone prompts me to take two more. What on earth do I tell him?

'If you are not too drugged up, do you think you can manage to walk, or are you too wired on herbal?'

My heart sinks as I recognise the all too familiar voice. Is this guy never going to go away?

'From here we can drive it in six hours, maybe seven at the most,' he says, walking away. What does he mean? I jump up grab the duty-free and laptop. Six hours, that means I will certainly make it for the rehearsal.

'Hey, wait, what do you mean?' I call after him.

The bastard is un-bloody-believable. He does not even wait for me.

'You aren't the only one who needs to be in Rome. I am hiring a car, are you coming or what?' he replies somewhat impatiently. Honestly, he is the reason I missed my flight and now he acts like he is doing me a big favour. He stops and I walk into him banging the whisky bottles against his leg.

'Ah, you're lethal do you know that?' he winces.

'Don't we need to get our luggage?' I ask stupidly, not even thinking to apologise.

'Ah, how many of those tranquiliser things do you have left? Or maybe I can supply you with a plastic fork? Were there many Yves Saint Laurent blouses in your suitcase?' I see he is mocking me again.

'Oh God, my suitcase is still on the plane isn't it? What stupid idiots.' I twirl around in anger.

With the will to live totally lost, I slump into the nearest seat. I can't breathe, and I certainly don't want to remember what was in my suitcase. Worse still, I am considering travelling across the country with a total stranger. I pull out my Rescue Remedy, then think better of it and throw it back into my bag. So, what would you have done? I mean, here we are, or at least here I am, stranded at an airport, with a fiancé waiting for me in Rome, and a family dinner booked. But, everyone tells you not to travel with strange men, right? And this is one irritating stranger. I try to think what Simon would want me to do.

'No, but thanks anyway,' I force myself to say.

He shrugs and heads out of the airport. I watch him from the door. Oh sod it.

'Okay, wait,' I shout and run after him.

At last, Rome here I come... hopefully.

Chapter Four

Marc Jacob jumper

'Okay, wait.'

I turn to see her running towards me and I very sensibly place my hand luggage protectively in front of my groin. The last thing I want is another bottle of duty-free hitting my balls. The woman is a walking disaster, certainly her thought processes shoot around like flying shrapnel. God, do I really need a whirlwind like her travelling with me?

'Thank you, I would like the lift,' she says breathlessly, skidding to a stop in front of me her hair flying all around her face which is streaked from crying.

It's settled then. I suppose that will teach me to fall for a woman's tears. I mean she doesn't exactly induce a heart-pounding adrenaline rush that's for sure. Having a fork put to your throat, albeit a plastic one, is a bit daunting. I mean, who does that? A psychopath that's who, or a completely over-the-top premenstrual woman, in which case that is all I need. That, of course, would explain the gush of tears that almost drowned the poor assistant at the desk. How can a dinner in Rome be that important anyway? Okay, I should stop being so cynical. It is obviously important to her and those tears were heartfelt. If I fell for them they must have been. Funny that. Maybe it was a combination of the tears, that stupid stain on the front of her blouse and the missing earring. I certainly am pretty immune to tears most of the time, these days. God knows, Claudine had literally flooded the apartment with them last night, hiccupping all over the place and sounding a bit like a frog.

'*You're* hateful, *you're* a bastard and you never think about me.'

Every *you're* emphasised with a sharp red fingernail pointing dangerously at my face that I feared for my sight, while punctuating *bastard* with a stamp of her foot. I'm a bastard? I'm hateful? All I did was move my flight back. It was just my luck that my decision collided with her impending period.

'I wanted us to travel to Rome together,' she had pouted.

'I'll be there a few hours after you. I have to go over these legal papers before I leave. It's one of those things.'

'That bloody lawsuit. It's all you ever bloody talk about. I suffer all the time because of it. I still don't understand why you didn't change both our flights. Honestly, you're such a tight bastard.'

'You know it is stupidly extravagant to change both. I had no choice. Get over it.'

Of course, she had flounced out saying she would die rather than spend time with my family anyway and she won't be coming. No sooner had I arrived at the solicitors she had texted to say she had changed her mind. Women. Surely life would be more bearable without them. Now, I have gone and burdened myself with this stuck-up, bad tempered, designer-obsessed madam. Will I never learn? She is a real weirdo with all that herbal dependency. A good glass of wine would do her the world of good if you ask me. She is now looking hopefully at me.

'Right, let's see if we can hire a car or something,' I say pleasantly while wondering what the hell I have let myself in for.

Chapter Five

'Is this all they have?' I stare miserably at the dented, sad-looking car which seems to reflect my own despair. The rental guy gawps at my bum and proceeds to stroke the bonnet.

'It is good car. I let you have for low price.' He licks his lips and I swear he dribbles.

My companion, who is lying on the floor, seemingly unconcerned about the Marc Jacob jumper but very concerned about the exhaust, ignores him. I sigh heavily.

'Well?' I ask, and get a grunt in return. He slides out from under the car and lifts the bonnet, much to my irritation.

'What are you doing?' I ask, trying to keep the irritation from my voice.

He lifts his head to look at me and bangs it on the bonnet.

'Damn. I am checking the engine, what do you think I am doing?' he replies impatiently.

'But, this car is terrible. We can't take this,' I retort exasperated.

'It is actually a classic.

'A classic piece of junk,' I argue.

He shakes his head.

'This is the third rental company we have tried and so far this is the only car available.' He slams down the bonnet, strides past me, yanks open the door and plays with the gears and steering wheel. I try hard not to grit my teeth. I look to the sales guy who winks lecherously at me. Jesus Christ, how did I ever get into this situation?

'I'm not paying the price you are asking, even with what you say you will take off, it is still too much,' he says.

What is he doing? I can't believe I am hearing this.

'You're not taking this, surely?' I say, struggling to keep the panic out of my voice. What will Simon's parents think if I arrive in this?

He ignores me. The salesman scratches his head and mumbles something in French which Marc Jacob jumper seems to understand.

'Another five per cent and we will take it,' he barters.

Please tell me I am not hearing this. Please let there be another car. The deal is seemingly done and with a smile the man hands over the keys.

'Oh no, you cannot possibly be serious,' I groan.

He nods.

'I agree, the last thing we want is a lemon, but if it's all they've got, we don't have a great deal of choice,' he replies, kicking the tyre.

'*A lemon*, what does that mean? It looks like scrap metal to me.'

'A Citroën, you know *Citron?*' he laughs, over-pronouncing the French. 'Great colour, you must admit,' he says kicking the other tyre.

Great colour? Is he totally off his rocker? Who in their right mind would buy an egg-yolk-yellow coloured car?

'Well, I am glad you're amused but I can't arrive for dinner in this,' I protest. 'It only has two doors.'

'How many doors do you need? Come on, this is a classic. Look a sunroof too.' He lifts the plastic and I watch horrified as it tears in his hands. 'You will arrive with your hair blowing in the breeze,' he laughs again.

'This thing probably won't even get us ten miles,' I say miserably.

'Kilometres not miles. Come on be positive, I bought it for next to nothing,' he says with a satisfied grin.

I look at him horror-stricken and then at the yellow piece of junk in front of me.

'Are you telling me, you have just *bought* this pile of junk? Are you totally nuts?' The words are strangled out of me. Jesus, we can't even hire another car now.

'Well, you didn't believe for one minute that he could hire this car out did you? You must have led a sheltered life. It's a fantastic bargain, an original classic French Citroën CV2.'

Like I know, or even care what the hell that is. He smiles, slides on his sunglasses and strikes a pose next to the Citroën. I roll my eyes and shake my head. My God, he is like a child with a new toy. My whole future hangs on this car, Jesus, what a suicidal thought. What the arsing head and hole is wrong with this guy? Has he no comprehension of the importance of my dinner? The sodding car is prehistoric. I decide to stand my ground.

'I am not getting in that thing. There is no way I can arrive in Rome for dinner in that,' I say resolutely.

The car gives a loud creak as he pulls the door open.

'Well, I can. I hate to burst your bubble but I don't think you are going to make that all-important dinner now, but if you want to get to Rome, get in and stop moaning. If not, it was nice knowing you,' he says flippantly and proceeds to get into the goddamn thing without me. Bugger it. I so hate this guy.

'It doesn't even have central locking,' I say appalled, wondering what else must be lacking in this useless piece of junk.

He bursts out laughing.

'You are seriously unbelievable. This car is wicked.'

Knowing I have no choice if I want to get to Rome at all, I reluctantly walk around the car to the open door, ignoring his look.

'What are you doing?' He blocks my way with his arm.

Oh Jesus, what now?

'I am getting in the car. You just told me to get in the car didn't you?' I retort between gritted teeth.

'Yes, but preferably in the passenger side, unless you are planning on driving, and I have to say frankly, I am not too comfortable with that.'

Shit, wrong sodding side. I twirl around without a word and fiddle with the handle on the other door. It doesn't bloody open. He sighs, walks around and pulls it open for me. I carefully place the duty-free and my laptop in the back and grimace at the odd fishy smell that emanates from inside the car. I watch as he pays. Well, he can think again if he thinks he is getting any money out of me. He gets in beside me and, against my better judgement, I find myself thinking that the jumper actually doesn't look so bad on him after all, in fact, maybe even better than on Simon. After several tries, and a few hiccups the engine splutters into life. God, it sounds terrible.

'Is it supposed to sound like this?' I ask without thinking.

'Like what?' he asks while fiddling with the knobs on the dashboard. Jesus, the guy is in love with the goddamn thing.

'Like my mother's sewing machine.'

He hands me a map which I unfold as we jolt out of the car park. He crunches the gears and I sigh heavily.

'We need the N71,' he instructs.

I struggle to find the N71 on the map while discreetly moving my knee away from his. The car surges forward and I give an involuntary cry.

'Is there a problem?'

You are the problem arsehole. He grinds the gears again, and I feel an overwhelming urge to jump from the car.

'Yes, there is a problem. Don't you know how to drive?' I quickly put my seat belt on and look at the map.

'I have to get used to the gears, where am I going?'

'God knows,' I retort crisply.

'Read the map woman.' He flaps at the map with his hand.

Oh this insufferable man.

'Damn, it's there,' he shouts, and I look to see what *is* there. Car horns blare at us as we shoot across the road. I close my eyes and scream.

'Shit, what are you doing?' I shout and instinctively push my foot onto a brake pedal, which is of course, not there. My hand grabs the side of my seat and I clench my jaw. The car bumps, shudders and then surges forward onto the motorway.

'I am getting us onto the N71, now can you read the map and stop swearing. By the way, your language is atrocious, where are you from, the East End of London or something?'

I am speechless. What an arsehole. I make the decision to speak to him only when it is really necessary. I fumble with the map. He seems totally unaware of me and is removing his sunglasses. I sneak a quick look at his face and am struck by his handsome features. He needs a shave, but somehow even I have to admit he is rather appealing. The laughter lines around his eyes are a clear indication he laughs a lot. I find myself glancing down to his firm thighs again and imagine, like Simon, he works out regularly.

'Surrey, actually, some distance from the East End in fact,' I say softly.

I am not sure if he has heard me as at that moment his mobile bleeps. For a second I could swear his face clouded over but he is back to normal in no time.

'Here, can you check that text for me.'

I stare at the iPhone he is holding out to me.

'I can't read your messages,' I say moving further into my seat.

He groans.

'In case you haven't noticed I am attempting to drive us to Rome, I can only drive. I can't read maps and text messages at the same time. I am not a Swiss Army Knife you know. I am relying on you for that and, so far, you haven't done very well.'

Bloody hell, that is it, I am not taking any more of this guy's shit.

'That is so unfair. I am reading your sodding map...'

'Oh sure you are, that is why I had to nearly kill us to get onto the N71,' he interrupts rudely.

God I am so close to hitting him.

'Don't blame your bad driving on my map reading. Bloody hell, you are sodding unbelievable.'

'I am unbelievable, ha! So far I have done everything in my power to get us to Rome and so far you have done everything in your power to make it as difficult as possible. Notice, I do not need to swear. So, do we need this road that is coming up?'

I find myself staring uncomprehendingly at him.

'I don't think you have any idea what I do or who I am,' I say trying to muster up some confidence.

'No, quite right, no idea whatsoever and no inclination to know, but I would like to know if we need this road that is coming up or should I stay on the motorway?' he says evenly looking ahead.

'What, oh shit.' I unravel the map again and see that we need the N274.

'And she swears again,' he sighs.

I ignore his sarcastic comment and strain to see the signs. Bugger, where is the N274? How can he possibly expect me to read this map? It's a French map for goodness sake.

'Oh oh, quick, we need the third exit on this roundabout,' I stammer.

'Ah, come on woman what are you doing?' He swerves in front of another car and I close my eyes. I feel sure my life flashed before me as the car spins round.

I hear him sigh.

'Okay, I managed to take the third exit, now just tell me where am I heading?'

'To hell, I hope,' I mumble.

'The N27 should be coming up, we need that I think,' I say aloud, waving the map in front of him hoping he will check.

He nods and hands me the phone, which I meekly take. I scroll into the text messages and see the message is from a Claudine.

'Do you want me to read it?' I ask hesitantly.

He turns and gives me a cross look. I let out an audible sigh and open the text. Oh God, I can't read this, can I? I feel a strange sensation when I realise there is a woman in his life and not just any woman, from the tone of the text. My God, am I feeling jealous? Don't be stupid Bels. You are just surprised that any woman could feel anything for such a moron.

'It's from Claudine. You really want me to read this?'

He sighs. Right, he asked for it.

'*Darling, why haven't you texted me? It has been hours now. I thought at least from the airport you would have been in touch. Hope to speak soon, miss you so much already and can't wait to....*'

I feel myself blushing. He is rubbing his eye and I am wondering if he is even listening.

'*Snoozy woozy you,*' I finish. 'Oh and there is a kiss.'

He does not flinch.

'There is an N274 coming up, signposted *Voie Georges Pompidou*, is that the one?'

I realise I am staring open-mouthed at him and quickly look back to the map.

'Erm, yes, that is the one and then we want the A39.'

He nods and puts the phone back in his pocket. I bite my lip trying to hold back the words that are fighting for release, fail miserably and blurt out.

'Snoozy woozy, I mean, what are you, like six years old or something?'

I see his eyebrows rise and the muscle of his cheek twitch. Still, at least he has had *a* text which is more than I have had. I can't understand why Kaz has not rung back or even texted me. I lean down and fumble in my handbag for my phone, except my hand gropes around clutching at thin air. Shit, there is no handbag. Oh shit again. I look to the backseat where my laptop sits cosily next to my duty-free bag. Treble shit, I must have left my handbag at the airport. Oh dear God, if you do exist, please send me the right words to use. Now my life is definitely not going to be worth living. I shan't need to jump from the car as he will probably just shove me out of it. Terrible visions of a dirty youth buying drugs with my credit card make me shudder. Come on Bels, drug dealers don't accept credit cards. Oh no, and how would you know that? I answer myself. The same dirty youth is probably trying to sell your Blackberry right now. Oh God this is awful, my whole life is in the organiser on that phone. In fact, my whole wedding is on my Blackberry. How could I have been so stupid? My stomach turns over and I feel sick when I remember that my passport is also in there and oh God, my Kalms and bugger, my contraceptive pill. Oh bugger it. How the hell do I get more if the bag is not there when I go back? I can't possibly ask Simon's mother. Only I could lose my contraceptive pill while heading into a Catholic country where just being in possession of them will have my cards marked as a modern day Mary Magdalene. What am I to do? I can't possibly refuse Simon on our wedding night. The chances of my getting pregnant then are growing by the minute.

'Okay, I can see a sign for the A39. I think we can relax once we are on that,' he says, unaware of my turmoil.

Bugger, come on Bels speak now for Christ's sake, after all things can't get any worse. You can't have a baby now. Not yet, maybe after a year but certainly not this soon. Somehow, Simon does not seem the fatherly type. Lord, why I am thinking these things now. Surely he is the fatherly type, isn't he? I will want children in time and surely he will too. Oh for Christ's sake, shut up and just tell him, otherwise the way things are going you will be lucky if you get there for your wedding, let alone bloody dinner and the chances of ever having a baby will be very slim but you certainly cannot have one yet, you need to get your pills and get them soon.

'I can't have a baby yet,' I blurt out.

'What? How did we get from the A39 to a baby? Did I miss something?' He seems so remarkably calm that my confidence grows.

'We have to go back, I have left my handbag at the airport and my pill is in there, my passport too. In fact, my whole life is in there.' Annoyingly I start to cry, bugger it.

There is silence. For a minute I think he has not heard me and am about to speak again but the continuous banging of his hand on the steering wheel stops me. My heart is beating so fast that I can barely breathe. He swerves right and into a slip road.

'You have left your handbag at the airport?'

I nod, unable to speak.

'Why would you do that?' I can hear the suppressed anger in his voice.

'I kind of got sidetracked I suppose, I'm sorry...' I realise I don't know his name.

He shakes his head. I am a wreck the whole journey back and spend most of it praying to a God I don't even believe in. Is my whole wedding trip destined to be at airports? It has been well over an hour since we left here. I feel my legs almost collapse with relief when the same lady I had spoken to earlier sees me and holds up my handbag.

'Ah, I am pleased to see you madam.' She smiles, obviously also relieved.

I gratefully take the bag and check inside for my Blackberry. Two missed calls and three texts. I thank her warmly and run back outside. He doesn't speak when I get into the car but just drives off. I check my messages. They are from Kaz and Simon, both asking what happened to my flight. The third one from Simon accuses me of punishing him because I haven't replied. What? Punishing him, is he mad? Bloody hell all I want to do is get to Rome, meet my future in-laws, have a family dinner and then get married. Instead, my sodding flight gets diverted because Mr Marc Jacob jumper has to stuff his face. Come to think of it the whole thing is his fault. I would be on the flight now if he had not fallen asleep.

'You have totally destroyed my life. I hope that makes you happy,' I say angrily reaching up in the vain hope there may be a sun visor with a mirror attached. Of course there isn't.

'Oh this sodding, stupid antique car.'

'Is that gratitude for bringing you all the way back to get your handbag?'

I punch in Simon's number and get his voicemail. Bugger it. I don't want to leave a message while I am with Mr Pain-in-the-arse. Why did he ask me what's happening and then turn his phone off? I fight back my tears and fumble around for the buttons to open the window.

'Look, I am sorry if I have destroyed your life. If it is any comfort it was not intentional. In fact if I could go back a few hours and just rearrange that life-changing moment when I asked you to join me for coffee, trust me, I would. But I can't, so here we are. Live with it,' he responds sharply and swerves around a lorry. Meanwhile, I shove my foot onto my imaginary brake again and wonder how long it will be before I am tempted to pull on the handbrake. What a maniac. I fumble in my bag for tissues. God, I feel so weepy. It will be hours before we get to Rome and I will never make it in time for the dinner now. Simon is annoyed, and I imagine his parents must be too. This could not be a worse start to my wedding. Marc Jacob jumper is fiddling with the radio and I take the opportunity to phone Simon again, only to get his voicemail. I send a text explaining I missed the connecting flight but it all sounds terribly feeble.

'Look, why don't we try and get on with each other. We have music, the sun is shining and we are in a classic Citroën. All seems pretty cool to me.' He sways to the music and I just stare at him.

'Yes, except the bloody windows don't open,' I say through gritted teeth.

He rolls his eyes at me, leans across me and quickly clips back the window. Honestly, this bloody car must be older than my sodding grandmother. I have never, in my entire life, met such an arrogant, reckless man. I mean, who seriously just buys a car on a whim when in a foreign country, and one without proper windows as well? Simon would be appalled. Thank God, I am marrying a sensible man. Never, in a million years would Simon have been so reckless with money, even if he did have it. No, Simon most definitely is not an impulse buyer. I feel confident that financially Simon will always be cautious. Of course, I do wonder if Simon is just a little over cautious. Perhaps consulting *Which?* magazine before every large purchase is a bit extreme. Still, I would rather he was over cautious than irresponsible like this guy. I did put my foot down when he started looking at the irons in the *Which?* guide. But, at least, he doesn't have debts. This guy, however, probably has credit card debts galore. Oh how I pity Claudine. What is he going to tell her? I suppose she is used to his extravagance. Thank God, I will be free of him when we get to Rome. The thought of Rome reminds me of my luggage and I grab my phone and again try Simon. Damn, bloody voicemail. Okay, I will try Kaz, she surely must answer. Shit, another voicemail. Where the hell is everyone? I look up and see that we are heading onto the A39. Christ that was quick. I sit rigid in my seat as we approach another lorry and overtake it at what seems great speed.

'Jesus, this is not *Top Gear*, you know,' I shout above the music.
'What?'
'I said... Jesus, why are you driving so fast?'
The cool air whizzes past my ear and of course, unlike him, I do not have a warm jumper. I fumble with the sunroof, a useless bloody thing that it is. Honestly, how could he buy a bloody car that doesn't have an automatic sunroof? He seems lost in thought. I take the opportunity to study him while he is unaware. The breeze is ruffling his thick brown wavy hair, which I can see now has been expertly cut. Another extravagance he probably can't afford. One hand is lightly holding the steering wheel while the other is on the gearstick. I remember I used to drive like that until Simon told me off. *A driver who has one hand on the gears is a bad driver. Always remember that, Annabel,* he had said. I follow my companion's hand up to his shoulder and can see his rippling muscles. God, he fancies himself. He most likely has membership to some very exclusive health club too, which he probably cannot afford. I have to admit, though, he looks good and is unbelievably relaxed, unlike me. I pull a scrunch from my bag, wind my hair into it and check my phone one more time. Damn, damn, why doesn't Simon phone me back?

'Do you have the map?'

I jump at the sound of his voice. Meekly, I open the map and want to cry when his phone goes. As always, it is his sodding phone. Where are all the people who love and care about *me*? He hands it to me without a word. Bloody hell, am I his secretary now? I give him a dirty look.

'Okay, fine. Hang onto the steering wheel will you?' he says calmly and removes his hand from the wheel and begins to tap into his phone.

'Shit, what are you doing you stupid wanker? I'll do it,' I yell and go to grab the phone but knock it out of his hand in my haste. It rings persistently, somewhere on the floor near his feet.

'You really are disaster on two legs aren't you? Can't you just swallow all that rescue stuff and fall asleep?' I can hear the restrained anger in his voice. I swallow back an apology and undo my seat belt.

'Oh no, what are you doing now?' he says fearfully. Oh yes, be afraid, be very afraid. I feel his legs tense as I bend across him to reach for the phone.

'Look, just leave it, really it isn't that important,' he says nervously.
No way Jose, I am sick of your insults. I purposefully bang his knee as I feel around the floor by his feet. Christ, the floor of the car is filthy. My hand touches something soft and wet and I scream and grab the edge of his seat. What the hell?

'Oh my God what is that? Oh Jesus there is something alive in the car,' I scream hysterically.
He yelps and I feel my hand being pulled from the seat.

'What are you doing? Move, move, I can't find the brake,' he roars.
I see my hand is tightly squeezing his thigh. I jump back with a start and am then thrown forward with a jolt as he brakes sharply and my head hits the dashboard with a thud.

'Oh great, well done. I am in the wrong lane and there is a police car behind us, they probably think you were giving me oral sex or something,' he snaps.

'In your dreams,' I scoff.
My head feels numb and I moan softly. Did he say the police? Maybe they can help me get to Rome and I can escape this lunatic. I turn to

see him staring at my breasts and shaking his head. I follow his gaze to the front of my blouse where a button has popped off and my Victoria Secret bra is on show. My face gets hot and I know it is turning scarlet.

'Classic,' he mumbles as the policeman approaches the car.

'Do me one big favour, please do not open your mouth, not even to take a breath. Got it?' he instructs.

I nod meekly and clutch my blouse. I feel totally deflated. I have never looked so awful in my whole life. Oh God why? Why are you doing this to me? I look down at the gaping hole in my tights. Shitty shit. The policeman approaches the driver side and Mr Marc Jacob jumper opens the door and hands something to him. I gasp, my God is that money? I strain to see, but it is impossible. They converse in French and then Marc Jacob jumper gets out of the car and then they are pointing and laughing at me. Bloody nerve, well I don't need to put up with this. Before I can speak the door is opened and my companion pokes his head in and winks.

'Honey, could you step out of the car for a second.'

Honey, what the hell. I open the door and walk round attempting a grin as I do so. Marc Jacob jumper gives me a funny look as I hobble towards them like an incontinent woman. The policeman is looking at my breasts too now. I quickly remember the gap and pull it together. Marc Jacob rolls his eyes and mouths, 'Why are you walking like that?' I nod down to the hole in my tights and smile warmly at the policeman.

'Hello officer, I am hoping you....'

'Honey, try not to talk too much. The officer understands and we just need to show him your medication,' he interrupts rudely, grabbing my hand and holding it tightly while smiling at the officer.

'What the hell are you talking about?' I pull my hand away.

He continues to smile at the policeman and shrugs apologetically.

'Come along sweetie, where is the special rescue medication.'

'Fuck you,' I retort and walk back to the car.

'Over my dead body huh, darling. I see the language hasn't improved,' he snarls still smiling.

I take the Rescue Remedy from my handbag and throw it to him. I can feel the tears welling up. Oh, I look such a mess. My forehead is red, my hair is a tangled mess and my blouse is torn and stained and

I have no other clothes and everything is his fault and worse still I have no idea what he is telling the police about me. I drop my head onto my chest and then see his phone. Gingerly, I lean down and grasp it. He is still talking to the policeman. I scroll into the messages and quickly read them. One is from someone called Josh and the missed calls were him too. Oh my God, it looks like Mr Marc Jacob jumper is a builder. Well, there is mention of building work being alive and well in Manhattan, so what else can it mean? His name is Christian it seems. Blimey, a bit posh for a loser like him isn't it? I check the other text which, yes, is from Claudine and she is calling him an arse, well I have to agree. So he is a builder. Say no more then. Well, he can drop those airs and graces with me. The policeman is waving to me and I cheerfully wave back. Marc Jacob, no, correction, Christian the builder, climbs back into the car. He is grinning from ear to ear.

'He loved the Lemon,' he says proudly, handing me my Rescue Remedy.

'Did he indeed, how fortunate,' I say caustically.

He starts the engine.

'Yes, but what really got us off was my telling him that you were my fiancée and you kind of have these jerks when you don't take your medication...'

'Jerks!' I explode. 'What do you mean jerks? The only jerk around here is you, and I most defiantly am not your fiancée, thank God.'

'No, but you are certainly someone's, poor chap,' he mumbles.

I feel my blood boil.

'And how would you know that?' I demand, fighting back an impulse to slap him.

'Well, the ring is a bit of a giveaway. Oh, and by the way, the wet soft alive thing was a sponge,' he huffs and pulls the car back onto the road. I am stupidly speechless. An arse indeed, Claudine was right about that. I don't imagine this guy has lasted more than a week in a proper functional relationship. Simon will be so appalled when I tell him about this loser. He hates builders with a passion. Oh I bet, Mr Christian, the builder, makes them wait and wait and spends much of his life handing out great estimates with much sucking in of breath. I bet he bleeds them dry and then spends it like water. He is probably on his way to Rome now while about three customers are going frantic waiting for him to turn up. I throw his phone into his lap.

'Claudine says not to be such an arse, rather impossible for you, I would have thought.'

He simply yawns and peers at the petrol gauge.

'Right, the Lemon needs some juice.' He glances quickly at me. 'And you, well you need everything don't you?'

If I hadn't been so thirsty I would have protested that I just wanted to go straight to Rome. Instead, I meekly nod. Hopefully there will be some clothes shops. The thought of buying some nice designer clothes cheers me up.

'Okay, I shall veer off at the next slip road and see where it takes us. We are not likely to get lost, right? All roads lead to Rome after all,' he laughs.

I respond with a dirty look.

'God, you are one sour woman,' he laughs again.

I bite my lip. Now is not the right time but the time will come and when it does, oh, I will relish it.

Chapter Six

Christian

What a bonus. The car is a gem, an absolute classic. I practically robbed the guy. Of course, it needs a good overhaul and the clutch is knackered, but all the same it drives like a dream considering. Not that madam appreciates it, of course. Jesus, she never stops complaining, and her language is atrocious. She certainly wouldn't be out of place on a construction site. In fact, I actually thought I was getting rid of her at one point when she stated she couldn't possibly arrive in Rome in my so-called rust bucket. What a blooming cheek. There was one highlight, when she said she couldn't possibly get into it. There was me thinking I had finally got rid of her when she goes and changes her mind again. Oh well, she is a diversion, albeit an irritating one. I glance at her to see if she is reading the map but surprise, surprise, she isn't. She has that glazed look on her face again. A little friendly jolt is in order then.

'Okay, I can see a sign for the A39. I think we can relax once we are on that.'

'I can't have a baby yet.'

What the hell? Who mentioned babies? Who even mentioned sex? Surely that comes before babies doesn't it? My God, she isn't going to scream rape is she? Oh hell, this is all I need. I knew she was a bit dotty but I didn't for one minute seriously think she was completely and utterly mad. Keep calm. The best thing is to humour her.

'What? How did we get from the A39 to a baby? Did I miss something?'

Like you screaming the word rape? And demanding money? But no, instead her face crumples and she blurts out that she has left her handbag at the airport with her contraceptive pill inside. I mean, is this really my problem? She then promptly bursts into tears. It's my problem. I'm beginning to think a Polar Icecap expedition would be easier than travelling to Rome with her. In fact, I actually think I would enjoy it. At least I could be sure of getting there. I really cannot bring myself to talk to her on the journey back to the airport and thankfully she manages to keep her mouth shut, although not for long unfortunately. I am relieved when she climbs back into the Lemon armed with the said handbag, and with, I assume, her pills safely ensconced inside. Everything would have been fine had she not opened that offensive mouth of hers. After fiddling with her phone she accuses me of destroying her life and insults the Lemon, calling it 'a sodding stupid antique car'. I fight the overwhelming desire to put my hands around her throat and bite back a stinging retort. I'm beginning to think a job as Colonel Gaddafi's chauffeur would be a walk in the park compared to chauffeuring Madam *Kiss-my-arse-I-think-I'm-Victoria-Beckham*. What an ungrateful cow. If that ring on her finger is anything to go by then some guy has actually chosen to be with her. He has obviously had a lobotomy at some point. He must be a bit of a strange guy though, because he hasn't phoned her once. I bet an evening with them is a bundle of laughs. Well, seeing as we are late now we may as well stop off for something to eat. That won't please her. I ought to phone Claudine. Women. They are all the same, a pain in the jacksie.

Chapter Seven

It is almost twenty minutes before we see any shops and in that whole time Simon does not phone or text. I feel a churning in my stomach. I just can't understand it.

'Hey, I can see what looks like a very big supermarket, which means there has to be a garage nearby,' says Christian the builder.

I let out a sigh of relief. Please God, let there be some decent shops here. Since our encounter with the police I have barely spoken to him. My thoughts have been focused on Simon and the wedding. I feel sure if I don't marry him, I probably won't marry anyone now. I keep trying to picture Simon with children, but it just doesn't happen. The only picture I get is of him in big business meetings and fancy lunches. I do want children don't I? Christ, I am driving myself mad with all this thinking. Of course I want children, why am I even asking myself such a stupid question? As long as I don't end up like my friend Maz. I mean, she was normal until she had kids and now she sits at dinner parties like a zombie and only seems to come alive when nappies or milk formulas are mentioned. Worse of all though is how a phone conversation with her is interspersed with sentences like. 'Shake little pee wee, that's a good boy.' Or 'Mummy is just talking to that nice Belsey Welsey,' which makes me sound like a face-dropping disease or something. I don't want to end up like that. Not with a face-dropping disease, I don't mean, obviously. But talking like a retard to my children.

I check the time on my mobile and want to cry. I have missed the dinner for sure. How the hell do I explain Christian the builder as well? What if they all think there is more to it? Oh shit. After all, it is a bit unusual to travel across the country with someone I hardly know. Simon's parents will think I have no morals and certainly won't consider me good enough for their son, with his soon-to-be own business. The problem is I have no other sodding way of getting to Rome.

'Are you coming? Here you had better wear this,' he says casually and pulls a jacket from his hand luggage. I take it cautiously.

'It's fine, I got all the fleas off,' he jokes as I wrinkle my nose.

I wrap the jacket around me, grateful for its warmth. The soft smell of an aftershave I can't quite place soothes me. I find it hard to thank him so just nod. He locks the Lemon and strokes the roof lovingly.

'Jesus,' I mumble.

'You called,' he laughs, walking ahead of me.

Arrogant bugger and to think for just a minute I almost liked him. Ahead of us is the entrance to a large supermarket and an underground mall. I make a mental note of all the things I need and pray there are some decent designer shops. As we enter the market my Blackberry shrills. It is Simon. I answer it and watch as Christian the builder walks ahead of me into the store. He chats to an assistant and seems to point downstairs.

'Oh darling, thank God you phoned,' I say, pleased to hear Simon's voice.

'Annabel, where are you? Your flight will be landing soon but evidently you are not on it unless the rule regarding phones on planes has changed.'

Oh God, he is very angry. Well, I can't blame him. Christian is holding up the most obnoxious blouse and nodding at me. I shake my head and pull a face.

'Annabel, are you there?' fumes Simon.

Why does he always have to sound like my father? Why can't he call me Bels like all my friends? How many times do I have to tell him that only my father calls me *Annabel*? I turn my back on Christian the builder and try to picture Simon. You know, Simon on a good day, when he is very loving, sweet and kind. I remember the Cadbury's Fruit and Nut in my handbag and break off a piece which I eagerly devour. I feel my blood sugar level rise and run a finger over my pimple.

'I am so sorry Simon. Didn't you get my text? There was an emergency landing and then I had an accident at the airport. When I came back from the loo the flight had taken off. They left much earlier than they had told us...'

'I just don't want Mum and Dad to think you are badly organised. You certainly didn't make it for dinner, now did you?' I hear the resignation in his voice and feel awful.

I turn back to see Christian, who is now holding up an even more obnoxious yellow dress and posing with it. I shake my head and bite my lip to stop myself from laughing.

'No, I...'

'Well, where are you? Are you even *trying* to get here?' barks Simon.

No, Simon, you stupid arse. Of course I am not trying to get there, what a silly question and why the hell won't he let me speak for goodness sake?

'Yes, of course I am, I...'

'Well, what flight are you on so I can look for it?' he interrupts yet again.

Christian is holding what looks like a bottle of sangria to his lips and miming, 'Yes, oh yes.'

Bloody hell yes indeed. I could drink the whole sodding bottle. I nod frantically. Christ, what am I doing? Come on Bels, tell Simon right now that Christian is bringing you in the car. Tell the truth and shame the devil.

'That's the problem, Simon. I couldn't get another flight and...'

'What?' I move the phone from my ear, best to get married without a burst eardrum. I feel totally exhausted by everything and am really not sure I can take this shouting from Simon for much longer. Christian is holding up drinking glasses now and nodding. I nod back.

'How the hell are you getting here Annabel, and when exactly are you getting here?' fumes Simon whom I can now picture frantically stretching his neck. Oh dear, he won't like this.

'Well, this...erm, couple, a middle-aged couple, also missed the flight and they have hired a car and I am coming with them,' I lie.

Bugger, not good. Why didn't I just tell him the truth? Because, you are totally out of order Bels and you know it. Three days before your wedding and you are travelling across France with another man who you know you find attractive, even if he is a pain-in-the-arse wanker with a penchant for extravagance. Oh dear, of all the times to be attracted to someone, I have to do it three days before my wedding.

There is silence for a second and I hold my breath. After what I imagine is much neck stretching he speaks.

'So, you won't be here until tomorrow then?' I hear the disappointment in his voice.

'I won't? I thought it was only about six hours away,' I say stupidly.

'Fourteen more like. I guess you will all have to stay overnight somewhere. This is a bad start to our future together...'

Fourteen hours? The bastard lied to me and I can't even tell Simon that the bastard lied to me because Simon does not know I am with the bastard. What a mess.

'Oh Simon, don't say that,' I jump in quickly, ignoring the fact that I have also lied to the man who will be my husband in a few days. 'I love you, and I will be there soon. How is your neck?' I finish tenderly. Not that there is anything remotely wrong with his neck you understand. Even a small disagreement with a colleague at work can result in Deep Heat or Bio Freeze being liberally slapped on to ease the tension. I have spent many a happy hour lighting fragranced candles to dispel the pungent smell of them. But, these are the things you do for love aren't they? I have even bought him with of those pain killing machines, you know, a nines machine, or is it a Tens machine? Anyway, I thought to buy one for him for Christmas. Of course, if the neck pain gets much worse I may have to let him have it earlier. Kaz said you can use them for labour pains apparently, so it will be useful all round. Shit, what am I doing thinking about Tens machines at a time like this?

'Sore, all this tension you see,' he says miserably.

'Yes I know, try to relax.'

Stay overnight? Oh bugger, there is no way I can do that. We will have to drive through the night. And I do love Simon and he will be my perfect husband because like Mum said, he is Mr Right.

'Oh Simon,' I add quickly. 'Will you collect my luggage? It is a real pain having to ask.'

His voice softens.

'Of course, and I am sorry honey, I just want to see you. I miss you.'

Oh God, why is the guilt punching me so hard. I have not done anything wrong, have I, except try to get to my fiancé, in time for my wedding? I watch as Christian pulls the Marc Jacob jumper over his head, ruffling his already messy hair and then pulls on a black fleece. I smile as he appraises himself in a mirror and then turns in the manner of a model, and grins at me while raising his eyebrows and nodding. I shrug and shake my head. The guy is nuts. He throws it into the trolley. Jesus, Mr Extravagance or what?

'I can't wait to see you too,' I respond. 'I'd better go Simon, we are at a service station and they are ready to set off again.'
Oh God, another lie and another pimple on my tongue.

'Okay, I love you darling, see you soon.' I hear him blow a kiss and attempt to do the same but it doesn't quite work.
I am relieved the phone call is now over, and feel guilty as hell. I reach Christian as he is throwing underpants into the trolley. I look at the clothes and grimace. Jesus, surely he is not intending to wear these things.

'I am going to look at the other shops,' I say stretching my arms and letting the jacket drop.
He throws socks into the trolley and grins.

'I wouldn't bother.'
I stop in my tracks.

'Why shouldn't I bother?' I ask, really not wanting to hear the answer.

'Well, you can bother. I guess it depends whether your plan was to buy designer clothes or get your hair cut, or indeed have a back massage. Of course if it is great sex you want, then down there,' he points with his thumb, 'is the best place, oh yes indeed,' he finishes.
I feel myself blush.

'You really are an obnoxious person, do you know that?' I say, grabbing a top and holding it against me, God, it is gross.

'I am just telling you. Is it my fault the ground floor has sex shops and massage parlours? That looks good on you by the way, you should get that.'
I roll my eyes at him.

'Oh purleese,' I scoff, throwing it back on the shelf.
He shrugs and dons a baseball cap.

'Cool, I'll get one of these.'

I look into the shopping trolley. It is a quarter full already with tops, pants, socks, biscuits, soft drinks, wine, glasses and a pair of jeans.

'You should try on some of these things,' he suggests, offering me a crisp from the now open packet.

'Shouldn't we pay first?' I say horrified. I have never in my whole life eaten anything in a supermarket before paying, well maybe a grape, but that doesn't really count does it?

'Oh purleese,' he mimics, uncapping the top from a bottle of Coca–Cola.

I grab the bottle off him and take a long gulp.

'You rebel.' He wags a finger at me.

I flinch as he places a baseball cap on my head.

'Come on let's check the food,' he smiles pushing the trolley forward. Why am I not surprised we are heading to the food counters? I yawn and shuffle my feet as he peruses the shelves.

'Do you like marzipan?' he asks, studying a box.

I shrug feigning indifference but my eyes have honed in onto the nougat. Oh, this is terrible. A few hours ago I would not have given a Hobnob the time of day and now I am studying the sweets like an uncontrolled addict. He sees me looking at the nougat and with a wink throws four boxes into the trolley.

'Right, let's get the petits fours as well. Oh yes.' He smacks his lips on seeing an array of them at the patisserie counter. 'Oh yes, what shall we get?'

He points to the Marzipan Cream Pyramids.

'Ah, if you like marzipan, you will love these.' He smiles and buys six. I watch astonished as he adds a dozen Nutella Ganache Tartlets and pushes one into my mouth. My eyes roll as the rich chocolate hits my tongue and he laughs.

'Fabulous, aren't they? Now we must have some opera squares and cream puffs.'

Bloody hell, I am supposed to be losing weight. I attempt to protest but he is already pointing to the colourful tray of macaroons.

'Choose a colour, any colour,' he encourages, and against my better judgement I find myself laughing.

We purchase six macaroons, twelve chocolate truffles, six chocolate éclairs and six coffee éclairs as well as biscuits, pain au chocolat, and crisps.

'Right. Cheese, olives, and some bread I think.'

He pushes the trolley to the cold-meat counter and I meekly follow my stomach rumbling. Fifteen minutes later he has talked me into trying on some of the worst-made clothes I have ever seen. I feel myself inwardly cringe as I pull the dresses over my head but I have to arrive in something other than a torn and stained Yves Saint Laurent blouse and laddered tights. Each time I pop out of the changing room something new is in the trolley. The shop assistant attempts to help, and thinking that Christian is my boyfriend, gets him a chair so he has pride of place in front of the changing room. He grins, eats all the crisps and gives me thumbs up for just about everything I try on, except for a long black cardigan and a shawl. A long flowery skirt and silk shirt gets two thumbs up, while a pair of high-heeled strapped sandals receives a wrinkled nose. I feel quite depressed to think I am spending even a small amount of money on such badly designed clothes. I try on one last blouse and step out for approval. He claps his hands in appreciation, proving he has no taste whatsoever.

'Perfect, just as nice as the Yves Saint Laurent thing, which goes to prove it is not who makes it but who wears it,' he observes knowingly while eating a biscuit.

I swig back some Coca-Cola with two Paracetamol. I am still fighting the desire to phone Simon again and tell him the truth. Oh yes, right Bels and just what do you intend to say? *Hi honey, just wanted to call back to say I actually lied about the couple I was travelling with. Actually, it is a guy, you know, just me and him. But it is fine, really, as he is an arrogant arse with an inflated wallet and a girlfriend.* I don't think so. Pushing Simon from my mind, I rummage through the underwear section while Christian throws in a can of shaving cream and horror of horrors, a toothbrush. Without even glancing his way, I quickly grab one too and toss it in. I mean, I have to face the fact that the chances we will have to stop somewhere are becoming pretty real. Well, at least I have clothes. Not the best in the world but surprisingly they look quite good and considering I spent about a third less than I would normally, I feel quite pleased. I see Christian watching me in astonished silence as I total up the value of my goods and my half of the food bill and convert the euros to pounds. Admittedly, a year ago, I would not have even considered it, but it really is quite astounding how much you can spend when you have no real idea of the currency. A month ago when I had to fly to New York for work, Simon had bought me the converter and advised me to use it. I really thought it was a waste of time but actually it was fantastic. I knew exactly how much I had spent. Now, I can see from the corner of my eye that Christian is shaking his head. Yes, well, wanker, at least I will be able to pay my credit card bill without having to up some poor bloke's building estimate to pay for my recklessness. I begin to separate the food so it is fairly shared between us when his hand slaps on mine.

'Okay, I can cope with the currency crap, just, but not this crazy *one bag of crisps for me, one drink for you*. We will be here all night if you start that. You pay for your clothes and other bits okay? I'll pay for the food, done,' he says flatly cramming things onto the conveyer.

'No, I can't be in your debt,' I insist firmly, whipping the cap from my head and throwing it onto the conveyer with the rest of my things. He huffs.

'It's a few bags of crisps, some chocolate, a few bottles of wine, whatever. Take my word for it, I don't want your body in return. I am well aware it belongs to somebody else.'

I feel my face redden.

'As in fact does mine, so there we are.' He seems to add this as a quick afterthought and I let out an involuntary gasp.

'It does?' I say sounding like a dimwit.

He nods and hands over a credit card.

'Yes, I have a fiancée, in New York, well she is in Rome right now.'

He stops packing the bags and looks at me.

'I thought you were keen on sharing, we could like pack together.'

I shake myself and start throwing things into bags.

'But, you are English,' I say stupidly and blush again.

He looks thoughtful.

'This is true, well spotted. And your point is?'

I shrug, carry on packing and pay my share. After transferring everything back into the trolley we make our way to the Lemon, where we silently pack the bags into the boot. I am about to climb in when he speaks.

'Just for future insults, do you have a name?' He winks, and I try not to smile.

I bite my lip and finally say,

'Bels.'

He nods.

'Ah ha, I thought that was a whisky.'

I sigh and fasten my seatbelt.

'I'm Christian, but I am sure you have thought of better names for me,' he grins.

I am struck dumb and take the biscuit he offers.

'You may need to drive in a while, is that okay Bels?'

I feel a tingle caress my spine when he says my name. Oh, this is just terrible. There is no way I can be attracted to such a person. I remind myself, I am on my way to be married, and to a most wonderful man at that. I decide there and then that as soon as I see Simon I will explain about Christian and why I felt the need to travel with him. I know he will understand. After all, I did not have much choice did I?

'Fine,' I answer lightly.

'Right, next stop is the garage then,' he says cheerfully.

I sneak another look at him. He has donned his sunglasses and the radio is back on. Annoyingly, I find myself wondering what Claudine looks like. I somehow imagine he would like his women blonde, slim and brainless. Well, I tell myself firmly, that is you out of the running then, so stop being so stupid and anyway you don't know that Claudine is brainless. In fact, maybe he does not even deserve her and perhaps she could do better than him. The man is a walking disaster. In just twenty-four hours he has spent an absolute fortune on total rubbish and not once phoned his girlfriend. The kind of man all women should avoid. The sun is quite hot now and the countryside is beautiful. I feel disappointed that we have to go on the motorway again. The green rolling hills and lavender fields are heavenly. The fresh air is a big change from smoggy London and for the first time since I left there I feel relaxed. I don't have to worry about being somewhere for dinner and it is quite a relief. Simon knows I am on my way, and there is no pressure to reach Rome by a certain time now. I will get there for the wedding rehearsal and that is all that matters. But, somehow, I am wanting the journey to go on longer and longer so I don't have to get there at all and that can't be right can it? It certainly has nothing to do with Christian the builder but a lot to do with getting married. I so wish Kaz would phone just so I could chat to someone. The truth is I am a bit concerned about marrying Simon after only knowing him for seven months while at the same time worrying if I wait much longer there will be nobody. Now, here I am stupidly attracted to the most unlikely man in the world, who probably finds me stupid and pretentious. Oh God, am I? I suppose he must think me very shallow with my Yves Saint Laurent blouse. Yes, well, come on Bels, he is a bit shallow himself with this stupid car, you must admit? I am relieved when we stop at the garage and I am able to use the loo and change into something decent.

The loo is disgraceful and I pee carefully, avoiding all contact with the toilet seat. After all, it will be the last straw if I give Simon a dose of something. I slip into the flowery skirt I had bought, which looks as good as any of my Laura Ashley ones, and throw on a lemon top finishing it off with a beige cardigan. It is hard to see how I look through the cracked, foggy mirror but I feel a lot happier. I bin my tights and slip on my newly purchased sandals. I feel all ready for a summer holiday. I splash my face with cold water and reprimand my fragmented reflection. Okay Bels, now for goodness sake get your act together. In just a few hours you will be with Simon and all this will be behind you. Christian the builder will head off into the sunset with Claudine and continue his holiday, and you will go ahead with your wonderful Italian wedding and you will never see or hear from Mr Christian again. This is just a passing phase and probably happens to everyone who is just about to get married. It just doesn't help that you are having doubts. Once you see Simon you will realise just how unattractive this Christian really is. I nod at myself confidently and make a note to self to get rid of Simon's Marc Jacob jumper as soon as possible although I feel sure once I see Simon in it I will not need to. I close my eyes and try to picture Simon, but it doesn't happen. I pull out my phone and scroll into the photos of us together and wait for that lovely warm feeling that always comes when I look at them. But, oh God, it doesn't come. I stare for a bit longer until I realise I am running out of time. Damn it, damn Christian. I race back to the garage. The Lemon sits contentedly in the sun and there is no sign of Christian. I take a deep breath and walk inside the garage shop and almost fall over a woman who is sitting on the floor. Stopping abruptly, I look down at her. My God, she is wearing a bright orange vest with a long beige cardigan, what a combination. Some women have no dress-sense whatsoever, and honestly, to sit on such a filthy floor. She doesn't even look up at me, or apologise, of course not that I would know she was apologising, but she surely does not have to look so serious. I suddenly realise she is not alone and see that there are several people on the floor in some kind of sit in. Great, I've walked in on some sort of a protest. I hope this isn't affecting Christian paying. It then occurs to me, I should offer to pay something towards the travelling. How to approach him about that without him getting all sour, I do not know. He seems to enjoy spending money so much that I doubt he will accept anything from me. Perhaps I could offer to buy dinner later. Dinner, what am I thinking of? I look at my ring and sigh. What a sad state of affairs it is when I need to look at my ring to remind myself I am getting married. Sidestepping round the woman in front of me and stepping over the man sitting beside her I try to see the cashier. Honestly, what a carry on. Surely petrol prices aren't that high that people need to protest in a garage. I look ahead of me trying to see Christian at the till and bump into a hoodie who I presume is waiting to pay.

'Sorry, excuse me, I am not pushing in, I just want to see my friend, well he is not actually my friend, he is more, erm ...' I say apologetically, realising I am rambling.
He turns angrily on me and barks something in French. Good Lord, can the French wonder that so many Brits dislike them, I mean, come on a bit of politeness doesn't hurt anyone. I then see Christian. Oh for goodness sake he is sitting on the floor too. I give up. The man is seriously deranged. Anything for attention it seems. His eyes meet mine and I open my mouth to speak. He gestures to the man in the hoodie.

'Sit on the floor, he wants you to sit on the floor,' his voice shakes and I feel my heart skip a beat.

'You have to be joking. I have just changed my clothes. I am not sitting on this filthy floor,' I reply uncertainly.

The man in the hoodie, who strangely enough is not sitting on the floor, seems to get agitated and starts to shout at me again. Oh, dear, I am starting to get a bad feeling about this. Why is it everywhere Christian the builder goes trouble seems to inevitably follow? I stupidly stare at the people who are either lying or sitting on the floor. Suddenly the hoodie points a gun at me. Jesus it's a bloody gun.

'Oh my God, oh my God,' I scream.

I only wanted the sodding loo for pity's sake. What the hell is going on? Surely we have not walked into the middle of a robbery? Classic or what? I mean, Jesus.

'Bels do whatever I tell you,' shouts Christian. Even with all the mayhem around me, I wonder, is that concern in his voice?

Oh Jesus, oh God.

'But what if I don't understand him,' I squeal. 'Oh my God is he going to kill us?'

'Think positive.'

Think positive, think positive, has he gone bloody mad? How positive is a man pointing a gun in my face? I close my eyes and feel my body tremble. Oh please God, let me get to Rome and marry Simon. I promise to be the best wife he has ever had. Please God, let Simon have the chance to have a wife. I promise not to think about Christian the builder ever again, except in a bad way. Just please please God, let us all live.

'Why did you bring us here,' I say through trembling lips.

The hoodie is in front of me and waving the gun menacingly. A woman on the floor screams again. I put my fingers in my ears in preparation for a gun shot.

'Oh please don't scream,' I wail.

'Will you do what I tell you to do, damn it? He is robbing the place. Do what I tell you and we will all be okay.' I hear Christian's voice as if from a distance and can only think of my lovely charmed life back in London and so much want to be there. Why couldn't we have married there? None of this would be happening. Oh Simon why are you not here? Instead, I am with this lunatic, Christian the builder, or is it Christian the robber. Oh my God. The gunman prods me in the back and I am propelled forward.

'Bels, please do as I tell you. He wants you to go to the till.' Christian translates with exasperation in his voice.

Bollocks, bollocks.

'No, not bloody likely,' I respond stubbornly and scream as the hoodie waves his gun again in my face.

'Oh my God, oh Jesus,' I sob, hoping Christian will jokingly respond with *you called*, but of course he doesn't, instead he says,

'Just do it Bels. Just go to the till.'

I walk slowly towards the till and hear the man bark again and Christian responds in French.

'Okay, get a carrier bag from behind the counter and put all the money in it.'

Does he have to sound so bloody casual?

'Am I robbing a bloody garage now? I can't do this. Why doesn't he do it?' I snap looking crossly at the hoodie.

Christian puts his head into his hands.

'Jesus, woman, please do as I tell you. Why do you argue so much?'

I don't argue that much, what is he talking about? I look at all the other frightened women and quickly punch the buttons on the till. My hands are shaking. Maybe I won't make it to Rome after all. Perhaps I will get shot in the middle of a stupid robbery. I was right about this mad Christian. He will end up getting me killed. I yank a carrier bag off a large bundle hanging behind the counter and begin throwing the money in. The hoodie is standing close to Christian and talking again. I so wish I had paid more attention in Miss Boursin's French class at school. As it is right now I have no idea if Christian the builder is even telling me the truth. I don't even know the guy. He could be in on the robbery for all I know. Although I have to admit he does not look like Christian the robber. Although, of course I have no real idea how robbers actually do look. Apart from *The Godfather* I can't say I have watched many gangster movies. Let's be honest, if all gangsters looked like Al Pacino, who would mind having a gun waved in front of their face? The hoodie is now fidgeting and pointing the gun at me. He yells at me angrily in French.

'I don't know what you're saying,' I say, looking at Christian for help.

'He said you are slow.'

'Well, I don't exactly do this every day do I?' I retort. Shit, my whole body is shaking and my teeth chattering.

The hoodie shouts again, and I thank God one of us knows French, or else he most likely would have shot me by now. What am I saying, us? When did 'we' become 'us'? For Christ's sake Bels, you are not a bloody couple.

'He wants cigarettes,' Christian translates.

What? I look at the packets of cigarettes. There are loads of them.

'Which brand?' I ask stupidly. Oh sod it. I throw the whole lot in. Hopefully the shagging robbing bastard will smoke himself to death.

'Throw those chocolate bars in too,' orders Christian and now I seriously do wonder if he is involved. I give him a sidelong glance and drop the chocolate bars into the bag. The hoodie, seemingly satisfied, points to the people on the floor. I look to Christian who attempts a weak smile.

'You're doing great. He wants everyone's purse and wallet.'

I slowly go from one person to another, apologising each time I take a purse or wallet and throw it into my carrier bag. I approach a young woman who is giving me a filthy look.

'Well, I am not giving you my purse, you will have to beat it off me,' she spits in what my mother would term a common accent.

'You're English?' I say feeling stupidly happy.

She purses her tight lips.

'Yes and I know exactly what you and your boyfriend are up to, and you are not getting my purse.' She clasps her bag to her chest. 'I know you're both in on it.'

The hoodie shouts at me again. I turn angrily.

'Okay, for Christ's sake, will you stop shouting at me?'

I lean down to the woman.

'I don't know what you mean...'

'Oh, you know what I am talking about, you and your boyfriend here, trying to pretend that you are innocent, well I know better,' she snarls.

'He isn't my boyfriend,' I insist hotly feeling myself flush.

The hoodie pushes me from behind and yells angrily.

'Just give me your purse,' I plead.

'No way lady, if you want it, you come and take it.'

I let out a sigh and turn to Christian.

'Well, Clyde, any great ideas?'

He bites his lip and looks at the hoodie.

'He has a gun just don't forget that, either of you.'

Great advice, I don't think. Butch Cassidy he certainly isn't.

'Right, lady I am not getting bloody shot because of you, so give me your sodding purse, now,' I snap, pushing her onto her back and grabbing the bag.

'You thieving bitch,' she hisses and kicks me in the shin. Bloody hell, is this the bit where I slap her round the face? Christ almighty, whatever next? At that moment *Bruno Mars* sings in my handbag. Kaz. It is the ringtone I have for her. I turn to my bag which hoodie is now holding.

'Kaz, Kaz,' I scream, 'We are being robbed.'

I see Christian roll his eyes. Hoodie moves towards me and attempts to snatch the carrier bag and, for some stupid reason, I struggle with him in an attempt to grab my Blackberry. He pushes me to the floor and in the struggle we exchange bags. He jumps up with the carrier in his hand and in his haste to escape, he falls over my leg and crashes to the floor, the gun slipping from his hand and landing directly in front of me. His eyes meet mine and then he is up, scrambling to get the carrier bag again before running outside. I quickly grab the gun and see it is a fake. I turn to Christian who ducks.

'Bels, for pity's sake put that down,' he yells panic-stricken.

The woman next to him screams and holds up her hands.

'Oh my God she's a psycho,' screams the British woman.

I look at her with disdain.

'Oh purleese, it's not even real,' I mumble and watch fearfully as Christian and another man race outside to chase the robber. The woman in the atrocious top jumps up and plonks a wet kiss on my cheek.

'Oh, merci beaucoup,' she cries hugging me.

I gently push her to one side grab my bag and race after Christian. The man who had gone with him has managed to retrieve the money. With shaking legs I walk to the Lemon and lean against it. The men walk towards me.

'Are you okay?' Christian asks gently.

I feel like crying, 'No I am not alright. I just want to get to Rome and to Simon and to feel safe again.' But instead I say, 'Can we just get going please?'

He looks hesitant.

'We probably should wait for the police but I guess as they got the money back… That woman is telling everyone you are involved though.'

'What woman?' I yell looking around me.

'The British woman, she is ranting a bit.'

I look pleadingly at him. He turns to the other man and says something in French and again I curse for not taking more notice in my French classes at school. He tells me it will be fine, and motions to me to get into the car. I close my eyes. Thank God. I make a decision not to move from the car until we are in Rome and also not to look at, or think about Christian anymore. I am on my way to get married, and in a few days I will be Mrs Annabel Lloyd and I cannot wait. I offer to drive and he accepts. I hand him the map and we set off again. Of course, I have no idea that the British woman will later tell the police that I was the one behind the robbery and have probably kidnapped Christian at knifepoint. I ask you, who would believe that?

Chapter Eight

I drive for about two hours while Christian the builder sleeps. In fact, I am beginning to think that sleeping and eating is what he does best. The Lemon is a bugger to drive and thankfully he sleeps through my gear grinding and cursing. The roads are deserted and I cruise along admiring the scenery, passing fields of lavender and sunflowers. Golden rays of evening sunlight pierce the tree-lined road. I pass an old stone farmhouse with faded green shutters and spy an elderly couple sharing a bottle of wine in the shade of an olive tree, and try to picture Simon and myself doing something similar in years to come. Of course the vision fails to materialise somehow and I feel quite mournful. I really cannot believe I lied so easily to him. That really can't be right can it? What if I am only marrying him because I seriously cannot bear the thought of being left on the shelf? No, that isn't true. I care about Simon, I know I do. Yes, but of course, the question is, am I in love with him? Oh dear, I am driving myself mad with all this thinking. Of course, I am in love with him otherwise I wouldn't have got engaged to him would I? Then again I suppose I would, if I was afraid of being left on the shelf. As the sky starts to change and dusk starts to fall I begin to feel a little like Thelma out of the film *Thelma and Louise*. Well, I was kind of involved in a crime so it does seem fitting. I pop square after square of Cadbury's Fruit and Nut chocolate into my mouth and feel like quite a rebel. I have been a reformed chocoholic for the past few weeks after Kaz had told me that every square was equivalent to one inch on my hips. I stop once to check my phone only to find the battery has died, which explains why no one has called. Christian's phone goes off several times but he does not wake up. I resist the impulse to look at his sleeping face. I have no idea what the time is but it is getting dark. I hear him stir and then let out a loud groan. He stretches beside me and hits me in the ribs.

'Ah, sorry, there is not a lot of room in this car is there?' he says lazily and yawns.

I move slightly so our knees do not touch. I see him check his watch from the corner of my eye. He yawns again, looks at his phone and then asks me the question I had been dreading he would ask.

'Where are we?'

'No idea,' I answer honestly and wait for him to explode.

He stops reading his text and stares at me. I continue looking ahead unblinking. Okay, so I should have woken him and I did try. I called his name several times but he didn't respond and there was no way I was going to touch him. I vaguely remembered him saying that the road I had been driving on was the one we needed, so I presumed it was fine. He fiddles with his iPhone and looks at the map. Don't you dare shout at me, I think aggressively, just don't you dare.

'How long have you been on this road Bels?' he asks softly but I sense he is trying to control his annoyance.

I shake my head.

'What does that mean?' he snaps.

I see a lay-by ahead and pull into it.

'It means I have no idea,' I shoot back.

There is a stunned silence. He struggles to turn the overhead light on and then strains to see the map.

'Why didn't you wake me?' he asks, reaching into the back and producing a chocolate éclair. I pop the last square of chocolate into my mouth.

'I did try to wake you. It just seemed like you needed to sleep.'

I look at his éclair and lick my lips. He says he will continue driving so I slide out of the Lemon while he climbs over the seat. I walk round to the passenger side and get back in to see a thunderous expression on his face.

'I can't believe you drove for three hours and didn't look at the petrol gauge, this car drinks petrol, and it's almost empty,' he groans.

I peek across him at the petrol gauge. It was half full, I know it was. I point to the gauge.

'Look I did keep an eye on it. Why do you keep having a go at me? There is half a tank,' I say crossly.

He shakes his head.

'Bels, that is the temperature gauge,' he says, and I hear the despair in his voice.

I gasp. Shit, shit.

'Oh, I am so sorry it's just in my car the petrol gauge is on the other side. I got confused,' I whisper apologetically. 'God, I'm so sorry.'

How can I have been so stupid? Oh my God, now we could be stuck here forever. I look at him hopefully.

'Do you think there will be a garage in the next town?' I ask, optimistically.

He nods and my spirit soars, and then he ruins it all by casually saying,

'Except the next town is about twenty miles away and we will never make it.'

A small sob escapes me. I can't believe I was so stupid. I look again at the petrol gauge as though by looking hard enough I can make the needle move upwards. He sighs and looks at the map.

'Right,' he mumbles.

Right what? How can he be so casual about everything?

'Aren't you worried? I mean, we can't just stay here,' I say irritably.

He gives me a sidelong glance.

'Will worrying make the car go further? If you were that worried why didn't you keep a proper check on it?'

Headlights dazzle me as a car races past and I consider jumping out and stopping the next one. Maybe they could give us a lift? I suggest this to Christian who just gives me an odd look. My heart sinks. I feel I am destined not to get to Rome. Is this fate telling me that Simon is not Mr Right?

'Okay, by chance I happen to have a friend who lives about ten kilometres from here, we may just make it.'

I clap my hands with joy, but he shakes his head.

'Don't get too excited because I have no idea if he is at home. I should phone. Signal is bad here.'

I clasp my hands together and find myself willing his friend to be home. I strain to see him as he walks down a short lane and am tempted to put the headlights on so I can see him better. After a few minutes he gets back in the car and hands me the map.

'Is he home?' I ask hopefully.

He rests his neck in his hands and stretches backwards. The Marc Jacob jumper stretches with him and a small amount of his chest is exposed. I look away quickly. He yawns again and combs his hair back from his face with his hand.

'They're home, but there is a slight complication.'

He groans lightly and I feel my heart sink. I try to think what the complication could be. I attempt to work out all the scenarios but not one seems to be a problem. If they are home and he is their friend what on earth can the complication be? I realise he is looking at me and the penny drops.

'I'm the complication?' I stammer.

He exhales.

'Well, yes and no. I, without thinking, told them that we had broken down and they just presumed that I meant Claudine and me.'

I gasp.

'Oh,' I expect more to pass my lips, but no, oh is all I can muster.

He looks at his watch. I try to make sense of what he is telling me.

'Did you explain I wasn't Claudine?' I ask hesitantly.

He rubs his nose and I curse.

'Oh for Christ's sake,' I moan and reach behind me. I remember the sangria and glasses. I place two plastic glasses on the dashboard and grab a pain au chocolat from the back. Jesus, I will look like Dawn French by the time I arrive for the wedding. I clean the glasses with a tissue and avoid looking at him. I sense his discomfort.

'They have family there for dinner so I'm hoping they will give us a can of petrol. Hopefully, you won't even have to get out of the car,' he says optimistically taking the glass of sangria I offer, along with half of the pain au chocolat.

'We'll just tell them the truth,' I say biting into the pastry and savouring the buttery chocolate taste. I must have eaten the equivalent of two packets of hobnobs in just the past hour. He throws the sangria back in one hit and coughs.

'Phew, that tastes like petrol; we should put it in the car,' he splutters.

I put my glass back deciding that I really do not need the Dutch courage after all.

'Just what is the truth Bels? We met at the airport, missed our flight and then decided to hire a car and travel together to Rome? This is not even mentioning the fact that we each have a fiancé, yet I haven't told Claudine I am travelling with you, and I am presuming you haven't told your fiancé about me?'

I feel my heart flutter every time he uses my name. I gulp. Oh my God. Of course he is quite right. How can we expect anyone to see this whole thing as purely innocent when we are both acting guilty? I shake my head miserably.

'Only because it didn't come up,' I say.

Yes, well, of course it didn't come up. I mean, how exactly would something like that come up in conversation? Not that Simon and I have had much in the way of conversation so far.

'If either of them found out, do you think they would believe us now? Besides rumours have a way of spreading and in my line of work bad press is the last thing I need.'

Bad press, in his line of business, what the hell is he talking about. Christ, it isn't like we are Posh and Becks. But then again, on reflection, he probably thinks he is the building world's equivalent to David Beckham. I groan and he nods while handing me the sangria.

'Just knock it back,' he encourages.

I throw it back in one hit and cough.

'Jesus, that is...'

'Lethal,' he responds.

I nod. He pours more into the glasses and chinks mine.

'One for the road?'

I am starting to wish I had told Simon about Christian the builder. At least I wouldn't be feeling so guilty if I had. The knowledge that we are both lying to our future spouses makes me shudder. I decide there and then that I will tell Simon everything the next time we speak. I throw back the sangria and try not to think of the calories. He hands me the map marking the road we need with a pen. We drive for some time and I feel that everything will be fine until the empty fuel light comes on.

'Oh no,' I say feeling totally helpless.

I feel myself getting tense as we drive, and keep expecting the car to conk out. I spot the road he marked on the map. We bump off the main road and snake round a narrow tree-lined country lane. I feel my heart sink. There are no houses, just trees and fields.

'Okay, this looks right. Look for a house called Treetops. It will be in English.'

I cannot face telling him that we have obviously gone wrong as there are no houses. We travel for some way before he turns into an uphill driveway. I see the Treetops sign but no house. Slowly we climb higher and higher until I can see the cars on the main road.

'This can't be right,' I mumble.

'It's a real tree house, it is on stilts actually. You will love it,' he says enthusiastically.

I will? Why would he think that? Even more interesting is how he knows these people. I see the house and take a sharp intake of breath. It is amazing. A real tree house and it is huge. Best of all, the lights are on. I want to sing with relief. It is the most welcome sight. Set back from the road and encircled by trees it is a real haven. The house is surrounded by small candles which wink at us like Christmas lights. I see someone sitting on a large balcony and, at the sound of our car they rise and walk into the house. Christian parks the Lemon next to two other cars that sit in the driveway and nods at me with a smile.

'By the way, how are you with American accents?'

'What?' Surely he does not think I am that dim. Obviously, I understand an American accent when I hear one.

'Claudine is from Texas.'

Oh shittity shit.

He is out of the car before I can speak and shaking hands with the man who has opened the front door. I stay in the car and wait patiently for Christian to come back with the can of petrol. Jesus Christ, he surely isn't expecting me to speak with an American accent is he?

'Christian, what a surprise, what are you doing slumming in Provence then?' laughs the man as he pushes a pair of spectacles onto his head. He sees me and waves. I wave back. A few minutes later Christian beckons me to step out of the car and my heart sinks. I slam the door shut and walk towards them.

'Claudine,' calls the man and I cringe. 'Lovely to meet you.' I am engulfed in his arms and fumble for the right words to say.

'Hi,' I say hollowly as I brush crumbs from the pain au chocolat off my clothes.

He smiles and nods.

'You are not what I imagined, but it is great to put a face to the name. So, come in,' he gestures to the house.

I look to Christian, who just shakes his head.

'I just told Christian that even if the garage were open, which it is not by the way, we couldn't possibly let you drop by and not have dinner with us.'

Oh yes, you could I want to shout. We really wouldn't mind in the least.

'Olivia, it's Christian,' he calls as we reach the front door.

I grab Christian the builder by his Marc Jacob jumper pulling him backwards.

'I thought we weren't going in,' I whisper.

Christian shrugs.

'Yes, well all best-laid plans and all that...'

'You haven't seen the house before, have you Claudine?' says Christian's friend proudly.

'Actually, I'm not...' I begin but a woman whom I presume to be Olivia, rushes out and I stare at her. I don't normally stare at women you understand, but immediately I recognise her as a model we have used for the magazine, and not just any model. It had taken us close on a year to sign her for just one shoot and by the time I arrived at the studio it was over. Finally, I get to meet Olivia Hammond, one of Britain's top models and I am speechless.

'Christian,' she cries giving him a hug. I wonder how the hell Christian the builder knows Olivia Hammond the model. She turns to me hesitantly.

'He has brought Claudine,' says her companion.

Christian smiles at me and drapes an arm around my shoulders. I attempt not to pull away and feel rather ashamed that I actually find it feels very nice. I blush slightly and am grateful it is dark.

'Claudine, this is Robin, whom you've heard of, of course, and this is Olivia.' He smiles releasing me and kissing her.

I open my mouth to speak but am saved by Robin.

'Oh for goodness sake come into the house.' He ushers us into the hallway of a most amazing house. I stand at the entrance of a long corridor and find myself surrounded by photos of Olivia. She looks embarrassed.

'Claudine, you must think me very vain. These are Robin's photos, as we go through the house you will see they are not all of me.' She smiles and I am already on the verge of asking her for beauty tips. She leans forward and kisses me on the cheek.

'Welcome to Treetops,' she says breathlessly.

Robin leads us into the lounge where I just glimpse some wonderful photographs. Out on the balcony another couple, somewhat older, are sitting and drinking wine. I immediately see a striking resemblance to Olivia in the older woman. She holds her hand out to me.

'Hello, I am Flora, Olivia's mother. I hear you and your fiancé ran out of petrol.'

I find myself shiver. I look to Christian who is accepting a drink from Olivia.

'Yes, very silly. I was driving and I got the temperature gauge mixed up with the petrol gauge,' I say, attempting my best American accent and ending up sounding like a Brummie. Christian gives me an odd look which I try to ignore.

Another man waltzes into the room carrying a tray of hors d'oeuvres. I feel my mouth water and realise that it has been some time since I had eaten properly.

'I just pulled these from the oven in case anyone is hungry,' he says smiling at me.

He puts out a hand that is encased in an oven glove.

'Nice to meet you, I am Olivia's father, Gerard. You must be Claudine, whose car has broken down.'

I tell myself I only desperately want to be Claudine because it will mean I will not have to lie anymore and for no other reason, although if I were really honest I was already enjoying myself.

'I did the same thing when we hired that car in Spain, do you remember darling? I got the gauges mixed up?' Olivia smiles warmly at me.

Flora is wearing the most fantastic outfit. I recognise it immediately as Christian Dior and am impressed but resist the impulse to comment. She has finished it off with a lovely cashmere scarf and small pearl earrings. I do not know how aware Claudine is about fashion. In fact, I have very little knowledge about her at all and feel myself becoming very nervous. If we do not get petrol tonight what are we supposed to do? I start trying to think of ways to get Christian to one side so I can discuss this with him. Mushroom vol-au-vents and smoked salmon flans are thrust into my face. The smell is irresistible and I find myself filling the plate that Olivia has handed me.

'Have an olive,' offers Gerard, plonking several onto my plate and squeezing my arm affectionately. Oh dear, I really should tell them Christian is far from my fiancé, and show them the photos that are on my phone. The thought of my phone reminds me that the battery is as dead as a dodo.

'Oh Olivia, do you think I could charge my mobile. I really should phone my fian... I mean my financial adviser.' I bite my lip the minute the words are out.

Gerard laughs, spitting out bits of mushroom.

'That's impressive,' smiles Robin.

Does he mean my accent, or the fact that I have acquired a financial adviser? Shit what a bloody mess. Why can't I just be good old Bels, who stupidly missed her flight and is now late for her wedding?

'For a minute I thought you were going to say fiancé,' laughs Gerald.

'Yes, I thought so too,' I say forcing a laugh.

'That's novel. Although I can well believe it is the only way you get to speak to him. But let me tell you young man, work is no substitute for a good marriage.' Gerard points knowingly at Christian and I try to hide my blushes. Christian nods earnestly.

Note to self: Try to remember that at least for tonight you are engaged to Christian.

'I thought you would have an American accent,' Robin says suddenly.

Oh God. What the hell accent does he think I have?

'Oh no, no not at all, I'm British, but everyone thinks I am American,' I blubber and blush again. Christian rolls his eyes and I wish the floor would open up and devour me. There is a second of silence and I make a determined effort not to speak just in case I end up sounding bloody Irish or something.

'So, what are you guys doing here?' Robin asks while uncorking another bottle of wine. 'It is lovely to see you, but it's a real surprise.'

I sit back and wait for Christian's reply.

'Well, we are actually on our way to Rome...' he begins, accepting the flans. I watch with horror as he places four salmon flans on one side of his plate, several vol-au-vents on the other side and then a pile of olives in the middle. As his fiancée, I feel decidedly embarrassed.

Robin hands me a glass of wine which I take thankfully.

'Rome. You are a bit off track old boy, Are you on a driving holiday then?' He laughs, and I can't help liking him. He is very like Christian and with a sudden punch to my stomach I realise that I am not missing Simon at all.

'Not exactly, we kind of missed our flight and, anyway, we bought a car,' finishes Christian and looks at me with a shrug.

Robin rushes to the end of the balcony and strains to see the Lemon.

'Yeah I saw the car, it's amazingly cool. Where on earth did you find it?'

Christian holds his hands up in mock protest.

'Not in front of Claudine, it's a sore subject,' he says between mouthfuls of flan. I watch with veiled disgust as he spoons more olives onto his plate.

'Brilliant car, you must take me for a spin. There is a garage in the next town but that won't be open till the morning.' He looks towards Olivia who is smiling at us.

'We have a spare can of petrol in the garage and we can use that to get down there in the morning, in the meantime, bottoms up.' He chinks glasses with Christian.

I am still hearing the words tomorrow morning! Oh please say he is joking.

'Tomorrow,' I say aloud and quickly bite my lip.

'It's fine, we have a spare room.' Olivia smiles warmly at me. Spare room? Oh my God this is just getting worse. I look imploringly at Christian who avoids my eyes. I excuse myself and wander upstairs to the bathroom, which is the size of my parents lounge. I sit with a puff onto the toilet seat and admire the photographs. The wall is totally covered in Robin's brilliant photography. I realise that all the photos are of Treetops in its varying stages of development, and Christian is in several of them. I wander over to the one of him in a hard hat posing by the swimming pool and sigh. So, he is an upper-class builder. Someone who helps rich toffs build their homes. Ah, that explains the *bad press* comment. God, what an inflated ego he has, he probably needs all that food to feed it. Dad would never approve of someone like him. I fiddle with the assortment of perfumes that sit on the shelf above the sink. What am I going to do? This is just getting worse. I have already eaten far too much that I feel seriously certain I must have gained a whole dress size. I should not have eaten those smoked salmon flans. I plead with God to deliver up a calorie-free dinner, or at least as calorie free as possible. I check my reflection in the mirror and do not drop dead from the shock. The pimple has almost gone and when I release the scrunch my hair falls in gentle waves. But what do I do now? This is a terrible situation. We were supposed to get a can of petrol and leave. Now, I am stuck here and probably for the night too. Still, I assure myself, I am obviously safe as Christian the builder obviously wants nothing to jeopardise his romance with Claudine. Whichever way it goes it is better than sleeping in the Lemon I suppose. Oh bloody Claudine and bloody Simon. I tell you I am beginning to hate both of them. If it weren't for them we would not be in this situation. Honestly, when I remember the pressure I was put under to get to that sodding dinner and now I am having dinner here instead. I decide to make the most of it and quickly tidy myself up before heading back downstairs. After all these are my last days of freedom, so I may as well enjoy them. I can refuse the dessert easily enough. With a feeling of total abandonment I go back downstairs.

Chapter Nine

Several hours later and I have eaten so much that I swear a surgical tummy tuck will be the only way to get me into my wedding dress. All my great plans to avoid high calorie food were thwarted by... me. Yes, none other than me. I have drunk three glasses of wine and have unashamedly eaten my way through at least two dishfuls of crisps, and a tasty succulent piece of duck with wonderful orange sauce accompanied by dollops of creamy mashed potato. Not satisfied with this, I then followed it up with chocolate cheesecake covered in double cream and strawberries, and delicious strawberries they were too. I am now polishing off the remains of a box of Belgian chocolates. Visions of myself looking like a big blob in a wedding dress pull me up sharp, and I refuse a top up to my wine glass. At least, I thought I had, but when I look again, my glass is half full. My God, the whole evening has flown by in a blur of wine and chocolate. Yes, well not a bad way to spend an evening. I have charaded my way through film titles, sang myself hoarse to 'New York New York' on their karaoke machine and danced 'the jig' until I dropped on the Wii. All in all I have had more fun tonight than I have had in a long time. Now, I am climbing all over Christian to get into my position on the twister game. Gerard laughingly hands me my wine, which I attempt to take.

'Give her an extra point if she can do it,' he shouts.

Of course, at that moment my Blackberry trills. It is Simon's ring tone and, in my panic, I lose my footing and fall onto the floor taking Christian with me.

'Don't worry, I'll get it,' offers Olivia.

'No,' I scream.

I am face to face with Christian, our noses almost touching.

'I give up,' he laughs nervously.

I jump up, feeling my head spin and turn to take the phone that Olivia is handing me. Oh shit. What do I say? I am drunk in charge of another personality.

'Hello,' I slur.

'Annabel? Is that you? I tried you earlier but your phone was off.'

Shit, bugger, oh to hell with him phoning me now. I am trying to do the best I can to get to sodding Rome, why can't they just leave me alone?

'Oh hi, how are you?' I say backing out of the room. 'The battery had died.'

'It's almost one in the morning, but I thought I would try you again. I expected to leave a message. Is everything okay, did you and that couple find somewhere to stay?'

I suddenly feel sick. The door opens and Olivia walks past mouthing 'coffee', to which I nod.

'Oh yes we did,' I lie again. 'We found a little bed and breakfast actually, very quaint.'

'Really, whereabouts?'

Whereabouts? What does he mean whereabouts?

'In the Provence area,' I say forcing a yawn.

'Provence? What are you doing there, surely that's a bit out of your way?'

Oh sod it.

'Oh, I'd better go, it's my turn for the bathroom,' I say quickly.

'Oh right. Okay, good.' He sounds flustered.

'I just wanted to tell you that Kaz is here and she said to tell you that the dress has been collected, and it's all okay. What time do you think you will get here tomorrow?'

I struggle to stop my speech from slurring.

'I'm not sure. I will phone you when I get near.'

He seems happy with this and, after a few minutes, I hang up and wander into the kitchen where Flora and Gerard are saying their goodbyes. After seeing them off Olivia shows us to our room.

'I'll fetch our bags darling,' winks Christian. I stare at the king-size bed and look around for a couch. There isn't one. How can Olivia and Robin have such a fantastic house with a fantastic spare bedroom, with an equally fantastic bed and not have a bloody fantastic couch?

'How can there not be a couch,' I moan, 'I can't sleep with him.' I turn to see Olivia at the door with the coffee. I bite my lip.

'He snores when he has been drinking,' I say quickly.

Christian steps past us carrying the supermarket carrier bags.

'Oh yes, like a pig I do. She always sleeps on the couch when I snore. I put our bits in these bags darling and left our suitcase in the car, is that okay?' He drops the bag onto my feet and I stifle a groan. What a bastard. He takes the coffees gratefully. Olivia stands uncertainly in the doorway and Christian hugs her.

'It will be fine,' he laughs. 'She snores louder than me when she is drunk.'

I try to laugh. Olivia gently closes the door and I grab my toothbrush from the bag, and storm into the bathroom. I fumble around in the cupboard under the sink for some toothpaste.

'I can't believe you've let this happen,' I say while throwing things onto the floor.

'What did you say?' He has followed me into the bathroom. 'By the way, you were awfully good when you were doing your Titanic charade. Better than Kate Winslet, I thought.'

He hands me a travel-size tube of Colgate. Why am I not surprised he has come prepared?

He pushes his toothbrush under the tap as I throw water at him.

'Bog off.'

'Ha, well I am in the right place to bog off. Now, as much as it pains me to do this, we have to share that bed.'

I spit out the toothpaste.

'We can't,' I stutter.

'We have no choice.'

I walk into the bedroom.

'Of course if you were a gentleman you would let me have the bed.'

He laughs and takes a petit four from a bag. Honestly does this man ever stop eating?

'I wish you would stop eating. I feel like I gain weight just watching you,' I say trying to cover my blushes.

`'Well, if you were a gentlewoman you would let me have the bed, and by the way, your karaoke... It was, how can I put it? It was... painful, oh it was so painful.' He bites into a macaroon and grins. I quickly snatch it from him.

'It has almonds in it, you can't eat that.'

He rushes to the bathroom and I shamefully finish the macaroon myself. Oh God, that's another pound on my hips. I picture my wedding being billed as 'My Big Fat Italian Wedding' and shudder. He returns from the bathroom and suggests we put something in the middle of the bed. I am so tired I really don't have the energy to argue with him. I rummage through the carrier bags for a T-shirt and dive back into the bathroom. I stare at my face in the mirror and realise I have to remove all my make-up. God, I can't let him see me without my mascara. I debate which would be worse, with the mascara now and panda eyes in the morning, or bare eyes now *and* in the morning. Whichever way it goes they are both totally dire. I choose to remove it, and clean my face of all make-up. I don the T-shirt and cover it with the towelling robe that is hanging on the door. I return to the bedroom and look at him shyly. He takes one look at my face and makes a sign of the cross with his fingers.

'Oh no, she is make-up-less.'

I shake my head.

'I should have let you choke on that macaroon,' I hiss, climbing into the bed which feels lovely. I pull the heavy quilt over me and smell lavender. To my alarm, the moment I lay flat my head spins. God, I am so drunk. I look to my clothes that I left scattered on the floor and wonder if should fold them. Before I can make a decision he is back from the bathroom with an armful of clothes which he throws on the floor next to mine. Images of Simon neatly folding his underpants flash through my mind. The mattress moves beneath me and I find myself shifting further from the middle of the bed. I have avoided all eye contact with him, in fact, when he emerged from the bathroom I kept my eyes focused on the painting opposite the bed as though studying it when the truth is I can barely see it as my vision is so blurred. I feel the pillows plonked at the side of me.

'Right, how is that? I don't think either one of us is in danger of rolling over and suffocating the other, do you?'

'Suffocation is too good for you,' I scoff as he pulls at the duvet.

'Charming, it is actually thanks to me that you have got this far.' I sigh.

'Yes, well, that is precisely my point.'

He bangs his pillow several times, and I fight an urge to groan.

'Yup, well goodnight. You were good fun tonight by the way.'

The last remark is said so quietly I barely hear him and then he clicks off the bedside lamp and I am left in darkness with my thoughts. Oh God it is terrifying, worse than being alone with Freddy Kruger. Once I hear his steady breathing, I relax. Don't you just hate night time? Every negative thought I have ever had I swear has come in the early hours of the morning. I force myself to think of Simon, and the wedding, but this makes my stomach churn. I concentrate on making my body relax by telling my muscles to relax and let go, but to no avail. After what feels like an eternity I am still awake. I try Mum's deep-breathing technique but no luck. Christian's steady breathing is beginning to irritate me. Bloody men, why is it they can always drop off to sleep so easily? I count sheep, I sing soothing songs in my head but nothing works. I am so tense that I feel I may spring from the bed at any given moment. I cannot possibly sleep in this bed with another man beside me. My whole marriage is at stake, my whole life in fact. I tense and then release each of the muscles in my body. This seems to have the desired effect. I feel myself becoming drowsy. I tighten my calf muscle and slowly release it and, oh God, I have cramp. Oh shit, the pain is excruciating.

'Oh my God, shit, shit...' I attempt to groan quietly and throw the quilt off. I am pulling frantically at my leg when he stirs. The pain is now unbearable.

The light is snapped on and I am in so much agony I really couldn't care what he sees.

'Oh my God,' I moan, kicking my leg out and hitting him on the shoulder. He yelps and jumps from the bed.

'Pull,' I cry.

'Is this some bedtime ritual of yours?' he snaps unsympathetically.

I squint at his black and yellow Simpsons underpants.

'Oh, your underpants are blinding me,' I groan. 'I've got cramp, oh God the pain.'

I throw my leg wantonly towards him. He looks at it with distaste for a second and then pulls it. I sigh with grateful relief.

'If it's cramp shouldn't you stand up and try to drink some water?'

'Yes, great advice but for now can you just pull it a bit harder,' I snap.

To my horror he grabs my foot with both hands and yanks. He pulls it so bloody hard that I feel myself slide down the bed and land with a thump onto the floor, my bottom stinging. I look to Christian who lies against the dressing table panting and I burst out laughing. He signals me to keep quiet and attempts to get up but loses his balance and falls down again, which sets me off laughing even more. I pull the sweatshirt over my knees and wipe my eyes with my hand.

'You said to pull,' he says grinning.

'Yes but not my bloody leg off,' I reply blowing my nose and climbing back into the bed.

He hands me a glass of water.

'Here, drink. I really do not want to be manhandling your anatomy for the rest of the night.'

'Huh, you should be so lucky,' I retort and blush immediately.

He turns off the light and within minutes he is sleeping soundly again.

I let out a soft sigh and tell myself firmly that this man is not for me. I have a wonderful, sensible fiancé, and my days of being with bad men like Christian are well and truly over. I am now a level-headed thirty-year-old woman. I remind myself that Christian might be fun for the moment, but an on-going future with someone like him only spells trouble. I make a mental list of all the reasons why I should *not* be with such a man. First I must not forget he is just an upper-class builder with upper-class friends. He is probably in debt up to his eyeballs and who knows who he owes money to. He is reckless, dangerous and not in the least bit responsible. This is not serendipity, for goodness sake. On that final thought I fall asleep and dream of my fairy-tale wedding in Rome.

I wake to the sound of birds singing and a ray of sunlight which has managed to push through a gap in the curtains. If I had not also woken up with the mother of all hangovers I may have enjoyed the lovely bright morning. I turn to Christian who has his head under a pillow and the duvet pulled up high. I climb quietly from the bed and tiptoe to the bathroom. After all, the last thing we both need is any embarrassment and let's face it men just can't control what happens in the morning, now can they? I shudder at the thought and quickly dress. Olivia is tidying up when I enter the kitchen. She greets me with a smile and an offer of coffee which I accept gratefully. I offer to help with the clearing up but she refuses.

'No, Martha our housekeeper will be here shortly. I just wanted a quick tidy up. So, you're getting married soon?' she says, taking me by surprise.

I sigh.

'Yes, tomorrow in fact.'

She gasps and puts her cup down.

'What? So soon, but I thought it was at the end of the year you were getting married.'

Shit, of course, she obviously means Christian and Claudine. They are getting married? Hell, I hadn't even really thought about that. I guess if they are engaged, they will be getting married. I open my mouth to correct my error, and before I know what I am doing I am blurting out the truth, and what a relief it feels.

'Actually, I am not Claudine.'

'I knew it,' she says triumphantly.

Oh my God, what does she mean? She puts a hand over her mouth.

'Oh Lord, sorry about the bed. Was it all right?'

'Oh yes, Christian was the perfect gentleman, but how did you guess?'

'It was your American accent, or at least the lack of your American accent,' she laughs. 'Also, your ring gave it away. I said to Robin it just isn't a Christian ring.'

I try not to look crestfallen, and she puts her hand over mine.

'Oh don't misunderstand me. Your ring is just fantastic. It looks really brilliant, but I just knew it would not be the kind of ring that Christian would have gone for and that meant you couldn't be the kind of woman he goes for. I knew it. Christian just wouldn't buy a garish ring.'

No, he probably couldn't afford one, I think, trying to ignore my hurt feelings. My ring is garish? I look at the single solitaire in its white gold filigree encasing. Simon had had it made to his own specifications in Hatton Garden. Admittedly, it would have been nice to have chosen my own ring, but all my friends had said how romantic it was that Simon had chosen the ring for me, and what does she mean I am not the type of woman Christian goes for?

'We both missed the flight and I need to get to Rome, for my wedding actually, and Christian has to be in Rome for... So we decided to travel together. So what kind of woman does he go for?' I find myself asking and flush.

She looks about to answer me when at that moment Robin bounces in. Talk about bad timing, although I hated myself for even asking. He hugs me warmly.

'Morning Claudine. Did you sleep okay?'

For so many reasons I want to be Claudine. I feel sad when I realise I will never see Robin and Olivia again. If I am totally truthful they are not the kind of people Simon would have for friends. Simon and I do not play twister, and we certainly do not sing along to a karaoke machine. Or perhaps I should say Simon doesn't. I must stop thinking all these negative thoughts about my future husband, what is wrong with me? I actually hate karaoke and always cringe at those silly people who do it, and as for charades... I know if I had been sober I would not have gone within a foot of the karaoke. No, these people and Christian are all wrong for me. I accept the toast that Olivia is offering and reach out for the jam. I stop with my hand in mid-air. Stop, stop now, says an inner voice, your stomach will soon resemble a Michelin tyre if you continue eating like this. I ponder thoughts of a girdle and wonder if Mum is in Rome yet and whether she can pop out and get me a few items, like a pair of Bridget Jones hold-it-all-in-knickers, just so I can do up the dress. Oh shit, it will be just my luck that it won't zip up. Well, maybe if the dress doesn't fit I won't have to get married. For God's sake what is wrong with me? I have to get married. I have a joint mortgage now, and an appointment at the bank to arrange a joint account. Oh sod a dog I don't want to be *joint*. I just want to be single. I reach out desperately for the Nutella and spoon a large dollop onto my toast and wonder what kind of clothes they sell in Evans, apart from the big ones, of course. I need a sugar boost I tell myself as I twist my ring round so that the offending stone cannot be seen.

'Fine thanks,' I answer Robin with a weak smile.

'Is the old boy up?' he asks and before I can answer he is bounding up the stairs calling Christian.

'I didn't choose the ring,' I say defensively. 'So what type of woman does he go for?'

'Well...' she begins but I cut her short.

'No, I don't want to know, I should not have even asked.'
She smiles and walks round to give me a hug.

'I will always be glad that Christian brought you and not Claudine, and I won't say a word.'
Robin bounces back in to the kitchen like an excited child.

'We're going for a spin in the Lemon.'
He rushes out for the can of petrol, and I fight a desire to scream. The bloody Lemon will be the sodding death of me. That car has been nothing but trouble since we left the airport.

'Christian wants you, he said there is something on the TV you would like.' What? I hate TV, what is Christian up to now? I excuse myself and head back upstairs and open the door slowly, just in case he is naked, as that really would be the end, I don't think I would survive that somehow.

'Hello,' I say loudly, while cautiously walking in. I stroll past the television and stand by the bathroom door where I can hear the sound of splashing water. I knock softly.

'Are you decent?' I ask quietly, not wanting Robin to hear me.

'No, I don't think I have ever been actually, but I am dressed if that's what you mean.'
I feel my blood boil and push the door open to see him shaving.

'Ah, morning. Did you see Robin?' he asks, casually leaning back for a towel. 'You should look at the news, you're all over it.'
He yawns and then smiles at me, his eyes sparkling. I stare at him. He leads me back into the bedroom and sits me gently on the bed in front of the television where a video of me emptying the garage till and taking the customers' purses is splashed all over the screen.

'You're famous. They are calling you *Madame Hood*.'
I fall back down onto the bed as my legs give way.

'Oh my God, do something, phone someone. I can't be a criminal.'
He walks back into the bathroom.

'It seems that the English tourist told the police you were some kind of female Robin Hood, you know, taking from the rich to give to the poor,' he shouts. 'The poor of France love you, but apparently you have kidnapped me, ha, now that *is* funny.'

Oh goodness, this cannot be happening. I feel my head spin and feel sure I am going to faint.

'I think I am going to pass out,' I moan dropping my head into my hands.

He walks back in smiling.

'Oh you're all right.'

So much for the overdose on sympathy, I make a mental note not to go down with malaria while with him. I stare at the photos splashed across the screen.

'I expect they will be all over the front page of the newspapers,' he laughs and I fight the urge to hit him.

'Oh God,' I groan.

He sits beside me and put his arm on my shoulder.

'It's not that bad. They just want to question you. It will probably soon blow over. The thing is, we could be held up for days if you do hand yourself in so to speak.'

'Hand myself in, *hand myself in, what are you saying?* I haven't done anything, in fact, you did more. You were the one *telling* me to fetch their wallets and purses. They should be photos of you,' I explode pulling his hand off my shoulder. 'Just because you spent the night with me, it does not mean you can touch me. Don't touch me,' I snap angrily.

He holds both hands up.

'Okay, okay, keep your knickers on. All I am saying is that we should try and cross into Italy soon as possible. That is all I am saying. The pictures won't be on the front page, I was only joking about that.'

I grit my teeth. To think just a few minutes ago I was asking what type of woman he goes for. He is nothing but a reckless irritating arsehole. I turn my face away from the television with another moan.

'I just want to die.'

He nods.

'Yes, of course and I have left plenty of razor blades in the bathroom for you. I am just taking Robin for a spin in the Lemon, and then we can have a quick coffee and head off.'

He leaves me standing in the middle of the room. Jesus, the man is un-bloody-believable. I stretch out an arm and fumble to turn the television off when I see a picture of a Citroën.

'Oh no, they know our car,' I gasp before I even realise I have said *our car*.

'Quick, what are they saying?' I yell.

He stops dead in his tracks, does a U-turn and stares with me at the television.

'Oh bother, not the Lemon. Oh well that's it then, we have to get moving now that the Lemon has a criminal record.'

I stare at him. Charming, when it is me, it doesn't matter, but as soon as it is the Lemon, he decides we have to get moving. I then see a half-smile on his face.

'Oh honestly,' I groan. 'Why is the hoodie not in the video?'

'Ah, well I imagine the reason he used you was so he could avoid the CCTV camera, unlike you of course.'

I turn to hit him, but he is out of the door.

'It seems it's you they are after,' he laughs again, 'great that the Lemon is famous though.'

Oh God, just a few days before my wedding and I am already infamous in France. I quickly check my phone. What if Simon has seen it? Thankfully there are no messages. Hopefully I haven't made the news in Italy. I can't even begin to imagine what Simon's parents would make of it. Can it get any worse? Why do I believe it can? I hear him whistling as he skips downstairs and I really believe he must hate me because of the way he glorifies my misery. Well, I hate you too you bastard, so there. You are just one of the bad boys, and I gave men like you up many years ago. I strip off in the bathroom and get in the shower, feeling more certain than ever that marrying Simon is by far the best decision I have ever made. Finally, I am going to be a respectable married woman, with a respectable and sensible husband, and all madness will be put behind me. I must not be influenced by this stupid builder person. Thank God, I am finally seeing reason. After my shower I rummage through the few clothes I had bought and pull on a pair of jeans and a loose top, and drape a cardigan around my shoulders, and pray that Christian won't be too long.

Christian

'What a hoot. Only you would have bought this, the engine sounds a bit funny though – is it meant to sound like that?' laughs Robin as he puts on his stylish glasses to study the Lemon. I smile as he inspects the dashboard. Finally, someone appreciates the Lemon apart from me.

'Claudine says it's a classic piece of junk.'

'I can fully understand you falling in love with this little darling. I'd never have forgiven you if you had left without taking me for a spin.'

We drive in silence for the next ten minutes and Robin tinkers with the radio, strokes the upholstery and fiddles with the windows, sighing every so often. He begins to study the sunroof and then reaches up to open it.

'Careful, it's a bit fragile,' I warn.

He laughs loudly.

'I can't believe you actually bought this. I mean, it's cool, but it's falling to bits.'

I tap the dashboard gently.

'Don't go insulting her now.'

'So, Claudine seems nice,' he says finally.

'Yeah,' I respond in a deadpan voice.

I feel him looking at me.

'So, what's the Rome thing all about?'

Oh no. This is just what I had dreaded. I am just so useless at lying.

'Oh you know? It's a family thing.'

Come on Robin, give it a rest man. But of course he doesn't.

'Uh oh, is that thing still on-going with your brother?'

I nod and watch nervously as he clips open the window.

'That will be a bundle of laughs then. Anyway Claudine is really nice. I didn't expect her to be such a good laugh somehow. How come she has a British accent?'

Luckily I am saved from answering as he points ahead to the garage and I pull in and brake sharply, too sharply in fact.

'Brakes are bloody good,' he observes. 'So, are you and your bro on speaking terms now then?'

'Well, only if we swear at each other and you know I hardly ever swear.'

Jesus, this whole thing is getting more complicated by the minute. Why I ever offered the woman a lift is beyond me. Well, of course, that isn't strictly true. I thought it would be nice to have some company. I never imagined I would actually grow to like her. Amazingly she has some very nice qualities, like her generosity for instance. She didn't make a fuss about taking her turn driving and the way she wanted to pay for her share of the shopping was rather nice. I fill the Lemon up with petrol while Robin gives her the once over.

'I wouldn't mind driving it back,' he smiles, and I throw him the keys.

'Just go steady on the clutch, it's slipping a little,' I advise.

At least the Lemon will keep him occupied. Hopefully he won't mention Claudine again. He crunches the gears and I laugh when I think what Bels would be saying now.

'Is the legal thing still going through?' Robin breaks into my thoughts.

'It sure is.'

Shit, Robin. He is like a dog with a bone. No letting go it seems.

'You never answered me. How come Claudine has a British accent then? I can't get my head round that. All of a sudden your Texan girlfriend is British?' he asks curiously and crunches the gears again.

'Steady on Robin, those gears are antique and probably irreplaceable. There is a knack to driving this car.'

'Okay, okay. So how come she has a British accent then?' he persists.

I sigh. It's no good. I can't lie, and he isn't going to give up.

'That's because she is British and her name is not Claudine. It's Bels actually.'

He swerves slightly and I feel myself tense and point to a lay-by.

'I don't want you to smash up the Lemon. It's my only mode of transport right now, plus Bels would seriously kill me. I have to get her to her wedding.'

He silently pulls into the lay-by and shakes his head.

'You've totally lost me mate. She isn't Claudine, and she's actually getting married? Bloody hell, you slept in our spare bedroom with her last night.'

Does he really have to sound so appalled? I exhale.

'Nothing happened, apart from her getting cramp.'

'It all sounds bloody complicated old chap.'

I shrug.

'It's not too complicated really. We're both going to Rome and the flight got diverted when this passenger got sick. We missed the second take off and it was kind of my fault. I bought the car and offered her a lift basically. She's going there to get married. Sorry for the deceit. It all just seemed so complicated at the time.'

He nods at me.

'Right, well these things happen, I suppose,' he says thoughtfully.

'Yeah.'

'So, you two had never met before the flight?'

'No, never set eyes on her.'

He nods again and then we are both silent.

'Does Claudine know then?' he asks suddenly.

'Hell, no,' I sigh, 'my relationship with her is a bit strained as it is. I tell you the way she spends money. Well, the way she spends my money is just ridiculous."

He turns the key in the ignition.

'You'd never think you two had only just met. Does she know about Claudine?'

I feel myself tense.

'Blimey Robin, so many questions I feel like I'm on *Who wants to be a Millionaire*, yes she does, well, no, she doesn't... That is she knows of her but, well I don't think she's that interested to be honest. Why should she be?'

'She's a good laugh. I liked her.'

I am relieved when he finally drives out of the lay-by and we are on our way to Treetops. In a few hours I can deposit her safely in Rome and into her fiancé's arms and I won't need to explain why I am with her. I will be able to continue with my life and forget we ever met. Although the way her damn perfume lingers in the car may make it a bit difficult. I'll have to get the car fumigated after we arrive in Rome. I can't help wondering what the hell she is doing with such an arsehole though. Robin crunches the gears again.

'Hey Robin, come on, treat her gently.'

He laughs mercilessly.

'You have to admit Bels has a point. The thing is a bit of a wreck.'

'Her fella sounds a right arsehole from what she has told me.'

'Oh yeah?'

'A classic arsehole in fact,' I repeat.

'She likes you.'

'Do you think?'

I don't say that I actually like her too. We slowly enter the driveway.

'Yup, but still as you say, she's getting married.'

I nod.

'Indeed, she is.'

'That's that then.'

Indeed, it certainly is.

Chapter Ten

Olivia and I are sitting in the lounge when Robin and Christian bounce in like two excited schoolboys.

'That car is bloody unbelievable for its age, it's a real classic, I'll get my book, I am sure there is one that old in it,' Robin enthuses.

'He loves the Lemon,' grins Christian. 'I told you, it is a brilliant car.'

He sits beside me on the couch and I move slightly. Robin returns with several books. I sigh when I see they are all books about bloody cars. He flicks madly through one and then shouts.

'Here it is. I told you, you got yourself a real bargain man.'

I roll my eyes at Olivia.

'Yes, I knew it. I would have paid three times that much if I had hired one,' Christian responds while nudging me.

'Oh ye of little faith, that car will pay me back a thousand-fold, I really felt I robbed the guy,' he says with a twinkle in his eye.

After a quick coffee we say our goodbyes with promises to return. As I hug Olivia she whispers 'phone me soon'. We are about to set off when Robin hands Christian a large frame.

'I thought you would like this. Let's face it, without all your hard work we would not be here.'

I strain to see the photo. It is of Treetops. So, I was right, Christian is an upper-class builder. He looks chuffed and hugs them both. Blimey, a bit extreme for someone who probably just arranged for the bricks to be there and maybe helped with a bit of plastering. Still, all the same, I envy him the photo.

'I hope you enjoy it,' Robin smiles, 'and it's been a real pleasure meeting you,' he continues while shaking my hand enthusiastically and giving me a curious wink. I wonder if Olivia has mentioned something about me not being the beloved Claudine. I realise that

Christian has not phoned or texted her for some time and strangely that makes my heart sing.

***

It is one day before my wedding and just a few hours before my rehearsal and I cannot bring myself to turn on my Blackberry. Just about everyone who is attending the wedding must be in Rome by now, except me of course. I seem to be the only one who can't quite seem to make it to Rome. I can imagine Simon seething. I don't even want to imagine what his parents are saying, let alone what they are thinking. Why is it, I can't seem to get there? My parents will have met my future in-laws by now. How fatal is that? Mother is bound to have waffled about her 'Touch the Spot' group. Oh God, that would just be dead embarrassing. In fact, she has probably just waffled. Oh my God, all I want to do is go home, but no one is at home anymore, they are all in sodding Rome. I think longingly of London and my cosy flat which I have to keep reminding myself, I will not be returning to. Most likely all my things are in the new, jointly mortgaged to the hilt, flat by now. The minor anxiety I had felt at the start of the week had escalated to panic, hence the visit to my mother, and now it is evolving into a nervous breakdown. Maybe I could develop amnesia and claim not to know Simon or my mother when I arrive. I look to Christian who has turned the volume up on the radio and is now doing a one-hand jive to Rihanna. He beckons me to do the same and turns the volume up even more. I hear Simon's voice. 'For goodness sake Bels, what will people think?' Poor Simon and his 'What will people think?' What will they think of my swearing, what will they think of my jokes, in short what will they think of *me*? I really should stop letting that man boss me around so much. I now own three Mahler CDs because Simon thought it was time I appreciated a good composer. Frankly I can very easily get through a day without Mahler, but have never told Simon that. Is it really so bad being thirty and not married? Oh God, yes. Now, I no longer have to find escape routes in bars when my blind date looks like Prince Charles, or sit by the phone waiting for the call that never comes. I no longer need to worry about my biological clock. I have gained respect from my married friends who no longer hide their husbands from me. Last week I was very happy, convinced that Simon was the perfect match for me. My mum adores him and Alex said a slightly older man was what I needed. I suppose they are right. Oh but why, right at this moment, do I feel a slightly older very responsible solicitor is the biggest mistake I could make? I pull myself from my reverie and fling off my sandals as though freeing my feet will help me hand-jive better. Five minutes later I am singing at the top of my voice with Christian doing the backing vocals. I recall the last time I had done something similar. It was the night I had met Simon. I had drunk far too much and was dancing to Lady Gaga and singing loudly. I had spun around and the Thames was looming. Simon had grabbed my skirt, not too gallantly, and with a twist of his hand I was in his arms, and my phone was in the water. 'Oh shit, my phone,' I had groaned. I had found myself looking into his warm hazel eyes. At that moment the music changed and he was spinning me round the dance floor. Later Kaz told me that I had been the first woman he had approached after a long-term romance of his had ended.

'He took it badly and was pretty messed up for a while. We all rallied around him but you know how it is. He's very available Bels,' she had said keenly.

It all felt so right, but it all happened so quickly and I soon found out that fun for Simon was the Law Society and their boring dinners.

'Life can't always be fun, it is time for you to take things seriously Annabel,' my mother had advised me. 'After all, you are thirty now.'

'I can't believe you knew all the lyrics,' Christian laughs as he turns the volume down.

I realise we are pulling into a garage.

'Right, Madame Hood, keep your head down. I want to pump up the tyres.'

He is not wearing the Marc Jacob jumper today, so I can look at him without being reminded of Simon, not that I am able to forget Simon, it is just that I would very much like to. He is wearing a light blue shirt open loosely at the neck and a pair of jeans. The white jumper he had bought in the hypermarket hangs down his back and the sleeves tied at the front. I remember Simon dressing in a similar way when we had gone punting one weekend in Oxford. Christian, I have to admit, carries it off much better. There is something very relaxed and calming about Christian, and the effect he has on me is quite intoxicating. I have a *devil may care* attitude when with him. He is smiling as he pours oil into the Lemon and pumps air into the tyres. I watch him walk into the store and see the man at the till looking at me through the window. I quickly slide down in my seat. The last thing I need is another run-in with the police. A car pulls up alongside and I slide down even further. Christian climbs back in and throws a newspaper at me.

'You are on page three,' he laughs, 'and looking very decent for a page three girl I must say.'

I open page three and cry out.

'Oh I look gross.'

'I think you look quite menacing,' he laughs turning on the radio. 'Let's see if you are still on the news.'

'Oh *purleese*. Sometimes, I think you enjoy this,' I sit up and pull my hair into a scrunch.

'Of course I do. It's fun.'

I look again at the pictures. This time the pain is less brutal. At least I look slim and thank goodness I had changed out of the Dior blouse and ripped tights. Actually, I look quite nice. What am I thinking? This is the most catastrophic thing that could happen. What if Simon sees it? I don't somehow imagine his first words will be.

'You actually looked quite nice.' They are more likely to be, 'What the fuck!'

'What if they see this in Italy?' I sob.

'Italy! You're not that famous, as it is you have only made the French version of *The Sun*. The higher class papers wouldn't touch you with a bargepole. Come on, be honest, you can't blame them.'

He laughs again and turns the volume up louder when the news comes on.

'By the way do they still sell *The Sun* in England?'

'I wouldn't know, I don't read such trash,' I reply snobbishly.

'No, you just appear in it. Ah ha, this is you on the news.'

I groan and cover my face with his cap.

'What are they saying?' I ask reluctantly although I really would rather not know.

His phone bleeps several times and his face clouds over. He is silent for a few minutes and I feel decidedly uncomfortable. I shift in my seat, hold my breath and finally blurt out.

'Do you want me to check that for you?'

He doesn't speak but chews his lip thoughtfully before reading the text. I throw the newspaper onto the back seat and spot the nougat. Oh God, this is just hopeless. I tear open the packet. Oh well, one won't hurt. I offer an éclair to Christian who shakes his head. I stare at him shocked.

'Good Lord, it must be bad if you're not eating.'

He starts the engine, turns the steering wheel and screeches across the road. I scream as he manoeuvres between several cars who hoot madly in response at us. He pulls into a small entrance, almost hitting the gate. The nougat flies off my lap and lands at my feet. Before I can speak, he is out of the car.

'I need some fresh air,' he says softly.

I sigh and watch him climb the gate and disappear down the deserted driveway. Bloody hell, what was all that about? I look at his phone. Should I or shouldn't I? If the texts are the reason he has left the car, then I should, because in theory, this affects me too. But supposing they aren't the reason? Supposing he just does not feel well? No, it was the texts I assure myself while reaching for his phone and clicking into them.

'Honey, you are such an arse. I am in Rome waiting for you and you are not here. I really hope you are not in France, you know how mad that whole business makes me. Anyway I have booked into Villa La Cupola Suite and don't annoy me by saying we cannot afford it. I want to spend some time together in luxury before meeting up with your family so text me for God's sake.'

I whistle. My God, Villa La Cupola Suite, Jesus, I thought only millionaires and politicians on expenses stayed there, oh and Fergie, of course. No wonder he has such big debts. So, he is going to Rome to see his family. I scroll to the next message which is an email and shamelessly read it. It is Claudine again.

'This is tedious and stupid Christian. Bloody phone me, it was only a bracelet for God's sake. I hope you are not in bloody France, I mean it.'

I gasp. Did some other man buy her a bracelet? I see from the email that her name is 'Claudine Williams'. I am about to read the most recent text when the car door opens and I sit guiltily holding his phone, which bleeps again as I pass it to him. I wince.

'Sorry,' I say, wishing I could crawl into a hole. Oh this is just dreadful.

He turns the phone off, throws it onto the dashboard and reaches for a biscuit. Oh thank God, he is back to his normal self, he must be feeling better. Relief flooding my body I also pop another piece of nougat into my mouth. I figure once I am married I can go on that Jenny Craig diet or something. I can't be arsed to fart around with all that point counting at Weight Watchers. I always cheat when I do that anyway, knocking half a point off here and half a point off there. No, Jenny Craig will be great. I can also arrange for a personal trainer or something. Yes, I will get fit easily enough. I will buy a Jane Fonda DVD and exercise in front of the television. Bloody hell, how boring is that? Perhaps I will go to Pilates with Kaz, although the last time I tried that I almost fell asleep rolling on the sodding ball. Of course, I could try yoga again. Bugger, I won't think about it now. As I pull myself out of my daydream I realise we are still not moving. I turn to look at him to see he is looking at me. Oh Christ, what now? Oh buggety bugger, he is leaning towards me and I lick my lips in anticipation. His warm lips land expertly on mine and my arm gently wraps itself around his neck. I feel his hand on my hair and close my eyes. I dare not think. Oh no, why does this feel so perfect? Why do my lips so naturally match his? I close my eyes and feel his tongue gently pushing. Oh, this is not just a kiss, it is pure heaven. I feel his hand gently slide round my back and hear myself moan softly. I really should push him away but instead my arms wrap themselves tighter around his neck. His lips gently stroke my cheek and then he is moving away from me and I open my eyes to see his face above mine. His lips are pink and his cheeks flushed. I exhale and gently push him further away from me.

'I probably shouldn't have done that, should I?' he states bluntly.

I am speechless and alternate between shaking my head and nodding it.

'I mean, you're getting married aren't you?'

I nod, still unable to speak. He looks at his phone.

'I am also getting married in about six months. I really should have known better. Are you in a great rush to get to Rome?'
I stupidly shake my head. Oh for heaven's sake Bels, say something, what is wrong with you? You are starting to resemble one of those nodding dogs that sit in the back of people's cars. I shrug helplessly and then find my voice.

'Sorry, I... That was lovely.'
Oh bugger, what am I saying? I can't possibly say our kiss was lovely. It was more than lovely it was amazing, mind blowing. In fact, it would qualify as the best kiss of my whole life, and you can trust me on that. I have kissed more than my fair share of frogs. In fact, I have probably been on more blind dates than anyone I know.

'I am marrying a very sensible man,' I say firmly.

'I'm sure you are,' he agrees, opening a bottle of lemonade.

'Is that diet?' I ask stupidly.
He produces two glasses and laughs. I watch as he pours the sangria into them and adds the lemonade.

'Here's to your wedding to Mr Sensible,' he says smiling.
We clink glasses and I wonder if just thinking of having an affair, before you are even married, counts as adultery. Both our phones are switched off and we are in a quiet secluded place. Oh my God, anything could happen. I must marry Simon, I must marry Simon, I repeat like a mantra. I knock back the sangria knowing it will not help my hangover and shudder as the liquid hits my tongue. I splutter slightly and he bangs me on the back.

'Come on, I want to show you what it is that Claudine hates so much about France, or are you in a great hurry to get to Rome?'
Shit, I only have a wedding rehearsal to get to, future in-laws to meet, and most likely a very angry soon-to-be husband waiting.

'No, I am not in a hurry,' I say.
He climbs from the car carrying the glasses and sangria. He hands me the lemonade and then leads the way through the gate. I follow him down the deserted driveway and realise I am acting like an insane woman. I don't really even know the guy and I am following him further and further into what seems like desolation. Good Lord, he could murder me. We are now out in the open again and are surrounded by fields of lavender and rolling hills. About fifty yards

ahead of us is what looks like the ruins of an old house. He walks towards it, turns and smiles.

'What do you think?' he says gesturing to the house.

I can see scaffolding and realise that the house is being restored,

'You own this?'

He nods proudly.

'Yup, six months ago. The house needs a lot of work but I bought it for a song.'

He is clearly very enthusiastic about his purchase. I stare uncomprehendingly. So Claudine hates it. Do I blame her? After all what is it except just another extravagant purchase by Mr Reckless?

'It's fabulous,' I say, because if I am truthful, it really is a fabulous place. I follow him inside the house. The floor has been laid with flagstones and beams straddle what I assume is a kitchen. The living room has a wide stairway to the side and spectacular view of rolling lavender fields from one wall which is made entirely from glass. The wall on the right is made from stone and has a fireplace big enough to fit a bed in it. I can imagine the room in the winter with a roaring log fire, a huge Christmas tree loaded with presents and decorations hanging from the beams.

'It's fantastic,' I say almost holding my breath.

He nods.

'Yes, I love it. It's perfect here and I fully intend to have the house finished by the end of the summer. I may be living here alone of course but anyway... I hate New York, it is too crazy there.'

I follow him back outside and he waves his arm in an arc.

'Here, I am going to build a veranda so in the summer you can sit out here and watch the sun go down. For the winter I am fitting an Aga in the kitchen and a log burner in the lounge.'

His voice rises with excitement and for a second I am pulled along with him until I remember that things like that cost money and I cannot imagine, even as a posh man's builder, that he can really afford it. I find his enthusiasm contagious and find myself hoping he really does achieve his dream.

'It sounds perfect,' I respond.

He pours more sangria into the glasses. Words dance around in my brain. I have to tell him that the kiss meant nothing, that it was a mistake and that I didn't really mean it when I said it was lovely. Oh buggety bollocks why did I miss the flight from France? Everything is getting far too complicated for my liking, and to make things worse, the more nervous I get about the wedding the more I eat.

'One for the road.'

I jump at his voice and see he is handing me my glass. I gulp it down in one hit and shiver with the bitterness of the sangria.

'Right, let's get you to your fiancé,' he says lightly.

I attempt a smile and realise it is very weak. Back in the car I check my Blackberry and then scroll into my Facebook account. I punch in *Claudine Williams* and hold my breath. My God, there are five of them. I dread looking at the photos. The first one has thick-rimmed glasses and looks all of sixty-five. Ooh, the next one is so pretty that I almost gasp. This must be her, no, she lives in Moscow. Okay, three to go. Next a sad-eyed slobbery bulldog, could that be her? This dog is so ugly, maybe this is her dog. They say that owners look like their dogs don't they? Or do the dogs look like their owners? Maybe she is not so pretty after all. No, this one is married. I scroll to the next one and up pops a photo of Christian with his arm around a beautiful blonde. I feel my breath catch in my throat. Oh my God, she is stunning. I click into her profile page, praying that she has loose security settings and yes I am into her photo albums. The album is titled *Christian's surprise thirtieth birthday party.* I stare at one photo where he looks so lovely that I can barely take my eyes off him. I look for a share button but sod it, there isn't one because, of course, she isn't my friend. Not that I would ever want her as my *friend.* I attempt to save the photo on my phone and after several tries I manage it. I close the application and then, with dread, check my own messages. I am a bit shocked to find there is nothing from Simon and just a simple text from Kaz, saying she looks forward to seeing me. Simon must be very mad with me. I throw the Blackberry back into my bag and sigh.

'There is a police car behind us,' Christian says in a matter-of-fact voice.

I slide down in my seat and try to see the police car in the wing mirror.

'Do you think they will recognise the car?' I ask worriedly.

'Never mind *the* Lemon, I just hope they don't smell the sangria on my breath.'

I kick the dashboard with my leg.

'Oh no,' I moan, 'Why did you drink that? Oh Jesus, this could be the end of my wedding.'

He sighs heavily.

'Your wedding, your wedding that is all we hear about it. I have to get to Rome too you know, you never ask why I have to be there.' He angrily grinds the gears. Bloody cheek, and to think I just downloaded a photo of him. Yes, shame on you Bels, why on earth did you do that? Is it my fault he drank bloody sangria and then drove the car?

'I am sure you have some flimsy reason for going to Rome. Your whole life is full of flimsy things,' I retort murderously.

I push myself up in my seat, see the police car is very near, scream and slide down again.

'Flimsy, you think I am flimsy,' he says changing gears with yet another crunch.

I grit my teeth.

'I don't *think* you are flimsy, I know you are. Can you not grind the gears please?' I explode.

God, this man is so damn arrogant kissing me like he did. He gives me a sharp stare and deliberately crunches the gears again.

'I am turning off here and we better hope they don't follow.'

'It's not my fault you drink and drive,' I say, sliding across my seat as he takes a sharp bend.

'Do shut up woman if you can't say anything sensible,' he says dismissively.

'How dare you,' I stammer.

Tears prick my eyes. How can he speak to me like this? All I want is to get to my wedding and so far everything that could go wrong has gone wrong and it has been his fault. He does not even care about my feelings. I fumble in my bag for a tissue and slip my sunglasses on so he doesn't know he has upset me. I cannot believe all this is happening to me. I am travelling in a rust bucket and wearing cheap supermarket clothes. My companion is a debt-riddled builder with a penchant for glamorous blondes and classic cars and now I am being chased by the police for a crime I did not commit. Simon please forgive me for the carnal thoughts I have had. I really am trying to get to you and I really will be the best wife ever. I am so busy begging forgiveness from Simon that it is a moment or two before I realise we are speeding along a country road. I grab the side of my seat.

'What are you doing?' I shout above the wind that is whistling through the sunroof.

He gestures behind us with his thumb and I turn to see the police car close upon us.

'Oh shit, do you think we should stop?' I say breathing unsteadily.

He shakes his head and for the first time he looks serious.

'I don't think so, not now there are too many things against us. They will probably want to question me for speeding and then they will realise we have been drinking and, of course, they may well recognise the car, and it hasn't helped we have tried to get away from them. I'm nowhere over the limit but all the same, the best thing is to try and get into Italy. I trust you still want to get to your wedding?'

I give him a long look.

'I can't think of any reason why I wouldn't want to get to my wedding, so I don't know why you are asking.'

He crunches the gears again as we climb a hill. I clutch both sides of the seat as we speed up the hill and squeeze my eyes shut in terror as we approach another car and madly overtake it. The police car has its siren on and I glance at Christian who is staring ahead intently.

'I think we should stop before this gets too dangerous, does this car have airbags?'

'The only airbag in this car is you Bels, can't you stop talking for one minute?' he snaps.

He pulls the car over and my heart sinks. Oh my God, what if they arrest me? I hate this man, I hate him so much. The police car overtakes and continues down the road at great speed. We watch as the blue light disappears within the dust trail that followed the car.

'They weren't following us,' I say with a relieved chuckle, 'I guess they couldn't smell the sangria on your breath after all.'

I lay my head back. Twenty minutes later we stop at a small shop and Christian disappears inside. We haven't exchanged a word since the police car incident. I feel stupidly hurt and grab my Blackberry to text Simon. I tell him, I will soon be in Italy and can't wait to see him. It rings immediately. I step out of the car to answer it.

'Simon, oh honey, I am so sorry it is taking so long.'
I hear his weary sigh.

'Well, at least you are near, when do you think you will get to Rome?'
I have no idea but I am not going to say that.

'I would not think it will take me long, how is it going your end?' I say, suddenly missing everyone.

'Good, I am just going to see this string quartet that Mum and Dad hired for the reception.'

'String quartet?' I repeat.
I hate bloody string quartets and Simon knows that.

'I thought we agreed to get a jazz band, you said you knew someone?' I say, sounding like a petulant child.

'Yes, well you're not here are you?' he says accusingly. 'And Mum and Dad said these were good.'
Oh for Christ's sake, am I destined to take shit from everyone? A thought enters my head.

'Simon, if I hadn't texted you would you still have phoned me about the string quartet?'
There is silence and then he coughs.

'Of course, look I have to go. I will see you quite soon, hopefully.'

'I love you,' I whisper but it sounds stupidly hollow. He responds with 'I love you too' and hangs up. Well, bugger me, this is a strange wedding. There is a small cough behind me, and I turn to see Christian.

'How long have you been there?' I bark and march past him into the shop. I am in there for a full five minutes before I realise I have no money to buy anything. I can see him through the window talking on his phone and every so often he laughs. So, he is making it up with the lovely Claudine. I feel myself getting jealous. I must stop this. This man is no good for me. Just because he has made me laugh and I had some fun with him, it doesn't have to mean anything. After all, I have had just as much fun with Simon haven't I? But the truth is, I haven't ever had this much fun with Simon. I emerge from the shop and he lifts his eyes to look at me.

'Your jeans have split at the back,' he states flatly.

I stamp my foot.

'Oh fuck.'

'Yes, that is the normal response from you. Here, I bought you a yogurt.'

He hands me the yogurt and climbs into the car. I meekly follow. I sit down carefully so as to not further rip the jeans. I struggle with the yogurt top.

'Sod it. Why can't they make these tops openable? It's the twenty-first century for goodness sake and they still haven't invented a yogurt top that just clips off?'

My hangover has returned with a vengeance. We finish the yogurts in silence and he takes my empty pot. I watch as he fumbles to open a packet of biscuits and laugh out loud when he finally rips open the packet and biscuits fly all over his seat. He looks at me and his eyes sparkle the way I have come to know.

'Sorry, I snapped at you earlier,' he says softly, 'the whole thing with Claudine is a mess.'

I shift in my seat as I remember my conversation with Simon. I really cannot believe he is going to let his parents hire a string quartet. Just because I am not there doesn't mean all our joint decisions should be changed.

'Mine is hiring a bloody string quartet for the reception. I hate string quartets. I think he is very cross,' I blurt out.

He nods and starts the engine. I check the map and see that we are getting close to the Italian border and my stomach churns. I had been almost two days trying to get to my wedding. At the start of the journey it was the most important thing in the world but now that I am so close it really doesn't seem to matter anymore. I clear the yogurt pots into a carrier bag. Soon, I know that the Lemon and I will part company and I will sadly miss the car I had once hated.

Christian

God, she even has a quaint way of snoring. I fight an overwhelming urge to slam my hand down hard on the steering wheel. Oh my God what the hell was I thinking of? I kissed her for pity's sake. She must think I'm a right wanker. I just can't take advantage like that. Of all people, I should have known better. She loves the arsehole. I heard her on the phone telling him so didn't I? He is obviously more her type than I am. Thank goodness there is little chance of it happening again because we will be in Rome in a few hours. But, she did say it was lovely didn't she? Lovely, is that all? Blimey, I ought to be insulted really. But she responded, I felt it and I am lucky it didn't go any further. For pity's sake, she is engaged and so am I. It's no good, I must phone Claudine. What the hell am I playing at not contacting her and treating her like crap? God, I once loved that woman so much. Surely, I can give her the benefit of the doubt. Talk to her about her extravagances. People make mistakes. I only have to look at how close I almost came to making one. I could have let my emotions take over. She wasn't fighting me, I noticed. I was so out of control. I really must not let it happen again. Her skin was so soft and her lips so yielding and her body so warm and inviting. Oh for God's sake stop torturing yourself. Bels is a welcome breath of fresh air, so enjoy it. Just don't go cocking it up. After all, you can be friends. The important thing is that I get her to this wedding. That's what she wants. As for Claudine, what is she playing at? Villa La Cupola Suite, what on earth? I check Bels is still soundly sleeping and carefully scroll into my contacts on my phone. Luckily she continues to sleep and I click it onto hands-free. The time has certainly come to stop Claudine's spending madness. I cancel the credit card I gave her and hang up feeling somewhat relieved. Villa La Cupola Suite, Jesus, sometimes I wonder if she actually loves me or just loves what I spend on her. Ah, come on man, give her a chance. Make something of an effort. What kind of response do you expect from her when you haven't made any contact? Fancy showing Bels the house, what was that all about? Now, that really was you acting like a tosser. I glance over at her and smile at her sleeping sweet face which twitches every so often. God, I'd love to kiss her again. She smells so fabulous and kissing her was pure nectar. I shake my head to push the thoughts away. This is not going to come to anything. For a start, she is engaged and not only that, she is crazy about the guy. She is probably suffering from some kind of pre-wedding nerves. She is after all a bit neurotic. Sweetly neurotic, of course, but neurotic nevertheless, with all that herbal stuff she carries around. She stirs slightly and I feel a bit relieved because I know I am going to have to stop the car for there is a mild tingling in my tongue. This is just marvellous. Now, I really will look like an idiot. When did I eat nuts? Oh Lord, I'd better stop the car. I try not to moan but I do and she hears me.

Chapter Eleven

My headache makes me sleepy and for a short time I doze. I awake with a start to the soft sound of groaning and think there must be something wrong with the car. We are on a high mountain road. I look at Christian and gasp. He is as white as a ghost and groaning like one.

'Christian, what's wrong?' I ask, using his name for the first time.

'I'm not sure. Did that yogurt have nuts in it?' His breath is rasping. Christ, this is the last thing we need. I scramble through the carrier bag and hold up his yogurt pot.

'It was a hazelnut yogurt, how could you not have seen that?'

'I thought it was vanilla,' he moans.

'Vanilla, why did you think it was vanilla? Hazelnut, vanilla, vanilla, hazelnut, how are they similar?'
He points to the tub.

'The colour of the tub, it's brown.'
I stare at him.

'What! Vanilla isn't brown,' I say incredulously.
He grips the steering wheel.

'Why are you shouting at me?' he asks, clutching his stomach and pulling over.
I hand him a carrier bag.

'What's that for?' He snatches it from me.

'In case you want to throw up or maybe breathe into it,' I say hesitantly. I don't know do I? I have never been with anyone who had an allergy before.

'I think, if I need to breathe into a bag, it is supposed to be a paper one,' he scoffs.

'How about if you drink water from the opposite side of the glass?' I offer helpfully.

He shakes his head.

'That is for hiccups, isn't it? You would make a terrible nurse.'

Honestly, some people are never grateful. I feel mild panic as I watch him struggle to breathe. Oh God, he isn't going to die, is he? I offer him water but he shakes his head. I climb from the car and gasp as a large gust of wind hits me. I walk round to the driver's side and open the door.

'There,' I say helpfully.

He grimaces.

'What are you doing?'

'I thought some fresh air may help.'

'I don't need fresh air, and it's cold out there,' he retorts slamming the door.

Oh for Christ's sake, it isn't that cold. I get back in the car. His shuddering breathing is scaring the hell out of me. Oh God, what if he collapses while we are in the mountains? I hand him the bottle of water again but he ignores it and reaches into the back seat for his hand luggage. I watch with a sense of relief as he removes a foil of pills and pushes one out and quickly swallows it. Beads of perspiration sparkle on his forehead and I exhale deeply when he relaxes his head back against the seat.

'Do you feel better?' I ask hopefully.

He opens one eye, looks at me and then closes it again. I pour the remains of the lemonade into a glass and knock it back. His breathing is still raspy, and I realise I have my hand on his knee. I debate whether I should move it and then decide it feels quite comforting and so leave it there. After what feels like an eternity his breathing becomes quieter and he seems to be sleeping. His hand has dropped onto mine and any plans I had of removing it are dismissed. I look at his face and feel my heart beat a bit faster. This is just so not good. Christian is the kind of man I have been avoiding for the past three years in a bid to find good husband material. Simon is exactly that, I remind myself and I must not do anything to spoil things. Christian is just a good-looking bad boy. His eyes open and I find myself looking straight into their deep pools.

'Do we have any water?' he asks quietly.

I slide my hand from under his and feel his fingers stroke it. I suppress a gasp and hand him the water.

'Do you want me to drive?' I ask casually.

He shakes his head. I pull the Rescue Remedy from my handbag and he grunts.

'I certainly don't want that.'

I unscrew the top.

'It's for me,' I state, throwing the drops into my mouth.

'Perhaps you would like the paper bag too.'

He is obviously feeling better and back to his old scathing self I see. Within minutes he has the car back on the road. He does not mention my hand on his leg and neither do I. In just a few hours I will be in Rome with my fiancé. I will say goodbye to Christian and never see him again. The thought depresses me and I reach behind for the bag of petits fours. I think of the wedding dress and throw it back. I then think of the string quartet and grab it again. I then curse and throw it back. Oh what the hell, one opera square won't do that much harm, and besides I need the sugar lift. I grab the bag again and take an opera square for myself and a cream puff for Christian. Satiated, I doze again. I awake to find we are in a car park. Christian is fumbling around in the back seat. I look at him sleepily.

'Ah, you're awake. There are toilets here and some shops. I thought we could get tidied up. We are a few hours away yet but we can't be sure there will be another place to stop.'

I nod miserably. Oh God I don't want to get there. This is terrible. I feel an overwhelming need to talk to someone. I follow him into the shopping mall and we head for the large supermarket but this time he does not joke about with the clothes but goes straight to the loo. I miserably head for the ladies and change out of my ripped jeans and don the white dress I had bought. I wrap a long cardigan around me and look in the mirror. My hair is still pulled up into the scrunch and I let it down, brushing it vigorously. My skin is glowing and I apply a small amount of blusher across my cheeks and am back in the store before Christian. I watch him come out of the loo. He is wearing jeans and a loose black sweater and I fight an impulse to pounce on him. My God, this is terrible. I am thinking about sex, and not sex with Simon. I am also thinking I really do not want to say goodbye to him. Oh God, if I could just get to know him a little better. Why now? I have been waiting to feel like this about someone for the past five years and he has to come along a few days before my wedding to someone else. He is walking towards me and smiling and visions of a quickie in the back seat enter my head and I can just tell he is thinking the same thing.

'Good God no,' I blurt out as he reaches me.

He stops in front of me, one hand loosely tucked in his jean pocket.

'Do you always say no before you are asked?' He grins at me.

I blush.

'Yes, I mean no. I mean, is this particular case yes.'

He looks quizzically at me.

'I was going to tell you about a wine-tasting event. It's advertised over there. We are about five miles from it. It seems a shame to go past.'

He is looking into my eyes and I feel hypnotised. I guess it would not do any harm, I mean, we are late after all and it is better than having sex with him. I bite my lip and he looks hopefully at me.

'I guess as we are already a bit late… and it's better than…' I stop quickly.

'Better than what? Did you have something else in mind?' he asks, smiling.

Oh good Lord, I swear he can read my mind.

'No, no, I mean, it's better than rushing,' I reply, sounding like a stupid bloody fool. 'And we are already late.'

'Yes, we are,' he agrees.

I nod my consent, and he smiles widely. I check my phone while he buys some poppy-seed crackers and cheese and shake my head when he holds up a hazelnut yogurt. My heart skips a beat when I see there is a message from Simon.

Text when you are near the hotel and I will meet you, we're all going for dinner when you get here.

I notice he does not put a kiss and I feel a sinking in my stomach. Am I blowing my whole future by being stupid with Christian? I check the time and realise I may not make it for dinner and feel a surge of relief. I slip the phone back into my bag and look at my engagement ring. It does look very big and indeed very garish. I fight an urge to remove it. Christian is suddenly beside me.

'I need to phone my fiancé,' I say.

He nods and walks outside. Simon answers on the first ring.

'Honey, where are you?'

God, why is that always his first question?

'Getting close,' I reply uncertainly and feel myself trembling. I am useless at lying. I either get all the words back to front or my voice shakes.

'How close?' he barks like the Gestapo and I feel my back go up.

'I will be there tonight but I may not make dinner, can you take Mum and Dad?'

He grunts, and I think I hear him swear.

'I was taking you for dinner after the rehearsal Annabel, are you now telling me, you won't be here for that either? Do you think you will make it for *our wedding*? I wouldn't want our marriage to put you out or anything.' He is raising his voice and I move the phone from my ear. Oh for God's sake, why do we need a rehearsal anyway?

'I didn't want a rehearsal Simon I was only doing that for you...'

'Fine, we'll have it without you.'

The phone goes dead and I find myself staring at my Blackberry. My God, the bastard hung up on me. Well, I suppose it serves me right. I really ought to go straight there. I decide to tell Christian that we need to drive straight to Rome when my phone bleeps with a text.

Sorry I was sharp Annabel, but you really try my patience at times. I expect you to be here for our rehearsal. After all, you are the only one who isn't bloody here. Please get here as soon as possible. What has happened to your sense of responsibility? You have really let me down badly Annabel.

I stare and stare at the text and then finally in frustration delete it. I feel tears run down my cheeks. I cannot believe I am travelling all the way to Rome to marry a man who constantly tries to control me. Oh why did I listen to my mother? Of course she wants to see me married. I imagine she feels a little like Mrs Bennett. Along comes a nice rich suitor and Mum can't resist. I suppose if I don't marry Simon, then I most certainly will end up on the shelf as nearly all the eligible men of my age are now married. Christian is standing by the car waiting for me and I make my decision. I will marry Simon and settle down. I am thirty and the time has come to do things sensibly.

Two days after my wedding I will attend the fashion show in Rome with my new husband and then we will fly to England and start married life in our new home in St John's Wood. I look at Christian again and feel my heart leap. I have just a few more hours before we say goodbye and I decide to enjoy them. Simon had a stag do in Rome and I am going to have a wine tasting in Italy. A final fling and why the hell not? After all, wine tasting is innocent enough. God, what am I thinking? The whole sodding wedding party is waiting for me and I decide I've got time to go to a wine tasting. I am seriously losing my mind. I gesture to Christian that I am going to the ladies. I rush inside almost knocking over a woman at the sink. She turns and curses me in Italian, at least I think it is Italian, and at least I think it is a curse. I lock myself in the loo and frantically phone Kaz. Thank God, she answers.

'I don't think I can go through with it, he is such a shithead and I know Mum feels like Mrs Bennett but I really can't help it,' I ramble down the phone.

'Bels, Christ, where are you? What do you mean? Oh fuck, let me go outside.'

Shit, she must be with Simon and his parents, and oh God, probably my parents too, oh bugger it. What was I thinking of?

'Bels, what's going on? Where are you? Everyone is waiting for you.'

I fall onto the loo and almost slide off as the seat breaks. Shit, for pity's sake.

'Oh God Kaz, I don't know what to do, I've met this guy...'

'What?' she screams and I wince. 'What the fuck, Bels. You are getting married tomorrow and you have all the bloody presents here. Simon is frantic, really frantic.'

I fall back onto the broken toilet seat and groan. I stare down at my cheap supermarket sandals and think how nice they look. Jesus, am I going mad? How can cheap supermarket sandals look nice? Get a grip Bels.

'Oh God, I hope people haven't spent too much money,' I say stupidly.

'Jesus Bels, of course they bloody have. Your wedding list was from John Lewis, remember? Bloody hell, I can't believe I am hearing this. How can you meet a guy coming to your wedding? Anyway where the bloody hell, are you?'

'I'm sitting in a supermarket loo,' I sigh.

'For fuck's sake Bels, exactly where are you in *Italy* right now?'

Kaz, my best friend aged thirty-two, single and spends her life speed dating and doing yoga. Kaz has had a string of not very nice boyfriends behind her and is always thrilled when any of her friends find Mr Right and my mum wholeheartedly approves of her apart from her swearing, of course.

'I'm not sure, does it matter? What matters is that I think I could seriously fall in love with someone else. How can I marry Simon if I can actually meet someone on my way to my wedding?' I ask, suddenly feeling very stressed and fumbling for my Quiet Life.

I hear her exhale heavily and picture her running her assortment of bangles up and down her arm, as she tends to do.

'Look, it is probably just wedding nerves and maybe Simon has handled it badly so far, to him, it just seems like you are not making an effort to get here. You hardly know this guy, who is he anyway and where did you meet him and where does this couple you are travelling with come into all this?' Her voice trembles and I feel my heart thud.

'Ah...' I mumble.

'For fuck's sake, don't tell me there isn't a couple?'

'Oh Kaz, he is so like me and...'

'Listen to me Bels, someone like you is the last thing you need right now.'

I slide on the toilet seat and look ahead to the broken tampon machine and wonder what the hell I am doing sitting in a filthy supermarket loo in Italy of all places.

'But, I feel so comfortable with him and...'

'Bels pull yourself together.'

'But how can I be sure that I do love Simon? I mean, surely I wouldn't be attracted to someone else if I was that much in love with him?' I wail.

'Well, the thing is...'

'And sometimes I think about Simon and feel nothing and then other times I just know I do love him and oh, I don't know.'

'I'm sure...'

'And when Christian kissed me...'

'What?' she squeals. 'Oh shit, and fuck it Bels.'

The tears rush from my eyes and I sniff loudly.

'God, I'm so confused.'

'You sure fucking are,' is her response.

I blow my nose loudly.

'What is happening there anyway, what are Simon's parents like?' I ask miserably looking at my chipped fingernails.

'Oh, his dad is lovely, his mum's a bit claustrophobic but your mum is getting on with her like a house on fire.'

'Oh Christ,' I moan loudly, 'what am I going to do?'

'Honestly Bels, I can't even let you travel alone to your wedding without you meeting a wide boy. That is exactly what he is right? A Jack-the-lad and men like that you just don't marry Bels. Think of the essential credentials, rich, handsome, reliable, eligible and responsible. Now, tell me, how many?'

Oh dear.

'Handsome, probably reliable, oh hell...'

There is a loud rapping on the door and I fall off the toilet seat.

'Bels, are you okay in there? We ought to get going.'

Shit, Christian. I clamber up and check my reflection in the mirror.

'Sorry Kaz, I have got to go, I'll see you soon.'

'Don't forget,' she shouts, 'Rich, handsome, reliable, eligible and responsible. Your whole future is on this and...'

I turn the phone off and open the door to a concerned Christian. He is frowning and holding a chocolate bar. He looks me up and down.

'Is everything okay?' he asks, pulling the wrapper off.

I nod.

'Yes, I think I am in the doghouse because I may not make the wedding rehearsal.'

He pulls a face.

'Why are you having a wedding rehearsal? Surely getting married should be spontaneous shouldn't it, not rehearsed? I mean, you don't rehearse your funeral do you?'

I watch him walk ahead of me and mentally tick the all-important list. Rich? I frown. Probably rich in debts, but does money really matter I ask myself, after all I earn a good salary at Versity. Yes, but what about when you have children, what then? I sigh. Handsome, I can tick that box, easily, reliable he certainly has been. Eligible he definitely is not, although he has been hinting that things are not good with Claudine. Responsible, well I have to admit he probably is not. I am shaking my head when he turns to look at me.

'There is something the matter isn't there? Would you prefer we went straight to Rome?'
He is offering me a piece of chocolate which I accept eagerly. There is no doubt that chocolate heals all ills.

'It's fine,' I say smiling and taking the map he hands me. Of course, it is far from fine, but I am really past any stage of caring.

Kaz

'Simon tells me, you're not married?'

Christ almighty, blunt or what? What makes women of a certain age think they can just boldly march up to you and probe into your love life? How would she like it if I boldly asked her about her sex life? I really could not imagine us discussing vaginal dryness over a glass of wine. From the look of her sour face I imagine she has had vaginal dryness most of her married life. Frigidity seems to become her.

'That's right. Tried it once, found it a bit limiting. You know, only one man in your bed and all that.'

She tries to hide her embarrassment, and I lay a hand on her arm.

'I'm only kidding,' I say quickly, realising the last thing I need is for Simon's mother to get upset.

She doesn't smile. Unless you call the slight turning up of the corners of her mouth a smile. God, where the fuck is Bels? Lunch with this lot feels rather like waiting for a funeral. Alex waves to me from the corner of the small dining room and I start to head over to her when Simon strides in, his face ashen. Oh God, what's happened?

'Simon, what on earth is the matter?' asks his mother before I open my mouth.

He inclines his head to me, and I quickly follow him outside.

'Bels just phoned me. It looks like she isn't going to make the rehearsal,' he says flexing his neck and unclenching his jaw.

'What the fuck. Where the hell is she?'

He shakes his head and looks so desperate that I want to put my arms around him. Now, that would have his mother talking.

'I've no idea but I just snapped at her. She may phone you. Try and get her to see sense for Christ's sake and try and find out what the hell is going on.'

I squeeze his arm softly.

'I guess she is dependent on these people that are bringing her.'

Why do I not bloody believe this for a second?

He sighs heavily.

'Whatever. I'm going to make some excuse to everyone.'

I follow him back in and wait for Kitty's little gasp which is a cross between a scream and a sigh.

'Oh for goodness sake,' bellows Alex's husband Tom and puts a protective arm around Alex who clutches her stomach. Simon's mother nods knowingly. Oh yes, she is thinking. I knew this girl was nothing but trouble. Hopefully my son will see sense soon. I watch as she whispers into his ear. What a poisonous bitch. Although, I really can't understand what the hell Bels is playing at.

'I find it very confusing dear, why is it, she cannot get here for her own wedding?'

Oh, she has a knack does his mother. That bloody husky voice of hers with just a trace of an accent really grinds on me. Why the hell she is wearing a cocktail dress is beyond me. Bloody hell, it was only lunch and she is dressed head to toe in Balenciaga. Kitty rushes up to us, phrase book in hand. God not again. Why does she not grasp the fact that we are all talking bloody English? I really don't think this is one of those bloody conversations that the sodding phrase book will cover and deliberately knock it out of her hand. We all watch it fall with a plonk into the tureen of soup which still sits on the table. Simon's father winks at me.

'Oh fuck, sorry Mrs Lewis.'

She cringes and I blush furiously.

'Oh shit, I mean...'

'Perhaps best not to speak at all dear,' says Julian.

'I don't know what you're confused about Mum. It's difficult for her not being able to get a flight and she feels terrible not being here,' Simon says firmly but I hear his voice crack. Poor bugger. I envision many hands around Bels' throat when she finally does get here. I nod in agreement with him and then quickly excuse myself when my phone shrills. Thank God. It is Bels, and she's sitting in a supermarket loo of all places. I mean, what the fuck? I see Simon straining to see me from the window. He looks devastated poor bugger. Why does she not see what she has in him? He is being so bloody patient with her. I turn away so he cannot see my face. I cannot believe she has met some wide boy.

'What the fuck Bels, you are getting married tomorrow.'

She doesn't hear a word of what I am saying. She is sobbing so much I barely make out what she is saying. It seems pretty clear though that this guy she met has a lot in common with her. Christ, what can I do to convince her that a wide boy is the last thing she needs now? Just as I think I may be getting somewhere she hangs up. Bloody hell Bels, what the fuck are you up to? Here is a guy I would give my eye teeth to be with and of course he barely notices me. You treat him like crap and still he waits patiently for you. Love sure is a crazy thing.

Chapter Twelve

The vineyard is further away than we had anticipated and, to make matters worse, we got lost, well that is, I got us lost. I was busy opening the pack of poppy crackers and didn't see our turning. I swear I have eaten in two days the sum total of all the food I would normally eat in a week. Visions of not being able to get into my wedding dress are pushed to the back of my mind every time my hand reaches for food. The Lemon travels effortlessly through the beautiful scenic wine country of Chianti Classico, and I lift my face to the sun. The narrow roads are lined with Cypress trees and I sigh at the beauty of quintessential Tuscany. We approach a medieval village and Christian smiles.

'Chateau de Velaruse should come into view soon.'

When it does I gasp at the sight of the majestic building standing at the top of the hill. The chateau looks like something from a Disney cartoon with medieval round towers capped with tall cones. I would not be surprised if Shrek were to pop his head out of one of the windows to welcome us to the castle.

'Well done my little Citroën,' he says proudly tapping the dashboard.

'Do you think Claudine will like the Lemon?' I say without thinking.

We stop at the chateau.

'No, she hates it when I spend money on myself, especially if she is not with me. Claudine prefers to spend my money on her.'

His lips have tightened, and I see his jaw twitch and then within seconds he has changed again and is smiling.

'Right, here we are, let's taste some wine then.'

A man wearing dungarees and a loose shirt is approaching us.

'Buon giorno. Buon giorno. You must be the British couple, excellent. Come in, come in. Welcome to Chateau de Velaruse.'

He strides towards us, and Christian shakes his hand warmly.

'Ah, this is the wife, how are you.'

He shakes my hand vigorously.

'Actually, I am not...'

'Don't spoil his fun,' Christian whispers in my ear. 'You have been elevated from fiancée to wife, well done,' he grins at me.

'I'm a quick worker, expect to be divorced tomorrow,' I whisper back.

'And I expect you will take me for every penny,' he responds sidling closer to me.

'You really can't afford me,' I reply while still smiling at our host.

Christian laughs out loud.

'You have such a low opinion of me,' he says draping an arm loosely around my shoulders. I give him a sharp look.

'I'm being a protective husband,' he smiles.

We walk into the house to be greeted by a rosy-cheeked woman, who I presume is the man's wife. It is the first time I have been to a vineyard, and it is really fascinating. The man introduces himself as Luciano and proceeds to tell us all about his vineyard. I learn so much about wine that after just twenty minutes I am feeling quite ashamed at having bought so many cheap bottles back home in London. More than once I forget to spit the wine out as instructed by Luciano, but I notice that Christian usually does. At one point it dawns on me that one of us has to drive the Lemon to Rome but it is a very fleeting thought. By the time we get to wine 'number eight' I am feeling quite tipsy.

'This is, of course, our pièce de résistance, *Chianti Velaruse*, this one you should really enjoy. A delicate wine with a hint of vanilla and raspberry and a little touch of black pepper. Wonderful with pasta,' enthuses Luciano proudly.

He hands us both a glass. I watch as Christian lifts his glass to the light, sighs heavily and then swirls the wine ever so slightly. He gives me a 'this is how you do it' look then takes a long sniff from the glass, finally taking a noisy gulp. I mean, honestly, what a show off.

'It is good, yes?' Luciano asks.

Christian nods.

'It is excellent; we must buy two of these.'

I widen my eyes.

'We must?'

'Here, try it,' he coaxes. 'It is actually the best yet.'

Luciano smiles and pats Christian on the back.

'I will let you stroll in the vineyard and then we carry on. Many people have told me, it is good for fertility to walk in my vineyard,' he says with a wink.

I blush.

'Wow, powerful vineyard,' murmurs Christian.

I feel myself sway as we walk. The field slopes away from the chateau, trapping the sun between the vines. The air feels dense with humidity and the sounds of crickets in the surrounding trees buzz loudly in my head.

'God, I think I've swallowed far too much,' I say shaking my head and walking into a bush. He grabs my hand and pulls me along. I see a bench sitting in a small opening ahead of us. I make my way towards it and fall down gratefully. The view is breathtaking and I sigh contentedly. Christian sits beside me, uncaps a bottle of water and drinks half of it before handing it to me and stretching out on the bench.

'So, in a matter of hours you will be getting married,' he states flatly.

'Yes,' I agree softly.

He turns slightly in his seat so he is looking at me. I pretend not to notice and stare admiringly at the view.

'Are you having second thoughts?' he asks bluntly and I turn to look at him.

'No. Should I be?' I retort more sharply than I mean to.

He bites his lip, goes to speak and then turns away stretching his arms and reclining on the bench.

'I have also swallowed too much wine,' he says throwing his head back and yawning. 'I just don't think you respect this guy that much.'

I bite back a stinging reply and wonder if the swallowing too much wine is an excuse for his boldness because I am sure he did not.

'How long have you known him?'

He looks at me again. I keep my head straight and continue enjoying the view. Every time I move my head the scene in front of me seems to spin. Oh God why is he suddenly so confrontational? I have managed to get this far without any discussion about Simon, why do we have to start now?

'Shall we talk about Claudine as well?' I snap back.

'If you like,' he replies softly.

Oh Jesus, this is not what I need.

'What do you want to know about Claudine?'

'Did some other man buy her a bracelet?' I blurt out before I can stop myself.

He laughs and again I find my heart leap at the sound.

'You've been reading my texts. No, she bought the bracelet with my credit card. I wasn't thrilled. It was her way of punishing me. It wasn't another man. I forgot our anniversary of being together for two years and so Claudine goes on a spending spree.'

He sighs, and I sneak a look at him. His hair is messy where he has run his hands through it. He turns and I look into his eyes.

'What about your fiancé. All you keep telling me is that he is responsible. Is he fun as well?'

I clasp my hands together and picture Simon in my head. Simon at the Law Society dinner, Simon at the crazy birthday party Kaz had thrown, Simon in the cinema, fussing when I open a bag of popcorn.

'No, he isn't much fun,' I answer truthfully. This is getting far too intense for me. I move to get up but he gently pushes me back down.

'But you're fun, so what are you doing with him?'

I turn sharply.

'It is time I became responsible, and anyway who are you to ask me? I could say the same about you, why are you with Claudine?' I snap, standing up and looking down at him.

He shrugs.

'I really don't think you want to be responsible, that's all. As for Claudine, I don't know to be honest with you. Her extravagant spending bothers me and sometimes I think we just drifted into getting engaged but then again I suppose we can't all have what Olivia and Robin seem to have. I just felt she was the right one, but I don't know...' he trails off.

Well, you are wrong, I think stubbornly. I do want to be responsible and I do want to be married.

'We should get back to Luciano and then get to Rome,' I say straightening my dress.

He nods.

'You mean I should mind my own business?'

I am saved from answering by Luciano approaching us.

'My wife has made nice cake for us, please come.'

Oh no, not more sodding food. Oh what the hell. In a few hours I will be married and then all this eating will have to stop. I decide to make the most of it. We are served delicious fragrant coffee and the most fantastic chocolate cake with whipped cream. I carefully spoon the cake into my mouth and suppress a sigh. It is lovely and crisp on the outside and moist and fluffy on the inside. Luciano's wife smiles at me and pours a small amount of raspberry sauce over it. Oh sheer bliss.

'We are very pleased you arranged to come today,' says Luciano grinning at us.

I look at Christian who looks away sheepishly.

'Do you not have any other visitors today?' I ask innocently.

I see Luciano glance at Christian.

'They are actually closed this week darling,' Christian says pouring more whipped cream onto his plate.

I shoot him a dirty look.

'Oh really darling, I must have forgotten you telling me that sweetheart,' I say with a Botox smile on my face.

He tries to hide his smile. I wait until Luciano and his wife clear the table and grab his arm before he can follow them into the kitchen.

'Did you get them to open just for us? God, how much did you pay for that?' I hiss.

He shrugs.

'Not much, anyway we have enjoyed it haven't we? You are far too intense.'

'You are far too extravagant and irresponsible.'

'Ah thanks,' he laughs and wanders outside. I exhale loudly and follow him.

'Wanker, you have to pay it all back one day,' I mumble.

'You say the nicest things to me darling. Now, Luciano wants to take us down to his cellar so we can collect our purchases.'

Before I can answer he is walking off and I have to run to keep up with them. Bugger him. Thank God I will be free of him soon but the thought sends butterflies churning in my stomach. I have spent the past few days with him and the thought of him not being around seems a pretty miserable prospect. I leave him to collect his wine and sit waiting in the sunshine. I look at photos of Simon on my Blackberry and try to capture the warm feelings I had felt on my flight from London. I quickly glance at the picture of Christian and then delete it. Why on earth did I visit my mother? I decide I will stab her to death when I arrive in Rome and then strangle Kaz. Have they lost their minds telling me Simon is right for me? The man is as wrong as any man can be. Christian is quite right of course, I do not respect Simon. I mean, I slept with Christian for goodness sake. Okay, I didn't have sex with him, but I certainly thought about it. The big question is can I tell Simon that I have changed my mind? Oh Jesus, if there was ever a *throw up in your handbag time* then it surely has to be now. This seriously has to be the worst time of my life. I begin to wonder if I could perhaps just not turn up for the wedding, but, of course, I can't possibly do that. I have two hundred and fifty guests and a heavily pregnant maid of honour who will most likely stab me to death if I call it off. Of course, it may be easier to just stab myself to death. At least everyone will be there to attend my funeral. I look at the time on my Blackberry and realise that no way am I going to make the rehearsal, and for a moment wonder who Simon will get to stand in for me as I know he will not cancel it. I sigh and check my Versity emails. I busy myself answering them until I see Christian emerge from the house with Luciano. He is carrying a crate of wine. I shake my head and find myself smiling. Anyone else would have bought a couple of bottles but Christian, of course, buys a couple of crates.

'Your husband has bought lots of wine for you,' says Luciano proudly, 'the best of my vineyard.'

'Why am I not surprised?' I say fighting to keep the scorn from my voice. 'Did the credit card cope with the battering dear?'

'My wife, the philistine, no appreciation but knowing her she will be sloshed on it before the night is out.'

I gasp in shock and am about to retort when he pulls me to him and kisses me roughly on the lips.

'You have swallowed too much wine,' I snap.

He shakes Luciano's hand vigorously.

'So, you must come back and get more for the new house,' Luciano says taking my hand and shaking it.

I nod dumbly. We walk towards the Lemon and a thought occurs to me.

'Who do you propose is going to drive the car?'

He laughs out loud and slaps his thigh.

'Propose, that's good, getting in the wedding mood are we?'

I grit my teeth.

'You have drunk too much and so have I.'

I watch as he carefully places the wine into the boot.

'You speak for yourself. I am fine to drive. Anyway, I have to get you to your wedding.'

He opens the car door for me. I carefully climb in avoiding all contact with him.

'You seem very keen to get me there,' I say realising that the thought hurts me a great deal.

'I said I would get you there and I will get you there. Besides I have to be in Rome also.'

I realise that I only have a few hours of freedom left. I look to Christian who is smiling.

'Chocolate?' he says simply.

'You know me so well,' I answer reaching into the back seat for my comfort. I think of the wine in the boot and wonder how he plans to get it back to New York. I shake my head deciding it is not my problem and offer him some chocolate. He winks at me and thoughts of carnal knowledge with him flood my brain like a haemorrhage and I quickly sing along with Bruce Springsteen to crowd them out. Within seconds he joins me and for the next thirty minutes we sing along with Lady Gaga, give Andrea Bocelli backing vocals and head bang to Status Quo while consuming copious amounts of chocolate. I ease my guilt by ordering, on my Blackberry, a keep fit video and sending an enquiry to Diet Chef, asking them to send me further details on their weight loss programme, hinting that we may feature it in the magazine. I feel warm, cosy and happy.

'Shall we stop?' I say breathlessly on seeing a lay-by. The views of Tuscany are breathtaking and I really want to savour them before finally reaching Rome. I feel him nod and the Lemon slows up. I leave him fumbling in the back of the car and stretch my legs. The sun is hot on my face and I shield my eyes to see the mountains in the distance behind us. The wind whips my dress around my legs and I inhale deeply. I turn to see Christian with a Nikon camera and laugh.

'I should have known you would have a Nikon,' I say trying not to pose.

I pull a face for the camera and then turn my back on him.

'I used to have a Canon, does that un-impress you? Come on, face the camera.'

I turn to look at him and the expression on his face takes me by surprise, and I realise this is the moment. If I really want carnal knowledge of him then this is the time, this is the place. His look clearly tells me, he wants me, and God knows I shamelessly want him.

'I am very unimpressed by a Canon,' I say feeling myself blush as he takes the pictures.

'I also have a very small instamatic, that is the ultimate in unimpressive isn't it?' He is coming closer, and I realise that I can barely move. I struggle not to laugh and an inner voice tells me to get back into the car but instead I say,

'I am about as unimpressed as I can be.'

He is very close to me now and I inhale deeply.

'I bet I can really un-impress you.' He moves even closer and I take a step backwards but there is nowhere to go and my back hits a fence. I open my mouth to speak but nothing comes out. I feel his breath close to my ear.

'The car was overheating. I was so relieved when you said to stop.'

I lift my hand to slap him but he catches it and looks into my eyes.

'You only have a few hours to get to your wedding rehearsal and I think we are on dangerous ground here.'

He releases my hand and I find myself nodding. My body feels like it is on fire and I take several deep breaths. I watch him lift the bonnet but I do not move, in fact, I am not sure I can.

'I need to top up the radiator. Poor little Lemon is struggling a bit.'

I let out a small groan and he looks at me.

'It will be okay,' he assures me.

Somehow, I do not believe him and the temptation to throw myself off a cliff is overwhelming, but not as overwhelming as the desire to rip all his clothes off. I find myself walking towards him and I can see him looking at me warily. All caution thrown to the wind, I approach him only to be stopped in my tracks by a familiar ringtone on my phone. Good Lord I have been saved by my own mother. Christian's eyebrows rise.

'My mother,' I explain.

I grab the Blackberry from my bag.

'Mother, hi, what a surprise.'

'It certainly is. I was beginning to wonder if my daughter had been kidnapped. Where on earth are you? Do you have any idea of the upset you are causing?'

I knew there was a reason I should not have answered the phone.

'Mum, I...'

'Listen to me. Simon's parents are lovely and they are being very good about you not being here but this is enough to send your sister into labour.'

'Well, at least that would take the interest away from me.'

'Bels, I have resisted the impulse to phone you until now, telling myself, you must know what you are doing, but now it looks like you are going to miss your own wedding rehearsal and I just don't understand why you would do that.'

I try not to sigh.

'Really, Mother don't you think a woman's wedding should be spontaneous and not bloody rehearsed. After all, no one rehearses for their funeral do they?'

Christian smiles at me.

'My sentiments exactly,' he whispers.

'Good Lord Annabel, where did such an idea come from? Simon explained...'

'Did you have a rehearsal Mother?' I ask boldly.

There is a moment of silence.

'Of course not, besides I got married in England.'

'What has that got to do with it, my wedding is going to be in English at least I bloody hope it is. Or has that changed now? And is he still getting that bloody string quartet?'

I bite my lip. Christian is staring wide-eyed at me.

'Language Bels, please. I don't understand any of what you are saying. What happened to your flight anyway? Alex flew here, and she is...'

'The only pregnant woman ever to fly, remind me to get her a medal,' I break in sarcastically.

'Annabel. Really, what on earth is the matter with you? All you had to do was get here for a dinner...'

I sigh and look again to Christian who is pulling faces.

'I will be there for dinner, just not that particular dinner.'

She exhales and when she speaks again I can hear she is controlling her anger.

'I can't talk to you when you are unreasonable. Your father and I will be waiting for you at the hotel and hopefully you will be here in time to have dinner with us. I will see you later.'

'Goodbye Mother,' I say quickly before she hangs up.

I click my phone off.

'My mother,' I explain again.

He nods.

'Who won the battle?'

I shake my head miserably.

'Oh my mother, she used her ace card, my forty-year-old pregnant sister. I can never quite compete with that you see. Seven months pregnant and she gets on a plane. I ask you, is there a bigger achievement than that?'

He looks suitably impressed, nodding slowly and with pouted lips,

'No, you're quite right, you can't compete with that. You have difficulty getting a flight, let alone staying on a plane.'

I fake a laugh and walk back to the Lemon. My mother has totally deflated me. I look at the view of the Tuscany countryside which, this time fails to lift my spirit. I feel his arm go around my waist and shudder.

'I never heard her argument but I am convinced it was flawed,' he whispers looking ahead to the view.

'You think so?'

'Yes, because I will get you there for your wedding.'

An overwhelming urge to cry engulfs me. What a fool I have been. Christian is not in the least bit interested in me, why on earth did I think he was? I have probably been light entertainment for him. My future awaits me in Rome, and I realise without a shred of doubt that I really do *not* want to marry Simon, but I now have little choice. I have left it too late. I know that I do not have the courage to call it all off now. With a sinking heart I follow Christian to the Lemon.

Chapter Thirteen

For the first time since we started our journey together, we barely talk. I spend much of the journey anticipating married life with Simon. Two hours pass and apart from stopping once, so I can take over the driving, we do not exchange a word. I listen as he phones someone, expecting it to be Claudine but instead he apologises for being late and asks someone to represent him at a meeting. After a while he drives again and scenes of Tuscany fly past me, and I find myself wishing something would happen so I don't have to arrive in Rome. My stomach rumbles and I look to the back seat. A half-empty bag of stale crisps lies there but nothing else. I look at his serious face and then at the speedometer. My God he is driving fast.

'We are out of food.'

He looks surprised.

'What about the croissants?'

I shake my head

'Are we out of chocolate too?' he asks, surprise in his voice.

I nod miserably. He looks at me quickly over his sunglasses and is about to speak when there is a loud bang. I scream and stare horrified as smoke billows from the bonnet and the Lemon shudders. Oh no. I know I wished for something to happen but, of course, I didn't really mean it.

'Damn it,' he bangs his fist on the steering wheel.

'You were driving too fast,' I say accusingly. 'Did we hit something?'

He shakes his head. The Lemon splutters and stops. Cars screech round us and hoot as they pass.

'I'm not sure what's happened. I can't look here. We'll need to get it off the road.'

'We'll be killed if we get out of the car,' I cry, covering my ears with my hands to block out the hooting.

'Don't be so dramatic. I need you to steer the Lemon while I push it into that entrance ahead. Can you do that?'

Oh my God, oh my God, of course I can't. But of course I have to because he is out of the Lemon before I can reply. I feel perspiration staining the armpits of my dress and want to curse. I wipe my forehead with a tissue and climb over into the driving seat. Fifteen minutes later I am still sitting in the Lemon and watch anxiously as Christian looks under the bonnet. He slams it shut and wrinkles his nose at me.

'I think the head gasket has blown but I can't be sure. Whichever way it goes I can't drive it to Rome.'

I bite my lip and suppress a groan. I don't believe this. He uses his iPhone to search for a garage and I struggle with a Blackberry that has low signal. Not that I have a clue as to what I can tell Simon this time. Christian finally comes off the phone and turns to me with a smile.

'Right, the garage should collect the car in about an hour and they will arrange a taxi to come with them, and that will take us to your hotel. So at a guess I would say we have just less than an hour for you to sort yourself out.'

I pull a mirror out of my handbag and stare at my face. I look terrible. Strands of hair have escaped the scrunch and are stuck to my neck. My cheeks are red from the heat and my dress is sticking to me.

'God, I look gross,' I moan as I attempt to straighten my hair.

'Indeed, you have looked better,' he agrees.

I throw him a dirty look. He leans into the back seat pulling his hand luggage forward.

'Right, I have some secret supplies in here,' he says smiling and I marvel at how good he looks in the blue short-sleeved shirt he had bought in the supermarket. His eyes are sparkling as he points ahead of us.

'There is a secluded field down there. I suggest we take the slightly grubby blanket that is in the boot and the supplies, and whatever clothes you need, and you can sort yourself out ready for... what's his name.' He waves his hand at me.

'I'll never forget what's his name,' I say absently and find myself laughing like a demented woman.

'Yes, well. Here, take this,' he says giving me an odd look.

I take the bag and watch as he grabs the carrier bags, my hand luggage, a blanket and a bottle of water. Meekly I follow him into the field, all thoughts of carnal knowledge wiped from my mind. In a few hours I will be with my family and my fiancé, and it all seems so wrong and yet I seem to have no way out. Christian falls onto the blanket and lies on his back with his face to the sun. Apart from the traffic in the distance the only sounds are the birds singing. I fall onto the grease-stained blanket and rummage through the carrier bag of clothes. I look at them in disgust. Finally, I choose a flowery skirt and a white T-shirt. I lay them carefully out on the blanket and then flop down at the side of him. I close my eyes and listen to the sound of his breathing.

'How did you meet him then?' he asks between yawns.

I smile and keep my eyes closed.

'It was one of those boat disco things on the Thames.'

I feel him move, and I turn my head to see him looking at me.

'Dead romantic was it? Did he sweep you off your feet then?'

His eyes are hidden by the sunglasses and I fight the desire to remove them. I lower my eyes and can just see the hairs on his chest. I shiver slightly and pull my cardigan tighter. I turn my head away and close my eyes.

'Not really.'

I'm sure I can feel the heat radiating from him.

'So, if the guy isn't fun, what is it you like about him?'

He sits up abruptly and rummages through his hand luggage, finally throwing a bar of Cadbury's Fruit and Nut at me before opening a bag of paprika-flavoured crisps for himself.

'Here, you can have the rejects, I don't fancy having carrier bags and Remedy Rescue forced on me again.'

Indulgently, I pop a square of chocolate into my mouth and take some crisps. Christian meanwhile has walked back to the Lemon and returns holding up a bottle.

'Fancy a wee dram,' he grins, holding up the whisky I had bought at duty-free. My God, that seems such a long time ago.

'This is good whisky, single malt, I am very impressed. Is it for your fiancé?' He stresses the word fiancé and grins.

'My future father-in-law, actually.'

He studies the label intently.

'Does he like whisky then?'

My stomach churns.

'I have no idea,' I admit honestly.

'Why two bottles? Is he an alcoholic or something? Do you not think one would be sufficient? We should open this one.'

I raise my eyebrows questioningly.

'Are you serious?'

'Well, two bottles is a bit extravagant anyway isn't it? It will calm you down, come on.'

I take the plastic cup of whisky and with wild abandonment pop more chocolate. What the hell, I am already on the slippery slope.

'So, what does he do this fiancé of yours?'

He chinks my cup with his and I stifle my sigh.

'He is a top solicitor. He is very successful.'

He feigns shock.

'Wow, impressive. He'll be able to get you off this garage robbery then, that's cool.'

I give him a disdainful look.

'Well it is better than being a builder,' I shoot back.

'Come on though, everyone hates solicitors don't they, you know they do.'

How dare he mock Simon in this way, at least Simon got to Rome without any hitches.

'He must be a very serious guy though. I mean, all this wedding rehearsal, string quartets and stuff. If you hate string quartets why is he getting one? It's your wedding too isn't it?'

I put my cup down and fall back onto the blanket. He follows me. He is quite right of course, why did Simon even consider a string quartet when we had already decided on a jazz band?

'He just likes to do things properly,' I say defending him.

'Did he buy you that stupid converter thing?' he asks with disdain.

Oh for goodness sake.

'It is not stupid, in fact...'

'Oh come on, either you are spending the money or you're not. What is the point of converting it, either you can afford it or you can't?'

Oh really, that is the limit.

'Ha, you can talk. In the past couple of days you have spent so much money I dread to think what your credit card bill looks like. The Lemon alone was an extravagance, and the wine, I mean that was just ridiculous. You are a fine one to talk... and the house in France,' I snarl, feeling very angry but not sure why.

'For your information, not that it is your business, I never buy anything I can't afford, and I would not hire a string quartet if my fiancée did not want one. I would hope to start married life making her happy. Anyway, I am going to take a dip in the river down there and freshen up.'

For a moment I wonder if I have really hurt his feelings. I have never heard him so harsh before. He leans over me. My skin seems to come alive and my heart thumps. His finger gently touches my lips.

'I expect you not to peep.'

'As if I could be bothered,' I say biting my lip, knowing damn well I certainly would be bothered and am already wishing I had a pair of binoculars. Minutes later I am straining to see him in the river at the bottom of the field, but of course, it is impossible and I do not have the courage to go any nearer. I look curiously at his hand luggage. Was he serious about not buying anything he could not afford? That would mean that he could afford the house in France and its renovation. Oh bloody hell, what am I doing even wondering about him? I pour more whisky into my cup and throw it back quickly and let out a shudder. Shit, the stuff is strong. Gingerly I pull the leather bag towards me and gently push my hand in, but guilt makes me quickly pull it out again. Damn it. Spotting the Nikon camera, I quickly grab it and focus the telephoto lens onto the river and gasp when I see him floating on his back. With shaking hands I lower the camera and knock back the remainder of my drink and pour more. I feel more courageous and push my hand back in his bag and this time I manage to remove a bulging blue folder. I quickly focus the camera again, sigh at his naked body and then open the folder. For a moment I cannot make out what the papers are and then I realise they are plans for a house. There are numerous diagrams which I push to one side. I go through the rest of the papers quickly and feel disappointment when I realise he is a builder just like I thought. I replace the folder and grab the camera again and check that he is still by the river. He is standing up now and I gasp at the sight of his bum. I strain to get a better look, but I am already slightly tipsy and everything seems blurry. Carefully, I focus in further and hold my breath. Jesus, what am I doing, in a matter of days I will be marrying Simon. For God's sake get a grip. Distracted by a buzzing, I turn to see a bumblebee the size of a golf ball. I jolt back, trying not to spill the whisky I am holding in my left hand. Balancing Christian's camera in my right, I shoo the beast away from my face while shaking my head to keep the insect out of my hair. There is a click from the camera and shit, shit, I have taken a photo of Christian's backside. I dive back down onto the blanket and peer to see if he is looking back at me but without the bloody camera I can't see bugger all. I replace the lens cap and take a deep breath. Hastily I wash my face and underarms with the wet wipes I had bought and release my hair from the scrunch. He returns with his hair wet and his face slightly pink. I feel my legs go weak. He puts on a short-sleeved top and flops down on to the blanket.

'You peeped,' he says, taking me by surprise. I feel my face flush. He leans across me for the whisky bottle and his arm brushes my breast and I gasp.

'Blimey, steady on Bels, you've had almost half a bottle.'
I shrug innocently.

'Is he older than you or younger?' he asks, offering me a paprika-flavoured crisp.

'Will you stop offering me bloody food, I never normally eat this much and, yes, he is older than me,' I reply pushing his hand away.

'You're not fat, you worry too much. Does he tell you you're fat then? I bet he wouldn't play twister like we did last night.'
I jump up. This is too much. I really cannot take much more. I have that horrid anxious feeling that you get when you to go to the dentist, that feeling when you are sitting in the waiting room and you hear the sound of the drill. Christ, this is terrible. I am dreading my wedding just like I dread a visit to the dentist. This is awful.

'God, I can't stand this, I am so nervous.' I take a deep breath.

'Here,' he pours more whisky into my cup. 'Why don't you take those Silent Life things?'

'Quiet Life,' I correct, taking the drink.

'Yes, those and that rescue stuff.'

I stare at him.

'What are you trying to do to me?'

He laughs.

'Nothing, just trying to calm you down. You seem to be getting a bit tense. You usually love taking those tranquilliser things,' he says calmly.

I exhale loudly.

'They are not a tranquilliser, they are just herbal.'

He nods.

'Oh, I see. That makes them safe does it?'

'They calm me down,' I snap angrily.

'So they are a tranquilliser?' he insists.

'Oh shut up will you.'

He shrugs as I grab the whisky bottle.

'Okay, just thinking of you. I suppose *he* approves of you taking drugs does he?'

I sigh heavily and knock back a gulp of the whisky.

'So, what kind of builder are you?' I ask, falling back onto the blanket, feeling a bit heady and grabbing a handful of crisps.

'You don't want to discuss your drug habit I see.' He is wagging a finger at me.

'Anyway, for your information I am not a builder. I design houses and have them built. I designed Robin's house for example. I designed the set for Olivia's big photo shoot for *Vogue* last year. Would you like a list of my clients so you can be absolutely certain that I really could afford that wine we just bought?'

I stare wide-eyed at him. He pulls the folder from his bag.

'This is the house I have designed for the footballer Bryan Marshall.'

I stare at the plans. Bryan Marshall? Oh holy fuck. He's only a bloody upper-class architect. He's only sodding rich. He's only successful and I'm only sodding speechless and staring at him with my mouth open.

'I am going to check on his house while I am in Rome. You could come and see it but I expect you will be busy honeymooning. Where has he decided to have the honeymoon by the way?'

I force myself to ignore his sarcasm and glance at the plans. Even if I don't know much about houses it is not hard to see that this will be a beautiful one. Oh my God, how could I have been so stupid? I pull a face.

'I thought you were...' I begin.

He nods knowingly and sucks in his breath.

'Can't do that for less than five hundred mate, and to be honest you might need a new guttering, but I will keep the price as low as I can. I should be able to do it for you next week providing I've got the materials. You really thought I was one of them. What a cheek.'

I nod shamefaced.

'Literally, with your bum cheeks on show,' I laugh.

He pushes me playfully onto my back and forces a crisp into my mouth.

'Ve vill make you fat for your vedding.'

The word wedding reminds me again of why I am going to Rome and I jump up and pour more whisky.

'You need more food,' he offers, getting up.

I glance at my phone and, to my relief see that I have no signal still. I seriously wonder if I can call the wedding off. Visions of Alex going into premature labour from the shock make me cringe, and then of course, my mother would have a fit and mourn my spinsterhood. Dad would probably take it with a pinch of salt and Kaz would just swallow more Valium than usual. Then, there is Simon and his parents. I imagine the three of them already want to kill me anyway, so I couldn't make things much worse could I? But there is the new flat and my things and oh, it is all so complicated. And of course by the time I get home I will be one half of a joint bank account and a joint mortgage and oh God, nightmare of nightmares, I now have a Tesco Clubcard as part of our joint grocery shopping plan. Then to make things worse there is Christian, and I have no idea how he feels about me. One minute I feel convinced he is not in the least bit interested in me and the next he is deliberately brushing my breast with his hand. Buggety bugger what am I to do? I take the hand he offers and allow him to pull me up. He has produced apples, olives a slab of cheese and some salami from his secret stash.

He pours more whisky into our cups and smiles. I take a sip and feel the warmth of the liquid run down my throat and hit my stomach.

'So, what actually is the situation with you and Claudine then?' I ask boldly, thinking I might as well find out just how available he is just in case. In case of what, I am not too sure.

'Whoa, Claudine, what can I tell you?'

He breaks off a piece of cheese and looks thoughtful. I bite into an apple and wait.

'It was our anniversary a week ago and I didn't completely forget. I had arranged dinner, but I got waylaid by a client and it didn't happen. So she went and bought herself a very expensive bracelet, and I mean expensive, with my credit card. It's my fault for giving her a credit card in the first place. It's the second time she has done something like that when she has not got what she wanted...' He shrugs and gives a weak smile.

I attempt not to look shocked but fail miserably. His smile widens.

'She will probably have bought up half of Rome by the time I arrive.'

I exhale loudly.

'Can't you do something?' I say stupidly.

He holds out a piece of cheese and I take it as if in a dream. Jesus Christ, is there anything else I can eat while I am at it? He throws an olive in the air and leans forward to catch it in his open mouth. I pull a face in disgust.

'I have, and she is probably ready to kill me. I cancelled the credit card the day after she checked into an expensive hotel in Rome. I imagine they have thrown her out by now, and my name is most likely mud. So I think the wedding will be off, mine that is, not yours, unless you are calling yours off too?'

I choke on a piece of apple and splutter. Why did he say that? Does he want me to? He hands me the whisky and I take a large gulp which only makes me choke more and break into a sneezing fit. I struggle to focus through my watery eyes and blow my nose frantically, only to sneeze again.

'Would you like a carrier bag?' he offers, grinning.

What a bastard. I wipe my face with a wet wipe and fall onto the blanket and realise I am feeling quite drunk, and it dawns on me that he is deliberately plying me with whisky. Oh my God, I must hold onto my wits and not let anything happen.

'I think you should hire a karaoke machine for your wedding and do a turn yourself. You're brilliant at karaoke,' he says flopping beside me.

I squint at him. Oh this is terrible. I should not be enjoying my time with him. I take another sip of my drink.

'You said I was terrible,' I remind him.

'Did I? Oh, maybe you were then.'

I giggle, although I am not sure what is funny. We finish the cheese and olives and share the last of his chocolate.

'So we won't see each other again will we. The taxi will take us to Rome and then we will say goodbye, forever,' he says looking straight at me. Of course, he is right. This is the last time I will see the Lemon, the last time I will rummage through the back seat for a bag of crisps, the very last time I will see his smiling handsome face. The last time I will hear his mocking voice. This is terrible. Now, he fits Kaz's essential credential check list, responsible, reliable, and obviously rich and now it seems, probably eligible and he is indeed handsome. Oh sod a dog, why now? Oh God, am I leaning towards him? Pull back Bels, you are drunk. His face is suddenly very close and his eyes are closed. Oh God, pull back Bels. But I don't and his lips lightly touch mine before he pushes me back.

'Your phone is ringing, again,' he says quietly. 'It's good at that.' I turn too quickly and my head spins. He hands me the phone and walks away. Shit and double shit, it is Simon. With trembling hands I answer it.

'Hi baby, are you all right? '

Oh God, he sounds so loving. I do love him, I do love him, I repeat in my head. I have known him for seven months, God, it seems such a long time now. I have known Christian for two days. I cannot possibly really know Christian at all. Guilt consumes me.

'Yes, yes,' I reply stupidly.

Obviously he is used to me sounding stupid for he makes no comment on my silly reply.

135

'Good, I just wanted to say that I hope you get here for dinner and that I didn't hire that quartet. I know you wanted a jazz band and I have found a good one and provisionally booked it. You can see what you think of them when you get here. I just miss you and so much want to see you.'

Buggety bugger, talk about great timing. I avoid looking at Christian.

'That is great and I really will try and make it for dinner.'

'Text when you are near and I will be waiting in the lounge.'

I smooth down my dress and pull my cardigan around me. I barely hear what Simon is saying as I am watching Christian fold away the blanket. At one point he waves to me and I wonder what he is thinking. I assure Simon that I will be with him very soon and hang up. I sway unsteadily towards the lake and when I am out of sight quickly change into the skirt and top. Please, please Christian, I find myself praying. If you really feel anything for me, say so. Just give me a sign that you would like to see me again, that you really wished I wouldn't go ahead with my wedding. I am so confused. Help me make some kind of sensible decision. I slowly walk towards the Lemon where he is still packing things away. The sun is in my eyes and I cannot see his face clearly but I see he is pointing down the road.

'They are here.'

I nod silently and wait for him to say more, to perhaps comment on what happened between us but he is silent. I fight to control my tears when I realise I was probably just a distraction for him. Just because he is posh and successful doesn't mean he still can't be a wide boy. He is a typical man, just having a bit of fun. Oh surely not. Surely that kiss wasn't just fun. How can I possibly marry Simon now? But how can I not? He would be devastated. I can't possibly do that to him. Finally, I meet a man who could be my Mr Right and it is all so terribly wrong. I take my last look at the Lemon. In silence we remove everything we need from the car and wait. In just over half an hour I will finally be in Rome and, for the first time since I set out on my journey I realise it really is the last place I want to be. I have never felt so sad.

Christian

I shouldn't have encouraged her to drink the whisky. The woman brings out the devil in me. The truth is I do know why I did it and it really isn't fair on her. Why couldn't she have loosened up and said that the marriage was a mistake? Damn her. She is so vulnerable and I can't even comfort her. I dare not. Of course, I could have misunderstood and maybe the scene I am visualising isn't going to materialise but I think I can pretty much stake my life on the fact it will. If only she had said something. Just given a hint of how she feels. Would it have made any difference? I suppose not, at least not if I'm right. Damn you Bels. How much booze did you need to say what I wanted to hear? And what the hell are you doing with him?

Chapter Fourteen

I sit listening to Pavarotti, who is blaring from the speakers in the back of the taxi, half expecting the driver to pop his head around the seat at any moment and hand us a couple of Cornettos. My hand luggage pushes uncomfortably against my foot. Christian and I sit squashed in the back with his laptop and my handbag being the only things that separate us. He has been texting ever since we got into the taxi and has not spoken to me at all. In fact, now I come to think of it, the last words he spoke to me were 'They are here.' I feel totally miserable and wish so much he would say something. I shift in my seat and cough but still he does not look up. I pull a mirror from the handbag and tidy my hair. I debate whether to apply some make-up but decide against it. I am very tipsy from the whisky and don't trust myself to apply it properly. I look across to Christian who seems intent on what he is doing. I cannot remember him ever being so serious. I keep looking at him until finally he lifts his eyes to me.

'I'm so nervous,' I whisper.

'Why don't we finish the whisky, there's not much left?' he offers.

I simply nod, grateful that he is still speaking to me and even more grateful that he kept the plastic cups. So it is thirty minutes or so later that we arrive in Rome, decidedly pissed but at least my heart has stopped racing. I text Simon to say I am near. The driver asks which hotel we need and we both say in unison.

'The Napoléon please.'

I stare at Christian who starts to laugh.

'Classic,' he grins. 'I don't believe this.'

A feeling of panic punches me in the stomach and I feel sick.

'You can't possibly come in with me,' I say quickly, sounding very unreasonable.

We have hit Rome and the traffic is dense. The driver starts honking his horn and I sigh. Oh to go back to the peace and quiet of Provence. I strain to see the sights but I really do not have much interest. I manage a glimpse of the Colosseum in the distance and some impressive columns by the side of the road but most of what I see is no different from any other city, except the crazy Italian traffic of course.

'Of course I can,' he responds matter-of-factly.

'But you are drunk,' I say accusingly, overlooking the fact that I must be too.

He laughs, throwing his head back.

'Not as drunk as you. I think you will be glad of my help when we arrive, unless you want to fall flat on your face at his feet. Although come to think of it, from what I have heard of him, I imagine he would probably like that.'

Oh this man. Whenever I start liking him, he always shows me what a bastard he is.

'Simon is not at all like that,' I snap.

His face clouds over and he looks thoughtful.

'Uh oh, is that his name? Simon? What a surprise. I should have known it was Simon. What an idiot.' His face turns thunderous. Oh God, something doesn't seem right.

'I don't understand,' I say stupidly. 'Do you know him? No, of course you don't, it's not like he's famous or anything.'

He doesn't reply. The car comes to a halt and I stare at the hotel entrance. Oh shit, we are here. Christian yanks open my door and I almost fall out of the bloody taxi.

'Are you coming?' he snaps.

He grabs my bags and storms ahead of me. I pull a face at the driver and, grateful for the flat sandals, follow unsteadily behind Christian. From the outside the hotel looks very plush and I glance down at my skirt, which I actually rather like now and can't help wondering what Simon will think of it. My mother will die if she sees it. Oh what the hell, they won't all be waiting in the lounge will they? My God, how wrong can a girl be? Christian waltzes through the revolving door. I follow but the door seems to spin faster than I anticipate. I manage to go through, but sod it, I find myself back outside, don't you just hate it when that happens? Determined to get it right, I wait for the doors to stop spinning so fast and make a second attempt. Finally, success and I find myself in the cool and dark inertia of the hotel. Pushing my sunglasses back onto my head I stop abruptly. Simon, with my parents, two other people and Alex are standing in the foyer looking at me. Simon is wearing his Marc Jacob jumper and I burst out laughing at the sight of it, as you do when you have had a little too much to drink. Christian stops walking and I bump into him. I feel my head thump and my face flush. Christian pushes me back and I steady myself just in time. I go to brush my hair back and realise I am holding the, now empty, bottle of whisky. Oh shit, and bollocks it. I then realise that Simon is looking at Christian and not at me. His lips are tight and he seems about to explode. I think about making a run for it but my head is spinning so much I really don't think I would get very far. I fix my sight on to the desk at reception and head slowly toward it. If I can just hold onto something this spinning may stop.

'You are drunk, and you are dressed like… well, words fail me…' Simon snaps, flexing his neck.

Jesus, why is he wearing that jumper?

'Ah, Marc Jacob jumper,' I scream. 'It's been with me everywhere,' I giggle.

I bite my lip and attempt to straighten my skirt with my spare hand but I am only just about managing to hold onto the counter. I carefully place the whisky bottle onto the check-in desk and smile lopsidedly.

'This is for your dad and this…' I slap the carrier with the handbag inside it against his thigh. 'Is for…'

Everyone has gone silent. I fumble to remember what I was going to say but I can't recall anything.

'You're two days late, you missed the family dinner and you walk in here pissed,' Simon says quietly. He resembles a bubbling volcano and I feel myself tense.

'I'm not pithed,' I argue. 'Just a bit tippy, that's all.'

He shakes his head.

'You reek of whisky,' he states flatly as he passes me.

I was sure he looked better in the Marc Jacob jumper. In fact, I was sure he looked very different altogether. He runs his fingers angrily through his hair and I spy several grey ones by his temple. Bloody hell, when did they sprout? Surely I would have noticed them before. I must be very drunk I think and feel rather ashamed.

'Simon,' I begin but he puts his hand up. Oh I see, talk to the hand time is it?

'Be quiet Annabel,' he says with a tone of authority.

I see Christian is seething and hold my breath. His face is thunderous and the muscle in his jaw is twitching.

'Don't talk to her like that, you're not her father,' he says sharply, walking to the counter and handing over his passport.

I cringe while at the same time feeling it is pretty cool to have two men quarrel over you.

'Did *he* bring you Annabel? Is *he* the reason why you're so late?' Simon barks at me. 'Did you lie to me about the middle-aged couple?' He stretches his neck from side to side.

I open my mouth to speak but Christian gets there before me.

'Is this how you talk to your wife-to-be? She has not been here five minutes and you are shouting at her.'

'Really, it is okay,' I say, while thinking it is not okay at all.

'Annabel, leave this to Simon,' orders my mother.

'What on earth are you wearing?' chimes in Alex, scathingly. I look down at the skirt.

'It's new,' I say smiling broadly and point proudly to my sandals.

'Okay, come on Simon. It really is no big deal,' says another man, softly, whom I presume to be Simon's father.

'Of course it is a big deal, Edward. After all, she is terribly late,' says his mother. What a bloody cheek. If the bride can't be late for her wedding then who can be?

I smile at his mother and hiccup.

'Christ, Bels,' Alex snaps, running her hands protectively over her bump.

'Sorry,' I mumble.

Simon wags his finger at Christian.

'I should have known it was you. Only you would be so selfish and irresponsible to get her here so late. I bet you did it on purpose. That is just the kind of thing you would do. You have both been drinking haven't you? You're disgusting.'

My God, do Simon and Christian know each other? I pray there will not be a fight as I really do not know whose side I will take. Simon moves closer to Christian and my breath catches in my throat.

'You are an embarrassment,' Alex hisses.

'I am not,' I say with as much force as I can muster, almost falling over in the process.

Suddenly, a young blonde woman flies past me and throws herself into Christian's arms. I stare at Claudine mesmerised. I feel a sense of relief when I see she is not as pretty as her photograph.

'Oh hello, are you, err?' I say louder than I expected, while holding out my hand to her in an attempt to look sober.

'Chris, where have you been? Why didn't you answer my texts honey?' she asks in a heavy Texan drawl and plonks a kiss on his cheeks, seemingly not at all perturbed when he gently pushes her away. *Chris*, why do I think I have heard the name before? I watch as Christian takes his room key.

'Well, I'm shattered…' he begins.

Simons stands in front of him.

'I am sick of your, *I don't give a damn* attitude,' he shouts, making me jump. 'And when it interferes with my life it is something else.'

I wobble slightly and grab the desk for support. I attempt to step between Christian and Simon with all of the conviction of Jack Bauer. The minute I do it, I realise I must be crazy.

'Simon, please calm down. I'm so sorry. It really is my fault…' I say tapping him on the arm. He pushes it away roughly while Christian looks crossly at him.

'Ah, come on Bels, don't do that. Don't start apologising when you haven't done anything,' he says softly.

'Don't you fucking call her Bels,' yells Simon, 'don't you fucking dare.'

Oh my God, Simon is going all blue in the face. I look to my mother who is visibly cringing at the double dose of the 'F' word.

'Simon, you're my brother, but sometimes you are far too intense for me.'

Brother, brother. Oh shittity fuck. Of course, Chris, that Chris, the brother Simon did not want as his best man? *'Chris is too laid back, I will never relax. Besides we have never been that close. I prefer if*

Jamie did it.' Shit, shit, shit. I am in love with my future brother-in-law.

'I'm fucking intense? Have you dropped your legal shit yet, have you? And you are too bloody irresponsible. How dare you be so arrogant to think you could bring her here?'

'Right, that is enough. I don't know what you two are talking about but Simon, you're going too far.' I look at Simon's father and realise there is a striking resemblance to Christian and my heart skips a beat.

'It's okay Dad,' Christian says quietly.

Simon shakes his head.

'I think you owe me an explanation Annabel. If there is something going on here you should tell me. Just exactly what have you been telling him?'

Everyone looks at me expectantly. I open my mouth to speak but nothing comes out. Oh dear, was there something I told Christian that I shouldn't have? Just what, exactly, was I not supposed to talk about? I feel sure I ought to know. I rack my brains and finally give Simon a puzzled look. He looks crestfallen, and I want the floor to open up and swallow me. I turn to Christian who is just looking at me.

'Of course there isn't anything going on,' I say finally. 'That's silly. I'm here to get married to...' I hesitate and spot the Marc Jacob jumper and point. 'And I'm not interested in anyone else,' I lie. 'He just gave me a lift. We both missed the flight,' I say, concentrating hard on the words, speaking slowly and as clearly as I can.

Christian shakes his head. His eyes are telling me something but I try hard not to look at them.

'Christian, what's going on baby?' drawls Claudine, seemingly three sentences behind everyone else, and I thought I was drunk.

'She's not my type Simon, so get over it,' Christian asserts.

I'm not?

'And he is certainly not Annabel's type,' pipes up my mum. 'She has had her fair share of men like that.'

I see Christian's eyebrows rise.

'Absolutely,' I echo, feeling stupidly hurt by Christian's words.

Christian marches towards the lift with Claudine running behind him leaving a trail of Poison fragrance in her wake.

'Well, now that is sorted I am going to have a rest. God knows, I need it after being with her for two days,' he says caustically.

I feel myself blush and am grateful when the lift door closes on him.

'I think you should sober up,' snaps Simon.

I watch as he walks away. I turn to my mum and grimace. She grabs me roughly by the arm.

'I can't imagine what you were thinking, behaving like this. God knows you were brought up differently.'

I grin at Alex and get a sour look back. I let out a long sigh and enter the lift where a young man takes my hand luggage.

'Welcome to Rome, madam.'

What I would not do to go back to France.

Chapter Fifteen

Christian

'Was it a misunderstanding honey?'

What a mess. My head aches from the whisky and I feel stupidly embarrassed. Why the hell did he have to mention the lawsuit and in front of Dad? What a wanker. I force a smile for Claudine and walk to the loo.

'I wish you hadn't have done that honey, you know with the credit card,' repeats Claudine.

I deliberately leave the bathroom door open. I've learnt something about women in the past few years and I really am not in the mood to have things thrown at the door. I splash cold water at my face and head and grit my teeth. What the hell is going through Bels' head right now? How the hell did someone like Simon get someone like her? She's smart, beautiful and too giving for him.

'Honey, did you hear anything I said?'

Okay, so she was a bit irritating at times but she has so many redeeming qualities. Does he even notice the way she licks her lips before being kissed or strokes her throat when she is aware of being watched? Does the look in her warm brown eyes and her beautiful smile make him feel he is walking on air? I don't imagine so. She is too good for him.

'That hotel is ridiculously expensive and you know it Claudine,' I reply, rummaging through her handbag for some aspirin.

'But we can afford it.' She stands in front of me and pouts.

I spot her dress hanging on the back of the door and remember my own luggage. I should have asked Claudine to look into that for me. Damn, another problem to deal with. Is he with her now, telling her what a bastard brother I am?

'Was it a misunderstanding then? Are you going to let me have it back?'

'What?'

'The credit card, of course, anyway as it happens your family have been really nice to me, even Simon.'

'That was big of him.'

How the hell am I going to cope with having Bels as my sister-in-law? Damn, I almost slept with her. If her phone hadn't have gone off would it have happened? Well, it doesn't matter. What does matter is that I don't let anything so stupid ever happen again. The stupid plonker already thinks I would steal his woman just to get at him. Does he not know me at all? The last thing I want is to give him ammunition against me. I find the aspirin and throw two back with some water.

'Can I have it back then honey?'

'What?'

'The credit card, darling.'

Oh, of course. Jesus, isn't she going to ask me why it took me so long to get here? Why I was with my future sister-in-law? Why I was partly drunk when I arrived? Or didn't she notice any of that? I sigh heavily and watch as she slowly removes her jumper.

'I bet you want to see me in the dress don't you? I bought it yesterday.'

She runs her fingers tantalisingly through her newly highlighted hair and grins at me. I smile reluctantly.

'Are you okay baby?' she sidles towards me.

'Sure, sorry I've been such an arse. Why don't you bring the dress into the bedroom and model for me.'

She flings her arms around my neck.

'I thought you would never get here,' she says snuggling up to me.

'So did I?' I mumble lifting her up and striding into the bedroom.

Chapter Sixteen

I hold my head in my hands and moan loudly. Kaz is holding out two Paracetamol tablets.

'What is the maximum dose? Surely I can take more than two,' I groan swallowing them with the second mug of ultra-strong coffee she offers.

'I wouldn't want to be your liver,' she jokes shaking another pill from the bottle.

'I don't want to be my liver. I don't particularly want to be me at all in fact. How many of these do I need to kill myself?'

We are sitting in my hotel room. Everyone has left me in disgust, it seems, although I do not remember the events in the foyer an hour earlier very clearly.

'Oh God,' I groan, 'I really don't want to go.'

I am to meet Simon for dinner with my parents and his in just under an hour, and I am dreading it.

'Have you seen Christian?' I ask hopefully.

She gives me a mean stare. I sigh. It seems like forever since we arrived in Rome and most of what happened in the foyer is a blur. Although I clearly remember Christian saying I was not his type. Jesus, why did I not realise he was Simon's brother? How could I have been so stupid? After all, I knew he was a famous architect living in New York and that he was younger than Simon, and of course, I was aware his name was Chris. Damn him, damn him for not being in the least like Simon. Damn him for being able to wear the Marc Jacob jumper better than Simon ever could. Damn him for being so easy going. Damn him, damn him for coming into my life. Damn him even more for showing me just how over-the-top responsible Simon is. Damn him for being so bloody young, or is it just that Simon is so old? Oh damn everything. Tomorrow at three I am to be married, and I have no idea what to do.

147

'I've become a joint person already, how the hell do I become un-jointed?' I ask Kaz desperately.

She dunks a biscotti in my coffee.

'Are you going to jilt him at the altar?' she asks, looking not in the least horrified.

Oh my God I can't possibly do that. I can't jilt someone at the altar. Oh Jesus, that means I have to get married then. Oh shittity fuck.

'Of course not,' I reply, trying to maintain some dignity.

'Of course, you could do it at dinner tonight. I guess that would be a bit more acceptable.'

It would?

'I can't jilt him in front of his parents, or in front of mine come to that.'

Bugger it. Kaz shrugs.

'I guess you're lumbered then.'

I grab a biscotti and immediately remember all the biscuits I had eaten with Christian.

'The thing is, if you don't marry Simon, you're not going to marry anyone are you?' she says sipping from her banana smoothie, while crossing her legs and slipping into the lotus position. I stare at the blue liquid and wrinkle my nose.

'Why is that blue?' I ask curiously.

'Blueberries and banana, and I have to tell you the soya milk here is just fab. Anyway, I think Simon is a real catch. You're very lucky.'

I sigh and walk towards the bathroom.

'*You* marry him then,' I call over my shoulder.

I pass my suitcase and feel tears prick my eyelids. Twenty-four hours ago and I would have been thrilled to see it but now it is just another reminder of all that has gone on in the past few days and I feel terribly responsible for the argument between Simon and Christian. I know I can't really jilt Simon for his brother. That would be just too cruel. Besides, I have no idea how Christian feels about me. I have never felt so trapped in my whole life. I step in the shower and let the hot water relax my muscles. Talk about feeling like a spare part at a wedding, what a bloody shame the sodding wedding is mine. I wrap myself in the soft fluffy towel and walk back into the room where Kaz is still sitting in the lotus position and is now stretching her neck. God forbid any breakdown of mine should interfere with her journey towards peace and spirituality.

'You've gained weight,' she states flatly.

Jesus Christ, great karma that is. I see she has made me more coffee. I begin to wonder whether it will be worth even getting into bed tonight.

'I can't have, not in a couple of days,' I deny hotly, very aware that my tummy is swollen with an impending period.

She peers at me with her head on one side.

'Uh oh, I think you have you know. You look far too big to get into that dress now.'

She points her nose upwards towards my wedding dress which is hanging on a hook and looks to me very much like a shroud. Oh I must stop thinking like this and pull myself together. Think of all Simon's good points. A full minute later and I am still bloody trying to think of them.

'You'd better stick to salad tonight,' she advises, clicking her neck. I grimace and pull clothes out of my suitcase.

Forty-five minutes later I am heading nervously for the lounge. Kaz had talked me into wearing my Monsoon dress and a white cashmere cardigan. For the first time in days I actually look really nice and instead of wishing Christian could see me, I am praying I do not bump into him. Simon is waiting by the bar and I approach hesitantly. Oh God, please don't let him be wearing the bloody Marc Jacob jumper or, I swear that will be the end of the evening. He turns to appraise me.

'Ah,' he says.

I stare at him. What the hell does 'ah' mean?

'Where are the stud earrings I bought you?'

Oh shit. I finger the gold dangling pearls.

'I... erm... I didn't bring those,' I lie.

He looks disappointed and finishes his drink without offering me one.

'Right, let's go, we are meeting everyone at the restaurant.'

'Everyone,' I echo, stupidly.

'My parents, Alex and her husband, Tom, and your parents, they get on very well by the way.'

He gives me a sidelong glance, and I feel my heart lurch.

149

'Of course Christian and Dina are invited, although I doubt they will come.'

I take a deep breath and attempt to act normal, but a small whimper, that sounds not in the least normal, passes through my lips. And how come he can manage to call her Dina but cannot ever call me Bels?

'Simon, what was that about a lawsuit?' I ask.

His face clouds over.

'You really don't need to worry your pretty little head over that.'

Do what? Have we lost a century or two somewhere and did someone forget to tell me? I don't need to worry my pretty little head? Good God, one month into marriage and I will be wearing a pinny, shelling peas and laying out his slippers if he has anything to do with it.

'I think my pretty little head can cope with it,' I retort trying to hide my sarcasm.

He sighs heavily.

'Christian is suing me...'

I gasp.

'Why?'

'Because he is fucking greedy that is why.'

I wince. I never thought of Christian as greedy.

'He is bitter because Dad handed the majority of the law firm over to me. He claims he should have been given half. Dad doesn't know about any of this. He left it to me to handle the takeover so don't blurt anything out, okay. Your wonderful brother-in-law is suing the family to get a share of what he thinks belongs to him. Now, let's go. I really do not want to talk about him. I am very much hoping he is sensible enough not to turn up at the dinner.'

'But...' I begin.

He sighs.

'But what?'

'Why would your dad do that? I mean...'

'For Christ's sake, can't a man do what he wants with his money? Now come on.'

God, I can't believe it. Christian just didn't seem that intense to me. What am I thinking? How well do I even know him? At some point he must have guessed that I was Simon's fiancée and did he let on? He was most likely using me to get at Simon. I feel a little prickle behind my eyelashes and fight back my tears. How could he hurt me like that? Oh God, please don't let him be at the dinner.

Simon steers me past the grand piano and towards the revolving door. I am about to walk through it when to my surprise Kevin, the businessman who had the heart attack on the plane, walks in. He stops in front of me and winks.

'Well, well, you made it for your wedding then?'

I stare at him. Jesus Christ, I don't wish to see the guy dead, but my God, isn't it his entire fault that I got tangled up with Christian in the first place?

'You're not dead,' I say sounding disappointed. Although on reflection, if he had been, it would not have helped my situation that much.

He laughs raucously.

'God no, it was just an anxiety attack. I got a private flight thirty minutes later, and I landed that contract,' he says proudly.

I nod, wishing I could throw up into my handbag. Private flight, good Lord, to think I was worried about him.

'Say, do you know what happened to that chap who held everything up? You almost killed him,' he laughs.

I open my mouth to speak but Simon tugs me by the arm.

'I'm sure she would love to chat, old chap, but we are running very late for just about everything,' he snaps.

I blush.

'See you Kevin,' I call over my shoulder as I am dragged through the doors, 'I am glad you got the contract.'

'Simon...' I begin.

'I really don't want to hear about your antics trying to get here Annabel.'

I take a deep breath and climb into the taxi. I sneak a sidelong glance at him and see his face is very tight. Oh God, I feel so deflated it is unbelievable. From the moment Christian had stepped into the lift I had felt so alone. I decide I must try and recapture all that I had once felt for Simon and gently lay my hand in his lap. He ignores it for the whole journey and strangely I do not feel hurt. I am relieved when we finally arrive at the restaurant and I dive out of the car almost before Simon has time to open the door. My dad is waiting at the entrance and I bounce into his arms.

'Hello darling, how are you bearing up?' he says hugging me and the smell of his aftershave almost has me blubbering.

Simon shakes my father's hand and propels me inside. The smell of food makes my stomach churn and I grab of glass of water as soon as I sit down. Alex who is sitting with both hands protectively on her stomach looks at me over her menu and nods appreciatively at my dress. I smile at Simon's parents and get a broad grin from his dad. His mother gives me a disapproving stare. Jesus, this is going to be some dinner and I find myself wondering if it is possible to escape out of the ladies loo window. I let out a heavy sigh and lean across to kiss my mother.

'Oh God,' says Simon loudly and I look up to see Christian enter with Claudine clinging to his arm. I fall back into my seat and feel my heart pound. For a second or two there is a heavy silence which he quickly breaks by kissing his mother and slapping his father on the back. I try hard not to look at him.

'Evening everyone, are we sitting here?' he asks with a half-smile while cocking his head at Simon. Then, before Simon can reply, he pulls back the chair next to Alex and waits for Claudine to sit down. I attempt to avoid eye contact with him and fail miserably. He catches my eye and winks before sitting opposite me.

'Well, we are glad you are finally here Annabel, especially considering the wedding is tomorrow,' my future mother-in-law pipes up.

I tuck my hair behind my ears self-consciously as I feel Christian's eyes on me.

'It is a great shame we did not have the rehearsal though,' she continues, removing glasses from her handbag, which I note is not the one I had bought for her.

'I wouldn't have minded if you had gone ahead without me...' I say boldly and stop abruptly when Simon gives me a piercing look.

'I imagine Simon has got everything well under control, haven't you Simon? What was the string quartet like, Bels?' Christian grins at Simon and then at me.

Oh fuck. Simon moves uncomfortably in his seat.

'We're getting a jazz band, try and keep up,' he bristles.

'Is that a La Dolce Vita handbag? I prefer Anya Hindmarch myself, much less pretentious don't you think? Did Simon give you my gift?' I say pointedly to his mother. Oh God could there possibly be a more beam-me-up-Scottie moment, than this one? She opens her mouth and closes it again. Simon's father smiles widely and offers his hand to me.

'My son tells us, you have a top job in fashion. He is very bad at introducing people. I'm Edward, Simon's old codger of a father, and this is my wife Rosa who just loved your handbag, didn't you darling?'

And you look exceptionally like your son, Christian and act like him, I think with a sinking stomach. Rosa nods and I take Edward's hand gratefully. He squeezes it and whispers,

'The whisky was superb, thank you.'

'You're welcome.'

'I've asked Tom to be in charge of the presents. The whole thing was getting out of hand. Some will need to be returned. That's what happens when people don't follow the guidelines Annabel. A lot of them didn't even buy from John Lewis, which makes it awkward,' tuts Simon.

'Oh no,' I gasp. 'God forbid people actually bought us presents that were not from John Lewis. I ask you, how selfish is that?' I don't even attempt to keep the sarcasm out of my voice. I mean, for Christ's sake, isn't it just nice that people bothered at all?

'Bels,' reprimands my mother, while looking at Christian. 'What is the matter with you?'

'Christian's influence undoubtedly,' murmurs Simon under his breath, slapping Deep Heat onto his neck.

'Talking of moi. Very guilty I'm afraid. We actually had something sent over from Harrods, didn't we Claudine? Of course, we could change it for something cheaper at John Lewis. After all, we would hate to step over the guidelines,' chips in Christian.

'So sorry,' drawls Claudine as she lays a hand on Christian's knee. I find myself staring enviously at it.

'Annabel is a bit overwhelmed, aren't you darling?' says Dad with a smile on his face.

'What's that smell?' asks Tom, wrinkling his nose.

We all look at Simon's very red neck but no one actually mentions the Deep Heat. Alex quickly changes the subject.

'Lovely restaurant, Simon, thank you so much.'

I glance at the wine list and to my surprise I see the name of the vineyard that Christian and I visited this morning. Memories of Luciano saying 'it is good yes' and Christian loading two crates into the boot of the Lemon seem a million miles away. How I wish I could be back at that vineyard right now. My daydream comes to an abrupt end as Simon barks to the waiter,

'We will have two bottles of Grattamacco, and I think two bottles of Pomino, and Alex, you won't want wine will you? Would you prefer water, or a soft drink?'

I stare horror-stricken at my fiancé. Jesus has he always been this bloody bossy?

'Water would be great,' gushes Alex.

'You won't want wine either will you Annabel?'

I widen my eyes.

'You have had more than enough,' he hisses into my ear and I feel my face redden. 'I'll order you water, shall I?'

'Actually, I would like the *Chianti Velaruse* please. It is a delicate wine with a hint of vanilla and raspberry and a touch of black pepper. It goes well with pasta, I think,' I say, recalling Luciano's exuberant description from the vineyard this morning.

'Here, here,' echoes Christian.

Simon turns to me, his eyes blazing.

'Bravo Annabel, Chianti Velaruse is an excellent choice. Your fiancé knows her wine Simon,' applauds his father.

I nod in gratitude.

'Don't you think you have had enough to drink already,' snaps my mother.

'Quite,' acknowledges Simon.

Oh honestly. Am I sixteen years old or something?

'Oh no, nowhere near enough,' I retort to her look of horror.

'Bels,' gasps Alex, clutching her stomach. My God this pregnancy is taking its strain on everyone. I for one will be dead grateful when she finally gives birth.

'You should visit the vineyard, 'Château Velaruse', while you are here,' suggests Edward, seemingly oblivious to the tense atmosphere. 'They do wonderful tours.'

I smile and relax. He smiles back knowingly and winks. I realise I am famished, and am grateful when the waiter comes with a basket of rolls. The waiter has a shifty look about him, and I ignore the odd look he gives me as I take two, a girl's got to eat after all. Out of the corner of my eye I see Simon move the butter out of my reach and feel myself fume. How the hell can I recapture my feelings for this guy when he keeps bloody aggravating me?

'Simon?' I say stretching over him to reach it.

'You know it's fattening.'

I feel myself fume even more.

'So, what if it is?'

He raises his eyebrows.

'Well, you don't want to get fat do you?'

'Maybe I do,' I retort.

'Oh don't be so ridiculous,' he patronises me.

'Don't you dare call me ridiculous,' I reply through gritted teeth.

'Keep your voice down,' he hisses.

'Oh for goodness sake,' I hear his mother mumble.

'Come on Simon, let her have some fun before she is tied down. Here you go Bels,' grins Christian, passing the butter. I fight an overwhelming urge to slap him.

'Honey, come on, don't interfere,' whispers Claudine.

Simon slaps it out of his hand and sends it flying straight into Alex's lap. Oh God.

'Don't you fucking call her Bels,' he snarls.

'Simon, for goodness sake,' snaps his mother.

I reach over and pull the butter from Alex's lap.

'Yes, honey, don't bloody interfere,' I say through gritted teeth, looking into Christian's eyes and feeling my knees go all weak.

'Everyone else calls her Bels, why are you penalising me?' Christian challenges while innocently biting into his roll. Meanwhile, Mother is frantically rubbing away at Alex's skirt with a serviette.

'Do you want to go and change?' asks Tom, lovingly. I mean, I ask you, there is barely a mark on the skirt.

'I don't know,' she replies anxiously. 'What do you think, Mother?'

Oh for goodness sake.

'No one is penalising anyone dear,' smiles Rosa, handing round the basket of bread.

I sigh heavily and flop into my chair.

'Her name is Annabel, and that's all there is to it,' snarls Simon.

'Bels, what do you prefer to be called?' asks Christian innocently.

'I asked you not to call her Bels,' yells Simon, jumping up.

Oh no not again. I'm beginning to feel like some femme fatale. Maybe I am letting out an unusual amount of pheromones. Yes, even Tom is looking at me oddly. My God, are all men going to turn into crazy tom cats around me? Do I dare intervene or will I just release more of the fatal chemical? I am just about to lay a hand on Simon's arm when Rosa bangs on the table and we all jump. Two breadsticks leap from the basket and land on my plate like manna from heaven.

'That is enough, both of you. For goodness sake what is wrong with you? If you have to argue, for goodness sake argue over something worthwhile.'

Excuse me? What exactly is she trying to say? I see Mother open her mouth and then quickly close it after Alex nudges her. Christian looks at Simon, his face thunderous and challenging. Thankfully the wine arrives, and as Simon waits to taste it, I take the opportunity to meet Christian's eyes and silently mouth,

'Please leave.'

He seems to nod and then leans over to Claudine who quickly rises.

'I hope you will excuse us. As lovely as the company is, we are both a little tired and I think it is beginning to show. Enjoy your dinner.'

Before anyone has a chance to comment, they are gone.

'Good riddance,' mumbles Simon.

I sip my wine in an effort to calm my nerves. The waiter with the shifty look is staring at me again, and I fight the impulse to poke out my tongue. Simon orders our starters and I sit obediently silent until they arrive. Halfway through my tomato, basil and mozzarella salad there is a commotion at the restaurant entrance. I see the shifty waiter pointing in our direction but think nothing of it until two burley policemen appear at our table. My mother looks horrified, and Alex immediately protects her stomach. I continue eating my salad until I realise that their eyes are on me and me only.

'Are you Annabel Lewis?' one of them asks in broken English.

The restaurant goes deathly quiet. I swear you could hear a pin drop. I feel my neck tense. Oh God, what now? Simon takes my hand and I grasp his gratefully.

'Can we help you officer? Miss Lewis is my fiancée, and we are to be married tomorrow,' he says pleasantly while calmly taking a sip of his wine. I gulp mine in one hit. I feel very safe being the fiancée of a top lawyer and for some silly reason I imagine I may even be invincible. I am no longer Bels but Simon's fiancée. Surely they can do nothing to me now. Oh how wrong can you be? The minute Simon confirmed that I was Miss Lewis more police appear, and the restaurant looks like a scene from *Die Hard*. I am half expecting Bruce Willis to slide across the floor and scoop me away. I wait with bated breath for someone to say 'We have you surrounded,' but of course they don't. Before I know what I am doing, I am holding my hands up in surrender.

'What the devil...' Rosa stammers.

My mother attempts to give her an explanation of sorts in Italian, but fails miserably.

'What is going on?' demands Edward.

'This is madness, my daughter is having a baby,' cries my mother and promptly crosses herself. I swear my mother has never crossed herself in her life and I figure it must be the Italian air or something. Alex gives me a murderous glare.

'If I have my baby in Italy I will never forgive you,' she gasps, grabbing Tom's sleeve.

'Miss Lewis, we are taking you to the station for questioning in connection with a series of robberies both here and in France,' the police officer announces.

I shake my head in denial.

'No,' I object. 'I haven't robbed a garage here I only *helped* rob one in France.'

Oh shit, what am I saying?

'Oh my God,' shouts Alex falling into Tom's arms.

My mother looks horrified.

'No, no what I mean is,' I stutter. Oh God, is there really any point?

'We have you on CCTV camera emptying the till and taking the customers' wallets,' the policeman declares solemnly.

'No,' screams my mother while appearing to faint. Oh God, this is seriously dire.

Simon releases my hand and I look at him. He is shaking his head.

'You'll have to go with them. I'll follow in my car. I am seriously hoping you have a good explanation for all of this.'

A good explanation? Good Lord, of course I have a good explanation. The guy had a bloody gun at my head. Somehow I don't imagine that will be good enough for Simon. What am I saying? Of course it will be good enough for Simon. I watch as he leaves the restaurant with his parents and wait for him to turn back and give me a reassuring wave, but he doesn't. Oh dear, this is not good.

'Come with us please,' orders another policeman and I shrug at my dad who nods encouragingly while waving smelling salts under my mother's nose.

'Don't worry darling, keep your chin up.'

'It's all a big mistake,' I call back to Alex.

'Do you know how many murderers have said that?' comments Tom dryly.

I give him a dirty look and follow the policemen. Oh well, things can only get better now because, let's face it, nothing can be worse than this.

Chapter Seventeen

'This is you in the film, you agree with me?' I am sitting in a dingy little room. I cannot believe they think I am a criminal. Where on earth is Simon? Surely he should have had me out of here long before now. He is a solicitor after all.

I stare both mesmerised and horrified at the video that is being played in front of me. I actually do look like a criminal. There I am, stealing people's wallets as cool as anything. But worse and this really is the worst of all, I cannot believe how awful I look. My hair is tangled and looks limp, and my face is deathly pale. I suddenly realise I am not a patch on Claudine and Christian probably never really found me in the least attractive. What a bloody fool I have been. Two policemen now sit opposite me and I wonder if they are planning on using the good cop, bad cop routine.

'Yes,' I answer miserably. 'I was not stealing their wallets though. You need to contact *him*,' I say leaning forward and pointing to Christian. 'He is my fiancé's brother and we were travelling here for my wedding and this other guy, the hoodie who kept away from the CCTV camera, he was the robber. He made me collect the money and…'

The police officer shakes his head and pushes the pause button.

'So you were forced to rob these people?' he says cynically.

I let out a small moan.

'He was pointing a gun at me, so yes I was.'

The other policeman jumps up and my heart starts beating very fast.

'You tell us where the hoodie man is,' he growls pushing his face close to mine, and I smell garlic on his breath. Oh God, this is awful. I am supposed to be getting married tomorrow. This should be the happiest time of my life.

'I don't know him,' I protest somewhat feebly.

159

'I don't believe you,' he shouts, thumping the table.

The other policeman holds out a packet of cigarettes and I shake my head.

'I don't smoke,' I say my voice trembling.

'You took a lot of cigarettes, we saw you on the video.'

Oh for goodness sake. Which bit do they not understand? Gun pointed at me? Forced?

'I'm getting married,' I say stupidly, like that explains everything. 'To Simon, he is a solicitor.'

'This man,' he points to Christian and I nod eagerly. 'This man, we know you were with because you travel in his car, but we cannot seem to trace him. Perhaps you know where he has disappeared to.'

'What!' I yell.

What does he mean, they cannot trace Christian? Does Simon know this?

'No, you're wrong, he must be here. He was having dinner with us this evening. He's going to be at my wedding tomorrow.'

At least I think he is. The policeman nods suspiciously at me.

'I see, and you say he was having dinner with you?'

I nod.

'Yet there was no sign of him in the restaurant?'

What is wrong with these people, how can they not know Christian? I try to think where he would go. Surely he would not leave the country. Maybe he is cross with me but I know he is responsible no matter what Simon thinks and I feel sure he will be at the wedding. Oh God, where can he be? Then, it comes to me.

'He is probably with Bryan Marshall, the footballer. He is building a house for him, you see.'

The policemen are silent for a moment and then suddenly launch into animated conversation in bloody Italian. I strain to recognise some words, but the only two that make sense are 'Bryan' and 'Marshall'. Then, before I have time to speak, more policemen come in and join in the discussion. One begins to demonstrate his dribbling skills and I shake my head in disbelief. What is it with men and football? It seems that all you have to do is mention a footballer's name and they all become little boys again, totally obsessed with kicking a ball around and showing off any skill they have, which in this case is pretty limited.

'Bryan Marshall, he is the best footballer and will play for Italy this year,' smiles my interrogator.

Ah, 'a result' as they say. The policemen leave the room and I drop my head into my hands. It feels like hours since I was taken from the restaurant. I'm sure that Simon has been here the whole time. Have I been a total fool? After all this, Simon may decide he wants nothing more to do with me. Of course, there may not be a wedding as I may well end up in prison. I shudder in my seat when it dawns on me that Simon probably cannot practise law in Italy. Please God, let them release me and I promise to marry Simon and be the best wife ever. I'll buy Nigella Lawson cook books and bake every day, well maybe not every day but most days and I promise to hand-wash Simon's shirts, or at least get someone else to but I won't ever put them in the washing machine like I did his Fat Face jumper. I'll never refuse him sex, even when I am tired, and I'll have lots of babies, well three anyway, just please God don't make me go to prison. I mean, I know it won't be like Thailand prisons and all that, but still, compared to England, it is bound to be a bit harsh. I just can't believe all this is happening to me. I came to get married for God's sake. It is all that bloody Christian's fault. The video starts up again and there is his annoying face. I groan and attempt to turn it off when the door is flung open and my dad walks in. I jump up and run to him and he enfolds me in his arms.

'Good Lord, this is some carry on. The women are in a fine state. I'll never understand the fairer sex.'

I hold back my tears.

'I don't want to go to prison Dad. I promise to be the best wife Simon has ever had,' I say desperately.

He pulls me away from him.

'I wasn't aware he had been married before,' he says frowning.

'What? No, he hasn't, why would you think that?'

'You said you promise to be the best wife Simon has ever had.'

I let out a loud groan.

'Dad, please. I will be his first and only wife. Can we just make sure I don't go to prison please?' I beg.

'Ah, it seems Simon got hold of Christopher...'

'Christian,' I correct.

He nods.

'Ah, that's it. I knew it was a religious name, Christopher, Christian...anyway.'

He can see I am growing impatient.

'Yes, well,' he begins, offering me my cardigan. I look eagerly at him.

'The police are releasing you. Simon is completing the paper work. Clever guy this Christopher. He...'

'Christian,' I correct grabbing my handbag.

'Ah, yes, sorry, anyway very clever chap. Your mother and I watched a programme about Bryan Marshall and they showed his house in Rome, fantastic. Of course, it's none of my business darling, or your mother's, but if you decide not to marry Simon, your life won't be worth living for a few months, but if you do marry Simon and realise he was not the right one, then your life won't be worth living full stop. Worth thinking about before you take the plunge.'

I am speechless. My dad, a man of few words and usually those are a muddle, but every so often he drops a gem like this, and you want to stitch it on a pillow. Generally though, he talks more to his plants than he does to either me or Mum. I look at Simon who is standing at the entrance watching the policemen kicking a football and know that I have no choice but to marry my fiancé. Dad's words had made me realise that there is only one person I want to spend my life with and that is Christian, but Christian is Simon's brother, so I must give up my foolish feelings and get on with my life.

Chapter Eighteen

'I don't believe this. There are lilies in your bouquet,' cries Kaz lumbering into the room carrying three large boxes.

Alex is twisting my hair into heated rollers so I cannot move.

'Oh no,' sighs my mother jumping up and almost falling over the hairdryer lead.

Lilies. Good Lord is someone trying to tell me something.

'Jesus,' gasps Kaz, seeing my mum in her face mask. I stifle my laughter and strain to see the bouquet.

'We have our own little beauty parlour here, Kaz, when are you joining us?'

She drops the boxes with a huff.

'If I can have a banana smoothie I will join you. By the way, the best man has the carnations sorted, and he says the inside of the church is beautiful, and he and Tom are taking the presents to the marquee.'

My mother holds up the bouquet with a frown.

'You can't have lilies. We'll have to send them back.'

I shake my head and lean forward to get my glass of water. Alex yanks me back. Jesus, letting a hormonal woman near my hair on my wedding day is probably not my best idea.

'I like them, they match my mood.'

It is several hours before the ceremony. My mother is in her dressing gown, and Alex is curling my hair as she waits for her toenails to dry. My head has been aching ever since I awoke at five this morning. I had spent the early hours reading my wedding cards, of which there seemed to be hundreds. Alex exhales loudly and lays both hands on her stomach before sitting down carefully.

'Right, your hair is setting, what time is the make-up artist coming?'

I shrug my shoulders.

'Actually, quite soon,' answers Kaz, looking at her watch. 'She has five of us to do.'

The phone shrills and Kaz jumps up to answer it. I check my Blackberry as Kaz reaches for the phone.

'The bride's boudoir,' she smiles. 'Oh hi, yes of course she is here, hold on.'

Kaz stretches the phone lead across Alex and hands it to me.

'It's Simon,' she whispers grinning.

I take the phone reluctantly. Please don't say anything to put me off you, I think desperately. I am holding my feelings together with just a piece of thread and I feel sure the smallest thing could see me unravel.

'Hi,' I say uncertainly.

'Hi, it's me Christian, your friendly builder.'

Butterflies dance in my stomach and I feel sick. Oh buggety bugger, why now?

I jump up knocking hair tongs into my mother's lap. I indicate to Kaz to transfer it to the bathroom phone and after stepping over towels and boxes of flowers I slam the door shut and flop onto the loo.

'Hi,' I say finally.

There is silence for a minute and my heart sinks when I think he may have hung up.

'Sorry, I probably shouldn't have phoned today, I just wanted to apologise for the dinner business. It was a bit of low point.' He sounds nervous. God, his voice never fails to send a shiver down my spine and I still can't connect him with Simon. How can two brothers be so different? I try to swallow but there is a large lump in my throat.

'There is nothing to apologise for, I...'

'Yes, there is. The truth is I think I knew you were Annabel long before I admitted it. Anyway, I just want to wish you all the best for the future and I think you and Simon make a great couple and I couldn't wish for a better sister-in-law.'

Sister-in-law. Sodding hell, why is the bastard phoning me now? Why the hell is he suing his own brother? In fact, why did he even have to come into my life? Well, of course, I know he would have come into my life; after all he is Simon's brother. I just wish he hadn't come into my life with such a bang and turned it upside down.

'Simon is a great guy,' I say holding back my resentment. Let's face it, the fact that he is Simon's brother most certainly means anything else between us is out of the question. Again there is silence.

'Anyway, good luck this afternoon, don't fall over the dress or anything,' he says finally. I notice he does not agree with me that Simon is a great guy.

'I'll try not to,' I say quickly, trying not to think of his lips on mine.

He laughs softly and I wonder if Claudine is nearby.

'It's the kind of thing you do isn't it?' I can almost see him smiling.

'I do not,' I reply indignantly.

'Yes you do and then you swear like a trooper.'

'What a cheek,' I say; grateful he cannot see my smile.

'Simon is marrying a fun girl and you're marrying...'

'A very serious guy,' I finish for him.

'The right guy,' he corrects me and I stifle my sigh.

'Am I?' I whisper.

There is a sharp intake of breath.

'Yes, you are. Anyway, break a leg.'

The phone goes dead and I stare at it wanting to shout 'trace that call and find out where he is staying.' But of course, I don't. I walk back into the main room where Natasha, the make-up artist is setting up her things. The only thing I can remember about our conversation is that he had said he knew who I was long before I knew who he was. Was this before he had questioned me about Simon? Before he had kissed me in the car? When had he realised I was Simon's fiancée? Damn the bastard. I probably *will* fall over my dress now and break a leg. I try to remember the seating plan for the reception. I could ask Kaz if she knows where he may be sitting but decide against it. Probably best that I don't know. I flop onto the bed and watch Natasha paint Alex's fingernails. Rosa strolls in and compiles a list of food and drink requests which she goes downstairs to fetch. I watch as if in a dream, all the goings on around me. The photographer sets up his camera and my hotel room looks like a film

165

set. Kaz watches Natasha as she begins to paint my mother's nails. Alex has propped her legs up on the bed and is gently massaging her stomach while my mother enjoys her manicure while looking very decadent in her Chanel dressing gown. I smile, my mum, fashionable even when going to bed. I check my Blackberry and realise I have just over three hours before I become Mrs Simon Lloyd and I have to take a deep breath to calm myself. Last night, on the way back from the police station, I saw the villa where the reception is to be held. I hated it. It is wonderfully medieval, and of course romantic, but it somehow reminds me of the vineyard at Chateau de Velaruse and I really do not need reminders of Christian on my wedding day. Rosa walks in with a tray of tea and sandwiches. I accept a cup of tea but decline the salami roll she offers.

'You should eat something darling,' advises my mother biting into a Parma ham roll.

I feel sick and slide off the bed.

'Actually, what I need is some fresh air; the room stinks of hair-setting gel and...

The room turns silent and all eyes are on me.

'What do you mean *you need fresh air*?' Alex asks.

'Do you want me to stop taking the photos?' asks the photographer looking confused.

Christ, am I a bloody prisoner now?

'There isn't time for you to go wandering,' Rosa chips in, nodding to Alex.

Wandering? What the hell are they on about? I pull the rollers from my hair and hear Alex gasp. I try not to sigh too loudly.

'I just need to get out of this room for ten minutes. Don't worry I will come back,' I pull on my jeans and grab my Blackberry.

'Well, don't be long,' says my mother.

I smile and close the door behind me. An enormous sense of freedom overwhelms me and I dive into the lift. The lounge is crowded with many of our guests and I quickly retreat from there and make my way to a small bar by the gym. I see Edward nursing a whisky.

'Ah, you've escaped. Well done.'

I join him at the bar and allow him to order me a diet coke.

'How is Simon doing? Is he nervous?' I ask, taking a small sip from my glass.

He looks at the whisky in front of him and twirls it around the glass.

'The whisky you bought me is really smooth. I opened it, I'm afraid. My son, Christian, well you've met him haven't you? He appreciates good single malt like his father.'

I nod. Why is it that everywhere I go Christian seems to follow me?

'Ah, Simon is fine. More to the point how are you?' He taps my knee gently. 'You look like you need something stronger than coke. Here, have a sip.'

I take a small sip, its warmth comforting me.

'You must not worry about our Simon, very business minded is my son, he takes after his mother. I hope you're not that serious, he could do with some light relief in his life.'

'He is a bit intense,' I agree.

He shakes peanuts from a dish and drops them into my hand.

'Yes, he is far too intense. Christian is more like me, thank God.'

Oh he sure is.

'But you don't have a nut allergy,' I laugh watching him throw a handful of nuts into his mouth.

'Ha, that is such a problem. Trying to keep nuts away from him when he was a kid was an absolute nightmare.'

Oh how I would love to sit and chat about Christian when he was a child. I look at my Blackberry.

'Oh sod a dog they will be shitting themselves. I promised I would only be about ten minutes. I feel like I just escaped Colditz, and now I am going back in. I must be out of my mind.'

I slide off my stool and quickly take another sip of Edward's whisky.

'That is really good stuff, right back to the wolves.'

He kisses me on the cheek.

'You make sure you are the boss of your own wedding and don't go falling over your dress.'

Oh my God. Did he really say that?

'I'll try not to,' I reply experiencing that déjà vu feeling.

I wave and rush back to my room. Everything is exactly the same as when I left it. Alex is still sitting with her hands on her stomach and Mum is having the second coat painted onto her nails. I sit back down and allow Alex to put the rollers back into my hair and try to smile at the photographer as he snaps away. Okay, this is it. In just two hours I will be walking down the aisle, and within minutes I will be Mrs Annabel Lloyd. I close my eyes and picture our flat in London. I am already one half of a joint mortgage so there is no going back. It certainly is time I got married and what better man to marry than Simon. He is rich, successful and handsome. How many men can you say that about? Well, Christian...No, no, I mustn't think about him. Eligible too, don't forget, Simon is eligible too and you can't say that about Christian. I sigh and hold my hand out for a manicure. Bugger it, why do I keep thinking about him? Alex takes my other hand and places it on her stomach.

'He's kicking, feel.'

Of course, I will probably have babies fairly soon as Simon is older than me so I don't imagine he will want to wait too long. We will probably spend a year together and then start our family. I picture us sitting in front of an open fire, or better still a log burner. Oh yes, I can definitely see our flat with one of those. We can toast marshmallows and teacakes on cold winter evenings. But, then again, maybe not, as I expect Simon will be too concerned about my weight. I expect all my dreams of being an earth mother and breastfeeding my babies all over the place won't happen either, as he will worry what people will think. Ah, well, I must think of all Simon's good points. The trouble is I seem to have great difficulty with that these days, shit, shit. But, of course, when I am pregnant, he won't worry about those silly things, like my weight and what people might think, but will indulge me in everything I like, and that is bound to include marshmallows and teacakes.

'Right, I will do your make-up now.'

I open my eyes to see Natasha poised with a brush close to my nose. I close my eyes again and feel the soft brush on my eyelids. I remember being so excited about having Natasha do my make-up. After all, how many women can say they had the same make-up artist for their wedding as Kate Moss has for her assignments? Oh God, I hope he doesn't call me Annabel for the rest of our bloody lives. I shall go sodding insane if he does. I may have to change my name by deed poll or something. I snap my eyes open and connect very harshly with the eyeliner brush.

'Ouch, shit. Sorry my fault,' I apologise allowing her to gently close them again but not before I realise Mum and Rosa are leaving.

'Are you going now?' I ask nervously.

'We will see you later and I just know you will look beautiful darling,' says my mum, kissing me warmly on the cheek. Rosa squeezes my arm and then they are gone. I watch Alex as she lays the wedding dress and bridesmaid dresses on the bed. Oh shit, back to daydreaming. I remind myself, I am thirty years old. If I wait much longer there may not be anyone left to marry. I mean, look at Kaz. I really don't want the highlight of my week to be a speed-dating evening or, horror of horrors, spending my weekends hugging a red rose and a copy of *Pride and Prejudice* while waiting for my blind date. Oh, it is too horrible to imagine. No, this is by far the most sensible decision, and as for Christian, well, why is he still single anyway? Yes, that is certainly something to think about. Although, didn't he say he hadn't met the right woman yet? Of course, he also said I was not his type. Shut up for goodness sake. In just a matter of hours I will be married and then all this thinking will be pointless. I feel my head being yanked back as Alex removes the heated rollers. I open my eyes and the light in the room blinds me for a second and makes my head throb. I look at my made-up face in the mirror. If this had been any other occasion I would have loved the attention.

'I just need to do your hair. Do you still want it up?' Alex asks hitting me in the back with her bump.

I nod and allow Natasha to kiss me carefully on the cheek.

'Good luck,' she whispers. 'See you later.'

I feel sick and lean over to read the time on my Blackberry. Surely I have a little while before I have to leave. My heart sinks when I see I have an hour. As soon as Alex has finished my hair I swallow two painkillers for my thumping head.

'What do you think? The million-dollar question is will I be able to pull a handsome Italian in this?' smiles Kaz, parading in her tight fitting maroon bridesmaid dress. I look at her slim waist enviously. I nod appreciatively.

'You can do it,' I say taking the bottle of Quiet Life from my bag. Oh God, my hands are shaking so much I can hardly twist the top off the bottle. How am I ever going to get into the dress?

'Can you open the balcony door?' I ask, struggling to breathe.

'We should get you into your dress,' commands Alex helping me up.

A loud rapping at the door makes us all jump.

'Croissants and jam for the wedding party, courtesy of the hotel management,' calls a breezy voice.

Jesus Christ, this surely cannot be happening. Kaz opens the door as I fall back into my chair. *Croissants and Jam.* I close my eyes and see Christian sitting in the small airport café surrounded by croissants. *Buy you a coffee*, his voice echoes in my head. I open my eyes expecting to see him standing in front of me.

'I can't go through with it,' I state flatly.

Kaz plonks the tea tray onto a table and a croissant bounces off the plate and onto the floor. Alex seems to somehow glide onto the bed like a human balloon.

'What?' snaps Kaz, picking up a croissant and putting it down again, 'What do you mean?'

'Oh my God, I hope they do epidurals in Italy,' moans Alex taking deep breaths.

'Oh fuck Bels, you can't be serious. Simon is probably at the church already,' groans Kaz, as my words sink in.

I watch as she leans against the bathroom door and slides down helplessly.

'Deep breaths, deep breaths, I think someone should call Tom,' moans Alex.

'You're not in labour,' I say feeling very calm.

'How the hell would you know that?'

'Because everything is in your mind, Alex, well, apart from the pregnancy. Have a cup of tea.'

'I can't believe this is happening. Who the hell is going to tell Simon?' Kaz sighs, while pulling at the roots of her hair. I stare at her.

'Oh fuck,' she groans dropping her head into her hands. 'I don't want to be the bloody messenger; they always shoot the messenger don't they?'

Alex is sobbing.

'You will now be on the shelf, you know that don't you?'

I sigh and look at Kaz.

'I am sorry Kaz, I really am, but you will have to tell him.'

She stares at the door. I follow her eyes to see my father.

'Oh Daddy, make her see sense,' cries Alex.

My dad looks from Alex to me and then to Kaz who is sitting on the floor. I pull my robe around me and attempt to smile.

'You have been giving this some thought then?'

I nod. Kaz jumps up pulling at her dress.

'Alex, can you get this off me. I swear I could kill you Bels.'

'Leave that to Mother, she will most certainly kill her,' shouts Alex.

I waltz into the bathroom.

'Well, frankly, I would rather be dead than marry Simon,' I say as I slam the door.

Chapter Nineteen

'I really thought his mother was going to lynch me.'
Kaz carefully lays a cold towel on her head and falls onto the bed. I really cannot believe I have done it. Of course, there is the flat and everything to sort out, but I can cope with that. It is such a relief. I can't believe how much better I feel.

'How was Simon when you left?' I ask apprehensively.
She pouts.

'How do you think? He was a bit shell-shocked, poor bugger. His mum started screaming and his best man called you a bitch. Simon's grandmother paced around wringing her hands saying *mamma mia,* as if someone had just died. Your mum burst into tears. Oh God, it was awful...They were all dressed to the nines and I turn up in my jeans. Your mum looked fit to faint as soon as she saw me.'

She lets out a giggle.

'Bloody hell Bels, you have got some guts, especially considering Alex was forever going into phantom labour. I mean weren't you afraid she finally would?'

I shrug.

'She isn't due for eight weeks. Honestly, that baby must be picking up all her anxieties. I swear it will be born with Valium in its hands.'

She sniggers. I hand her a mug of tea and sit hugging my own.

'Simon's brother, what's his name?'

'Christian,' I reply my heart skipping a beat.

'Yeah, he looked a bit stunned and disappeared in all the commotion.' She grabs a stale croissant from the plate. 'So what are you going to do now?'

I think for a moment.

'Go home I suppose. Try and get my flat back,' I say, without much conviction.

'I wouldn't go outside the door for several hours, if I were you.' Kaz is quite right of course. I am now Rome's most wanted, dead or alive. My Blackberry hasn't stopped bleeping. Mum has knocked at the door several times but I could not face seeing her. I have four voicemail messages from Simon's mother and six from my mother. After Kaz leaves, I run a hot bath and soak for a while. I then phone the airport and arrange a flight for tomorrow afternoon. Kaz had eagerly agreed to stand in for me at the fashion show so I could go home and wallow without feeling guilty about not attending. As I lie on the bed contemplating my future my mobile shrills and flashes Simon's name. I reluctantly answer it.

'Simon, I am really sorry,' I say meaning every word.

'The thing is I really *don't* want to see you Annabel. I know there is a lot to sort out and I am capable of doing it. I will take care of the bank and mortgage, and the flat. I would really prefer it if you didn't get in touch. I am sure you had good reason for doing what you did but I can't say I understand it.'

Oh bollocks, he really hates me. I suppose if I were him, I would hate me too.

'I'd like the ring back,' he states flatly, just as I am feeling sorry for him.

I nearly fall off the bed.

'What?'

'The ring, I bought it from a very good jeweller friend in Hatton Garden. He will give me a good price for it,' he says, coldly.

I sit upright and look at the ring on my finger.

'But you gave the ring to me,' I argue.

'Yes, well now I want it back and the bracelet that I bought you when we first met.'

I push myself to the end of the bed and swing my leg.

'Are you really serious?'

'Be grateful you don't live in America Annabel, it is the law there and I would not even have to ask.'

I should have known. Only Simon would know all the legalities of a relationship breakdown.

'I hope you don't ask me to give you the earrings back,' I snap irritably.

'They were earrings for pierced ears so I can't get my money back on those,' he responds coolly.

'Well, that is just as well, seeing as I lost them on the flight here,' I say with cruel delight and bite my lip quickly.

'Typical,' he sighs.

Bloody hell, was I really going to marry this guy? What a lucky escape. Oh yes, a lucky escape all right, except now I am not only single but probably homeless as well. However, I console myself getting divorced from this guy would have been a legal nightmare. He most likely would have found a loophole to have me deported. A bit of an exaggeration but you get my drift, never marry a lawyer.

'I'll leave them at reception for you.'

'No, my dad will come and collect them this evening. He will give you my wedding ring, of course.

Oh this is so mean and horrible. I really cannot believe he is going to return the wedding ring I had bought him.

'You can keep that,' I say, attempting to be nice but realise I sound very condescending.

He laughs and says cynically,

'And why would I want to do that? I never married you remember. I just thank God for that.'

I say goodbye and hang up, not wishing to be insulted anymore. I look at the ring for a short time and then take it off placing it carefully into an envelope I had found in the dressing table. I search for the bracelet in my travelling jewellery bag and pop that in too. I pull my laptop from its bag and Google *flats for rent in St John's Wood* and yes, there is my flat. Good Lord, he has put the rent up already. I stare astonished at the new rate with a sinking heart. I was already paying more than I could afford but this is daylight robbery. Shit, shit, what a nuisance. I send the landlord an email making myself sound more sorrowful than I actually am, asking if I can continue with my lease. I think it best not to mention the increase in rent. I mean, perhaps he will take pity on me and let me continue with the same agreement. Dream on Bels. My fingers hover over the keys as I consider Googling Christian, not that I believe he is *that* well known in the building world. All that talk of bad publicity ruining business was just him showing off and trying to impress me. Of course, if that were the case he is not likely to be on Google is he? With that comforting thought, I type in his name and oh my God, he is all over Google, and there are even photos of him and lots of them too. My heart is beating so fast you would think I had just entered a hard-core porn site. I am stunned to see he is treated like a celebrity, talking of which, according to Google, he seems to know a lot of them. Oh Jesus, there are even photos of him winning awards and pictures of Olivia's photo shoot. I click the 'Connect with Christian Lloyd' on Facebook and find myself staring at his profile. I hover over the request friendship link and then, with a deep sigh click the page shut. He is not interested in me, I remind myself. I must not forget that I am not his type. A small envelope symbol pops up on the screen and my gloom is lifted when I see Jake, the landlord, has replied already. I click into the email and wrinkle my eyes, too afraid to look. I see the first two lines and feel a surge of hope.

'Hi Bels, sorry to read of your bad news but hey, it happens all the time...'

It does? Bloody hell, all those jilted men. I wonder if they all asked for their engagement ring back.

'I would be happy to have you in the flat. Better the devil you know.'

Bloody cheek.

'Afraid the rent has gone up a bit, old gal.'

Bugger bugger.

'But I can meet you halfway on the increase. Let me know. Cheers Jake'

I can cope with that, just. I email back to say I will take it, and with a sense of relief I fall back onto the bed. But within seconds I am back on Google and looking at photos of Christian. I am still looking at them when Edward knocks on the door. I let him in shyly.

'Hello, how are you bearing up?' he asks kindly.

'You asked me that a few hours ago. I never did get to fall over my dress.' I attempt a smile.

He sits on the bed and produces the wedding ring from his pocket, carefully placing it on the bedspread without looking at me.

'Sad state of affairs this. Still, better now than after you've been married five years, Italian divorce law is a legal nightmare you know.'

I nod and hand him the envelope which he pushes into his pocket.

'Would you like a drink? There must be something in the mini bar here,' I say pointing to the fridge.

He nods.

'That sounds civilised, why not.'

I empty a small bottle of whisky into two glasses.

'Not the best I wouldn't imagine,' I apologise, handing him a glass.

He points at me knowingly and smiles,

'You should know.'

I bite my lip.

'I actually bought you two bottles,' I say feeling more confident with the whisky in me. 'But Christian talked me into opening the other one.'

Edward laughs raucously.

'He said it was a good whisky and one would be sufficient for you, of course, he didn't actually know it was you,' I say smiling.

'That's my boy,' grins Edward.

'Is he your favourite?' I say swallowing more from my glass.

He clinks his glass against mine.

'Ah, a parent never admits to having a favourite, but he is more like me so I relate to him better than I do Simon. He should have known better, opening that whisky when you were so close to Rome.' He shakes his head, as though in despair, and finishes his drink.

'Don't go worrying about Simon. Better now, than five years into your marriage. These things happen. He'll get over it.'

He sighs and stands up.

'Thanks for the drink. I would love to stay for another one but we already have one bad boy in the family. You take care.'

He gently squeezes my shoulder. I exhale.

'I didn't realise Christian was so... well known.'

'Yes, he has done well and fortunately he doesn't take it too seriously. My influence I like to think.'

I lean forward to say goodbye and kiss him on the cheek. I close the door softly behind him. Poor Edward, he has no idea his sons are fighting over his law firm. How could they? But I can't blame Simon. Kaz is quite right. I do let wide boys sway me. I seem to lose all sense of reason. Of all of them, Christian was the worst. What a fool. I've thrown away everything just because of a funny feeling in my stomach when the words croissants and jam were mentioned. Oh I feel so angry with myself. How could I let him make such a fool of me? Getting me drunk like that? Damn him to hell. What a rotten bastard to sue Simon. He is nothing but a cheating liar. To think I threw my marriage away because of him. That's not strictly true. It wouldn't have worked with Simon. All the same he would have made a decent husband, and there must be lots of women who marry good men. After all, not everyone can expect to find their soul mate. I pack the last bits into my suitcase and make a mental note to buy one of those *cooking for one* cook books at the airport.

Chapter Twenty

Mother is devastated, Father resigned and Alex, well Alex is totally beside herself.

'How can I ever wear that outfit again? It will always be my daughter's non-wedding outfit I ask you, how embarrassing is that?' says Mother bitterly.

'Some people would be very happy to be embarrassed in a Stella McCartney outfit I would think,' says my dad helpfully.

Both my mother and Alex give him a 'you stupid man look' while I tap him affectionately on the arm.

'Well, I am so ashamed. I can't look anyone in the eye,' Alex moans, one hand lying protectively on her stomach.

'Look at another part of their body then,' suggests Dad, lifting my suitcase. I grab the hand luggage and walk to the door with him.

'Honestly, Dad, you are insufferable. You are always on Bels' side,' complains Alex.

Dad looks at her over his glasses but says nothing.

'You will feel guilty if Simon kills himself won't you?' Alex glares at me.

I stop in my tracks. Oh my God, is he suicidal?

'He's not talking suicide is he?'

'Good Lord,' gasps Dad.

We hover in the doorway. Alex looks sheepish.

'No, but the fact he hasn't mentioned it, surely means, he is more likely to do it,' she says confidently.

Dad gives her a puzzled look.

'I didn't know that,' he says nodding seriously.

Oh for God's sake.

'I really don't think he is going to be suicidal over me. In fact, he has offered to take Kaz to the fashion show,' I say in my defence.

I look at Alex and send a silent prayer to God, asking him please don't ever let me be *this* hormonal if I ever get pregnant.

'Don't upset yourself darling, think of the baby,' chips in my mum. As if Alex does anything else except think about her baby, her pregnancy and her bloody epidural. I feel like I am on epidural overload.

So here we are, or at least here I am, sitting in the hotel lounge with my parents and sister, trying to think of an excuse to leave and sort my life out. It had occurred to me to try and contact Christian. There isn't anything illegal in that but I finally decide against it. I feel sure that if he wanted to get in touch with me, he would. The last thing I need to do is make a bigger fool of myself than I already have done. Edward had phoned to say goodbye, but there had been no word from Rosa. In six hours I will be back home in my own flat. I had booked a week off for the honeymoon and have decided to go to a spa in Milton Keynes for a few days and spend the voucher Mum and Dad gave me for Christmas. I thought I would go shopping while there. Not that I have ever been to Milton Keynes mind you, or even fancied it to tell you the truth, but the name sounds cool.

'I had better go and pack,' says Alex with a tone of finality and a peck on my cheek.

'I have no idea what to tell them at the WI. I mean, they are expecting photos and everything. I told them about my Stella McCartney dress and your designer wedding gown. Oh, it is just too embarrassing. It wouldn't sound so bad if he had jilted you,' says Mother, wringing her hands.

I stare at her.

'Wow, thanks Mum,' I say finally.

It comes to something when your mother is more worried about the Women's Institute than she is about you.

'Well, you didn't think about any of us when you jilted Simon,' she admonishes.

I try not to sigh. I kiss Kaz and Mum goodbye and hug my dad before climbing into the waiting taxi. At last, I am on my way home. Once at the airport I relax. I check the flight board and then sit in the departure lounge. I stupidly expect Christian to walk in, but of course, he doesn't. I board my flight on time, find my seat and fiddle with the in-flight magazine.

'Good Lord,' exclaims a voice that I can't quite place. I look up to see the beaming round face of Kevin, the businessman from the London to Rome flight. I find myself staring at him and then look around suspiciously as though expecting Jeremy Beadle to jump out of the cockpit.

'Wow, this is uncanny,' I say eventually.

'Did you get married?' he asks bluntly, looking pointedly at the empty seat beside me.

I shake my head.

'I heard about a big wedding upset back at the hotel. I did wonder if it was you.'

Oh great, I am big news.

'Perhaps I'll be in the hotel newsletter,' I say cynically.

He taps me on the knee.

'I'll buy you a drink after we have taken off.'

Of course, I end up totally opening my heart to him and in return, Kevin gives me what I can only term the worst advice ever.

'It sounds like that landlord is ripping you off for a start,' he says knowledgeably, nodding his head. 'I know a thing or two about the rental business you know.'

Ripping me off? Well, I guess on reflection he is taking advantage of my situation. But, I explain to Kevin, I have nowhere else to go and that another flat may well cost me more.

'He has you by your balls then, if you'll pardon my French.'

I pull a face in agreement.

'Trust me on this. You need to move back to your parents. That's the best thing,' he assures me with a wink of his eye.

Good God, no one could possibly call that good advice. How can I possibly live with my mother? I would commit matricide in less than a week, well maybe a month, but I would most certainly kill the bloody dog before a week was out. I'd be drinking strange tea, meditating and watching re-runs of *Strictly Come Dancing*. God I would rather slit my throat.

'Also, when it comes to relationships I have a sixth sense, it's as clear as day to me. You want to cut all ties with that family of Simon's and you don't want to see that Christian ever again.'

I don't? That seems a bit drastic.

'Give up your job and make a new start, be a secretary or something. That's the way forward for you my dear.'

Be a secretary? Jesus, don't you need to type with all your fingers for a job like that? The only thing that walks across a keyboard when I type is my right and left index finger. Of course, he doesn't buy me a drink. Instead, he sleeps the best part of the journey, mostly on my shoulder and what's more, he not only snored but dribbled as well. My French supermarket top is very wet by the time we arrive in London. Oh, but what a wonderful sight is a British airport. Kevin helps me with my luggage and even offers to share a taxi with me. I refuse politely. As nice as Kevin is, I really don't want too many reminders of my trip. I collect the key from the landlord and make my way to my flat, almost crying at the sight of it. So here we are, or at least here I am, back in my London pad. Thirty years old and still single, and the prospect of carrying red roses and paperback copies of *Pride and Prejudice* looking more likely by the minute. I glance at my wedding finger, now devoid of a ring and wonder if Simon really will return it to the jeweller. I am suddenly very aware of my age and the fact that my body clock is ticking like a time bomb. I lug my suitcase into the bedroom and dump it on the bed and sit beside it. Right, the fridge will be empty, as will all the cupboards. Oh dear, this really is like starting all over again. I take a deep breath, grab my handbag and head to Waitrose, without a bloody Clubcard thank God.

Chapter Twenty-One

It's been well over a month since the wedding that never was and I still can't seem to get my head around work. I spend hours staring at my keyboard and wondering about Christian and whether he ever thinks of phoning me. Whichever way it goes, he never does. Then I spend hours on end being grateful that he hasn't and hope that he has lost my number. So, it came as no surprise when my boss called me in for a meeting.

'Bels, sweetie, do you want to tell me what is going on?'
I flop into a chair and look across the large mahogany desk at Justin. I pull a face at the purple streak in his hair.

'Purple suits you,' I lie.
His eyebrows arch.

'I didn't call you in here to talk about my hair and don't bloody lie,' he replies, running his hand through his shoulder length locks.
I sigh. Oh well, no harm in trying to change the subject.

'I'm sorry,' I mumble. 'My mind has not been on work.'
He nods.

'Is it Simon?' he asks kindly.

'God, no,' I reply quickly and bite my lip.
His eyebrows rise again and he looks at me questioningly.

'You write a shite article, forget to arrange a car for Kathy Monroe, no less...Thank God, she has forgiven us, and you faff around the office like some bimbo.'
I cringe.

'But worse, you send Gabrielle to cover the Paris fashion show exactly one month too early. I mean, I can't abide lateness but that was ridiculous.'

'Yeah, I really don't know how I got those dates mixed up,' I say wrinkling my forehead.

He shakes his head.

'And the hotel you booked for the sports fashion exhibition was ten miles from the centre. Are we all expected to run, in our fashionable sports kit, from the hotel to the exhibition hall?'
I pull a face.

'In my defence, I have sorted that out now,' I argue feebly.
He stands up and towers his lean body over me.

'I want you to take a holiday.'
I also stand up and my head collides with his chest.

'But I've just had...

'Am I the boss, or am I the boss?'
I nod.

'Okay then. Now, in just over a week we have the big McQueen shoot with India Pilano and I need you here for that because you have organised everything. But, after that, I want you to take yourself off somewhere for two weeks.'

'Two weeks,' I cry. My God, what am I going to do with myself for two whole weeks? I've already been to the spa and shopping at Milton Keynes. Shit, he really cannot be serious, surely?

'But, really Justin, work is the best place to get my mind off things,' I say, trying not to plead.

'Yes, but most of the time your mind is *off work*, sweetie. You are the best features editor I have, but right now you are bloody useless to me. Yesterday you spent longer making coffee and washing up than you did on your bloody computer. I don't need a bloody Stepford wife working here.'
Oh dear. I open my mouth to speak but am saved from pleading by the ringing of the phone. Justin leans behind him and clicks on the speaker phone.

'Justin Rowley,' he barks.

'Oh Justin, it's Bels' mother, Kitty. I did phone her office and Kaz said she was in a meeting with you. I wonder if I could have a quick word. It's a bit urgent.'

'Ah, Kitty, you have another emergency. Never quiet in your house is it?'
Justin frowns and I pull a face.

'So, how is the dog, I forget its name? Did you sort out that little emergency with its paw yesterday?'

Mother gives a little embarrassed cough.

'Oh yes.'

He rolls his eyes,

'Ah good, as I would hate to think I called Bels out of an important photo shoot for nothing. So what is the emergency today Kitty? Does the dog have worms now? Oh no, that was Monday's problem wasn't it?'

I feel myself cringe.

'Oh, I won't keep her five minutes,' reassures my mother.

'Well, that's fine. We're only on a conference call with Brad Pitt. I'll just put him on hold on line two while you discuss your little emergency. I am sure he won't mind in the least. Your mother, I believe,' says Justin, handing the phone over. I blush furiously.

'Mother, what are you doing phoning me at work again? I am in the middle of an important meeting.'

'Oh Justin doesn't mind. I didn't know Brad Pitt was a client. You never mention it.'

I quickly turn off the speaker phone so she doesn't hear Justin's deep sigh.

'Mother, you can't keep phoning me at work like this, what is it this time?'

She makes a tutting sound.

'I need you to come over after work and help me sort through all the things for the auction, and I don't want you making any plans for Saturday. It's the fund raiser for Kat's son.'

I let out a groan,

'Mum, I am not coming to the fund raiser. I will be bored to death.'

'Corinne's son will be there. He is recently divorced and very well off. He is desperate to get married again. He is...'

Oh no.

'Not now Mum. I'm at work.'

'Don't eat, okay? Dad can fetch you and take you back, that way you can have some wine with us. We will discuss it later.'

The phone goes dead and I stare apologetically at Justin.

'She's worried about me,' I explain.

He flicks his hair back.

'Sweetie that is why I am giving you a holiday, so you can go away for two weeks and give us all a break from your mother.'

I nod reluctantly, knowing he is right. I have been back at work almost three weeks now and they might as well hire a dishcloth for all the good I have been. My mind seems to be constantly on my spinsterhood. I did worry for the first week about Simon and if he was coping okay. Kaz, however, has seen him a few times now and tells me, he is doing just fine which is more than can be said for me. Christian has not been in touch, not that I really expected him to be. I have finally stopped looking at his photo on Google and abandoned all ideas of requesting his friendship on Facebook. I spend my evenings eating cheese on toast or marmite sandwiches and watching old episodes of *Friends*. I mean, how bloody depressing is that? Mother phones twice a day. Once at work and again in the evening when I get home, and I beginning to wonder if I am on suicide watch. Justin taps me on the shoulder.

'Go home early sweetie and look for holidays on the Internet.'

A holiday for one, oh yes, very appealing, *not*.

***

'It is very generous of him to let you have two weeks like that.'

I place wine glasses on the table and smile at my dad who looks at me over his spectacles.

'Yes, but a holiday alone, I mean, where can I go?' I try not to sound too ungrateful.

'I think India would be a wonderful place to go. It is so exotic,' says my mother, almost dropping a steak and kidney pie onto the table mat. I return to the kitchen and fetch the salt and pepper while my dad carries in roast potatoes. My stomach rumbles at the smell of them and my mouth waters at the sight of the apple crumble sitting on the hob. I attempt to ignore the Stella McCartney 'mother of the bride dress' that hangs in the hallway. Mother has decided to auction it off at her fancy fund raiser for her cleaner's son who is going blind. I have no idea why he is going blind or even why my mother wants to get so involved in raising money for his private treatment. The problem with having a do-gooder mother is that you almost always get dragged into her good works.

'Maybe Annabel doesn't want exotic,' argues Dad.

I pile roast potatoes onto my plate and wait while Mother cuts the pie.

'Of course she does,' replies Mum taking my plate and piling it high with steak and kidney pie.

I shrug at my dad who sighs resignedly and hands me the gravy dish. At last some decent food. After tucking into forkfuls of pie and potato I finally take a gulp of wine and sigh contentedly. My mother's pastry really is superb and the steak is beautifully tender and moist. But best of all, are her roast potatoes, golden brown and perfectly crispy. I must admit, if anything could tempt me back home it has to be Mother's perfect roast potatoes.

'Are you meditating?' she asks, carefully spooning peas into her mouth.

I nod, although of course I am not. I did try lighting the joss sticks she gave me but after just ten minutes the smell of them had given me a thumping headache and instead of meditating I had gone to bed with two Paracetamol. Candice barges through the lounge doorway and proceeds to lick my feet. I cringe and pull them up underneath me.

'Your mother tells me, you are helping with the fund raiser on Saturday,' says my dad pulling Candice off me.

I nod reluctantly.

'Of course she is helping. It will keep her mind off things. Besides I want her to meet Jack Russell.' Mum looks at me over her glass of wine.

'Jack Russell,' I splutter. Who the hell is Jack Russell? And do I really want to meet him? Jesus, couldn't he have had a better name than a breed of dog?

'Mum, I really don't think it is a good idea. I mean it has only been a few weeks...'

'Nonsense,' she snaps, cutting more pie and plonking it onto my plate. 'It is like riding a bicycle. You have to get back on again quickly.'

I stare open-mouthed at her. Like riding a bicycle? She surely is not serious?

'Well...' I begin.

'Jack is very nice and the perfect catch. Okay, he may not be a solicitor but he earns just as much. He is a self-made man and you have to respect that,' she says looking hopefully at my dad who sits with half a roast potato poised by his mouth. He swallows quickly.

'Well, I agree, he is nice enough but I really don't know if he is Bels' type.'
My mother jerks her head back and looks as if she is about to have an apoplectic fit.

'What do you mean? Of course he is her type. He is rich, successful and wears fashionable clothes.'
Oh, that sums it up then, my type in three words, rich, successful and fashionable. Bloody hell, I sound shallow.

'Preferably, with a bit of a brain,' I add.

'And not brash and showy, which he most definitely is,' throws in my father between potatoes.

'He can afford to be brash. Besides, it is probably a cover for the pain he had to endure by that terrible wife of his. Corinne said she is perfectly beastly and only had her eyes on the...'

'I thought you said he was available,' I break in, pouring more wine for myself and Dad, feeling we both may well need it if we intend to take on my mother.

'He is divorced, darling. I did tell you. It has been six weeks now, but oh dear she did take him to the cleaners.'

'*Women,*' exclaims Dad, as he throws a potato to Candice.
I really am not in the mood for men right now, well at least not this one. A vision of Christian leaning over the Lemon enters my head and I quickly push the memory away.

'Why do you need my help with the fund raiser anyway?' I say miserably, beginning to think that a two-week holiday, or at least a two-week break, from my mother would not be such a bad idea after all.

'I still have so many things to price up and I need you to start the bidding for the dress. It will look really good if you introduce it, you being in the fashion business and everything.'
I sigh heavily.

'As long as I don't have to say you bought it for the wedding that never was.'
Dad forces a laugh.

'Of course not,' my mother reassures me, while giving Dad a dirty look. 'It will be a good opportunity to meet Jack. He is bringing Corinne, his mother. You remember Corinne, she had that stroke a year ago and...'

'I remember,' I lie, although I couldn't for the life of me remember anyone who had a stroke and had a son named Jack who was, Oh God, what is he?

'What did you say he did?' I ask, holding my breath.

'I didn't dear, but he owns his own company and is very comfortable. He is a scrap metal merchant.'

Bloody hell.

'Wonderful,' I mumble, grabbing more potatoes. Exactly what I need, a rich fashionable scrap metal merchant named Jack Russell.

Chapter Twenty-Two

I cannot believe I have agreed to allow my mother to set me up with her friend's son. I really am not in the least bit interested in men, unless you count Christian, and I unashamedly spent the whole of last night on Google, trying to find as many photos of him as I could. I had hoped I would find out if he was still with Claudine, but all I get are photos of him and photos of his houses. One night, I almost phoned Simon to ask him and just stopped myself in time. It seems that Simon has been seeing something of Kaz although she is being very cagey about it all, and insists they are just friends.

'I'm a shoulder to cry on, you know how it is,' she had said airily.

That is all very well but shouldn't her shoulder be for me? It is Saturday morning and I am to meet the very eligible Jack. I let out a deep sigh and wander into the bathroom to get ready. I really should make an effort. After all, I am well aware that Christian is not interested in me. I am not his type. He is probably preparing for his own wedding this very minute. I cannot even check Claudine's Facebook page anymore as she has made it very private. Twenty minutes later dressed in jeans and one of the blouses I bought from the French supermarket, I set off to the Methodist church hall, where the fund raiser is to be held. I must make every effort to like Jack. The Methodist hall looks quite jolly with the bunting outside. Two boys shake their collection boxes and stand like sentinels at the doorway.

'Help raise money for the blind,' they chorus.

I give them a friendly smile and walk through the entrance door to the hall. I smile at the vicar who looks absently at me.

'Ah, here she is,' declares my mother, before I can even take a breath.

The Methodist hall smells of damp and freshly sprayed pledge. I force a smile and wipe my sweaty palms on my jeans and wonder what on earth was being said before the 'Here she is,' announcement.

'Hello everyone,' I say, nervously, to a sea of smiling faces, all women, thank God. Maybe he couldn't make it after all, I think hopefully. I recognise some of Mother's Women's Institute friends and shudder. Three of them swarm down upon me and I feel myself getting claustrophobic. A lady with blue hair leans close to my face and I splutter as her sickly perfume catches in my throat.

'We are all so sorry dear,' she says loudly, and I feel colour enter my cheeks.

I splutter loudly.

'Your perfume,' I explain, blowing noisily into a tissue.

'Timeless, by Avon,' she says proudly. 'I have a catalogue; I'll give it to your mother shall I?'

Good God, no. I fight back the impulse to tell her, it certainly is timeless.

'Lovely, thank you, that is so kind,' I say forcing a smile.

'It must have been so hard for you, being jilted like that,' her friend chimes in. What? Wait till I get my hands on my mother. I open my mouth to speak but nothing comes out.

'Where do you want these?' booms a man's voice.

Oh no. A man who I sense is the eligible Jack Russell, walks from the kitchen, carrying a large tray of teas. His thick gold bangle clangs noisily against the metal tray.

'Oh 'ello,' he says on seeing me, and I see my mother cringe ever so slightly. Oh please, don't be Jack Russell.

'Ah, Annabel...' says my mother, eager to rescue me from the blue hair brigade. 'This is Corinne's son, Jack.'

She smiles widely and he holds out his hand.

'It is nice to meet you Annabel, I'm Jack Russell.'

I begin to scream hysterically at this point, much to my mother's horror and Jack's disappointment. I attempt pointing to the wall behind him but his red face suggests he thinks I am pointing at him and obviously screaming with amusement at his ludicrous name. Well, let's be honest, it is ludicrous but even I have better manners than that.

'Oh someone, please, kill that huge spider,' I cry, expecting, of course that the *someone*, will be Jack.

He freezes and, to my dismay, jumps forward, almost sending me flying.

'Oh God, is it massive?' he asks through trembling lips.

Before I can answer him, Mother has scooped the spider into her hand and shaking her head walks past us.

'Really,' she scoffs.

Jack sighs with relief and with great gusto holds out his hand which I politely take. Oh dear, do I need a man who is afraid of spiders?

'Nice to meet you,' he smiles.

I pull my eyes away from the heavy gold bangle and rub my hand where his gold signet ring had dug into it.

'Hello,' I smile sweetly. 'Are you helping too?'

He laughs loudly, exposing slightly crooked, white dazzling teeth and a gold filling. Good Lord, the man has gold everywhere.

'Sure am.'

'Yes,' answers my mother. 'Isn't that lovely of him?'

'Lovely,' I echo looking around for an escape route.

Mother nudges me gently in the ribs and wanders off. I politely excuse myself also and rush out the back to help bring in the auction items. I grab her arm roughly.

'Did you tell the women at the WI that I got jilted at the altar?' I ask crossly.

She bites her lip and looks shamefaced.

'Well, I couldn't say you did it could I? Not after I had spent so much money on the dress. Anyway, don't think about all that. Come and meet Colin, he is running the auction.'

'Mother, how could you?' I say miserably and edge towards Colin who I recognise from the local Waitrose store.

'Colin, this is my daughter Bels, she will be doing the introduction to the dress. You must know Colin, he is the manager of our Waitrose store and he has made a generous donation to our cause.'

I look suitably impressed.

'Ah, you will be doing the introduction to the mother of the bride dress, wonderful,' he says slapping me on the shoulder. I look crossly at Mother.

'Does everyone know? Well, I am certainly not introducing it as 'the mother of the bride' dress, so forget it,' I mumble but she has already walked away.

I spend the next twenty minutes setting up her stall. Jack helps his mother with her things and doesn't even glance my way. Relieved that he does not seem interested in me, I begin to relax and help price up the last few bits for Mother's stand.

'Jack has agreed to bid against you for the dress, you know, just to get it started,' whispers Mother as the auction begins.

I whirl round to face her.

'How much is he bidding? I need to know when to stop,' I hiss back.

She looks baffled. Oh great. I find a quiet corner and sit with my head bowed until Mother calls me up to introduce the Stella McCartney dress. The hall is almost packed now and I climb onto the stage. Jack gives me a little wave.

'I bid twenty-five pounds,' shouts a lady sitting at the front.

Mother gives her a look to kill.

'Martha, you have to wait until we start the bidding. Bels has to give an introduction first.' She nods at me.

I cough slightly and then launch into my boring little speech to which Jack applauds very loudly before I have finished. Luckily the bidding goes very well and I begin to think I may not have to spend any money after all.

'Good, I have forty-five pounds and I know it will look really good on you Mabel, now who will bid me fifty?' shouts Colin.

The vicar, sitting in front of me, suddenly raises his hand. I wonder who on earth he can be bidding for.

'Thank you vicar, fifty pounds it is. Do I have fifty-five?'

I think fifty pounds is great until my mother nudges me.

'Go on, bid.'

Bugger, do I really have to? I raise my hand gingerly but Colin still spots it.

'Fifty-five pounds for the mother of the bride dress and a bid from the bride herself no less, what an unlikely turn of events that is everybody. Do I hear sixty?'

I slide down in my seat. Jack's hand shoots up and he winks at me.

'Sixty, wonderful, thank you Jack. Who is going to give me sixty-five?'

I look warily to my mother who encourages me to bid sixty-five. Jack, then, of course, bids seventy. Good God, I cannot bid seventy-five pounds for this stupid dress. Before I even have time to think, Mother is raising my hand.

'Shit, what are you doing?' I hiss, pulling it back.

'Seventy-five pounds, thank you. Anymore, do I hear any more?'

Oh please.

'No, sold then, to the bride herself no less.' Colin slams down the hammer.

'Oh Jesus Christ!' I say loudly.

The vicar squirms in his seat and turns to glare at me.

'Sorry,' I mumble, feeling my face grow hot.

Shit, shit.

'Congratulations, you have just bought yourself a Stella McCartney dress,' says Colin, carefully handing the bloody thing to me.

'Well done, I didn't quite make it,' smiles Jack. I find myself grinning back through gritted teeth.

'It's for a good cause,' my mother reminds me.

I waltz over to the cold drinks stall and pour myself an orange juice.

'Your mother tells me, you could do with some cheering up.'

Jack has followed me, and I swear I can feel his breath on my neck. I turn quickly and bang my hand on his bracelet. He is flattening his hair down with his hand and I spy a small bald patch.

'Oh I am fine, honestly,' I stammer.

'No, seriously, I could do with some cheering up too. Maybe you would like to come out to dinner after this is over. I know a great place, they do the best steak and often there are famous people eating there. Do you like steak? It usually comes with new potatoes and stuff but you can have chips.'

I am staring open-mouthed at him. He slaps his cheek.

'Blimey O'Riley, are you one of them vegetarians? I mean, that's okay, they do good veg too, and they know me there so they will make a good dinner.'

I close my mouth and swallow. A good dinner! Mother stands behind him and nods.

'Erm, actually I had something...'

'Else in mind,' interrupts Mother coming to stand beside me. 'Bels was thinking of another restaurant weren't you darling?'

I was? I look wide-eyed at her.

'I think she would like this place. Famous people go there,' Jack asserts.

Oh well then, it must be good if famous people go there. What sodding famous people is he talking about?

'Won't be a sec,' I smile, grabbing my mother and pulling her into the loo.

'Are you mad? I can't go out with him. Have you looked at him? He is dripping with gold. It is worse than being with Del Boy and besides, Dad was quite right, he really is not my type.'

'For goodness sake, Annabel, are you in a position to be picky? We can't have you on the shelf, now can we? People will talk. I've told you already it is just like riding a horse. You fall off and you just get back on again.'

'It was a bicycle the other night. And I don't care if people talk.'

I splash cold water on my face.

'One dinner won't hurt, and it will do you good to get out for an evening. It is only one date after all, and he does like you, and he is comfortable. You could do a lot worse Annabel. You haven't given the poor man a chance.'

There is no way my mother is going to let this go, sometimes she is like a dog with a bone. I sense I am not going to win this one. I exhale and dab my face dry with the tea towel she offers.

'Okay, but just the one date. I will give him a fair chance but that is it.'

She gives a relieved smile and walks out ahead of me. So dinner is arranged. Mother tells Jack to collect me from home. I stand beaming like a beacon until my face aches, while wondering what I am letting myself in for. The afternoon is a blur of fairy cakes and bunting. I had managed to avoid eligible Jack and every time I tried to get a sneaky look at him, I found he was staring at me. I finally convince myself that a night out will do me good. Feeling that maybe the whole thing was not such a bad idea after all, I drag home the

Stella McCartney dress and prepare to get ready for dinner, with Jack, while telling myself that a new man in my life is the only way to forget Christian.

I hear the phone shrilling as I turn the key in the lock and fly through the doorway, almost falling over the hem of the Stella McCartney dress.

'Hello,' I shout breathlessly into the mouthpiece.

'It's me Kaz.'

I sigh. I never understand why she always has to say, 'it's me, Kaz'

'Put the television on,' she instructs.

I switch on the TV, throw the dress on the couch and walk to the bathroom.

'Designing houses is in my blood.'

The familiar voice stops me in my tracks and I turn to see Christian smiling back at me from my television screen.

'They are doing a feature on him,' shouts Kaz, excitedly.

I flop onto the couch and watch as Christian lays out designs in front of the presenter. My heart is thumping and I have to clasp my hands around the phone to stop them shaking.

'These, of course, are the designs for the footballer Bryan...' the presenter says but I barely hear him. Christian is now looking straight at me. Oh my God, I never realised how much I missed him.

'In the programme tonight we are looking at dream homes and in particular the work of designer architect, Christian Lloyd.' The presenter is smiling at Christian.

'I'm surprised you didn't know,' Kaz shouts again, obviously concerned that I have not replied.

'I... How did you know about it?' I ask finally.

'Simon told me,' she squeals.

'He didn't tell me,' I retort, sounding like a spoilt child.

She makes a clucking noise into the phone. I hang up after telling her I need to get changed. I click on the record button and reluctantly turn the television off. After all, there is no point dwelling on something I cannot have. I turn back to double check it is recording and finally get changed.

Christian

'You can't possibly wear lavender honey, it just don't suit you.' Claudine's face drops and I pour more whisky. The wedding plans are more complicated than any building plan I've seen. George holds out his glass and I pour whisky into it even though Stella is giving me a stern look. Why we couldn't have had lunch while discussing wedding preparations is beyond me. But the women are on a pre-wedding diet it seems and George, well George just does as he's told. I offer him some crisps but he dutifully refuses after getting a look from Stella that would seriously have scared me, and that's saying something.

'Now, darling, I don't want you getting drunk. You need to know your part in the proceedings.' Her sweet voice belies the sharp look she gives us both. Claudine smiles nervously at me.

'Don't worry 'bout the mule woman, just load the wagon,' George retorts knocking back the liquid. Jesus, why can't these people speak English? This Texan drawl of Claudine's parents is a language all of its own. I raise my eyebrows and Claudine giggles.

'Are there many mules coming to this wedding? It's just I thought we might have it in France and I will need to get some stables set up,' I say tongue in cheek.

'Honey, we all agreed we can't have it in France,' says Claudine her bottom lip trembling.

'Who's all? I didn't agree anything.'

'Look, Christy, can I call you Christy?' asks George.
I smile.

'Not if you expect me to answer.'
Claudine sighs and shoots me a dirty look. George shifts in his seat.

'Look Chris, Stella has kind of set her heart on having it at the ranch.'
Has she indeed.

'I just about told everyone, and it's what my Claudine wants,' chips in Stella.

'Well, Claudine and I are still discussing it so I guess the decision has not really been made yet.'
Stella stands up suddenly.

'Well, we understood that it would be at the ranch. You did say it was settled Claudine.'

'Ah, well as you might say, 'Just because a chicken has wings doesn't mean it can fly',' I say standing up also.
I put my arms around Claudine and kiss her softly.

'I'm just going to make a phone call. Why don't you discuss all the other arrangements with your parents, like the invites and stuff? We can talk about the venue later.'
I ignore their dirty looks and sigh as I close my office door. I make several phone calls to France to check on the house, finish my accounts while keeping one ear cocked for when the front door closes. This is the third meeting Claudine has had with her parents about the wedding and each time we seem to get no further. Finally the door bangs and Claudine pops her head round.

'I'm just going to have a shower. Do you want to order some lunch from Barney's? I'm starving. We can have a chat over lunch if you like and then watch your programme. I recorded it last night.'
I pull a face. Sounds like fun, I don't think. I nod and scroll down my contacts for Barney's number and find myself scrolling just a bit further to Bels. It's been weeks since the wedding was called off and I stupidly thought she might phone me. It wouldn't be hard to get my number. The office number is on the web. Obviously my stupid concerns that she called off the wedding because of me were unfounded. Does she ever wonder about me? This is damn stupid, not calling her. We were friends after all. We got on well. It seems crazy not to give her a call. I scroll into her number and press call, only to quickly click disconnect. Lord, how many times have I done that now in the past few weeks? What the hell am I doing? I'm still engaged for pity's sake. I shake my head and put the phone on the table only to pick it up again a few seconds later. I could text her, ask how she is. For goodness sake, how stupid is this? There is no harm in calling a friend is there? I press call again and listen to the ringing tone…

Chapter Twenty-Three

Jack arrives. He screeches to a halt in a blue MG convertible and honks the horn several times. Discreetly, I ignore him and spray myself with Jo Malone's Grapefruit, while I wait for him to knock at the door. I am just grabbing a pashmina when he does so. I open it and reel back from the overwhelming smell of his aftershave.

'Hi,' he says wafting in.

I sneeze uncontrollably and feel my eyes water.

'Oh dear, here you are.' He offers me a tissue which I accept gratefully.

'Your aftershave,' I explain, feeling like all I do these days is comment on people's fragrances, or the overwhelming aspect of them. Thankfully he does not tell me it is Avon.

'You look very nice,' he says giving my dress an approving look.

I hadn't gone to much trouble really and was wearing a simple black dress, but I had dressed it up a bit with some pearl earrings and a matching necklace. I am about to respond when my Blackberry rings. I shrug helplessly, and he smiles. I don't even glance at the screen and stupidly presume it is Kaz again.

'Kaz, I am just going out.'

'Bels, hi, how are you? It's Christian.'

I feel my legs give way and grab the back of the couch for support. Christian? How can that be possible?

'But I just saw you on television,' I say stupidly and immediately want to kick myself.

'Sorry to interrupt Bels, is the toilet through there?' asks Jack quite loudly.

'Oh yes, help yourself.'

Help yourself? Shit, what the hell am I saying? How dare he phone me right out of the blue like this? Get a grip Bels for God's sake. He is a cheating liar, don't forget.

'And what did you think?' Christian asks, and I wonder if he heard Jack.

'Oh I haven't watched it all yet,' I say, sitting down, feeling sure if I don't, I will fall down. God, my heart is beating so fast I feel sure it will burst right out of my chest.

'Ah, well I hope I'm not a disappointment.'

I don't know what to say in response and cringe when I hear the loo being flushed. Jack strolls out of the bathroom and pointedly looks at his watch. There is silence at the other end of the phone and I wait a few seconds.

'So, how are you?' he repeats finally.

I take a deep breath and stand up.

'I'm on my way out actually,' I say attempting a cool voice. I find myself willing Jack not to speak, but he does.

'Actually, we really should go Bels; the table is booked for seven.'

There is a silence and I feel my head spin. Why now? Why does he phone me now? If only Jack wasn't here. I could have asked him why he is being such a bastard to his dad and Simon.

'Oh, right, okay...' He seems to hesitate but gives no indication he has heard Jack. I wait and then think I hear a door squeak open.

'Perhaps if you're around tomorrow, I could call you. Or you can call me if you like?'

He gives his number and I frantically look around for a pen. Jack kindly hands me one along with a scrap of paper. What am I doing? This is crazy. I jot it down and then hear Claudine's Texan voice call out in the background.

'What are you ordering honey?'

Oh the bastard doesn't change.

'I'd better go,' I say coldly.

'I'll phone tomorrow,' he says quickly. We both say bye and I hang up feeling more confused about him than ever. Jack is holding open the door and I follow him out making a firm decision to forget Christian for the rest of the evening. Jack is wearing a blue open neck shirt and I glimpse far too much of his, oh my God, very grey hairs and thick, chunky gold necklace. He opens the car door for me and patiently waits while I climb inside. By now, the overpowering smell of his aftershave is beginning to make me quite heady and I attempt to open the window.

'I'll put the top down,' he says cheerfully and pushes a button. The top slides back noiselessly and memories of the Lemon's tatty sunroof come back to me and I feel an urge to cry. The wind whips at my hair and I struggle with the pashmina to keep myself warm. There is barely any room for me to stretch my legs. I am so cramped, that I feel certain I will have curvature of the spine by the time we arrive.

'You will love the restaurant,' he shouts. 'It is the best in St John's Wood.'

My hair is blowing into my mouth and I struggle to keep it back. He pushes another button, which I hope is the one that puts the top back down, but sadly it isn't. Pink Floyd blares out at me from the speakers.

'It sounds lovely,' I shout back and fight with the pashmina. By the time I have my hair and the pashmina under control we have pulled up outside the restaurant. I watch in horror as he parks, with a screech, into a disabled parking space directly outside the restaurant.

'Here we are,' he announces.

'But you can't park here,' I protest.

He opens my door.

'I park here all the time.'

He leans towards me and offers his hand. A large gold Saint Christopher swings dangerously towards me. I duck.

'But it's for disabled people,' I say looking up at him and my teeth collide with the medallion. For one awful moment I think we are going to get tangled in his necklace but he pulls away carefully and smiles.

'I don't think a disabled person will be coming here for dinner. I mean, let's face it, their allowance wouldn't even pay for the starter,' he guffaws.

I force a smile and wait for my teeth to stop throbbing. Bloody hell, what am I doing? The waiter acknowledges us and shakes Jack's hand.

'Lovely to see you again Mr Russell, your usual table is it?'
Jack smiles proudly at me. I struggle to tidy my hair and follow the waiter to the table. Much to my relief it is in a corner. I accept the menu and try to relax. I let my mind wander back to Christian and the TV programme and feel a warm glow travel through my body. Oh please God, don't let him marry Claudine.

'What would you like to drink?' Jack asks as he carefully places his phone and wallet side by side on the table.

'A champagne cocktail, please,' I reply, feeling a strong need for something alcoholic.
He looks at me for a second and then beckons to the waiter.

'We'd like a bottle of your best champagne please.'
A bottle! I open my mouth to say a champagne cocktail would be fine but close it again when he says,

'So, your fiancé Simon, dumped you at the altar then?'
I feel my mouth open and then close again. Finally forcing a smile I say,

'Actually, no, I jilted him.'
For a second he looks confused but quickly composes himself and absently checks his phone. I struggle to think of something to say.

'Are you interested in fashion?' I ask sweetly.

'Ah, yes I am. All my clothes are designer. I won't spend less than sixty quid on a shirt.'
I attempt to look dead impressed and sigh with relief when the waiter approaches with the champagne. I knock back the first glass. Good Lord, was I out of my mind agreeing to a date with him? He is not my type at all. In fact, even I am not sure what my bloody type is anymore. Simon was my type I suppose. I guess if that is anything to go by then in theory Jack should be close to my type. Oh what the hell, does it matter? The fact is, there is only one type for me and that is the Christian type. In fact, to be more correct, Christian is my type, Christian and only Christian. Time to face it Bels, Christian is the one you love and the truth is he does not love you. I hold my glass out for more champagne feeling more miserable than I thought possible. Jack is talking about the menu and I attempt my best smile.

'Of course, the lamb is wonderful too but if you want a really good dinner I would recommend the steak. You're not a vegetarian are you, or God forbid, one of those vegan people?'

I shake my head. I must make an effort. Mother is right, I can't be on the shelf for goodness sake. I must not forget that I am thirty and men are in short supply. Oh God, what a thought. I allow Jack to fill my glass and ignore the swimming in my head. After all, when was the last time I let myself go? Memories of my arrival at the hotel in Rome swarm into my head and I quickly shake it to get rid of them.

'Are you sure?' Jack asks.

'What?'

'I asked if you wanted a starter but you shook your head.'

'Oh no, I mean yes, I would like a starter, and sorry I was miles away.'

I look at the menu and blink several times to see the print.

'I am having the smoked salmon, I can recommend it.'

Considering I cannot see what the starters are, I agree to the smoked salmon too and a crab salad for the main meal. A waiter rushes towards us as I close my menu.

'Two smoked salmon starters. One sirloin steak and I will have chips with that. The lady will have the crab salad and could you bring a bottle of your best red wine. You do like red don't you?' says Jack looking up at me.

I swallow the last of my champagne.

'Well, with the fish I should probably have white...' I say hesitantly.

He waves a hand dismissively.

'Ah, have red if you like red. Yes, bring your best red plonk and I'll have an extra portion of chips. Do you want chips Bels?'

Shaking my head, I cringe in my seat and attempt to smile at the waiter as he pours the last of the champagne.

'Great and I would like my steak very well done as usual. The chef knows how I like it.'

The menu is removed and I look across the table at Jack. Oh God, I have already had too much to drink. I make a mental note to have one glass of wine only and to make sure it is not topped up. He checks his phone again and then relaxes in his chair. Okay time to make an effort. After all, he is nice enough. So what if he orders a well-done steak and red wine with fish and of course horror of horrors an extra portion of chips with his chips, but generally he seems nice and he is making a big effort to impress.

'Your mother told me you are going on holiday soon.'

Oh good Lord, he undoes another button on his shirt. How many more of those grey hairs can I stand?

'I haven't booked anything.'

The waiter returns with the wine and pours a small amount for Jack who knocks it back in one hit and then lets out a satisfied sigh. I close my eyes and picture Christian at the wine tasting. I can't help wondering if he thinks about me as much as I do about him. I shake my head again to push out the thoughts.

'Whenever I can get a break, which isn't very often, I always fly out to my place in Spain.'

My eyes snap open. Now, this is impressive.

'You have a property in Spain, how nice? How often do you try to go?' I ask, leaning back slightly so the waiter can place the smoked salmon onto the table.

'Well, I can only use it for two weeks of the year, so...'

My stomach rumbles and he smiles at the sound.

'It's a timeshare is it?' I say trying not to look disappointed.

He nods and tucks into the food, which I have to admit is delicious.

'I would offer it to you but I have used up my allowance for this year.'

He looks embarrassed, and I begin to feel a bit sorry for him.

'At least you have a timeshare. That's more than I have,' I console him with my best smile.

We eat in silence for a while. I sip from my glass and try to sneak a look at him over the rim. Why do I have to compare every man I meet to Christian? I shall never find a new man if I go on like this. But no matter how hard I try I cannot find anything appealing about Jack. The waiter removes our plates and I struggle for something to say.

'My mother tells me you're in scrap metal is that right? I have never met anyone who was in scrap metal before,' I say stupidly.

'You've heard the saying, where there's muck there's brass? There was never a truer saying than that one,' he answers, opening his wallet and removing a small blue card which he proudly hands me.

'I do house clearances, lots of muck in those places and I can tell you, a fair bit of brass too.'

He breaks his roll in half and cuts a large slab of butter. I suppose he must have dealt in a lot of muck to be able to afford this, I find myself thinking, and dearly hope after dealing in so much muck that he has washed his hands. I take the card hesitantly and pretend to study it. I am relieved to see the waiter approach and am saved from making any comment. I gasp when his steak arrives. It is so well done it is almost charcoaled. I thought he said this was the best restaurant in St John's Wood. I open my mouth to complain but stop when he nods at the waiter.

'Wonderful. They cook it to perfection here.' I roll my eyes without thinking and tell myself to stop being such a snob. The waiter leaves us and walks to the door to greet a group of people. I look up and then quickly look away again. Oh no, is that Simon? Surely, it can't be. I sneak another look and cringe. It is him. Oh no, I really don't want him to see me with Jack. I slide further down in my seat and see he is coming our way. Bugger it, bugger it.

'Annabel?'

I pull myself up and run my hands through my hair. I strain to see the people who are with him but they are already heading to the bar.

'Simon,' I respond. 'What a surprise.' And none too pleasant either, but of course, I don't say that.

Jack splutters on a chip and grabs his serviette.

'Simon, this is Jack, and Jack, this is Simon,' I say, feeling myself blush.

Jack quickly holds out his greasy hand which Simon barely touches.

'Jack Russell's the name, pleased to meet you Simon.'

For a second, Simon looks baffled.

'Jack Russell, isn't that a breed of...'

'Yes Simon,' I interrupt. I pour myself more wine and see that Simon is now looking at my crab.

'You should be drinking white wine with that crab surely?'

Bloody hell, Simon never changes. I smile at Jack who looks embarrassed. Oh sod this for a game of soldiers. I lift the glass to my lips.

'Jack and I like to break the rules, don't we Jack?' I smile, taking another sip of the wine.

Jack goes to speak but Simon breaks in.

'Well that is true, I can't argue with that. You always were a rebel.'

His critical eye travels over Jack's shirt and finally lands on the well-done steak. He opens his mouth to speak but I stop him with a cough. The last thing I want is Jack to feel more embarrassed. Simon looks at me with a grin.

'If you'll excuse me, I am dining with friends. It was nice seeing you.'

I watch him walk away and exhale, giving Jack a devilish look.

'I think we rattled his cage.'

'Oh dear,' he remarks loading more chips onto his plate with his hands.

I pour more wine into his glass and laugh.

'Actually, it is really rather nice breaking all the rules.'

Jack looks decidedly uncomfortable and, much to my relief buttons up his shirt.

'Is it difficult seeing him?'

'Good Lord no,' I say airily and lean across to steal some of his chips. Simon has encouraged me to 'go where no woman has ever gone before' which in this case is to eat chips with my crab salad while drinking the forbidden red wine. Jack visibly relaxes and continues telling me about the timeshare in Costa de Sol. I try to look suitably impressed but fail miserably. Finally, dessert comes and with great relief on my part we are drinking our coffee.

'Would you like to go for a drive in the MG?' asks Jack as he pays the bill.

I shake my head apologetically.

'Actually, I have an early start in the morning.'

He nods knowingly and helps me with my pashmina.

'Oh, you're leaving already.'

I snap around to see Simon with a group of people from his law office. Two of his snobby friends are sniggering. I link my arm through Jack's.

'Actually, we are just about to go on to a casino, aren't we Jack?' I say breezily.

Jack's mouth opens and just as quickly closes again. I pull him out of the restaurant to the car in the disabled parking space. I cringe with embarrassment and step into the road to allow an elderly gentleman with a walking frame pass along the pavement. I pray he doesn't speak, but of course he does.

'Well, you sure look disabled,' he spits at me.

Jack quickly pulls the parking ticket from the windscreen and climbs in beside me. I watch, deeply ashamed as the man walks slowly into the restaurant.

'No one ever wants to park here normally,' moans Jack, under his breath.

We pull away with a screech and I see Simon's face staring at us from the restaurant window.

'What casino do you want to go to? I usually go to one in the West End. It is good, and they park the car for you,' says Jack, his face lighting up.

Buggety bugger.

'Let's go there then,' I say sighing heavily. All plans of watching Christian later this evening instantly dashed. I pray that Simon does not follow. I mean, it is just the kind of thing he would do. I stifle a yawn and wrap my pashmina tighter round me as Jack pushes the button that puts the top down.

'What about your early night?' he shouts.

I shrug.

'Great car this isn't it?' he shouts again.

It was Simon who had once told me that MG convertibles are hairdresser's cars.

'Those little sporty numbers are hairdressers cars' I can hear him saying, 'especially the ones with soft tops,' meaning the cars and not the hairdressers I presume. Honestly, Simon is such a snob and to think I was so close to marrying him. I sneak a look at the time on the dashboard and curse myself for needing to get the better of Simon. All my plans of a cosy evening drooling over Christian have now gone, not to mention the precious time I could have spent praying to a God I do not believe in, to ask that Christian will not marry Claudine. Bother, bother, bother. I am now faced with several hours of blackjack, roulette and poker, and I have no idea how to play any of them. It occurs to me that I should tell Jack this is my first visit to a casino. I really don't know why I let Simon get to me. I should be happy he has moved on, and the truth is I am. I just want him to think I have to. I really do not want him to think that I am like the walking dead, trailing in the shadow of Christian, even if that is the truth.

'I could have arranged for us to have had dinner there if I had known you enjoyed the casino,' shouts Jack.

I jump in my seat at the sudden sound of his voice.

'To be quite honest with you, this is actually the first time I have ever been.'

He covers his shock and grins excitedly.

'You'll love it. I'll show you how to play the roulette table.'

And so what I had intended to be a short evening did not end until almost three in the morning. The atmosphere of the casino is electric and I am swept along by the excitement almost immediately, and if Jack had seemed a little dull in the restaurant he certainly made up for it at the blackjack table. Clutching my chips, I move from one table to the next growing more confident with each chip I put down. When we become tired and hot, a lovely waitress fetches us a cold drink and some sandwiches. The roulette table has me hooked. When I am not playing I am an avid spectator. The smell of the place intoxicates me and the excited chatter of the gamblers makes me heady. I can't imagine why I have never been before. At two thirty, having lost all our chips, we have a last drink before driving home. I am high on adrenalin and feel sure I will not sleep, but of course, the gentle movement of the car induces me to doze and before I know where I am Jack is waking me up. We are parked outside my flat and the clock says two forty-five. Jack leans towards me. I fumble quickly with the door handle and practically fall out.

'Whoops,' I laugh.

I am at the front door before he has even climbed from the car.

'Do you want to do something tomorrow, I mean tonight?' he asks pushing his hands awkwardly into his jacket pockets.

I swallow and fumble around in my head for a reply that won't hurt him.

'I would love to go out again but I think I will be very tired tonight. I don't want you to think I am getting involved though Jack. It is much too soon for me.'

I bite my lip. Oh dear, I was much too blunt. I wonder if he has heard me, for he replies.

'Great, I'll call you in a couple of days.'

I blow him a kiss and go inside where I flop straight onto my bed and fall fast asleep.

Chapter Twenty-Four

'Finally, she comes into work.'

I give Justin a dirty look and pour coffee from the cafeteria.

'I have been working from home this morning,' I lie.

'You look like shit,' he states none too kindly.

'She was at a casino until two this morning,' Kaz informs him as she carefully lays out the seating plan for the magazine's celebrity fashion dinner.

I scoff loudly. He ignores us both and looks closely at the plans.

'Okay, this looks good. Has everyone confirmed?'

I nod and Kaz shakes her head. I look questioningly at her.

'Did you both miss the news?' she asks disbelief on her face.

I look to Justin who shrugs.

'India Pilano, our main model?'

We both raise our eyebrows. Kaz sighs.

'She broke her leg in a skiing accident yesterday, so, unless you want her to model fashionable leg plasters, we are screwed.'

I let out a little scream and stamp my foot.

'She can't have. She signed a contract with us which stated she was not to ski from the day she signed until the contract was up. I don't believe this. She was the main feature for the show and she was booked to do the McQueen photo shoot. Everything is set for next week. This is terrible news. It took me six months to get that contract with her.'

Justin chews his lip.

'Get onto our lawyer, that's the first thing. She has broken our contract, damn it.'

Kaz picks up the phone.

'We need a replacement,' he says carefully, and I can see his mind working overtime. He looks thoughtful and I take the phone from Kaz.

'Olivia Hammond! Get her and I will give you the best rise you have ever had. It seems she is retiring to have a baby and...'

I drop the phone.

'She's having a baby?' I echo.

'God, Bels, where have you been?' Kaz sighs.

Olivia is having a baby? Does Christian know? For God's sake, it seems like the whole bloody world knows except me. Oh God, was that why he phoned? Did he want to share the news? I should have known it had nothing to do with me.

'But, if she *is* having a baby she isn't likely to sign with us...' I object.

'Think about it Bels. She does her last shoot before retiring, and it's with us and even better if you can get her to stand in at the celebrity dinner fashion show. You can do it, make it your goal before you go away. We can do the McQueen shoot anytime she wants. I only want the best.'

He points a wagging finger and heads for the door.

'And I want Olivia Hammond,' he says bluntly and slams the door shut behind him.

Kaz stares out of the window.

'Jack really liked you then?'

I lift my head to the ceiling. Oh why did India have to go sodding skiing?

'Not really,' I say absently.

'Oh I think he did.'

I give her an odd look. What is wrong with her?

'What is wrong with you?'

'You'll see.'

There is a knock on the door and she rubs her hands with glee.

'Oh he luuuuved you,' she says opening the door.

I gasp. Standing in the doorway is the largest bouquet of flowers I have ever seen. The young man delivering them lumbers in panting.

'Miss Lewis?' he breathes heavily.

I mumble a yes.

'That's a relief. I don't think I can carry this lot much longer. It weighs a bloody ton. I already went to the wrong department.'

Kaz struggles to take them off him as I stare open-mouthed.

'So, you don't think he likes you,' she laughs handing me a rose she had plucked.

'Did someone die? Did I die? There is a hell of a lot of lilies here.'

The delivery man shakes his head.

'A man can never get it right can he?'

My God, I will never have enough vases for all these flowers. I open my mouth to give a sharp retort, but nothing comes out.

'I saw him wandering around with them earlier. I guessed they were for you. Can I have some?' squeals Kaz.

I take the card she offers and fall into a chair.

'Thank you for a wonderful night, you are truly special. J. x

Oh Jesus, a bit over the top or what? I look to Kaz who is making up her own little bouquet from my oversized one.

'God, it is obscene. Can you put them into vases and spread them around the building or something? You had better phone the solicitor too, and if Jack should phone please tell him I am unavailable.'

She salutes me with a grin and waltzes off with the bouquet over her shoulder. Damn, damn, Jack obviously was not listening to me last night. I dive in my bag for some aspirin and swallow them with more coffee. God, my head aches. Never again will I drink so much. I bury my head in my hands and think about Olivia Hammond. I didn't admit to Justin that I had her personal mobile number. I decide it is much better if he does not know about that. I wait until my headache eases and then pull out India's contract from my drawer. It is time to phone her agent and deliver the bad news. Twenty minutes later Kaz buzzes me.

'Our legal people are in discussions with her legal people, do you want me to keep you updated?' I hear the smile in her voice.

'Yes and can you get Olivia Hammond's people on the phone?'

'Yes, boss. Oh, and Jack left a message while I was delivering flowers. He said he will call back.'

I groan. At five o'clock Justin pops his head around my door.

'Good God, did someone die? Are we a bloody florist now? I know you like flowers but isn't this a bit over the top?'

I shake my head.

'I didn't buy them. It was a humongous bouquet from Jack, thanking me for last night.'
His eyebrows rise.

'Good Lord, what did you promise him? No, don't answer that.'
I pull my hair up and twist it into a scrunch.

'I don't intend to.'

'So, what's the news on Olivia Hammond?'

'I've been trying her agent all afternoon. I have left three messages,' responds Kaz, walking in with doughnuts. I grab one eagerly.

'Let me know when the deal is signed.'
Justin takes a doughnut and walks out. I let out a deep sigh.

'Good God. What the hell...' he shouts, making us both jump.

'Ah,' smiles Kaz.
I give her a quizzical look.

'Custard, Justin. They didn't have any jam doughnuts,' she yells.

'I frigging hate custard,' he moans loudly. We hear his office door slam shut and we both laugh hysterically.

'I don't like to mention it but shouldn't you phone Jack and thank him or something,' Kaz says casually as she bites into a doughnut, squeezing out a blob of custard which lands with a plop onto my desk.
Bugger, this is getting tricky, very tricky.

'God no, I need to think this through and if he phones, tell him I have my head down the loo.'
She shakes her head.

'You get paid to lie,' I snap.

'I do not,' she snaps back, licking sugar from her lips.
I grab a doughnut and sneeze. Jesus, there is more pollen in my office than in my dad's garden.

'Well, tell him I will phone him later,' I sniff.

'What are you doing?' she demands. 'The guy is loaded, he likes you and he seems really nice. Not many men would even think about buying flowers, let alone a bouquet like that. Trust me Bels; there aren't that many nice rich eligible bachelors out there.'
She flounces to the door, taking the doughnuts with her.

'Please, don't nag me. I have enough of that from my mother,' I say miserably.

She stretches her arms behind her back and moves into a yoga posture.

'You are so stressful to be around. I need to go and meditate,' she says huffily and walks out.

I throw all the plans for the celebrity dinner into my handbag and turn off my laptop. Neither the coffee nor the doughnuts have taken away my headache. I decide, a quiet night, in front of the television is what is needed. To be precise, a quiet night, watching Christian on television, is what is needed. My intercom buzzes and I bark into it. It is Justin.

'Christ, what did I do?'

'Sorry.'

'Get your arse in here can you. I want to go over a couple of things before you go home.'

I come out twenty minutes later. Kaz is painting her nails and I tut loudly. I look past her to the empty doughnut plate that sits on her desk.

'What? I've done loads for you today and all you've done is snap my head off,' she complains. 'By the way, Jack phoned your Blackberry and seeing as you weren't going to say anything, I did.'

'What!'

'Don't have an epileptic fit. I only said you loved the flowers and would phone him later, probably. God forbid you just might.'

I sigh.

'Okay, I guess I should text him or something.'

She jumps off the desk grabbing her bag.

'You haven't forgotten my lingerie party tomorrow night have you? I am relying on you to bring the pizzas.'

Shit, shit and double shit. It has been all of ten days since she mentioned this party and I totally forgot about it. I must have let out a small moan as she looks at me despairingly.

'Don't say you forgot? You are going to come, aren't you? I only said I would have it because you told me you were depressed. I thought it might cheer you up.'

Damn, damn and double damn.

'It is only lingerie isn't it? There won't be vibrators and wind-up plastic penises will there?' I say pulling a face.

'Good God, penises? I feel sick, pass your handbag. Of course not. We're having pizza. What a horrible thought, pizza and penises.' She sticks her tongue out. 'Anyway, the Ann Summers party I went to didn't have any penises.'

'Okay, maybe I will bring Mother with me, she likes lingerie.'

I kiss her on the cheek and walk down the corridor to Justin's office. He is on the phone so I pop my head round the door and wave. The thought of my cosy flat and the Christian programme is very appealing, and I push all thought of work from my mind. I check the time on my Blackberry and wonder when Christian will call. I arrive home to three messages from Jack. With a sigh I delete them and quickly send him a text saying I will call him in a few days as I have gone down with a rotten cold. He sends a lovely text back saying he hopes I feel better very soon and that he will phone me in a few days and not to worry. I grab a yogurt from the fridge and settle down to watch Christian. The sight of him has me trembling so much that I need to take three Quiet Life tablets with some Rescue Remedy. I had almost forgotten how handsome he is. I hold my breath throughout the programme, expecting at any minute to see Claudine. Much to my relief she is not mentioned and I let out a deep breath as the programme finishes. I rewind the recording ready to watch again and then prepare myself some beans on toast. I check my Blackberry in case I missed his call but there is nothing. A half-opened bottle of wine sits on the kitchen counter and I pour the contents into a large glass. I am much calmer during the second viewing and find myself staring at Christian like a lovesick teenager. Oh God, please don't let him marry Claudine, I pray desperately, while searching on Google for any news that may indicate he already has. After an hour of fruitless searching I close the lid. Five times I attempt to phone him but hang up before it rings. Surely if he wanted to speak to me he would have phoned by now. Twenty minutes later with a false sense of security helpfully induced by my alcohol intake I tap into my mobile Olivia's number and listen to the long international ring tone.

'Hi, this is Olivia. Sorry I can't take your call. Leave a message and I will call you back as soon as possible.'

Damn. I leave a short message and my home number and hope she remembers me as the nutty woman who came to visit with Christian.

I click off my phone, yawn and head for the bedroom when the phone rings. Hesitantly, I answer and Olivia's bright cheery voice wakes me right up.

'Annabel, thank goodness you phoned. I lost your phone number. Christian phoned and told us everything and said that your wedding had been cancelled...'

'I cancelled it,' I break in quickly. 'I found out that my fiancé is Christian's brother. It is an awful mess and I haven't seen Christian since. Is he okay, do you know?'

Oh God, why did I ask that? What if she tells me he is fine and just about to be married to Claudine? She does not speak but I can hear her breathing. Oh dear she cannot tell me.

'Oh no, you were engaged to his brother? We haven't seen Christian,' she says finally. 'He phoned here several weeks ago now, it was a few days after you left and he said that you had cancelled your wedding, that everything was a bit crazy and he was going back to New York. He never mentioned his brother. Oh poor you and I know how much you liked Christian.'

I breathe a sigh of relief. He isn't married, at least not yet.

'So, you haven't been invited to his wedding then?' I bravely ask.

'No, we haven't heard anything about that. Anyway, tell me about you?'

So I do and after another half glass of wine I am brave enough to tell her I am features editor with Versity and several sips of wine later I ask her if she would replace India at our celebrity fashion dinner. To my glee she agrees and offers to fly to England the day after tomorrow to do the McQueen shoot before her pregnancy shows too much. I insist on collecting her at the airport and we finally say our goodbyes. I finally retire to bed feeling more miserable than I ever thought possible. I have to face it. Christian has no intention of phoning me. Surely he isn't waiting for me to phone him. Just who does he think he is? I have some consideration for Simon, even if he doesn't. God, men, they are so bloody arrogant sometimes.

Christian

The meeting seems to be going on forever and my mind is drifting away. I yawn, pour myself more coffee and then open the window. The smog of New York hits my nostrils and I feel myself sigh. Why Claudine is so insistent on living here is beyond me. It is frighteningly mad, often depressing and without doubt claustrophobic.

'How about these interviews Chris, do you want us to agree to all of them, or do you want to limit yourself?'

I turn to Matt, my PA and shrug.

'Sorry Matt, I wasn't listening.'

He grins.

'Marriage is changing you already, and you're only at the planning stage.'

I give an evil laugh.

'I'm the spanner in the works mate. Everything she arranges I put an obstacle in the way. Or at least so she tells me. Anyway, what interviews?'

'I've managed to organise the Munich trip around that weekend you're in Europe, is that okay?'

I sit back at the table and force my mind back to work and nod at the appropriate moments but annoyingly I find myself checking my phone. I guess she must be pretty serious about this Jack guy then. Or at least he sounds pretty keen on her. She certainly isn't going to phone now. I check the time for England and see it is almost one in the morning. I really ought not to phone again. What would be the point? I really didn't see her as the type to be that impressed with an over-the-top bouquet of flowers. It just goes to show. Women, they are all pretty much the same. I suppose I should have corrected Bels' assistant's mistake when I phoned earlier but it was near impossible to get a word in. Besides if she mistook me for the Jack guy it was probably best to leave it at that. The last thing I want to do is mess up any new relationship Bels has. It would have been nice to have explained about the lawsuit. I wish I knew what the hell he had told her about that. Surely she would understand why I need to do it. I have a right to what is morally mine. I can't just let them get away with that. Damn it, do I really care what she thinks? I barely know her. I must forget about her now. She doesn't want to be friends, that much is clear. I gave her my number, I said I would call her or she could call me. Well, she has chosen not to call me and I did phone her so that's that. I look at her number again and then click into the delete button and find myself hovering. No, that would be rash. After all, we were good friends and had a laugh. God, I'm tired. I throw the phone on the desk and lean back closing my eyes. Matt's voice along with everyone else's fades into the background. It rings making me jump and I grab it quickly. I feel a small stab of disappointment when I see it is not her. I answer it on the third ring.

'Honey, when are you coming home? I'm so excited. We have found the perfect dress. It was just sitting there waiting for me in Proposals,' Claudine squeals.

'That's great baby,' I say and make a mental note to delete Bels' number after I hang up. I realise the guys are packing up and push it into my pocket deciding to do it later. Everyone is drifting out of the door and I grab my jacket from the back of the chair.

'Chris, could we have a word before you leave?'
I turn to my accountant Bryn feeling irritated. Matt is looking embarrassed.

'What is it? I really want to go home. This meeting really went on far too long.'
Matt closes the door, leaving just me, Bryn and him in the room.
Bryn looks to Matt and I feel myself getting more irritated.

'What the hell is it? Is it to do with the lawsuit?'
They both seem to shift uncomfortably on their feet.

'It's a bit delicate, Christian...'
'Just spit it out, I don't have all day.'
Bryn produces several sheets of paper and shoves them in front of me.

'Did you sign these? I mean, if you did, that's fine but you really should run this stuff by me. I can't do my job properly if you don't.'
I look at the contract and swallow. Matt seems to nod and reading my thoughts, he opens a window.

Chapter Twenty-Five

'You said there wouldn't be wind-up penises,' I say accusingly, walking into the kitchen. I pour cola into a glass for my mother. Kaz hands me a glass of wine.

'I can't, I'm driving Mother home and first thing in the morning I am collecting Olivia Hammond from the airport.'

My mother rushes in and looks hurriedly around the kitchen.

'Can I slice celery or something,' she asks nervously, her cheeks twitching.

Kaz hands her a knife and points to some French bread.

'The one I went to wasn't at all like this,' justifies Kaz as she steps over a plastic penis.

'Come on, those ladies hiding in the kitchen,' calls the hostess. 'It's time to play pass the parcel.'

Oh God, do we have to?

'I'll stay in the kitchen and cut the bread,' Mother offers.

I reluctantly follow Kaz into the lounge and take my seat for the pass the parcel game. Typically the parcel lands in Kaz's lap just as the music stops. I am about to take a sigh of relief when she throws it into mine.

'What?' I cry, but it is too late and the hostess is beaming down at me.

'What is your forfeit?' she asks, excitedly.

I look around at the other women who are now pleasantly tipsy from the wine. What on earth am I doing? I only came because I thought there would be lingerie, after all that is what Kaz had said. Instead, we had walked into what my mother had called 'a soft-porn film'. Although, I did wonder, how she even knew what soft-porn was. Mind you, after tonight she would be left in little doubt. The room is full of soft-porn DVDs and books. I open my forfeit.

'Cup your breasts and sing the first lines of 'I've got a lovely bunch of coconuts.'
Encouragingly, the hostess cups her own breasts and nods at me. I squeeze my eyes closed, grab my breasts and sing for all I am worth. I open my eyes to see the hostess is holding out a colourful tube. Oh God, what now?

'Well done, Bella, didn't she do well? Here, have a free tube of tingle pleasure cream. Now who wants to win a Rampant Rabbit?'
My mother claps from the kitchen doorway.

'Ooh, that sounds nice, we should get one for Alex's baby,' she coos.
I groan.

'Mother it is not a toy, well it is, but not a soft toy, as such.'
Kaz smiles at me as several guests parade from the bedroom in the lingerie.

'I'll heat the pizza,' I offer and join my mother in the kitchen.

'This is just too awful,' sighs Mother popping the pizza onto trays. 'Why did she think your name was Bella? You really should tell people to call you Annabel.'
The idea of a holiday is becoming decidedly more appealing by the minute. The women are giggling loudly, and I see Kaz has put a frilly red bra over her dress and is now parading around the room.

'And pray, tell me, what exactly is a Rampant Rabbit?' Mother asks, offering me a pickled onion, which I decline with a shake of my head.
The phone shrills in the corner and I am saved from any graphic descriptions of Rampant Rabbits that I may have been able to offer. Mother and I look at each other. Kaz is now loitering dangerously close to a large pink vibrator, and I hesitate to take the phone into her. Mother nods decisively at me and answers it.

'Oh hello,' she says, looking taken aback. 'Well, she is a bit busy at the moment. We are having an Ann Summers party and there is a lot of... well, stuff going on.'
She shakes her head as I pass by her to retrieve the potato salad from the fridge.

'Annabel is here though do you want to talk to her? Hold on.'
I look nonplussed at her.

'Simon,' she mouths.

I shake my head frantically. She covers the mouthpiece with her hand.

'What do you mean no? Of course you want to speak to him.'

I do?

'He obviously wants to speak to you.'

He does?

'Why didn't he phone my mobile then? He must want Kaz.'

'Don't be ridiculous.' She pushes the phone into my hand leaving me with no choice but to speak to him.

There is a scream from the living room and I look back to see Kaz sliding seductively around a pink pole that has been erected in the middle of the room. Oh dear.

'Hi, Simon,' I say hesitantly.

He coughs loudly.

'Is Kaz around?'

'Actually, she is kind of draped around a pole at the moment. Can I give her a message?'

'What kind of pole?' he snaps.

Well, it's not the North Pole, is it? What is he doing phoning her anyway? He is supposed to be pining over me.

'You know, pole dancing, sexercise, I think it's called.'

'I'll call back,' he says gruffly and hangs up.

Mother is smiling at me.

'He wanted Kaz,' I snap and roughly spoon the salad into a dish. By the time the pizza and salad are ready, Kaz has finished her pole dancing party piece and sways drunkenly into the kitchen.

'Isn't it a hoot?' she laughs.

'Simon phoned and wanted to speak to you. He seemed a bit put out when I said you were pole dancing,' I say sharply and walk into the living room in a huff. I pour myself some wine and wonder why I am so upset. After all, didn't I jilt Simon at the altar? Aren't I in love with his brother? So why the hell am I angry with Kaz because she and Simon are getting along well?

'Here we go ladies, now here is what you have been waiting for, the Push My Buttons Clitoral Vibrator,' cries the hostess enthusiastically and the guests squeal excitedly.

'Time to go, I think,' I say resolutely, standing up and stepping on a plastic penis. The hostess heads towards me smiling.

'Oh dear,' sighs my mother.

'You can't go,' cries Kaz rushing towards me from the kitchen, tripping over yet another sodding penis.

'I do hope you will order something,' smiles the hostess, shoving an order form in my face while collecting up the bits of broken penis. Oh for pity's sake.

'No, thank you,' I say politely taking my handbag from the couch and grabbing Mother by the arm.

'There is so much to choose from there must be something you liked?' she persists.

Kaz is blocking the doorway and I sigh.

'How about one of our bullets, they are very popular and...'

I see red.

'Lady, I do not want a bullet, or a gun that fires a thousand volts up my arse while stimulating my clitoris. I am a woman who is not even having sex right now, so even your crotch-less knickers would be a total waste on me,' I shout.

The room goes silent and my mother blushes for me.

'Goodness Annabel, that was rather graphic.'

Kaz grabs me by the arm, tearing me from my mother and pulls me into the kitchen where she slams the door shut on yet another plastic penis, which bites the dust on impact.

'Okay, I have been seeing Simon, but don't forget you guys broke up. I have always liked Simon, but, of course, I never said anything when you were together. I thought you wouldn't mind. I thought it was Simon's brother Christopher that you liked.'

I stamp my foot in frustration.

'Christian, his name is Christian.'

There is a loud thumping on the door and Kaz and I look at each other. I sigh and open it to see my mother wringing her hands.

'They are about to play orgasmic bingo, you can't leave me out here on my own,' she says, panic written all over her face.

God almighty, why is an Ann Summers party beginning to feel like showdown at the OK Corral? I allow my mother into the kitchen and we all stand quiet for a while. Kaz finally breaks the uncomfortable atmosphere.

'If you really don't like me seeing Simon then I will stop.'

'Are you coming out for the orgasmic bingo?' calls the hostess cheerily, obviously not in the least upset by my outburst. Mother cringes.

'Go ahead without us Sam. I will be out for the jam tart game,' Kaz calls back.

'Jam tarts?' questions my mother.

'Don't even go there,' I say wearily.

Kaz winks at me and I exhale loudly. I feel an overwhelming urge to cry. The truth is I really don't mind Kaz seeing Simon. In fact, I want them both to be happy, but more than anything I want to be happy. I apologise and give her a hug.

'Of course I don't want you to stop seeing him.'

'Her period is due,' chips in Mother, as though this explains everything.

'Honestly, what you won't do to get out of buying a Rampant Rabbit, Bels,' smiles Kaz.

Mum convinces her to let us out the back way. I let Mum walk ahead of me and then turn quickly to Kaz.

'Does Simon ever mention this business with his brother?' I whisper.

She shakes her head.

'I only know what you've told me. Why?'

'I just can't believe Christian is capable of something so awful. I mean, to sue your own father...' I trail off.

She pulls a face.

'You hardly knew him Bels. You probably don't know what he is capable of.'

I nod miserably. She is quite right I suppose. I kiss her goodnight and hurry to my mother who is waiting by the car. We are silent the whole way home and I am grateful for that. I pull up outside my parents' house and Mother kisses me on the cheek.

'I told your father it was a Tupperware party. I would prefer it stayed that way.'

I nod.

'You look tired dear, you need that holiday.'

I return her wave and decide she is absolutely right. I do need a holiday. I decide to start looking at brochures the very next day.

Chapter Twenty-Six

'India did us a great favour slipping on the slopes, so to speak.' Justin gleefully closes the portfolio and claps his hands.

'Olivia, you saved our corporate arse.' He smiles at Olivia and clinks his champagne glass against her orange juice.

Justin has kindly arranged a farewell lunch for Olivia, who will be leaving today, and as a special surprise, we arranged the whole photo shoot into a portfolio for him.

'I had something to do with it too,' I clink my glass also and feel quite proud of myself.

'I would suggest you take a holiday, but I have already instructed you to do that,' Justin grins at me.

'Where are you going?' Olivia asks.

I cut into my smoked salmon and memories of Jack enter my head. I feel rather bad about him as I never did return his calls. On reflection, of course, he may have decided he did not want to see me anymore. I push him from my mind and smile at Olivia.

'I have still to decide.'

She looks thoughtful, picks up her fork and then puts it down again. I look at her admiringly and realise much of the male clientele is doing the same. She looks stunning in a simple Versace dress which clings to her hips almost sensually. A white linen jacket is draped around her shoulders and I stare enviously at her long jet-black hair, which falls in soft curls around her cheeks. She is a beautiful woman and one of the nicest friends. We had spent two whole weeks together. Working in the studio in the mornings, then shopping in the afternoons and finally, dinner together in the evenings. Robin phoned every day and it was nice speaking to him too. We only discussed Christian the first night and I never mentioned him again, and neither did Olivia. There seemed little point if she had not seen him since our visit. I was desperate for news of him, however, so it was quite disappointing to think he had not been in touch with either of them. It seems his time is very much taken up with Claudine and their wedding preparations.

'This is an awful cheek Bels, but I don't suppose you want to come to France do you?'

I feel my eyes widen. France? Oh God, all those memories of Christian. I couldn't possibly go back to France.

'I'd just love to go to France again.'

Justin pours more champagne and cocks his head to one side.

'French men, ooh la la,' he laughs.

Olivia's eyes light up.

'It's just, we booked a holiday in India and Martha, our housekeeper… Do you remember me mentioning her?'

Justin looks quizzically at me over his glasses. I avoid his eyes. I hadn't told him just how I contacted Olivia, but now I suppose I will have to.

'Yes, I remember.'

'She always keeps a check on the house. The house is our pride and joy, well you saw it.'

Justin removes his glasses, coughs slightly and stares at me.

'I visited Olivia in her home on the way to my wedding,' I explain, sensing his curiosity would not go away unless I said something.

'Ah,' he nods, as though that explains everything.

Olivia goes on to explain that Martha normally stays at the house when they go away, but her daughter recently had a serious car accident, and Martha has decided to go and stay with her for a month to help the family out. So, I find myself agreeing to house-sit their home in France. Two weeks at Treetops. I tell myself this is serendipity. After all, I had been having difficulty choosing a holiday destination and now here it was.

'Here is the address,' says Olivia handing me her card. 'You can use our car and I will leave a map of all the best places to shop. You will have a great time. I will leave the key in the outhouse in a jar marked *pulses*.'

Her excitement is contagious and I find myself looking forward to it. I punch the house alarm numbers into my phone.

'You have my mobile number, so phone me if you think of anything. We fly out in a week so there is time for both of us to think of things. I will get Claude, our gardener, to collect you from the airport. Oh this is so great Bels. I can't think of a better person to have in the house, and you will love it there.'

The rest of the lunch just whizzes by as Olivia and I discuss the house, her plants, places I should visit, people to phone if there are any problems and the best places to eat.

'I will tell Georgia, she owns our favourite restaurant that you are coming, she will reserve a table for you every night. You will adore the food.'

By the time I kiss her goodbye I am trembling with excitement at the prospect of my trip. Any nagging doubts I had concerning memories of Christian are quickly forgotten. Justin arranges a car to take her to the airport and I wave her off happily.

'You had better toddle off sweetie and do some holiday shopping,' laughs Justin and after kissing him on the cheek I do just that.

***

'France? I thought you were going to India,' exclaims Mother from beneath her face mask.

I drop my shopping bags onto the floor and stare horrified at the large slices of grapefruit on her eyes and then smile at Petra, my mother's Polish beautician who I'm sure has no idea what she's doing.

'Shouldn't you have *cucumber* slices on your eyes?' I ask, attempting not to sound critical of Petra.

'Oh, we couldn't find any,' she says, gently removing the grapefruit from one eye and peering at my shopping bags.

'Ooh, you've been to Monsoon,' she says enviously.

I pull my purchases out and scatter them around me. Petra applies wax sheets to Mother's legs and I feel myself tense.

'Actually, I never said I was going to India. Do you want some camomile tea?' I ask thoughtfully as Petra grabs the sheet and yanks it.

'Ouch. That would be lovely dear,' she replies in a strangled voice.

My father comes lumbering in carrying a very wet Candice. I watched horrified as the dog drips onto the lounge carpet.

'I just gave her a nice bubble bath and hosed her down. She loved it,' smiles Dad.

I look at the shivering Candice and grimace as her tongue lolls from her panting mouth.

'Please don't let her drip all the over the floor, dear,' gasps Mother as Petra yanks another sheet of wax.

'Good Lord, Kitty, whatever you do, don't look out of the window, people will think it is Halloween,' says Dad flatly as he walks into the kitchen. Candice flops wearily onto the kitchen floor. I step over her and fill the kettle. Petra comes out and quietly mixes together a green powder with warm water in one of my mother's best dishes. Dad and I exchange wary glances but don't say a word until she leaves.

'Good God, what was that?' I say laughing.

'Every week for the past three years she has mixed that stuff and your mother never looks any different. Never have understood paying fifty pounds for agony you could just as easily inflict on yourself. I did offer to put grapefruit on her eyelids but it would not be the same, she said.'

I stifle my laughter and take in the tea for my mother, who is now having her left leg waxed.

'But France,' she repeats. 'Why would you want to go there? Especially after the terrible journey you had in France to get to your wedding? Oh good God, you're not going to see that Christopher are you?'

She gasps as Petra yanks at the wax strips.

'Be a dear, Petra, could you do my nails while I talk to Bels?'

I hand her tissues and she dabs at her watery eyes.

'I understand why you shave,' she whispers and we both quickly smile at Petra.

'His name is Christian, and no, of course I am not going to see him, he is in New York,' I say shoving a custard cream into my mouth.

Mother holds an elegant hand out to a gum-chewing Petra, who proceeds to paint the nails in a blood-red polish. I pull a face.

'Is it too dark?' asks Mother worriedly.

'Matches your Halloween look,' comments my father turning on the television.

'Not now dear, we are talking,' sighs Mother.

He calmly turns it off and walks back out into the garden. I explain how Olivia needed someone to house-sit. I do not mention that I had been there before but gush at how lovely the house is and how spectacular the views are. By the time I have finished with my graphic details, Mother is as excited as I am. I show her the dress and top I had bought in Monsoon and the new earrings from Camden market. Mother instructs me to phone at least three times a week and to send photos via email.

'We will phone if Alex goes into labour,' my mother shouts, as I climb into a cab.

'You'll probably hear the screams in France,' smiles Dad.

I wave enthusiastically before collapsing in the back of the taxi. Now is the time to get into holiday mode.

Chapter Twenty-Seven

I decide to think French. On the way home from my parents I stop off at Virgin records and browse the French artists, finally buying a box-set of popular French albums and four French films. This time, I decide, I will be better equipped and look through the French language courses in Borders. After all, this time I won't have Christian to depend on. I finally choose *French for Dummies* as they are out of stock of *French for Idiots and Morons*. Later that evening, while listening to one of the new CDs, I tell myself, it is time to start thinking about romance again. After all, I am going to romantic France aren't I? I spend a leisurely amount of time in the shower, shaving my legs, and bikini line. I will forget Christian, after all he has obviously forgotten about me. Yes, I will go to France and hopefully make everyone happy by returning with a handsome beau in tow, although personally I would like to give men up for Lent, even though Lent is nine months away. I slowly dry my hair so it falls in gentle waves around my shoulders and then pack my suitcase and hand luggage. Finally, sitting with a hot mug of cocoa, I text Jack, apologising for not getting back to him sooner. I thank him for a lovely evening and the beautiful flowers but explain that I don't think we are quite suited and that it is probably me still smarting from the break up with Simon. I figure a small lie does not hurt in the grand scheme of things. Everything now ready, I pull my legs under me and settle back to watch the film *Moulin Rouge*, thinking that this time tomorrow night I will be watching a French film at Treetops, and swallow some Quiet Life to ease the excitement.

***

The taxi driver hoots and I wave from my window. I do a quick flat check and lug my bags downstairs.

'All right darling, where you off to then?'

'France,' I say airily, climbing into the back of the taxi. I fumble in my bag for my Blackberry and sigh heavily when I can't find it. The cab driver goes to speak to me, but I hold up my hand.

'Sorry, I have to make a phone call. Straight to the airport please,' I say quickly and grab my phone which I dropped on the seat.

He shrugs and climbs into the driver's seat. I pretend to punch a number into my phone. I mean, don't you just hate chatty cab drivers? They always talk nine-to-the-dozen, and you can never get a word in. Of course, while they are doing so they take you all around the houses and of course you don't notice, because you are so busy chatting away about your holiday or your love life, that when they present you with the bill, you feel terrible mentioning how high it is, especially as they had been so nice and everything. Oh yes, I was not born on a banana boat, as my father says. I begin a pretend conversation on my phone.

'Oh, how wonderful Gina, tell me all about it. Oh no it's fine. I am in a cab on my way to the airport. We've got about twenty-five minutes, thirty tops.' I quickly check the driver has heard me. I continue my pretend conversation for the full thirty minutes and end the call when I see the airport signs. The driver looks at me through his rear view mirror. Throwing the phone into my bag I run my fingers through my hair.

'Oh good, we are here,' I say, feigning surprise.

He swerves into a parking space, switches off the engine and turns in his seat.

'That was an impressive phone call.'

I stare at him.

'This is yours; you dropped it as you got in the cab. I tried to tell you, but…' he says with a smile, gently throwing my phone into my lap.

'Oh bugger. Whose phone did I just use then?'

I feel myself blush as I pull the stranger's Blackberry out of my bag, and hand it to him.

'Sorry,' I mumble.

'It's not a problem. I'm just impressed you made a thirty-minute call on a phone with a dead battery.'

Shit, shit, shit. I hand him a twenty pound note, and waltz with my head held high into the airport. Feeling very cross with myself, I march to the check-in desk and swallow some Quiet Life as I queue. This time I have packed my creams and perfumes in my suitcase. I have no intention of giving more away to Jade and Tracey. My handbag is tidy this time around, and I find my passport easily. I glide through passport control and within minutes am standing back in the departure lounge where I first saw Christian. Unwillingly I find myself walking towards the Sushi bar stupidly thinking I will see him, dressed in the Marc Jacob jumper and stuffing his mouth full of Sushi. Of course, I don't. In fact, the bar is practically empty compared to the day when I had first set eyes on him, and I begin to wonder if my journey across France in the Lemon had been a dream. I blink rapidly. I really must try and forget about him. Is the man ever going to leave my thoughts? I check the flight board. I see I have forty minutes before boarding and decide to go to the Internet café to Google Christian for the last time. As I type his name into the search bar, I tell myself that once I step on the aeroplane I will not think of him ever again. 'News for Christian Lloyd' pops up and I click again. A new post stares at me and I click into it with a thudding heart. Oh God, has he married Claudine at last? I stare in frustration at the photo and short caption which is in German. I stare at a picture of a demolished building and then a photo of Christian, which I had seen on other sites. It would have to be in German wouldn't it? I spend half of last night, learning sodding French, and when I desperately need to know another language it turns out to be bloody German. Would you believe it? I check the time on my Blackberry and then quickly copy the text and paste it into Google fish. I stare with fascinated horror. Oh my God this surely cannot be right.

'In Munich today the building 'Grampian house' collapsed on Christian Lloyd as he donates thousands of euros to the school. Mr Lloyd was driven to the hospital in Munich.'

I feel sure my heart will stop. Without a second's thought, I scroll to Simon's number in my Blackberry and wait with my hands clenched for him to answer, but his answerphone clicks on. Oh no, he is probably at the hospital in Munich with his parents. I leave a short message asking him to phone me as soon as possible. Oh my God, oh my God, I have to get to Munich. I print the page so that I can take the address of the accident with me and race to the information desk and garble my plight to the assistant.

'Sorry, madam, did you say someone had died?' she enquires frowning.

'Oh God, they may have done. I am just praying you can get me on a flight to Munich. The building has collapsed,' I sob, fumbling for my Rescue Remedy.

'One moment, let me get you some water,' she says softly.

'No,' I cry, 'I don't need water, just a flight to Munich.'

I swallow five drops of Recue Remedy and wait for it to take effect. I watch impatiently as she looks on her computer.

'I really don't think we can offer you anything today...' she says hesitantly.

I let out a small sob, and she looks pityingly at me.

'However, if it is an emergency, I should be able to find an airline with a flight.'

'Oh it is, it is, a building has collapsed on my friend. It's on the Internet, look, I have a copy of the page here.'

I wave the printout at the clerk. Oh God, it sounds so tragic when I say it out loud. The passengers behind me gasp and one lays a comforting arm on my shoulder.

'May I read the article?' asks one man in the queue. I nod, feeling wretched.

'His name is Christian Lloyd. The news is in German, it happened in Munich you see. You will have to Google fish the article.'

He smiles kindly at me.

'I speak German. Let me see.' He reads silently and then looks quizzically at me. Oh no, what is it?

'What does it say?' I ask, holding my breath.

'You Google fished this?'

I nod. Oh God, is it worse than I first thought? He shakes his head. I feel faint.

'Here it says, and I'll translate for you, '*In Munich today the building Grampian house was demolished as Christian Lloyd donates thousands of euros to the new school being built, on the site, to his specifications.* I can't see where the building fell on him. Google fish probably mixed the words up and picked the word collapsed for demolition.'

Oh What! I stare with my mouth open as he reads on.

'Ah, here, further down, is slightly more. *Building demolished as Christian Lloyd donates thousands. Mr Lloyd made a generous donation to the children's hospital in Munich, in addition to other charitable giving to the arts foundation for much needed restoration work.'*

'He is fine,' he smiles.

I continue staring at him. Oh buggety bugger, what an idiot. My phone rings, I mumble a thank you and turn away to take Simon's call. Shit, shit.

'Hello?' I say softly, feeling the other passenger's eyes on me.

'Annabel, what's wrong? You sounded frantic on my voicemail.'

Oh shit and double shit, what the hell do I say?

'I'm at the airport, on my way to France, and I suddenly got worried....' I say flapping around in my head for an excuse.

'Worried? What are you worried about?' he replies, doubt in his voice.

'I think I left the cooker on, can you get my mum to check? I can't get hold of her,' I lie and hear a woman snigger behind me. Oh, this has to be the most embarrassing thing ever. Simon scoffs.

'You hardly use the thing, so I doubt you've left it on and...'

'Thanks,' I say loudly. 'I must go, they're calling my flight.'

I hang up, throw the phone into my bag and race to the flight board. Jesus, the gate is about to close. I run to the boarding gate like an Olympic sprinter and arrive panting and with perspiration running down my face. I hand over my boarding pass and get on the plane where I am greeted by hostile stares from the other passengers. I quickly take my seat and hunch down. Note to self: have nothing to do with men while on holiday and never ever think of Christian Lloyd again. The man is having a whale of a time, knocking down buildings, erecting new ones, donating money to all and sundry and probably planning a wedding. I don't imagine he has given me a second thought. What a bastard. I decide from this day forth I shall dislike him intensely and I will not give him the time of day if he should contact me. Depressingly, however, I have to admit that the chances of him ever contacting me are decidedly slim. I look enviously at the *Hello* magazine that the girl next to me is reading and miserably pull out the in-flight magazine from the holder in front of me. Right, it is time to start my holiday with some duty-free perfume, a glass of wine and some peanuts, and oh yes, up yours Christian Lloyd.

Chapter Twenty-Eight

I arrive in France feeling quite heady. Being back at an airport that looks uncannily like the airport at *Chatillon-Sur-Seine* where I had seen Christian eating croissants and jam makes me feel very strange indeed. I stop close to a café and inhale the coffee aroma that emanates from it. I imagine I hear his mocking laugh but when I open my eyes I see it is a stranger walking out of the café with his girlfriend. I realise he does not sound in the least like Christian. With my head dizzy from memories I contemplate my holiday. Two whole weeks in Côte d'Azur and I find myself feeling rather nervous. The thought of eating alone in the French restaurants is a bit daunting, but as I leave the airport and walk outside into the sunshine I feel better. Claude meets me with a smile and a warm handshake, and I am greatly relieved when he speaks to me in English.

'Welcome to Côte d'Azur, you have been to France before, oui?'
I allow him to take my laptop and hand luggage, and lead me to the small Fiat in the car park.

'I came to France when I was a child, but I passed through Côte d'Azur a few weeks ago,' I answer, while squeezing into the Fiat as elegantly as I can. Claude starts the car, and we shoot off immediately. I grasp the side of my seat tightly while fumbling to fasten my seat belt with my other hand. I quickly check there are airbags.

'I need to fasten my... Oh God,' I scream as the car mounts the pavement to avoid a cyclist. An old man walking his dog shakes his fist at us. I jump as Claude hits the horn. Feeling myself start to sweat, I hastily click the seat belt on and grasp my seat with both hands. I fight an impulse to squeal each time he overtakes. I allow myself a quick glance at the speedometer and feel quite faint.

'You like shopping?' he asks, pushing his hand onto the car's horn again. I jump at the sound and he smiles.

'You very nervous,' he observes.

Christ, did he say nervous? The man is a lunatic, and I am scared shitless.

'Erm, yes,' I reply, not taking my eyes off the road. 'I like shopping. I like driving slow too, so I can look at all the sights.'

He obviously does not hear the driving slow comment as the car picks up speed as we join the main road. I fight an overwhelming urge to scream.

'I hate cities, they make me, and how you say in English, claustrophobic? I get out as quick as I can.'

Oh isn't that just my luck.

'I give you my daughter number. She knows the best shops for clothes and will enjoy taking you.'

Taking one hand off the steering wheel he leans forward to the dashboard for his mobile phone. I gasp as a pheasant runs out in front of us. He swerves expertly while glancing at the phone.

'Here, you write it down. Her name is Camille.' He passes the phone to me. I reach out for it without taking my eyes off the road. Finally, he takes a sharp left and slows down. I let out a very audible sigh of relief. The scenery looks familiar and my stomach somersaults as I remember the Lemon travelling along these roads. I find myself wondering what happened to the Lemon. Did it get repaired, or did Christian just abandon it? I shake the thoughts from my head and copy Camille's number into my Blackberry. The views are stunning, and as we are driving at a more sedate pace I can enjoy them without my stomach churning. It takes close on fifty minutes to reach Treetops. Hard as I try not to remember my visit with Christian, the memory flashes with crystal clarity into my head. We pull up sharply and I am thrown forward, banging my hand on the dashboard. Claude retrieves my bags from the boot while I fetch the key. It is exactly where Olivia said it would be. I replace the lid on the jar and walk towards the house where Claude is waiting. The house is even more magnificent in the daytime and I decide to marvel at it after Claude has left. He carefully places my bags in the hall and hands me a small card.

'My phone number, you phone if you need anything, okay? The town, Côte d'Azur, is twenty minute from here. You have map?'
I nod enthusiastically.

'Oh yes, I brought one with me. Thank you.'
I stand outside and stare in awe at the house. It really is a giant-sized tree house and to think I thought Christian was a builder. Oh what an insult that had been. Now, I cannot even tell him what a great architect he is. I shake my head and walk into the house. Lumbering upstairs with my luggage I avoid the room Christian and I had stayed in and head for the master bedroom as Olivia had instructed. A four-poster bed dominates the room and I resist the urge to dive straight onto it. I study the artwork on the walls and understand why Olivia and Robin were nervous to leave the house empty. A note lies on the bed which is addressed to me. It is from Olivia. *'Bels, welcome. We hope your flight was good. We have left two bottles of wine in the kitchen for you and fresh bread in the bread bin. Enjoy and have a wonderful stay, all our love Olivia and Robin.'* I check there is a lock on the bedroom door and sigh. I shall feel very safe in this room. I unpack, and then go downstairs to look around. I open the fridge for a peek inside.

'Those who indulge bulge,' shouts a voice.
I jump and spin round.

'Jesus Christ, who was that?'
I slam the fridge door shut.

'Naughty pickers wear big knickers.'
What the hell? I am beginning to feel like a naughty girl who has been caught with her fingers in the cookie jar. A large flashing *Diet Decision Maker* cupcake is winking at me from the fridge door. Blimey O'Riley, Olivia has a deterrent fridge magnet that gives a verbal equivalent of a slap on the wrist whenever you are tempted. Is this the secret to Olivia's slim figure I wonder? I turn away with a smile and make myself a cup of tea and sit outside on the balcony to enjoy the stunning view. Any hope of putting Christian out of my mind is impossible. Everywhere I look there are reminders of him. I open the fridge for milk and inside are the cheese and olives that he loved so much. On the kitchen counter are the chocolate biscuits that he ate so many of. After drinking my tea, I decide to drive into the town for some shopping. Olivia's Peugeot, I am thrilled to see, is

automatic, so armed with my map, I set off to the town. The sun is shining and I find I feel quite happy. Stopping at a lay-by, I check the map. I take the next left and follow the quiet country road. A man waves at me and I wave back. I sigh contentedly until a car zooms around the corner. I scream when I realise the maniac is coming straight towards me.

'Get out of the way, you maniac,' I shout in a shaky voice.

He swerves around me shaking his fist. I exhale as I see him disappear around a bend and lift my foot slightly off the accelerator. My God, the French are bloody mad drivers. Following the sign to the town I turn right at the lights only to have another maniac come towards me. I see a pedestrian waving frantically at me. Oh Jesus Christ, it's not them, it's me. I am on the wrong side of the bloody road. I swerve the car sharply to get it onto the right side, forgetting the cars that are already there. They all sound their horns at once and I scream as the car mounts the kerb.

'Stupide femme,' a driver shouts at me and I blush. I have no idea what the insult is, but an insult I am sure it was. How dare he? After all, I am British, so in theory he is in the wrong and I am in fact driving on the right side of the road. Well, I would be if I were in England, I assure myself as I park the car in what I hope is a car park. I look around for a ticket machine, but there isn't one. I debate whether to leave the car or move it when I see a lady walking towards me.

'Oh, bon petite senora,' I stutter, thinking it doesn't sound right at all. Oh why did I not learn French properly at school? I always was pants at languages. She looks at me quizzically and then behind her and then back to me.

'Can I park here?' I say loudly and clearly.

She shakes her head and then shrugs. I point to the Peugeot.

'I stop car here,' I say nodding at her.

She shrugs again. Oh sod it. I thank her and walk to the shops. Olivia told me to use the general store as they speak English. The smell of freshly baked bread hits my nostrils as I walk in and instantly my stomach rumbles. I approach the assistant, an elderly lady who wears an apron and has her hair tied back severely.

'Bon petite senora...' I begin and then realise it is most certainly wrong.

'Shit, sorry, that's Spanish, bon petite madam.'
The girl stacking the shelves sniggers and I feel myself blush.

'Bonjour madame, how can I help you?' answers the elderly woman pleasantly.
Oh shit, shit, of course its bonjour, Oh bugger, bugger. I feel the blush suffuse my body.

'I'm staying at Treetops and I need some provisions, would you be able to help me?'
Jesus Christ, what is wrong with me? Provisions? Am I in the Wild West now? I'll be asking where the nearest saloon is next. It was so much easier when I was with Christian. Oh bugger, why do I keep thinking of him?

'Ah yes, Olivia told us about you.'
The young girl sniggers again and I wonder what on earth Olivia told them about me.

'I am Rosa. My daughter owns 'Clarisse' the restaurant. You will be dining there tonight?'
I shake my head and then wonder if it was a question or more of a statement. It did sound a little Gestapo. *You vill be dining there tonight.*

'Oh no, not tonight but tomorrow I vill, I mean will,' I reply and bite my lip.

'I book table for tomorrow, eight o'clock good for you? We have nice British man who eats with us every night. I sit you with him?'

'Oh no,' I shout and quickly look behind me to see if anyone has heard me.
She raises her eyebrows.

'I thought you look for a new man, and he is English just like you, and no girlfriend.'
Good Lord, do I look that desperate that I would dine with a stranger on my second night?

'That's very kind of you but don't you think you should ask him first? Actually, I will eat alone and about six thirty, if that is okay?'
Good heavens, I have not been here five minutes and matchmaking is in progress. I would really prefer to see what this man looks like before sitting down to dinner with him. What kind of man is he anyway if he agrees to eat with a woman he has never met, and who

might look like the back of a bus for all he knows. A desperate man, that's what, and a desperate man is probably an ugly man. Unless, of course, he knows nothing about this matchmaking malarkey, in which case it would be dead embarrassing all round.

'I am sure he will not mind. He comes most nights to eat and chats to everyone. I think he would like the company at dinner.'
I cough uncomfortably.

'Well, I would prefer to get to know him first, but thank you.'
I thank my lucky stars for the escape and allow myself to be guided to the cheese counter. My mouth waters at the sight of the succulent meats and assorted cheeses. I purchase a selection along with some freshly baked bread and olives and, of course, Christian enters my head again. Oh this is ridiculous. The whole country reminds me of him. The girl wraps the cheese and points to a poster on the wall.

'You would like it, and there will be men too,' she says nodding excitedly.
Good Lord, what on earth did Olivia tell them about me? One hour in France and it seems I am already known as the 'man-eating English woman'. They will be locking up their men before you know it.

'Lovely,' I remark, looking at the poster and not understanding a word.

'It is a cheese tasting with wine. You will like it. It is in French of course, but we will pair you with someone who speaks English as well as French. I will put your name down,' says Rosa, pulling out a pad and scribbling in it.
Heavens, these French women are pushy.

'But, when is it?' I ask hesitantly, not wanting them to think that their idea of finding me a man is not appreciated.

'Wednesday evening. That is good for you? Ah…' She puts a finger to her head. 'Claude is helping you, I remember, he can bring you, and you can drink some wine. That's good.'
I go to protest but she wags her finger at me and I know it is pointless.

'Great, that sounds really great,' I say, attempting to sound enthusiastic and moving quickly to the door.

'Bon Jovi,' I say exiting quickly and cringe. Bon Jovi? What am I saying?

I trudge back to the car with my purchases and am piling them into the boot while trying to think of an excuse to get me out of the cheese evening when a yellow Citroën zooms past. It couldn't have been the Lemon, surely? After all, isn't Christian in Munich? Or if not in Munich then in New York, but most definitely not in Côte d'Azur. Anyway, I am supposed to be forgetting him aren't I and meeting someone new? Perhaps I should have dinner with the British man, after all he may be decidedly handsome for all I know. No, what am I thinking? No men for a while. I put the Citroën out of my mind, switch on the engine, check what side of the road I should be on and pull out slowly. Visions of a large glass of red wine, a warm bath and my French language programme push all thoughts of Christian from my mind. My first day getting to know the locals has gone very well, I think. I drive slowly on the wrong side of the road. Well, it is in fact the right side but it certainly does not feel like it. My mind travels to Christian and something occurs to me. I turn into the driveway leading to Treetops, park with a screech and dive out of the car. I race upstairs to Robin's office where I had dumped my laptop. I open it and Google 'Christian and French home'. It takes almost ten minutes before I have the information I need. There is a small photo of him wearing a hard hat, and a very unglamorous jacket, but to me, he still looks sexy. The caption below reads *Celebrity architect builds his own home in France*. I read the article and clap my hands in glee. This is exactly what I suspected.

Christian Lloyd, the celebrity architect has bought a home in Europe. Born in Surrey, England, Mr Lloyd has often voiced a desire to build a home in France. It is thought that Mr Lloyd paid an estimated half a million euros for land which is deep in the French countryside in the village of Carte d'Or, close to the town of Côte d'Azur.

I jump up and do a little dance and then realise my phone is ringing downstairs. It must be him. I fly down the stairs almost falling down the last two. He must have seen me in the town also. I grab my Blackberry and stare mesmerised as Simon's name shows on the screen. Oh good God, what now?

'Hello,' I say cautiously.

'Annabel?'

For Christ's sake, if he phoned me, it must be me mustn't it, so why does he ask such a question? And why in heaven's name doesn't he call me Bels like everyone else, sod it.

'Simon, hello.' I attempt to sound less cautious this time, but I can't help wondering why the hell he is phoning.

'You arrived there okay then?'

His voice sounds funny but I can't work out in what way. My eye spots the bottle of wine that Olivia had left sitting on the kitchen counter and I then remember the shopping I had left in the car in my haste to get to my computer. I walk outside.

'Yeah, I got here fine,' I say pulling the car door open and retrieving my shopping.

'I didn't know whether to call you back or not but I figured you wanted me to.'

'What!' I shout, slamming the door on my foot and wincing.

'Can you hear me?' he shouts back.

Shit, what the arsing head and hole is he talking about? Why is he being so nice to me? What does he mean *he figured I wanted him too*? I limp to the lounge and drop the shopping bags and then myself onto the couch. I look down to my foot and wince. My toe is very red, and oh good God, very big.

'Simon, I'd better say goodbye. I think I've broken my toe,' I say, attempting to wriggle it.

'Good God, how did you do that?' he exclaims, surprise rather than concern in his voice.

I sigh and don't bother to respond.

'Do you want me to come to France to see you?'

'What?' Jesus Christ, is the only word I can utter, continually going to be *what*?

'No no, I don't think it's anything serious.'

I stare longingly at the kitchen to where the wine sits and slowly ease myself up and begin to hobble towards it. Clicking my phone onto hands-free Simon's voice booms out,

'I wasn't talking about your foot. It's just I checked your flat and well, you hadn't left the cooker on... the thing is...'

I look to my phone and see the battery has died. Oh God, what was he about to say? Surely he does not think I phoned with the pretext of leaving the cooker on as an excuse to talk? Oh bugger. I pull the cork out of the bottle and a wave of pain shoots through my foot. I fill a glass in the hope it will send me some kind of divine inspiration. I look at foot and groan in disgust. It is starting to turn a very nasty purple colour now and throbs like hell. I grab Claude's card from the coffee table and limp to the house phone. He answers on the second ring.

'Hello, Claude, sorry to bother you but I think I have broken my toe,' I say flatly.

Chapter Twenty-Nine

I wake up feeling quite happy until I move my foot. The agonising memory of the door slamming on my foot returns with alarming clarity. I grab my Blackberry which is now nicely charged and see I have missed two calls from Simon. Oh bugger it. Pulling the quilt off I stare at my now very large toe. Of course it is just a bad bruise. Claude's wife came over last night and rubbed some atrocious smelling cream on the toe and gave me a bottle of strong painkillers. I was also equipped with a pair of crutches. The painkillers had knocked me out for the night. I can't let a bruise stop me, I think courageously and forty minutes later cautiously test my bad foot on the pedals of the car. Feeling assured it would be okay I grab my bag, map, crutches and Blackberry and set off to an art exhibition that is being held in a church in the hamlet where Christian has his house. I considered looking for the house but remembered it was so well hidden that the chances of me finding it were very slim. No, the best idea is to go to the hamlet and ask questions, well *try* to ask questions. I hope that someone there will speak English. All through breakfast I had debated whether to phone Simon, finally deciding it was best not to. I will see him when I get back and by then he would have seen sense, hopefully. I edge the car out of the driveway and make sure I am on the right side of the road. I stop after thirty minutes to check the map and then continue for another thirty minutes until I see the sign for Carte d'Or. My toe is throbbing now, and I am delighted when I see a sign for car park in English and French. After manoeuvring the Peugeot into a space I lift my throbbing toe from the pedal. I am in the heart of the countryside, and the smell of lavender is divine. I close my eyes and listen to the birds singing and imagine that I am sitting in the Lemon with the sunroof off. After a short time I reluctantly open the door and step timidly from the car. Armed with my crutches I hobble down the cobbled pathway. I see people walking towards me and hope that they speak English, but not feeling very confident I pull out the notes I had made in French. I approach hesitantly.

'Bon Jour Senorita, can you show me le eglise?' I ask, drawing the shape of a church steeple with my hands.

They look at me blankly. Oh God, stupid bloody language course. I feel sure eglise is the French for church. I begin to wonder if maybe they speak some kind of French slang and so do not understand me. There must be regional accents here too.

'You English, yes, I understand,' says a woman smiling.

Oh Lord.

'No, no, you don't understand. I'm not English, well I am English but, oh dear...'

'Ah, Swedish?' she says.

Swedish! Do I look bloody Swedish? I didn't recall having blonde hair and plaits the last time I looked. There suddenly seems to be a lot of shouting. Within minutes a mob has gathered and they are all staring at me expectantly. Good God, if I had been in the East End of London, I would not expect to get out alive.

'Bon Jour, everyone,' I say pleasantly, only to be met by a stony silence.

'Ah, of course, I must use the plural as there are a lot of you. Bon journo,' I repeat and this time, at least, they look at each other.

'I want to go to le eglise. Yes?' I pretend to pray and feel I am getting closer and closer to God by the minute.

'Ah, eglise, yes,' says one woman excitedly and my heart leaps until she starts firing directions at me in rapid French. Oh sod it. Obviously in this part of France they do not speak English or at least not very much. Another woman joins in and I attempt to write down the few words I understand, which are, turn right turn left and then turn right again. I spend five minutes writing things down and crossing them out, as they argue amongst themselves. Finally, armed with directions, I thank them kindly and make my escape. My foot throbs and my stomach feels decidedly acidic from the wine I had drunk the night before, and I could seriously murder a coffee. Hobbling away from the mob I try to follow their directions by using my small phrase book. God knows, the bloody Beginners French course has been totally useless so far. By the time I reach what few shops there are I am parched and in desperate need of my painkillers. I see an elderly man walking towards me and, although I am certain it will be a waste of time, I approach him.

'Excuse me, can I get a coffee anywhere?'

He snorts, points to what looks like a corner shop and continues walking. Good Lord, friendly lot or what? I open the door of the coffee shop and fall down a step.

'Shit, that's a bit dangerous,' I yelp, glaring at the pretty shop assistant who smiles kindly at me.

'Are you all right,' she asks in perfect English and I almost hug her.

'You speak English,' I say excitedly.

She nods.

'I love the English language, I so much want to go to England and see Cilla Black.'

Well, that's novel. Most people want to see Kate Middleton, and there was me thinking the French hated us.

'Are you from Liverpool?' she asks, her face brightening. I stare at her. Good God, do I sound like I am? I shake my head. How did I go from being Swedish to a Liverpudlian?

She rushes out the back and comes thumping back with a chair.

'Here, you have to rest your feet.'

I discover her name is Greta and she loves everything English, especially re-runs of *Blind Date*. She makes me coffee and while I sit drinking it, she lists all her favourite British things, all of which are Cilla Black related. When I can finally get a word in, I ask her if she knows where Christian Lloyd lives but she looks blank.

'I not know a Chris John,' she says after thinking deeply.

'No, Christian, it's all one word,' I correct.

She shakes her head again. I wait while she asks several of the customers but no one has heard of him. I thank her and hobble up the step.

'I can ask my father, he takes the post to everyone.'

I stop with my hand on the door. Bingo, at last. Surely if Christian lives nearby, Greta's father will know.

'Does he deliver outside the hamlet?' I ask hopefully.

'Yes, it takes him all day.'

I limp back down the step and offer her my phone number. Perhaps the yellow Citroën I saw yesterday was the Lemon, and perhaps Christian is in France and not building schools and hospitals in Munich after all, well it's worth a try.

'Please call me if he knows him. It is very important that I get in touch with Christian Lloyd.'

She looks at the number keenly and smiles.

'I'm sure if he lives here my father will know, but I don't think he does. Maybe you have wrong town?'

I think maybe I have the wrong country. She waves as I start the long walk back to the car.

'*Blind Date* is on tonight, you watch it,' she calls.

I nod and walk miserably back to the car. What a fool I am. It most likely had not been the Lemon that I saw. It is obvious no one has ever heard of Christian. I drive back feeling decidedly fed up and very determined that I shall not allow men into my life for a very long time. I shall remain a spinster, read all Jane Austen's novels and learn how to knit. I won't have to worry about pleasing a man because there won't be one. Of course, I think cheerfully, this means I can eat as much chocolate as I like. Hobnob overdose, the chocolate ones, here I come. I stop and buy several boxes of chocolates and a family bag of popcorn on the way home. After all, a little bit of comfort eating does one the world of good. Armed with the warm feeling my chocolate feast shop had produced, I step into Treetops saying the words 'I don't need a man' over and over again. I open a bottle of wine, make myself a large cheese sandwich and peel an avocado. I huddle on one of the long couches, turn the TV on and surround myself with chocolate and wine. After the second glass I attempt to phone Christian, but hang up before it rings. Surely if he really wanted to talk to me, he would have phoned again. After all, he did say he would. Damn him, why did he even phone at all? I phone Justin instead, hiccupping and tearful.

'Sweetie, what on earth is wrong?' he asks anxiously.

The first of a two-hour *Blind Date* marathon has begun and I am feeling more desolate than ever.

'I thought I saw the Lemon, but it was just another Citroën,' I hiccup with my mouth full of chocolate. 'I came here to forget him, but everywhere I look I am reminded of him.'

'Oh honey. It's never too late you know, why don't you phone Simon?'

Simon? I am stunned into silence and all that can be heard is a dubbed Cilla, who doesn't sound like Cilla at all. How can Greta possibly enjoy this rubbish? It's bad enough when I know what is being said, but this is pitiful. All I can think of is that if Christian Lloyd was a croissant I would be the jam because I want to be all over him. A tear splashes into my wine and I sniff loudly.

'Why does everyone talk about Simon? Why would I want to phone him?'

I rack my brains to try and understand.

'Ah, well, he was the one you were going to marry, so I just assumed... I'm gay darling, what the hell do I know?'

'I wish I were gay,' I mutter, studying the bruise on my toe.

Justin laughs merrily.

'Of course you don't.'

'I do too,' I say rummaging through the chocolates for a praline, only to realise I have eaten them all and there are only the toffee ones left. 'I wouldn't have to worry about men anymore. I would have mad passionate sex with every woman I see and I wouldn't even have to think about contraception.'

I hug a cushion, knock back more of the wine and try to remember who I had phoned.

'So, who are we talking about sweetie if it isn't Simon?'

God it's hot in the house. I look to the window as though willing it to open.

'I mean, he may have phoned but I wouldn't know. He said he would, but he hasn't. I can't phone him can I? To make things worse they don't have 1471 here, or if they do, it doesn't work on this phone. I don't normally like 1471 but it is awful when you haven't got it, do you know what I mean?' I lean over to turn the TV down, and almost fall off the couch. I put my Blackberry down for a second and punch 1471 into the house phone only to get an unavailable tone. I pick up the mobile again.

'No, it does not work,' I shout into the mouthpiece. 'Perhaps I should try 141.'

'No sweetie. That is when you don't want people to know that you are calling them.'

That doesn't make sense.

'But, why would I call them if I don't want them to know I am calling them? That's silly,' I scoff.

'Listen darling, if it's not Simon we're talking about, who is it?'

'Simon?' I bellow. Why on earth does everyone keep talking about Simon?

'It's...' I falter. Who the hell am I talking about? I close my eyes and the room spins. I snap them open and fumble for the chocolate.

'Marc Jacob,' I shrill excitedly, as the Sushi bar memory launches itself at me.

I look at the window again and think it might be quite nice to hang my head out of it.

'I need some air,' I say struggling to get up and falling over my shoes.

'Bels, is this about that guy, Christian?'

'Ah, yes, yes.'

The window is starting to resemble a prison break out and I fall exhausted back onto the couch.

'He doesn't love me either. He is probably snoozy woozying Claudine as we speak. No one loves me. Who am I going to have dinner with when I get home?'

'What about that guy Johnnie that you were seeing last year? He seemed quite nice.'

I snort.

'Our whole romance became a series of twitter updates. I was nothing but a twit to him.'

'I think you mean tweet darling,' he laughs.

'Bloody insult that is all I remember.'

'Bels, why don't you go to bed?'

Hmmm, sounds like a good idea. I click the TV off.

'I think I will, thanks for phoning Jus.'

I click the Blackberry off and pile cushions on the couch. The window seems a million miles away, and I abandon all plans to open it and instead fall back with a sigh onto the cushions. I stare at my toenails and then my fingernails. Maybe, I will have a manicure tomorrow I think dreamily before sitting bolt upright. Oh hell, is that an age spot on my hand? I stare at the small brown mark on the back of my hand, willing it to go. Oh good God, this is absolutely dire. Never mind a manicure, it is probably a sodding facelift I need. I pull the small vanity mirror that Mother had bought me for Christmas from my bag and study my face for other brown marks. I breathe a sigh of relief after not finding any but feel somewhat alarmed at the sight of crow's feet around my eyes. I throw my head back onto the cushions and sob. Oh Jesus, what am I to do? I am seriously close to my sell-by-date and shall soon be on the shelf and, let's face it, who is ever interested in out of date goods? I guess this means I don't have time to give up men. The brown spot beckons me and I study it again, realising it is chocolate. I lick it off, pop two painkillers with the wine and flop back on the cushions, thinking I really should phone Simon tomorrow. The last thing I remember is deleting Christian's phone number and slumping onto the bed.

Chapter Thirty

I wake up the following morning with a strange craving for fish and chips which seems very odd, but make do with a bowl of muesli. I eat it with some very odd-flavoured yogurt and check the bottle that contains the painkillers and see that they should not be mixed with alcohol. Perhaps that explains my strange memories of last night. I decide I will phone Simon after showering and overdosing on coffee in the hope that my head will be a bit clearer by then. Christ, how much did I drink last night? And what the hell did I say to Justin? Heavens, those pills must be strong. A very hazy memory of announcing that I wished I was gay haunts me. I now have nothing but an overwhelming urge to soak in a large bath full of lavender essential oil, with an ice pack on my head and a copy of *Hello* magazine, but have neither oil nor magazine. It is pissing down with rain to top it all, so I certainly won't be sitting on the balcony this morning. Instead, I force myself into the shower and huddle over another cup of coffee while recovering from the exertion. My laptop sits open on the kitchen table and I lazily log into my Facebook account. I scroll down my profile page and almost faint.

'Annabel Lewis and Claudine Williams are now friends'
What! Claudine accepted my friend request? Oh God, I vaguely remember requesting it on my phone after my third glass of wine. My heart palpitates and I reach for the Rescue Remedy. I don't click into her page until I have had almost half a bottle of the stuff. I stare at her profile picture and then read her status, which totally floors me.

'Four sleeps to go and then the big day.'
Oh my God, what big day? I scroll further down to read some of the messages on her wall.

'Good luck Claudine, sorry we can't be there but it will be great.'
'Can't wait to be with you on your big day.'

'Don't be nervous. Remember, it will be a once in a lifetime day.'

I slam the laptop lid down and exhale. Oh my God, Oh my God, she is getting married. What else can it mean? What a lying, deceiving bastard. To think he even kissed me. My God, I ought to go there and stand up when they ask that question, you know the one, when you have to speak now or forever hold your peace and all that rubbish. He is a lying deceiving, two-timing, shagging bastard is what I will say. I lift the laptop lid and click into her photo albums and sigh with relief five minutes later when I do not find any of her with Christian. If she is marrying him then I have four days to stop it. Good Lord, what am I saying? Even Julia Roberts didn't manage that in *My Best Friend's Wedding*, so I've no chance. My phone pings, it is a text from Mum. Oh wonderful.

Hello darling, your father and I are just off to a garden party at the Johnsons'. You remember them don't you? You stole apples from their garden once when you were scrubbing. Their son just got divorced. His wife was one of those German Greer women, burning her bra and all sorts. Turns out she was a lesbian by all accounts, too awful for words. It must have been frightful for him. I think you would like him. Write soon. X

Oh no, that's all I need. I quickly answer.

France is great apart from the rain. It's Germaine Greer by the way and I was scrumping not scrubbing and I really don't want to go out with someone who is emotionally scarred from having a lesbian wife thank you very much. Love you both. X

I look again at Claudine's profile, annoyed that she doesn't say if she is in a relationship. I put the lid down and phone Simon. I tip out some Quiet Life while I wait for him to answer. Perhaps I will get his voicemail and I can offer to meet him when I get home.

'Simon Lloyd,' he barks making me jump and drop the Quiet Life bottle.

'It's me,' I say meekly.

'I'm in a meeting,' he says brusquely.

I feel myself go all timid and am about to stammer a reply when he speaks again.

'Hold on, I'll go outside.'

I hear a murmur of voices and chew the inside of my lip nervously.

'Did you see that I had called you?' he asks gruffly a few seconds later.

'I tried to call you back but signal is really bad here,' I lie.

'I just wanted to say that if you wanted to try again...'

'Try again?' I repeat.

'Yes, try again...'

'Why would I want to try again when I have already tried?' I ask, feeling like we are stuck in a maze.

'Well, you phoned about leaving the cooker on,' he says raising his voice slightly.

'But I didn't leave it on.'

'I know, and I know that you know I know.'

Jesus Christ, do I need a Peter Piper picked a pickled pepper conversation when nursing a hangover?

'You know I know what?' I ask and immediately wish I hadn't.

He sighs.

'That I know you know.'

'I know you know that I know, sodding what though?' I shout.

'That you want us to get back together. I know that is why you phoned and pretended you had left the cooker on.'

I drop my head in my hands and rub my eyes. Oh this surely is not happening. Why did I ever phone him in the first place?

'Oh Simon, it really isn't like that. I thought you liked Kaz.'

There is silence and for a second I think we have been cut off.

'But you sounded desperate to talk to me. The thing is I do like Kaz and I think she likes me but I feel I owe it to you to give it another shot if that is what you want...'

'Simon,' I try to break in.

'I'm attending a wedding in France in a couple of days. We could chat then if you like?'

Oh my God, so Christian is marrying Claudine, and here in France. What a bastard to get married when I am here. Honestly, like he hasn't hurt me enough. Why have they suddenly decided to get married? I bet she's pregnant. Oh no, this just gets worse.

'I really did think I had left the cooker on,' I lie.

I can see him nodding in the way that he does.

'You don't mind me seeing Kaz?'

I exhale.

'No, I am very happy for you. Really I am.'
I hear someone call his name.

'Ah, I'm needed, I should go. Glad we got that sorted though. By the way, did you know that Christian is in France?'
I struggle to stop my voice from shaking.

'Oh really, no I didn't know,' I answer trying to sound casual.

'He's doing a place up in Provence. Kaz said you're staying somewhere in Provence?'
Ask him now for goodness sake, and put yourself out of this misery.

'Your trip, is it for...' I begin.

'I've got to go, millions of dollars rest on it. You know how it is. Have a great holiday. I'm glad we had this chat.'
Then he is gone and I never got to ask if it was Christian's wedding he was attending. Damn it. What a disaster. I take a choc-ice from the freezer and devour it while driving to the patisserie in Cote de Mont. I will have lunch there and take a walk to see if I recognise anything. Christian's house can't be that far away. Surely, something will look familiar. Greta greets me with a wide smile. The patisserie is busy and the smell of coffee and warm bread makes me hungry.

'I have news for you. I was going to phone you after lunch. Here you sit.'
She pulls a chair out at a small table by the window. I sit down gratefully and study the menu. All around me are couples. Is everyone married but me? Even Christian is getting married it seems. I expect most of the women here are expecting babies, or have already punched out a couple while I plod along heading towards my forties, crashing into one dysfunctional relationship after another. God, I am falling apart. My ex is seeing my best friend and they will probably marry each other, and ask me to be maid of honour. The man I love is marrying someone else and has probably forgotten that I even exist. My mother is trying to match me up with every medallion man in sight and Justin thinks I want to be gay.

'What would you like?' Greta breaks into my thoughts.

'I'll have the chicken pesto pasta please. Could I have a coffee?'
She sits opposite me with her pad.

'I will bring a pastry with the coffee. A macaroon maybe, but first I have to tell you that I know the man you asked me about. Of course, I didn't realise until I spoke to my father that you meant Chris.'

'Chris,' I echo and stare at her. She seems unaware of my stare and animatedly describes how she had asked her father about an Englishman named Christian Lloyd, and how for a moment even he did not know who she was talking about. She laughs loudly at this. I seem unable to find my voice. It seems I have finally discovered that Christian is here in France and I am stupidly struck dumb. She points to the hill opposite the patisserie.

'We've been invited to the petite reception. I'm very excited.'

'Reception,' I echo finding my voice.

'That is why you are here, isn't it, for the party?'

'No, not really,' I answer forlornly as I remember Claudine's Facebook status.

I watch as she draws directions for me. I feel my stomach churn. Finally, I know where he is and I really don't know if I have the courage to see him. I eat my chicken thoughtfully and with excitement rippling through my body, I pay the bill and climb into the car. I drive to the top of the hill and turn left and recognise the beautiful views. Lavender fields are on both sides and I inhale the fragrance deeply in the hope it will relax me but nothing seems to calm my quivering body. Pushing my sunglasses onto my head I open the window. The instructions tell me to take a sharp left and the driveway that Christian had walked me down comes into view. I gasp and brake suddenly. The house sits about a hundred yards from me and has been magically transformed. The porch he had so lovingly talked about now gleams in the sunlight. A rocking chair sways slightly in the breeze and a white cat stretches lazily and stares at my car with interest. The door squeaks open and I slide down in my seat. A middle-aged man in overalls steps out and, without looking at me, shakes a dustsheet. I wait until he goes back inside and then reverse the car back out of the driveway. Satisfied that I am out of view, I look back to the house. I am now facing the side of it and sigh when I see the Lemon parked there. It is cleaner than I remember and, even from this distance I can see the sunroof has been replaced. I am admiring the car when Christian walks from the house. I freeze. Damn it, I can't bloody move. He doesn't look my way but gets into the Lemon. I wait with my breath held for Claudine to follow him but there is no sign of her. Oh my God, is he coming this way? I look around desperately and realise I have nowhere to go. I bend over the passenger seat so that I can't be seen. My heart thumps madly and I tighten my muscles as I hear him drive past. He does not slow up and I allow myself to relax. I wait until my racing heart has calmed down and then get out of the car. I walk gingerly to the porch, constantly glancing behind me. The cat stretches and begins to meow around my legs. I can hear banging from inside and am just about to knock, with no idea of what I will say to Claudine, when the door is opened by a grey-haired grim looking woman holding a saucer of fish heads. The woman jumps back and screams, throwing the saucer into the air. A fish head lands on my foot and I grimace.

'Madame, you give me heart attack,' she cries.

'I'm so sorry,' I say looking down at my foot where the cat is purring lovingly and rasping its tongue over my toes. I shiver and attempt a smile.

'What a lovely cat,' I say stifling my gasp as it dribbles onto my foot. Oh Lord, don't scream Bels.

The woman runs into the house and returns with a wet cloth that smells disgustingly of disinfectant. She shoos the cat away and beckons me to use the cloth. Several minutes later and smelling of pine, I am ushered into the house followed by an eager cat who has decided I am his dinner. My shoes click on the kitchen flagstone flooring. There is banging coming from upstairs and I look up expectantly. I have no sodding idea what I will say to Claudine if she walks down the stairs. The cat sweeps its tongue round my ankle and I give it a discreet little kick.

'Shoo, shoo.' The woman boots it out onto the porch. I suppress my gasp and wonder if I should tell Christian that his housekeeper manhandles his cat when he is out.

'It come from the fields, it here every day, I don't know why he wants us to feed it. How can I help you?'

I struggle to think of a reply and she beckons me to follow her. I clip-clop reluctantly into the shiny new kitchen where she waves her arm around with a satisfied sigh. The kitchen has been transformed from the building site that I remember from the day Christian showed me around. It looks as if it has been taken right out of *Hello* magazine with shiny dark granite worktops and oak cupboards complementing the flagstone flooring and dark beams. An oak table in the middle of the room sits under an impressive rack of copper saucepans. I look in envy at the large built-in hob with an equally large chimney hood.

'Come, come,' my enthusiastic hostess insists, pulling me by the arm to the kitchen window behind the double sink. She pulls up the Austrian blind to show the view. It is breathtaking, with rolling hills and, in the distance, the Alpine mountains.

'And look,' she continues, opening the cupboard doors to reveal the dishwasher and washing machine.

'It is finished at last. Come this way.'

I follow her outside where a marquee is being set up. My heart sinks at the sight of it. Any hopes I may have had that he wasn't marrying Claudine are now dashed. I stare in awe at the magnificent preparations. Lights are being set up around the marquee and a small bandstand is being erected. She excuses herself to direct the men at the bandstand. I wander across to the marquee and peek inside to see rows of tables. At the far end a man is testing a mike and I visualise Christian making his speech. Oh bugger it all. I see the woman walking towards me and I step out of the marquee.

'Sorry, as you can see we are preparing for a…how do you say?'

'*Petite reception*, yes I know,' I finish for her.

She smiles.

'It has been a long wait but worth it, are you coming?'

Shit, shit.

'Erm, actually I lost my invitation and it had Christian's number. I am still not sure if I will make it, could you give me his phone number again?'

She gives me an odd look and walks into the kitchen where I watch her write something on a piece of paper.

'Here.' She hands it to me. 'I have put house phone number and time for Friday, I hope we see you.'

So it is Friday, and that fits with Claudine's 'big day'. There is a noise upstairs and my heart thumps in unison with the footsteps.

'Oh good Lord, is that the time?' I ask, looking at the clock on the kitchen wall. 'I must dash, thanks so much, see you Friday.'

I fly from the house back to the car and miserably drive home.

Chapter Thirty-One

After rifling the fridge I scoff half a trifle with hardly a minute's thought. Well, that is not strictly true. I did hesitate when the talking cupcake shrilled *'naughty pickers wear big knickers'*. I really can't imagine how many pounds I have gained in the past month, but big knickers it most definitely will be, soon. I console myself with great plans to start a diet as soon as I get home. In fact, I will sign up for the local gym as well as starting Weight Watchers. Mind you, the thought of counting all those points is enough to put you off dieting for life. Still, it will all be worth it in the end. Fired up with my good resolutions, I reward myself with half a bottle of chocolate milk that is sitting in the fridge and two éclairs. If I can't eat when I am lovesick when can I? With this thought in mind I go back to the fridge and remove some strawberries and ice cream. I arrange my own little feast on the floor and turn on the TV to watch an episode of *24* on the Sky channel. By the time it ends, I am bloated and a little drunk after finishing some champagne, while watching Jack Bauer escape from his terrorist captors despite being drugged and tied to a chair. For two whole hours I manage to forget that Christian is getting married tomorrow. The realisation hits me again, and I wobble to the fridge. The crutches lie against it and I remind myself, I must return them. I yank back the door to the cries of *'carrot cake is not one of your five-a-day'*. Shaking my head at the talking cupcake I pull out a yogurt which I take upstairs with me. After climbing into bed and eating half of the yogurt, I lie down and stare at the ceiling. I feel my body shudder and then freeze. Above my head is the largest spider I have ever seen. It must be the size of a saucer at least. I stare in fascinated horror at it and feel all my muscles tighten. Oh shit, it's moving. Oh please God, don't let it fall on my head. I lie rigid, watching it crawl along the ceiling. I let out a small sigh of relief when it is no longer above me. I debate spraying it with some hairspray. I read somewhere that if you do that it freezes their legs. I shudder at the thought of the legs and want to turn away but know that I dare not in case it disappears. The hairspray idea is quickly abandoned in favour of keeping it on the ceiling. The thought of it dropping onto the bed has me shaking with terror. Oh God, what if it is poisonous? Who knows what kind of spiders they have in France. It could well have a killer sting. Oh shit, shit what am I going to do? I watch as it crawls to the end of the ceiling and only then do I feel it is safe to sit up. I realise that I have to plan some kind of a strategy. I try to imagine how Jack Bauer would handle it and wish to God I had a gun so I could blow the sodding thing's brains out or shoot its kneecaps off. Mind you, I would never have enough bullets to shoot all those kneecaps. I feel sick and curse the damn thing. It sits unmoving above the door which means I now can't escape. I grab the glass of water on the bedside cabinet and drain it. I watch with a shiver as the thing starts to walk down the wall towards the floor and let out a small shriek. I must get out. I move as quietly as I can, after all, the last thing I want to do is disturb it and make it run under something. The thought of losing it makes me shiver. I carefully pull the wicker chair that sits beside the bed, towards me and dive onto it where I can now see the spider better. It is now crawling behind the curtain, oh no. I jump back onto the bed and grab my Blackberry where I punch in Christian's number. Oh what the hell. After all, he is the only person I know in France. I listen to the long tones and wonder why no one answers when I remember it is the early hours of the morning. I am about to put the phone down when the spider crawls out from behind the curtain and up the wall again. I scream just as the phone is answered. It's Christian, thank God.

'Christian?' I squeal as the spider runs above the door.

'Bels, is that you? Are you all right?'

Is that concern in his voice? Oh God, I hope it is.

'I need your help,' I say hesitantly and quickly add, 'I'm sorry I know you're busy with things...'

'Not at two in the morning I'm not.'

Oh shit, two in the morning? What if they were... well, were? Oh hell and bugger it. How do I tell him I want him to remove a spider?

'I'm at Olivia's and...'

'Olivia's,' he raises his voice disbelievingly and I think I detect excitement in it.

'Oh God, I am so sorry to call you so late and everything but there is a spider in the bedroom and it is huge and I am sure it is one of those poisonous ones.'

Of course, I am not in the least bit sure but I don't want him to think it is just a tiny thing.

'A *spider*? You phoned me because you want me to come and kill a spider?'

I sigh.

'Well, I don't want you to bloody photograph it with your Nikon do I?'

Oh honestly, some people never change. He laughs.

'It's almost an hour's drive and...'

The spider seems to fall, wobble and then climb back to above the door.

'Oh God, please come,' I scream.

I hear him sigh,

'Okay, calm down. Take some Silent Life or something. I'll be there in a bit.'

He hangs up and I feel tears prick my eyelids. Oh please hurry, I beg. I spend the next forty minutes checking the time on my Blackberry. The spider is still above the door and I am bursting for the loo. Forty five minutes after I had phoned I hear the distinctive sound of the Lemon. I walk carefully to the window and see Christian. My hands tremble at the sight of him and I realise I look horrendous. I am wearing my nightie, and my hair is sticking up in places it shouldn't stick up in. I try to pat it down but you know how it is, the more you try to pat it down the worse it sticks up. He knocks on the door and I lean out of the window.

'I can't get out,' I call.

He looks around to see where the voice is coming from. Oh God, he looks so gorgeous even with his hair tousled and flopping over his forehead. He is wearing a light green shirt which he had obviously thrown on quickly as it hangs out of his jeans.

'I'm up here.'

He tucks in the shirt as he looks up at me and I feel myself drown in his warm hazel eyes.

'What do you mean you can't get out?' The familiar irritation in his voice somehow makes me feel all warm inside.

'The spider is just above the door. Oh my God, oh my God, it's moving,' I cry and feel my body shudder.

I hear him laugh.

'You're a sorry case. Throw me the keys so I can come up and slay the monster.'

I snort and walk carefully to my bag where I quietly retrieve the keys and throw them from the window. As soon as he catches them I run back to the bed and wrap a cardigan around me. I hear the front door slam and desperately wish I could shower, blow dry my hair and apply a fresh layer of mascara before seeing him. The thought of mascara reminds me that I hadn't removed it from yesterday. Oh, I must look atrocious. It is the first time I have seen him in weeks, and I look like something the cat has dragged in. I hear him mounting the stairs and I stare at the door.

'Come in slowly,' I yell in a trembling voice.

But of course he doesn't. The door is thrown open and he jumps in brandishing a toilet brush.

'Where's the beast, let me at it. Do you want it tortured first?' he says, waving the brush.

I fight back the urge to giggle and point to the monster above the door. Christian looks at me and I pull my cardigan tighter. He is even better looking than I remember and it feels like all my insides fall out when I think of him marrying Claudine in just over twenty-four hours. Would it really be so terrible of me to try and stop it?

'That's the spider? I thought you said it was huge?' he says in amazement. I watch horror-stricken as he reaches up and scoops it into his hand.

'Don't drop it,' I scream.

He throws it out of the window and I rush to the loo. I take the opportunity to tidy my hair and wash my face. I study my reflection in the ornate gold-rimmed mirror. I actually look better than I had imagined and step back out feeling a bit more confident now that the spider has gone. He is waiting by the window and turns when I walk in.

'So, how are you, apart from having a nervous breakdown that is?' I detect a slight tremor to his voice. Oh my God, what does that mean?

I pull the wicker chair towards me and sit with my legs curled underneath. This is just too awful. I should not have phoned him. I really must not spoil anything. Christian is not a man to do anything he does not want to do. If he is marrying Claudine it is only because he wants to. After all, didn't he say I was not his type? I must not demean myself by thinking there is more to this than meets the eye. He is the type of man that would come out at two in the morning to kill a spider isn't he? He does nice things for people.

'I am so sorry for bothering you at this time of the morning. I mean, I know how busy you are, preparing for things...'

Oh Lord, what am I rambling on about? I stop and attempt to give him a half-smile. He looks for a chair and not finding one, perches on the window sill. He runs a hand through his already tousled hair and looks at me thoughtfully.

'I was wondering how you had my phone number here in France?' he asks bluntly and I feel myself blush.

'Olivia gave it to me,' I say quickly. 'I am only here for a few days to keep a check on the house. Olivia did a shoot for the magazine I work on and...' I tail off. How stupid I have been. Of course he is not in the least interested in me and probably never has been. He must have women running after him all the time. Obviously, blonde bimbo types are for him, and hence the wedding to Claudine.

'Anyway, I can't be away too long, I have deadlines at the magazine and of course there is my boyfriend Jack Russell, who is so busy with his successful business that he couldn't even take time off to come with me.' I stop abruptly and pat at my hair nervously. This is just too awful for words. Why on earth did I phone him? Why didn't I think to phone Claude for goodness sake? And most importantly of all, why the hell am I saying all this rubbish about Jack?

'Jack Russell?' he repeats looking into my eyes. 'That's interesting, because when I spoke to Simon the other day he said you weren't going out with anyone, and anyway, isn't that a breed of a dog?'

He talked about me to Simon? What a bloody cheek.

'Well, I don't report my every move to Simon, and I'm certainly not going to tell him about a new boyfriend,' I snap.

He looks at me intently for a second and then stands up.

'The monster is slain and I should get back.'

I watch him walk to the door, a thousand words running through my brain but the only thing that comes out is.

'I'm bloody surprised Simon is even speaking to you. He is obviously a bigger person than you. I think what you are doing is loathsome.' I immediately bite my lip but it is too late. As my mother would say 'It's out there now.'

He stops in the doorway and I see his shoulders and neck tense. He turns slowly and his expression is stony.

'And what would that be?

'You know exactly what I'm talking about.'

'I actually don't think you have any idea what you're talking about.'

What a bloody nerve, to patronise me. He is hateful. Kaz was right. I barely know the guy. I feel myself shaking and cannot speak. His face softens slightly.

'By the way, I've done a lot to the house in the past few weeks and, if you are still here tomorrow night, there is...' he pauses.

'Your petite reception?' I offer miserably. 'Thanks but no thanks.'

He looks quizzically at me, moves to the door and then turns back.

'You don't know any of it, you know,' he says softly.

God, I am so angry with him. I am so angry he deceived me. So damn angry he is a bad boy. Damn angry that he can make me feel this way. Why does he always manage to make me feel like this? How can I feel hateful towards him while at the same time wanting to put my arms around him? I won't cry. I won't.

'You can't even phone when you say you will.'

What am I saying? He is getting married and I am making a fool of myself.

'I did phone actually. Your friend thought I was your wonderful boyfriend Jack and gushed about the wonderful bouquet he'd bought you,' he snaps, giving me a pained look.

'Well, there was no need for you to. After all, you made it quite clear I wasn't your type and...' I shrug.
I have never felt so foolish in my entire life. Why did I even imagine he was interested in me? He was being kind to me that was all. Helping me get to my wedding in Rome as any decent man would. This is probably the best thing that could happen. He is getting married tomorrow and I have no reason on earth to continue moping over a man who never wanted me in the first place. Of course, this doesn't explain why he discussed me with Simon, unless of course, he just wanted to be sure he wasn't the reason Simon and I split.

'I made the right decision not marrying Simon, and I think Jack is the right man for me. He is honest and has integrity, which is more than can be said for you.'
I can see from his face that I have hurt him and hate myself. He leans forward and kisses me on the cheek. I fight the swoon that seems to engulf me and attempt to remain dignified.

'All the same, the invitation is still there for tomorrow. It would be nice if you could come. We can remain friends can't we?'
Friends, oh Lord he can't possibly be serious. After all the things I have just said, how can he even consider it? Besides he does not realise that, if we remain friends, Claudine does not remain alive.
'It really wouldn't work,' I hear myself say as I shake my head. 'After all, you've got your life to live in New York and I have a life ahead of me, with Jack...'
I trail off. A life with Jack, what am I talking about? As nice as Jack is, I would rather slash my wrists than sit at another dinner table with *him*. He salutes me playfully.

'If you need any other monsters slain, I'm your man. Feel free to phone while you're here.'
Oh yes, of course. I'm sure Claudine would be delighted, not. I watch him walk through the doorway and it feels like my heart will break all over again. Why do I fall in love with men who only want me as a friend? The front door slams and I rush to the window to see him walking towards the Lemon. He waves.

'Thank you,' I call down.

'It was my pleasure. Apart from your filthy temper and spiteful tongue it was actually nice seeing you again.'

I think I hear wistfulness in his tone. Could I have it all wrong? Does he really like me? Oh my Lord, is he close to calling off his wedding too?

'It was nice seeing you too,' I say without thinking. He hesitates at the car. I sigh when he says,

'If I remember correctly, you said that I wasn't *your* type either. Sleep well.'

He climbs into the Lemon and before I can blink, he is gone. I get back into bed and struggle to remember when I had said Christian was not my type. I recall my mother saying it but had I agreed? If I hadn't meant it at the time does that mean he hadn't either? I toss and turn for the rest of the night and finally doze off as the sun streams in through the crack in the curtains.

Chapter Thirty-Two

The bleeping of my phone wakes me and I squint at the clock. I groan when I see it is almost eleven. My head aches and my mouth feels like the inside of a sewer. I groan and roll over, taking the Blackberry with me. I bury my head under the pillow as memories of the night before hit me. The phone bleeps again and I reluctantly pull myself up and check it. There is a text from Justin and an email from my mother. I read Justin's and decide to leave my mother's email for later.

'Hey you foxy lady, how are you doing? We landed the Rouge contract, thought you would like to know. Come back happy and refreshed.'

Oh yes, of course, Justin. The only snag with that is that the man I love is marrying someone else today. I cannot believe I am not ecstatic about the Rouge contract. I groan and dive under the quilt. I lie there miserably for some time until my phone rings.

'Oh for God's sake,' I moan miserably.

It is Kaz, bright, cheerful and full of news.

'We got the Rouge contract,' she screams excitedly.

'I know,' I sigh. 'Justin sent me a text.'

'You don't sound very pleased,' she observes.

I am thrilled, of course. Rouge is the biggest cosmetic company in the country and I had done everything but sleep with the director to win the contract, but it seems so insignificant compared to Christian's wedding. I search through my handbag for the painkillers, figuring that if they are good enough for the pain in my foot then they will do perfectly well for my headache.

'Where have you been anyway? I thought you might have phoned,' she says accusingly.

'I went to New York to have lunch with George Clooney, only got back an hour ago.'

'Oh well, that's all right then.'

'Christian is here, in France and he is getting married to Claudine today. I want to kill her, but as I can't, I might as well kill myself,' I say dramatically, reaching for the water by the bed.

'Are you sure? Only I would have thought Simon would have been going.'

I choke on the water. What is she talking about?

'He is going. Only the other day he told me, he had a wedding to go to in France, I mean, it is obvious it is Christian's.'

Although, of course, the way they are at each other's throats it does seem a bit surprising, I have to admit.

She clucks down the phone at me.

'Bels, he's going to Kieran's wedding, remember Kieran? We all had invitations to this wedding six weeks ago, including you, and anyway it's not until tomorrow. Don't you remember I couldn't go because of Mum and Dad's anniversary party? Jetting off to New York and gallivanting with celebrities has scrambled your brain. Still, I expect it would mine too.'

What? This doesn't make sense. Surely Christian would have asked Simon. Oh sod a dog; don't tell me, he is not getting married. Oh no, don't tell me I said all that stuff about Jack, while all the time he was not even planning on marrying Claudine. But what about Claudine's Facebook status update?

'But, I read it on her...'

I stop when I realise I never actually read she was getting married on her profile page, just that she had so many sleeps to go before the 'big day'. So what was happening on the big day?

'I have to go Kaz, I'll phone you later.'

I click the phone off and almost fall down the stairs in my rush to get to my laptop. How could I have made such a stupid mistake? Sitting in my nightie with an old cardigan slung around me, I open the laptop and my breath catches in my throat when I see Claudine's profile picture. It is of a pink ribbon day skydiving event. I squint at her status, half of me wanting to see it and the other half knowing that I will slash my wrists if it does say what I dread.

The big day, parachute jump, here I come!

Parachute jump? I look again to check I have read it right. She is doing a parachute jump. I let out a huge groan and stamp my feet.

Pain shoots through my foot and I bite my lip. What a stupid bloody idiot I am. And what the hell did I say last night? I cringe at the memory. Oh God, did I really say Jack was the right man for me? Not to mention the other things that came out of that vile mouth of mine. Oh damn, bugger and piss it. Why is that now I know he may no longer be with Claudine, do I feel he deserves the benefit of the doubt? I yank the fridge door open to the chorus of '*A second on the lips is a lifetime on the hips*' and scoff two éclairs in front of the cupcake and slam the door to '*Naughty pickers wear big knickers*', while giving it a two finger salute. With a large mug of black coffee in front of me I debate how on earth I can put things right and wonder what the hell he was celebrating tonight. A marquee, a bandstand, crikey it has to be something special, but what? I fiddle with my phone and finally call Georgia at the restaurant. Of course, it all makes perfect sense now. The kitchen finally finished, an Englishman eating every night at 'Clarisse's' and the man without a girlfriend. Oh you stupid fool Bels. Here is the man of your dreams with all the right credentials, responsible, reliable, rich and very eligible it seems, so what do I do? I let him slip right through my fingers. Rosa answers the phone and after I explain who I am she fetches Georgia.

'Is it to come for dinner this evening that you phone?' she asks politely.

I open the pantry door and remove a packet of biscuits, relieved not to be serenaded with the likes of '*Those who indulge, bulge*'.

'No, I don't need dinner tonight, I...'

'That is good because we are not open this evening,' she says bluntly.

I perk up excitedly.

'It's about the Englishman who is having the petite reception, the one who comes to the restaurant, you know who I mean?'

'Yes of course.'

Okay, time to ask the million-dollar question.

'Is he getting married today?'

There is silence for a moment.

'Monsieur Lloyd?' There is surprise in her voice. 'Why would you say that?'

I can't believe Georgia knows Christian. I spent all that time searching for him, when all I had to do was ask her.

'The petite reception he is having, is that not for his wedding or maybe a parachute jump?' I ask feeling more stupid by the minute.

'I think perhaps you should ask Monsieur Lloyd himself about his party,' she replies sharply and hangs up. Shit, shit. I debate whether to call her back but decide it would be a bad idea. Instead, I shower and throw on a pair of jeans and a black vest.

I decide I need some fresh air to clear my head. After checking the weather, I grab a shawl and leave the house for a walk. I head down the driveway and cross over into a small country lane. It is deserted and I walk slowly. I force myself not to think of Christian but every lavender field I see reminds me of him. The lane is deserted and I savour the peace. I close my eyes and listen to the birds. Oh what a heavenly break this could have been, instead I will go home more of a wreck than when I came. The harmonious sound of the singing birds is broken by a babbling of French voices. I open my eyes to see hundreds of banana-in-hand pink ribbon walkers, heading towards me. Oh for pity's sake, where is a woman supposed to go to get some peace. They are marching towards me and visions of being trampled to death by the pink army brigade look frighteningly real. These are women on a mission. There is nowhere for me to retreat to. Their long skinny legs bounce on new trainers, and their breasts strain against the pink material. My God, are they all wearing the same top? Manes of blonde hair and bright red-glossed lips engulf me. As they get closer the pink fuses into one big mass. Oh my God, how many of them are there? I'm all for Breast Cancer Awareness but not at the expense of being trampled to death, or even worse: breaking another toe by slipping on a banana skin. I look for an escape route. I see a gate ahead of me and vault over it. Amazingly, not one of the walkers seemed to notice me. I watch them march on, chatting and banana eating. Good Lord, for a second I thought I was going to be the ultimate sacrifice for the pink ribbon cause. That would have raised awareness all right. I am temporarily blinded by a sea of pink and dazed from the heavy scent of bananas for a minute or two. I remember Claudine's parachute jump and feel slightly guilty that I am not doing anything for Breast Cancer Awareness and decide to buy a pink ribbon pin and a banana later. Blimey, I bet the old banana growers love this, not to mention the pink T-shirt manufacturers. As soon as the coast is clear I climb out of the field and walk slowly back to the house. I decide that I have to go to Christian's party and spend the rest of the afternoon choosing an outfit and checking Claudine's Facebook page. At four o'clock, there is a status update and I discover that Claudine is most definitely not marrying Christian.

'One *giant leap for womankind – done! See you all at Copacabana.'*

I let out a sigh of relief. While Christian is hosting what I now presume to be his house-warming party, Claudine will be dancing the night away at one of New York's top nightclubs. I race back upstairs and look in desperation at the clothes that are strewn across Olivia's king-size bed. I glance into her walk-in wardrobe and spy a pair of Jimmy Choo sling back sandals.

'Ooh,' I gasp.

My eyes also land on a beautiful black dress, which I recognise as Chanel. I carefully part the scarves until I find one to match the dress. Oh, I would look spectacular if Olivia would let me borrow it. I text her and get an immediate response telling me to borrow whatever I like but she advises me to remember that Christian does not do classy. Oh no, now what do I do? I claw through my clothes which are strewn all over the room and spot the floral skirt and lemon top I had bought in the supermarket with him. He did say he liked them at the time. I put them on and study my reflection. Oh I so hope Olivia knows what she is talking about. I find some heated rollers and apply my make-up while the rollers get hot. I decide to keep it simple and brush a thin layer of mascara onto my lashes and stroke my cheeks with Bobbi Brown blusher. I put the rollers in with shaky hands and sit at the dressing table sniffing the assortment of perfume bottles. I finally decide to use one from my Jo Malone selection. Finally, as satisfied with my face as I can be, I pop in some pearl earrings and brush out the rollers. I slide my feet into the Jimmy Choo shoes, which are a little tight but bearable for one evening, and stare at myself in the mirror. With a nervous sigh, I nod appreciatively at myself, grab my clutch bag and walk slowly downstairs. A flashback of the night before haunts me. How could I have been so hateful? What if he doesn't want to talk to me? I really don't think he will give me many more chances. After all, why would he want to keep spending time with a woman who keeps abusing him? This may be my last chance to put things right so please God, don't let me blow it. My stomach churns as doubt stabs me in the solar plexus. I can't justify his behaviour towards his dad, I just can't. How anyone could sue Edward is beyond me, but for his own son to do so is unforgivable surely? I pull my Blackberry from my bag and dial Simon. It really is time to ask him what this legal battle with Christian is all about. It disappointingly goes to his voice mail. Damn it. He is probably on his way to France. I throw the phone into my bag, take a deep breath and leave the house.

Chapter Thirty-Three

Cars are everywhere. The small bit of confidence I had felt earlier has all evaporated. My toe is throbbing in the shoes and my heart is beating so fast I think I might be sick. I park the car behind a dozen others and sit listening to the faint sound of music that emanates from the house. I had not wanted to arrive too early but now it seems like I am too late. I check my reflection in the mirror and convince myself that I look awful. I let out a nervous sigh and wish I had brought my Quiet Life. I take several deep breaths and climb from the car. Okay, think super model, and ooze confidence. I hobble towards the front door attempting my best Claudia Schaefer impression and fail miserably when my foot wobbles and the heel goes under.

'Shit,' I mumble.

'Are you all right,' asks a soft voice in broken English.

I turn and pain shoots through my foot causing me to grimace. I stare into the face of a very pretty woman who is wearing a black strapless dress in a way that I can only dream of. She throws a light pink shawl around her shoulders and looks warily at my foot. The will to live is slowly disappearing and I feel like I am the ugly duckling who has just bumped into Cinderella. I haven't got a clue who the woman is, but feel almost sure she is romantically involved with Christian and feel a *Fatal Attraction* moment coming on. Does she have a pet rabbit that I can boil I wonder?

'Did you hurt your foot?' She smiles at me.

People are walking around us, and I hobble to one side.

'Actually, I hurt it a few days ago, and these shoes are now murdering it.'

She laughs revealing white even teeth.

'Take them off, no one will mind. I'm Maria by the way.'

I take the hand she offers.

'I'm Bels. I am here on holiday.'

She slips her arm into mine.

'Well, as my husband is late, why don't we escort each other?'

She's married. Thank God. For a minute I was convinced she was Christian's girlfriend. What if he does have a girlfriend? What if I have got it all wrong? Oh my God, what if she greets us? The thought of getting through the evening with a false smile on my lips is unbearable. There is no going back now, however, as Maria is leading me towards the house and another car has parked behind mine, making it impossible for me to leave. I attempt to ignore the pain that is now relentless and look ahead to the twinkling lights. The soft melodic tones of Norah Jones reach my ears. Loud raucous laughter makes me jump. I am as nervous as a kitten. In fact, if Maria was not leading by the arm, I would most certainly turn back and hide. We walk round the back of the house and the marquee comes into sight. The smell of a hog roast makes my stomach rumble. Fairy lights lead the way around the field and I follow Maria into the marquee. Groups of people stand around laughing and chatting with champagne flutes in their hand. To the right is a long table housing a mouth-watering buffet of roast duck on platters, surrounded by smaller plates of guinea fowl, French bread, cold meats, and egg segments. Further along the table are a number of bowls filled with different salads and sauces.

'Hey, Maria, you made it. Where's Jean-Paul?' asks a man who I vaguely recognise and I try to remember where from.

'Finishing that roof, where else do you think Monsieur? Bels, this is Alain, he laid all the floors in the house for Christian.'

Of course, I had seen him at the house.

'Yes, I saw you yesterday.'

He smiles and salutes.

'You probably did. Most of us here today have been doing something around the house the past few weeks. It has been hard work getting it done so quickly. It is great what Christian has done to show his, how do you say in English... gratitude?'

I nod. Talking of Christian, just where was he? I glance around but there is no sign of him. Maria waves at someone and rushes away. Alain grins at me and leans behind to the table with champagne. I shake my head when he offers me a glass. I really feel I need to keep a clear head for once in my life.

'You would prefer water perhaps?'

'Thank you.'

He walks away and I toddle outside to where a group has congregated by the bandstand. I watch as the musicians mount the steps and I wait in anticipation for them to start. More people join and the excitement builds. I find myself forgetting Christian for a few moments and sway with the music. It is a jazz band and I find myself smiling. It is only when I feel chilly that I venture back into the marquee where many are sitting eating. I look around for Christian and begin to wonder if he is actually going to make an appearance at his own party. I see Maria waving to me from a table at the other end of the marquee. I wave back and walk towards her.

'We saved you a seat. There will be the speeches soon. This is Jean-Paul, my husband, and this is Matt Rivers.'

Jean-Paul is a small man with a big smile. His brown eyes twinkle at me. I shake his hand and accept his offer of food. Matt grins widely at me and leans forward to take me into a big bear hug.

'Nice to meet you Bels. I'm always thrilled to welcome a fellow Brit. I don't know about you but I can't speak a word of French. These bastards, however, insist on speaking their lingo when around me.' He laughs.

'That is because we are talking about you most of the time,' smiles Maria and begins talking in French to Jean-Paul.

I quietly sit and eat my roast duck with sauerkraut.

'I'm Christian's PA by the way, probably should have said. What about you?' Matt smiles and offers me some bread.

'No, I'm not a PA,' I answer seriously.

He laughs loudly and his cheeks dimple. I smile and wonder if I could ask him about the lawsuit. He seems very approachable.

'I'm a friend of the family, well a friend of Simon's actually.'

His expression seems to change and I think I see his face cloud over but very quickly he composes himself and is smiling again.

'Ah, a friend of Simon's. Well, do accept my condolences.'

I let out a small gasp and he shrugs.

'I'm sorry, that was a bit rude.' He looks sheepish.

'Simon isn't the one suing his father,' I say bluntly and immediately wish I had kept my thoughts to myself.

He cocks his head to one side and studies me before reaching forward for some champagne. He pours some into a glass and hands it to me before refilling his own.

'That is quite true, but when you have acquired three quarters of a law firm through dishonest means, I guess you don't have to sue anyone do you?'

I stare at him.

'I don't understand.'

'Well, that's understandable if all your information came from Simon. As a family friend, however, you surely should know that Edward is no fool. Although having said that, he was a bit of a fool to trust Simon with the legal side. The guy has wanted full control of the business for years... Anyway, I have said too much. My loyalty is to Chris, so I apologise for being rude.'

'But that is what Edward wanted,' I say realising I sound as naive as I feel.

I feel my head spinning and wish I could phone Simon and ask him to explain everything.

Maria watches us and smiles.

'The food is very good, yes?'

I sip some champagne.

'It is excellent,' I agree.

She looks pleased.

'My mother, me and my sister, prepare all the food today.'

I gasp.

'You did?'

She nods proudly.

'Yes, we did everything but the pig roast. The desserts are in the kitchen, you will like them.'

I almost ask her where the bloody hell the host is, when at that moment he walks in to cheers and applause. I feel my face redden and my heart quicken. He is every woman's dream, at least I think so. I find I can't take my eyes off him. He is wearing the Marc Jacob jumper and the memory of when I first saw him in the Sushi bar floods back into my mind. I watch as he grabs a piece of bread and then climbs onto one of the tables to more cheers. He raises his glass of champagne. Maria leans across to me.

'How do you know Christian?' she asks with a smile.

God, I must be so transparent. I pick my glass up with shaking hands and take a long gulp.

'I almost married his brother,' I answer honestly.

She looks wide-eyed at me and Matt seems to nod knowingly. I turn back to look at Christian who is asking for silence and holding a microphone in his hand.

'I'm not going to ramble. I am really glad you are all here and I just want to say eat, drink, be merry. I am so grateful to all of you for all your hard work and for helping me get the house finished in record time.'

His lifts his glass and smiles broadly.

'Santé.'

Everyone lifts their glasses and echoes 'santé'. As they do Jean-Paul climbs onto the table. He takes the microphone, sending a loud squeak through the PA system.

'I know I can say this in French as Christian, you speak our language very well, but we have quite a few British people here so I say it in English. Christian, we look forward to having you as a neighbour and we are very pleased you have chosen us over New York. Welcome to a future in Provence.'

There is more applause and I see Christian's gaze land on me, and for a few seconds, our eyes lock. Then, as though nothing ever happened he holds his hands up for quiet again.

'Thank you everyone, enjoy. One last thing, those of you who fed that damn cat, you're not getting paid.'

There is much laughter as he jumps from the table. I wait hopefully for him to come over to me but instead he is eaten up by the crowd, and I lose sight of him. Please God, don't let me have made the worst mistake of my life by coming this evening. I wait a few minutes longer but there is no sign of him. Any hopes I had of him approaching me are quickly dashed.

'Shall I fetch you dessert?' Maria asks while looking at me curiously. 'Are you all right? You look a little flushed. Do you need water?'

I jump up, wanting the ground to open up and swallow me. I had made a terrible mistake. I had misread all his signals and worse than that I had been unbelievably vile and not even apologised. I grab my handbag and limp slowly towards the exit only to see it blocked by a crowd of people. I limp back and head for the other exit that leads to the side of the house. My foot is killing me and I am relieved when my phone rings and I can stop for a bit. It is Simon.

'I have a missed call from you,' he states bluntly.

I can hear airport noises in the background and memories of my first meeting with Christian rush into my head.

'Simon, I am at Christian's. Did you try to fiddle him out of the law firm?' I answer equally as bluntly.

There is a shark intake of breath and I curse. Sod it. Those awful things I had said about Christian having no integrity and being dishonest. How can I ever put them right?

'I've admitted to making a mistake, didn't he tell you that?'

Oh God. Me and my big mouth never actually gave him a chance to tell me anything. What an idiot I am.

'I really didn't think he would care. He's got his business and God knows it's doing a hell of a lot better than Dad's law firm ever could. I just wanted some control. I didn't think he would get so uptight about me having the larger majority. I'm sure if Dad could have done it that way he would have done...'

'But your dad didn't?'

I hear loud raucous laughter and someone calling Simon's name.

'Look, I have to go. All's well that ends well, huh? Have fun.'

I click my phone off and feel wretched. I remove my shoes and continue until I am outside the back door of the house. I can see the desserts laid out on a large oak table.

'Can I offer you dessert?' asks a voice from behind me. I freeze unable to look at him.

'We have croissants and jam. I remember how you liked croissant with your jam.'

I turn to see him looking playfully at me and I nervously pat my hair. He walks past and the familiar scent of him calms me. I hobble in to the house and watch as he cuts a croissant. I open my mouth to speak but nothing comes out. He closes the door to shut out the music from the bandstand. My mouth is dry and my foot throbs unmercifully.

'That looks nasty,' he says, pointing to my toe. 'You never did say what happened.'

He spoons jam onto the croissant and hands it to me, pulling out a chair as he does so. I flop down into it and sigh. He sits in another next to me and cuts a slice of cake.

'I slammed the car door on it,' I say, and then blush.

'Well, that's the kind of thing you do isn't it?' He grins at me and bites into the cake. 'I bet the air was blue that day.'

I shake my head in exasperation.

'You've not lost your appetite I see,' I retort.

'That's a nice top,' he says softly, not looking at me.

My stomach is churning and not even the fresh cream trifle can tempt me.

'About my vile tongue...' I begin, wondering if there is a chance in hell of putting all this right.

'Yes, not your best quality, I have to agree. You have a lot of nice qualities but the vile tongue and filthy temper does tend to erase those from one's mind.'

I sigh. Why is he always so bloody irritating?

'It's just I thought...'

'I know what you thought,' he interrupts passing me a slice of cake. 'You really should try the desserts, or is there another dress you are struggling to get into?'

I smile awkwardly.

'You're not suing your dad?'

He shakes his head.

'Right now, I'm not suing anybody. But, I would have gone through with it if Simon had not seen sense. As it happens he finally did. Frankly, the truth is I couldn't care less about the firm. I don't mind admitting that everything I know about law can be written on the back of a postage stamp. He is welcome to run the place but Dad wanted his two sons to own the business and that's what mattered to me. Simon's welcome to be in charge but I wanted everything to be morally right for Dad's sake. '

I take a half-hearted bite of my cake.

'What I said about not being my type, well it wasn't true,' I say quietly.

'Oh, and there's me thinking Jack Russell's were more your type.'

I frown at him. Why can't he ever be serious? He pours lemonade into a glass without looking at me.

'I only went out with Jack once, I haven't seen him since. I only went out with him because my mother insisted. I am sorry. I just could not cope with being friends with you if you were married to someone else.'

He smiles and pulls off the Marc Jacob jumper to reveal the top he had bought on our journey to Rome.

'I realised you weren't marrying Claudine and I thought...' I stop and swallow in an attempt to lubricate my throat. What had I thought? He is looking at me.

'Oh Lord, what did you think? No, don't tell me. Claudine, as it happens played me for a fool and not many people do that...'

'And live,' I smile.

'I was lenient. I just called the wedding off. She was so desperate to live in New York that, behind my back, she tried to put a spanner in the works with the house. I would have to have sold it.'

'Oh,' I sigh, the relief evident on my face.

'Of course, things weren't helped by her discovery of some photos taken here in France, especially a very fetching one of my backside, which she discovered on my camera. She had some kind of an anaphylactic fit on seeing those,' he continues, with a twinkle in his eye.

I clap my hand to my mouth to suppress my gasp and feel myself blush.

'The house looks nice,' I say embarrassed.

'You're sure you don't want me just for my spider-catching skills,' he says seriously.

'No, no, of course not, I...'

'Just as well, because secretly, I can't stand them.'

I struggle to keep the disappointment from my face but fail miserably and simply say.

'Oh well...'

I stop when I see the grin on his face.

'You're so gullible, you believe everything I say.'
I could hit him.

'I'm so glad you came,' he says softly leaning towards me.
I feel my body sway towards him and the kiss, when it finally comes takes my breath away. My hands curl around his neck and I sigh with pleasure.

'Although your spider-catching skills help, of course,' I whisper.
His hands encircle my waist.

'Just don't expect me to get you to any more weddings.'
The door creaks open and we both turn to see the cat saunter in. The cat looks at us and meows.

'That's it then, the cat approves,' he says laughing.
I wrap my arms tighter around him. At last, I have found Mr Right, and he is everything he ought to be: rich, successful, reliable, responsible and best of all, eligible. Mother will be pleased.

Our Favourite Recipes

Snoozy Woozey Sangria and Lemonade

Mix a little lemonade (diet or otherwise, what the hell) with a large glass of cheap sangria. Compensate for the bitterness with a square of Cadbury's Fruit and Nut chocolate. If you suffer from a nut allergy, like Christian, avoid the nuts at all costs. Once consumed, continue your shared drinking experience with a good single malt whisky.

Caution: Avoid bumble bees if outside.

Kaz's Banana and Blueberry Smoothie

Take two organic Pink Ribbon bananas, blend with a cup of organic blueberries and half a litre of unsweetened soya milk. Add a teaspoon of organic honey, a pinch of cinnamon and serve as an energising beverage.

Best drunk in the lotus position.

Edward's Whisky and Nuts

Select a good single malt whisky, matured for at least twelve years. Enjoy with a handful of roasted nuts. Nice and simple.

Best drunk in a quiet corner, away from the crowds.

Jack's Chargrilled Steak

Take one large sirloin steak and place it under a hot grill for thirty minutes or until nicely burnt. Serve with a large quantity of chips and a glass of the best champagne. If anyone questions your choice of steak and champagne, tell them you like to break the rules.

Best eaten with a large side order of chips, before a night at the casino.

Christian's Sushi Overload

Purchase as much Sushi as you can, preferably from the local Waitrose (Kitty knows the manager). While there stock up on olives, cheese, crisps, chocolate, pastries and cakes. Grab a couple of bottles of wine too while you're at it. Money no object.

Sushi best eaten until you feel sick.

<u>Bels Jam with Croissants</u>

Purchase two croissants from a reputable boulangerie (If you are anything like Bels, then you have never baked anything in your life, so why start now?). Acquire a pot of home-made raspberry jam from Mother's kitchen. Apply liberally.

Best enjoyed in the airport departure lounge.

<u>Justin's Doughnuts</u>

I don't care where they come from; just don't cock it up again sweetie. They must be jam doughnuts, JAM and not frigging custard. Can you at least get that right? Am I the boss or am I the boss? Bloody hell!

Best eaten in the office.

The Dog's Bollocks (A Romantic Comedy)

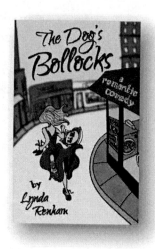

On arriving home after a friend's posh wedding, launderette worker Harriet, finds her life changed when she discovers her flat ransacked and her boyfriend missing. In a matter of hours she is harassed by East End gangsters and upper crust aristocrats. Accepting an offer she can't refuse, Harriet, against her better judgment becomes the fiancée of the wealthy Hamilton Lancaster, with dire consequences. What she had not bargained on was meeting Doctor Brice Edmunds. The Dog's Bollocks is Lynda Renham's funniest novel so far. A cocktail of misunderstandings, three unlikely gangsters, a monkey and a demented cat make this novel a hysterical read. Follow Harriet's adventure where every attempt to get out of trouble puts her deeper in it.

Pink Wellies and Flat Caps

(A Romantic Comedy)

Alice Lane has everything; a wonderful fiancé, a responsible job and a lovely flat in Chelsea, but after she has a bra fitting her life goes tits up. Homeless, and with just a sparkling engagement ring as a memory of her previous life Alice accepts a live-in farm manager s job and discovers that things actually can get worse. Come with Alice as she makes her hilarious career change and struggles to cope with her moody employer, Edward. But can Alice turn her back on romance and resist the dashing Dominic or will the past come back to bite her?

Rory's Proposal (A Romantic Comedy)

When 29-year-old Flora Robson reversed her car into Tom's Audi she had no idea who he was. Only after she has started to fall in love with him does she discover the gorgeous blue-eyed Tom is the man who is trying to close down her hairdressing business. It seems that Tom will stop at nothing to get what he wants, but Flora is not giving in to anyone. Can she win the battle against her multimillionaire enemy or will her feelings for him get in the way? Follow Flora's hilarious journey of love, hot chocolate and marshmallows, and the man who changes everything.

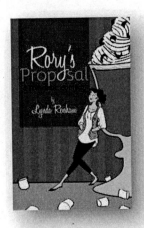

It Had to Be You (A Romantic Comedy)

When 29-year-old Binki Grayson is offered a Christmas bonus by her boss at the office party she didn't imagine he meant a quickie over his desk. Things for Binki just go from bad to worse and by Christmas Day she is not only jobless but boyfriend-less, so when she discovers her late Aunt Vera has left her something in her will she thinks things can only get better. What she doesn't realise is that her inheritance comes with a complication by the name of William Ellis.

A mishmash of misunderstandings, sex-shop escapades, high finance and a blooming romance make It Had to Be You another hilarious romantic comedy by the uproarious Lynda Renham.